# THE GUARDIAN PROJECTS

# THE GUARDIAN PROJECTS

James Herbert Edwards

Copyright © 2007 by James Herbert Edwards.

Library of Congress Control Number:	2007902006
ISBN:	Hardcover	978-1-4257-4893-7
	Softcover	978-1-4257-4891-3

All rights reserved. No part of this book may be reproduced or transmitted in any form or by any means, electronic or mechanical, including photocopying, recording, or by any information storage and retrieval system, without permission in writing from the copyright owner.

This is a work of fiction. Names, characters, places and incidents either are the product of the author's imagination or are used fictitiously, and any resemblance to any actual persons, living or dead, events, or locales is entirely coincidental.

This book was printed in the United States of America.

**To order additional copies of this book, contact:**
Xlibris Corporation
1-888-795-4274
www.Xlibris.com
Orders@Xlibris.com

37660

# CONTENTS

Foreword ..................................................................................9

Introduction ............................................................................13

Chapter 1   Lost and Found ...............................................15

Chapter 2   Home Sweet Home .........................................31

Chapter 3   Dead and Buried .............................................52

Chapter 4   Tweedledee and Tweedledum .........................62

Chapter 5   Do Not Pass Go ..............................................94

Chapter 6   Meaty, Beaty, Big, and Bouncy .....................122

Chapter 7   Through the Looking Glass ..........................167

Chapter 8   Doctor Livingston I Presume ........................187

Chapter 9   Somebody Call a Cab ....................................216

Chapter 10  The Black Spot's Gone ..................................247

Chapter 11  The Last Word ...............................................287

Chapter 12  The Devil, an Owl, and the Pussycat ............313

Chapter 13  Drunk and Ugly ............................................338

I dedicate this book to my wife, Joan, who makes it all worth it.

# FOREWORD

Dear Readers,

I met the author, Jim Edwards, a few years ago, quite by accident if there are such things. Our mail, bless the U.S. Post Office, had gotten mixed up, probably because our last names are similar, or maybe just because they both start with an *E*, who knows. The mailman had knocked on my door with a letter, and it had looked important, so I signed for it without really looking at the name on the envelope; my mailman is always in a hurry, believe it or not, and I took it inside. If I remember correctly, excuse, excuse, it was from our mutual alma mater, WVU. So I opened it, and after inspecting the contents—something to do with his alumni status—I realized it wasn't for me, but rather for someone named James Herbert Edwards. I almost threw it away but didn't because I had signed for it, and Lord knows what the USPO might do to me if I tossed out someone else's mail. I naturally put it somewhere safe; I tossed it on my pile of monthly bills.

I didn't think about it until a week later when I was at my office, looking over applications that my secretary had gathered from the file cabinet that morning while I was sleeping off a late night of babysitting a new well for a client who wanted to hire my production company to maintain his well but hadn't bothered to finish the well. It had taken my crew a lot longer than what we had anticipated to finish the work; chalk it up to being shorthanded. Which was why I was at the office and not still sleeping. I was sick and tired of being shorthanded and had vowed to put an end to it, once and for all.

Call me naïve.

Jim's application was in the pile. His name did not ring any bells, but I did notice the man had worked for other production companies and was now also working as a landman, leasing land and doing oil and gas title work for various companies—not a very steady line of work at the time. Yet to me, it meant he was smarter than most of the dumb-asses I had hired in the past, and I have hired some idiots, believe me, especially since he did title work in the local courthouses. Record rooms are not someplace they usually let idiots into, considering everybody's deeds are there, unless of course you are an attorney and an idiot. I never said that.

I set up some appointments to interview my prospective workers—Jim was one of them—at a bar in St. Mary's, West Virginia. Not all business is done on a golf course, plus the bar was an end-of-the-day gathering place for oilfield workers, so I figured I might even get lucky and find a few good ones. Actually, now that I remember it, I had left a message on his machine, letting him know where I would be that afternoon. I called my secretary into my office and handed her the stack of bills that I had brought in with me from home. I got the dirty look when she saw what they were, followed by another dirty look when I told her where I was going and started to load the employment apps into my briefcase.

She started to rise from the chair and leave my office, dragging her ball and chain for effect while leafing through the stack of envelopes, whining about late fees and my irresponsible filing skills. That was when she threw Jim's letter from WVU at me. I stuck it in the briefcase and made a quick getaway before she could find the really late bills and begin her preaching.

An hour later, I entered the bar with a good friend I met in the parking lot, forgetting my briefcase in the trunk as I imagined a cold Stroh's Beer sliding down my throat. Not to mention my friend had a joint and was needing a little help finishing it before entering the establishment.

It was a typical redneck, country music blaring, smoke-filled bar that naturally attracted all kinds of people who liked that shit. I found a table toward the back and sat down. The waitress knew us and was right behind us with a couple of mugs of beer, not to mention a nice ass too. Why I was there vanished from my consciousness as the stories began flowing like the beer. I had mine, and as more guys joined us, they had theirs. The stories were about the oilfields; gossip, bullshit, and rumors mixed together with an ounce of truth. And as stories get told and retold, the stories begin to change until they aren't quite the ones you heard the last time, so new ones get top billing at any table. The latest one was new news to me.

"So let me get this straight," I said to the guy at the table telling the tale, "a dozer operator said he was working for a geologist who told him that he and another guy had uncovered an alien creature, and it had attacked the guy before escaping into space." I wondered what he had been smoking.

"Yup!" he barked, not liking my look of disbelief.

"Who was the dozer operator?" I challenged him.

"It was Big Mackie, from Greenland Excavating," he retorted.

I looked at him like I didn't believe that either. I knew who Mackie was, a helluva dozer operator, which didn't make him any more credible than a bad dozer operator. I pointed that out to the well tender.

He scowled. He wasn't real happy about coming to St. Mary's for a job interview and finding me half sloshed.

I hadn't apologized to him, but I did buy him a beer. I didn't like his manner; he was a bully. I didn't hire bullies.

"Who was the geologist?" That man would be credible, had to be.

"I don't know his name, but he's the one who looks for UFOs at night," answered the tender. His tone told me what he thought of the man. I thought different; I couldn't for the life of me remember his last name, but I knew him, I knew him as Rick the Trekkie. He was a great geologist, very independent and not a bit nuts. I liked sci-fi too, and I wasn't nuts. I decided I had heard enough from this jerk. I didn't like to drink with bullies either.

"Well, look, I have your application, and I'll call you when I've made my choices." I stuck out my hand. It hit a mug of beer. The beer tipped and spilled onto the table, running toward the man's lap. I didn't mean to do it. Oh well.

He jumped up and avoided the river of brew but bumped a guy behind him who was holding a plastic cup of soda. It splashed all over the place. The man looked at the bully. The bully started swearing at him and me. Then a strange thing happened. The man's eyes got black as coal, his entire eyeball not just the pupil.

He said something in a language I had never heard before.

The whole experience was like being the first vehicle at an accident with multiple fatalities. You're not involved, but the horror is right there in front of you.

It unnerved the bully who turned and fled, bumping into other guys like a fucking pinball machine ball.

The man turned to me and stuck out his hand, his eyes deep blue and quite normal now.

"I'm Jim Edwards and for the record, the creature didn't attack me, it attached me." He sat down as I offered him a seat. The other guys at the table got up like he had the plague.

"Tell me all about it," I said to him.

"No problemo." He smiled.

What you are about to read is his story. I read it a few years later.

I told him he needed an editor.

He told me that would be impossible. He said the way he wrote it is his own style, and he believes that if he changes even one word of it now, it won't be his story anymore. He hopes you won't be offended but tough tits if you are.

Be forewarned.

And if you do meet him one day, tell him I've got a letter for him.

Thanks.

Ray Edmonds

# INTRODUCTION

I will be the first person to admit that I am not a great writer, and I do not see myself becoming a literary figure of great renown. Hell, if the truth were known, I am neither a great speller nor a very good typist. But I get it done. I have on occasion told a good joke and even a good story or two, but this is neither. This is what happened to me, and now I really need to put it down in writing because I think it's important that people of this planet know as much about the *Projects* as the rest of the population of the "known" universe. Also I should mention that I have a lousy memory, which has probably gotten worse as I grew older, if I could only remember. And, if you're like me, you hate to be the last one to hear something new.

So now you will be able to read about what's going on out there with the rest of the universe, at least what I have experienced so far (and haven't forgotten). Remember also that I won't give you detailed scientific explanations about what I saw, heard, and used, because out there, things are different. For example, a Boeing 727 must have a zillion buttons, bells, and lights in the cockpit; my ship has maybe a couple of dozen! See what I mean. Different. Sometimes I just let it happen and tried not to figure it out, whatever it was, because I didn't have the time nor the intelligence, and it might give me a headache. What surprised me was that sometimes shit happened that was just like TV Land. Or it would surprise me when I expected TV Land and got the exact opposite instead. Endings were like that, as you will see.

So I will do my best to describe it all, but remember, I'm not Einstein, and some of the stuff I saw even he couldn't explain, so don't expect a lot of fancy shit, OK. I mean, who can explain what happens when you start your car? A mechanic, right. So maybe someday I can take an expert with me; just remember, I'm not a mechanic. A lot of the places I traveled to, and aliens I met had their own name for things, though I sometimes couldn't pronounce, let alone spell them. So I did my best to get through it without any problems, and when I had to, I gave it my own name or used the ones we use here on Earth.

Finally, we all look back and wonder why things happen to us and try to figure it out. I think this is true of what happened to me and why I'm writing this, a little closure maybe. I certainly didn't ask to become a "Guardian" and if doing something nice for someone caused me to be singled out, oh well. It happened, and that's that. One other thing I will add before I begin is that to my knowledge, no one else has ever been outside the solar system besides me, except those of you who claim to have been kidnapped by aliens. So rest assured that although I have been accused of being a bullshitter, no one in the coming years will accuse me of being a liar, even if I'm not perfect. Which is not to say that when my life was in danger a few times, I didn't lie like hell; as you shall see, it was what kept me alive to write this. So let's begin.

# CHAPTER 1

## Lost and Found

In the early 1980s, I drilled some oil and gas wells in western West Virginia, with the help of an extremely smart geologist who also happens to be my good friend. The story begins at one of my locations in Tyler County at the end of a long hollow called Copperhead Hollow. We had staked a location the previous week and, after receiving the permit, had made arrangements to meet a bulldozer at the proposed site to clear the location and construct a road for the rig to come up the hill. You always let your geologist pick the well site; he's the expert at finding the oil and gas, and he usually picks a location halfway up the side of a mountain, which requires many hours of preparation with a dozer, timber that has to be cut and stacked, and a small mountain of rock to spread on the road and location. I was forever bitching about this fact, and today was no exception. We arrived at the location or rather the old farm road directly below it just ahead of the dozer-loaded flatbed truck. I had requested a D-9 dozer since it is the biggest one you can bring out the roads around there. The blade is about sixteen feet across, so it has to be taken off the dozer before moving and put back on it when it gets where it's going. This process gave Rick and I a chance to survey the proposed site one more time. I had brought my pistol with me to shoot at copperheads if we saw any; after all, this place was uninhabited and had been for a hundred years, and I didn't want to make a liar out of the person who gave it its name.

"Rick," I began bitching, "I believe we only have to move half the hillside this time."

"Look, Jim," he replied as we picked our way up the hill, "I picked this spot because of the anticline underneath it, so quit stewing, will you." He was smart and patient too.

"I know, I know," I admitted. I knew the anticline; a geologic formation that would bring in a good well, and he was right as usual. I just once wanted to drill on a flat spot. Something moved out of the corner of my eye near Rick's path. I pulled the gun out of my pocket; I was wearing my winter coat since it was a typical chilly October day. Sure enough, it was a snake of unknown length headed straight at Rick. He saw it just as I squeezed off a shot at it. The shot hit the ground right in front of the snake, and it seemed to bolt off into the brush beside Rick as he jumped the opposite way with a shout. The noise from the gun echoed back and forth across the hollow as he swore at me.

"Christ, Jim!" he yelled, "you don't have to shoot me, I'll put the location anywhere you want it!" We both laughed and continued on up the hill. I wondered out loud if the surveyor we sent out here to do the staking had seen any snakes.

"He didn't say anything to me about snakes," answered Rick as we arrived at the stake, all decked out in pink flag ribbon, "but he did tell me that the place gave him the creeps. He said that while he was here he felt like someone was watching him and when he started to leave he swore to me that he heard someone or something groaning." He looked over at me and gave me his "no bullshit" look. Below us we heard the dozer arrive.

"No kidding, and did he see the headless horseman too?"

"No really, Jim, you know Bill Jarrett, he never kids around about anything. The man has no sense of humor at all."

I had to agree with Rick on that score; hell, Bill was about as much fun to be around as your mother-in-law.

"So when were you going to tell me this, Rick?" I asked. I was as superstitious as any oilman, and this was not a good sign. I began to inspect the area for more trouble but could find nothing to shoot at for the moment.

"I didn't want you to get worried," he replied, looking down the hillside at the approaching dozer. It was shoving over a tree as it started to make the oil well service road, crunching over the ground with an inhuman intensity as it shoveled the tree off to the side.

"I'm not worried," I lied. I could feel the hairs on my neck just starting to stand up. If Rick believed Bill then there was a damn good reason for me to worry. I had thousands of dollars tied up in this lease, not to mention many hours of work in putting together a drillable lease, both legally and geologically. The dozer had shoved over a few more trees and was now halfway up the hill. The operator was smart enough to come up first before cutting down the roadbed. I looked down and recognized the guy. It was Mackie the Maniac, a savage operator who no doubt would someday be on the top ten hate list of Greenpeace.

I liked him. He could clear a location in half the time it took other operators, but he sure was hard on Mother Earth. He saw me coming and flipped me the "bird."

With him, it meant he liked you, which was a good thing since he was almost as big as the dozer. He brought the dozer to within ten feet of us and throttled it back. He untangled his huge bulk from the controls and climbed down to greet us.

"Hello, boys," he grunted, wiping his sweating brow and spitting a wad of chew the size of a softball, "how's it hanging?" His huge hand dug into his pants pocket and removed a large Mail Pouch tobacco pouch as he prepared to load another wad of tobacco into his now-empty flapping cheek. He was so disgusting that you found yourself staring at him out of curiosity, like you would an animal at the zoo.

"So this is the spot," he grunted at us. His face returned to a cherubic roundness as he stuffed in another wad.

Rick smiled and nodded. He couldn't help watching him either.

"Stake's right there." Rick pointed. "The rig will be here the day after tomorrow." You didn't really have to answer Mackie's greeting; he didn't care how it was hanging anyway.

"Good," he spat, "me and Bertha will be done by then." He motioned back at his dozer. He named all his dozers after his latest girlfriends, who, by the way, were approximately the same size without the blade on the front.

"Been doing any hunting?" I asked him.

Rick looked over at me as if to say, "Don't get him started," but it was too late. For the next fifteen minutes we heard about his exploits. You listen to him, and you feel like arming the poor deer so they can fight back. He was a true country boy for sure.

Finally he finished his tale of mass species' annihilation and with a grunting good-bye, turned and lumbered back to old Bertha. The way he climbed onto the dozer, I wondered if he knew which Bertha he was climbing. The dozer had been idling while we talked, rumbling like a great beast about to charge. With a smoking snort, it began to move forward on the hillside, like a bizarre rodeo ride.

"Come on, Jim, let's go check the Gibson well," said Rick, glancing up at the late afternoon sun, "then we can swing back here and see how much destruction he's done."

We started down the hill and stopped at the sound the dozer was making. Mackie had apparently started cutting down to "level" and had struck something the dozer could not easily move aside. The pitch of the motors' sound rose, and the volume was deafening in the hollow. You could see Mackie straining as if he were doing the moving, and then suddenly the dozer lurched forward and quit running. We watched Mackie's big arms grab at the various controls as we walked back up toward the big guy. We were almost to the dozer when Mackie let out a roar and lunged off his seat and dove to the ground, scrambling to his feet much quicker than I thought he could, and ran toward us.

"Fuckin' snakes!" he screamed. He hated them with a passion, and I wondered what he would do to me when he found out the name of this hollow. He puffed up to us, winded from the short sprint, arms flapping, chest heaving, and his mouth belching wads of spit and tobacco. Slowly he regained his composure, his face a reddish hue like when he gets pissed. I decided it might be advisable to move some other direction.

"I'll handle this," I assured them, pulling my gun out and advancing on the dozer. The side we were facing looked clear of wildlife, but as I rounded the back of the machine, I saw them. There must have been twenty or thirty of them climbing up over the treads and casing. They looked like Mackie, pissed. I shot at the tread and hit one right in the head. At least I thought I did, but then I didn't see any blood or guts as it fell back into the squirming pile of copperhead snakes. Those hairs on my neck began to rise again, and as I stood there watching, the snakes slid down off the dozer like liquid and disappeared into the ground, like they were organized or something. A little red light went off in my head, the same one that goes off when someone yells "red alert" on the bridge of the starship *Enterprise*, know what I mean? I backed away from the dozer and rejoined Rick and Mackie. Rick did not like the look on my face.

"Snakes are gone," I bluffed unconvincingly. I tried to look relaxed.

"Horseshit," exclaimed Mackie, "there must have been a hunnert of them damn things crawling up at me from outa the dirt. You sure the hell didn't kill them all with one shot." With a look of utmost disgust, he walked sideways to see the other side of the dozer and came back shaking his head in disbelief. He was not a happy camper.

"You ride up there with me," he commanded. I don't think he expected an answer, so I nodded, and we walked over to the safe side of the dozer. He pointed up at the seat, so I climbed first, putting me between him and the snake-pit spot. I looked back at Rick, and he smiled and waved. I gave him the finger and turned my attention to the side of the dozer, pulling my gun out again. Just as Mackie succeeded in starting the motor, I saw the ground move, not like when a small animal, or snake as the case may be, wiggles under the leaves, not like when big dozers move around, but like the whole area suddenly shifted; and as Mackie started to move forward, it happened again, a shudderlike movement, as if the whole planet shifted. Mackie swung the dozer with one tread and turned it to face the spot where the snakes had come and gone. I climbed down and walked over toward it. Rick came over to me, wondering what the hell I was up to now.

"Something's wrong, real wrong," I remarked to him. "I saw the ground move, Rick, like it was alive." He saw the look on my face and knew it was my "no bullshit" look. I picked up a branch from the ground and walked to the spot and thrust it into the ground. It sunk about one inch and snapped off in my hand. I jumped back expecting a stampede of wigglers, and none appeared. I walked to the center of the spot and turned to Rick.

"Where the hell are the snakes?" I wondered out loud. Just as I was starting to kick away the leaves, the ground, which had just had a ten-ton dozer sitting on it, gave way under my feet, and I sank so quick I couldn't even shout my surprise. No, it felt like I was being pulled under, sucked down like a nail to a magnet, and I didn't even have a chance to kiss my ass good-bye. My senses went into overdrive. Now, wherever I was, I could barely hear the dozer, and it was black as night. I felt like I was drowning in something, but I couldn't open my mouth. It was warm, but I couldn't feel any snakes slithering on me, just this totally smothered feeling. I couldn't move, and I didn't like the feeling one damn bit. If I could have, I probably would have shit myself. I stopped struggling and tried to relax, which was easier to do body wise but not brain wise. I seemed to be breathing, yet I wasn't actually inhaling or exhaling. My heart was beating because I could hear the kettledrum in my ears. The whole feeling reminded me of the time when I was in college and took a whole bunch of muscle relaxers to see what it felt like; this is what it felt like all right, brain going a mile a minute, body totally numb. *This wouldn't be so bad if I could see where I was,* I wondered to myself.

As if someone had read my mind, the darkness seemed to lighten up, like when your eyes get adjusted to a dark room. Then it got even brighter, until finally I was in a completely white cloud—yes, just like being in a cloud. It felt like a toilet paper commercial; I felt fluffy and white. Thank God claustrophobia is not one of my weaknesses, or I probably would have had a heart attack by now. The light seemed to help, but the "trapped like a rat" feeling was still driving me nuts. *How long have I been in here,* I wondered, *and how come Rick and Mackie hadn't dug me out yet? Those pricks.*

Suddenly, right in front of my eyes, I could see Rick standing in the same spot I had been standing in, and I knew it had only been micromoments ago. In the corner of my view, I could see Mackie approaching with an armload of shovels and picks from the flatbed truck. He handed a shovel to Rick who proceeded to stab at the ground with a vengeance. The shovel handle snapped in half like a toothpick, and he turned to Mackie in amazement. Now it was Mackie's turn as he approached the spot with a pickax in his huge hand. With his big arms, he raised the pick over his head, and I could almost hear the air whoosh as he brought it down on the spot. I could have sworn I felt a slight vibration as it hit the ground above me, and then it too broke below the ax head, leaving Mackie standing puzzled with only the handle in hand. He turned to Rick and said something; I wished I could hear what they were saying.

"Could try to scrape the ground with Bertha," Mackie said to Rick, "maybe I had the blade too deep before."

Holy shit, I could hear them. I tried to calm down and figure this out rationally. *Whatever had trapped me here seemed to grant every wish I made. Maybe I was in the belly of a hungry genie, who liked his meals to suffer a little bit before he actually ate them. Nah, that was stupid,* I thought. *Any self-respecting genie would have grabbed Mackie first, hell, he was a smorgasbord I'm sure, but at the same token, I wasn't little either.* With no reaction to that thought, I relaxed a little more.

"Let's give it a try," replied Rick to Mackie, "but I really don't think it is going to work. I think we're dealing with an unknown force here."

I could tell he was concerned but also tantalized by what was happening. Mackie looked at Rick like I used to look at my calculus professor, then he walked out of my sight; I imagined him climbing up on the dozer and shortly saw it come into sight. As the dozer reached the spot, it quit, not running but moving. I could hear it running and feel the vibrations of the engine, but for some reason, and I could see Mackie straining, it would not budge an inch. It gave me an idea. I wondered if I could talk to them and tell them I was all right; at least assure them that I wasn't dead and buried. It worked like a charm.

Well, almost like a charm. I still wasn't free, but now my head was sticking up out of the leaves where they could see me. Rick looked puzzled, as in Trekkie mode, and Mackie looked like he had seen a ghost.

"Jim," exclaimed Rick, "what the hell is going on? Are you OK? Are you stuck?" I could see his gears turning in his head. Mackie just stood there looking bewildered and, I'm sure, for the first time in his life, scared.

"Yes, I'm OK, and yes I am stuck," I began, and suddenly I was back in the white world. I had to think up a better wish next time; that's for sure. The old brain clicked in with a good idea, and I decided to try it.

I wondered to the genie if it might not be a good idea if we talked about the situation before it got any worse, especially for me. The voice that came into my head was both masculine and feminine; I know that sounds crazy, but I can't describe it any other way, other than it was a warm comfortable sounding voice, very soothing, which I badly needed right about now.

"I will tell you what you want to know," began the genie, "and you will hear me in your thoughts. I do not want to hurt you. I want you to help me. I need what you need." A pause, and the Genie continued, "Freedom."

"Are you a genie?" I asked; I figured, first things first.

"No, I am a creature from a distant star group, and I have been stuck here for a long time. I would like to be free so I can return to my home."

*So would I*, I grumbled mentally. *So would I.*

Instantly I found myself standing on the spot I had disappeared from; Rick and Mackie were looking at me rather strangely. I can't say that I blame them; I felt rather strange. The whole experience had been a bit mind bending even for an old hippie like me. I wondered if I would have to "go underground" in order to communicate with the creature; after all, I did want to help it. At least it set me free.

"You may call me Pracon." The voice made me jump. I turned to Rick.

"Did you hear that?" I said to Rick. He looked at me like I was more nuts than usual.

"Hear what?" he replied suspiciously. Mackie was still giving me the weird eye. He was speechless, which was fine with me.

"So you can hear me," I wondered out loud. I knew I shouldn't have after I said it. Now they both gave me the "nuts" look.

"Yes, but only you can hear me unless you want me to let your friends hear also," answered Pracon.

I looked at Rick and Mackie. Rick could handle it; Mackie would go crazy.

"Who are you talking to?" Rick asked.

*Can you do just Rick?* I wondered to myself, pointing toward him.

"Yes I can," came the answer.

I knew from the look on Rick's face and the way he stiffened slightly that he had heard Pracon. He handled it well.

"I'm talkin' to Pracon," I said to Rick, "and he is now 'talking' to both of us."

Rick was an old Trekkie too, so this thought-transfer thing was no big deal for him.

"What the fuck are you two idiots doing?" Mackie spat; he was clearly not a happy camper, and his uneasiness translated into crabbiness. "Have you lost your minds?" This man was no Trekkie, not even close.

"Mackie," said Rick, grabbing a hold of the situation, "why don't you start cutting the road. We can do the location tomorrow." He looked at me, and I nodded.

This seem to pacify the big guy, and he lumbered over to the dozer, climbed up, and began to move it away from the spot and off the location. Soon he was cutting at the edge of the proposed road site and seemed to be lost in his own little destructive world. I turned back to Rick.

"Thanks, that was quick thinking." I nodded. He was good at that too.

"I figured we needed privacy, and I didn't think Mackie could hear what I heard." He nodded back.

"He didn't," I answered. "I wanted to keep the mental giant outa this."

We both laughed. And I quickly filled him in on what happened to me down under.

"So I figure Pracon is trapped under the hillside and we need to extract him somehow." I was pretty quick myself.

"That is correct," Pracon agreed. "I am not able to do it on my own."

"But you made the ground move, didn't you?" I asked.

"Only to you, it was only a projection in your mind."

"You made the snakes appear too?" Rick asked.

"Yes, I have done that for years," Pracon began, "until now it was necessary to keep the life-forms away from here." He sounded sad but relieved.

"All illusions," concluded Rick.

"Yes," answered Pracon.

"No wonder they named this place Copperhead Hollow," I also concluded. "You've been scaring away the locals for the last hundred years, that way no one would bother you, until the right person showed up?"

"That is basically correct," it agreed. "I determined when I contacted you, that you were capable of comprehending my problem and helping me get free. I must admit, at first I thought you were much too violent a life-form, at least from your thoughts, but your ability to understand, made me risk taking you inside me and communicating as we have done."

"So you need us to uncover you?" Rick asked. I knew from experience that he had something in mind besides that question.

"Yes," it answered, "and I do not have the ability nor the desire to destroy your home, Rick."

It must have read Rick's thoughts; the look of surprise on his face was obvious to me. That certainly gave it the advantage in my book. I laughed at Rick. I could get away with that; not many people who knew Rick would even dare. He had taught me everything I know about fighting, but not everything he knew. Not by a long shot. He flipped me the bird and grinned.

"So how do we dig you out, since all our shovels are broken? Thanks to you, no doubt," I demanded. I looked over at the tools on the ground. They weren't broken; it had been an illusion too. This time it was Rick's turn to laugh at me. He always enjoyed it I must say. I flipped him off.

"I'm afraid you will need the dozer to accomplish it," Pracon commented. "Is it possible that you can do that without the big life-form, Mackie?"

We both laughed at the mention of his name.

"I can probably operate the dozer, Pracon," I offered, "but don't expect miracles." If he only knew what happened the last time I used one.

"You mean when you drove it off the cliff on the Noland well?" Pracon answered. I looked at Rick, and he smiled. He looked guilty too.

"You read his damn mind, didn't you?" I yelled at both of them. Then we all laughed, even Pracon, and its strange laugh made Rick and I laugh even harder.

"Seriously, Pracon," said Rick, "Mackie is one of the best operators in the state."

"I know that," it answered, "but his heart will not take the shock of uncovering me. He would likely die due to an enlargement in the organ. He should not be straining his cardiovascular system, not the way he is presently constructed.

Pracon' s words were a real reality check for Rick and I. This creature possessed some remarkable abilities; that was for sure. Rick and I set off down the hill to find Mackie and see if he would let us borrow the dozer at lunchtime, which according to Rick's watch (I don't wear one) was very near for old Mackie.

"Hey, Rick," I said as we trotted down a well road wide enough to be a four-lane expressway, "what are we going to tell Mackie about using his dozer?"

"Nothing," he said, "let's just get rid of him." He turned and smiled at me as we walked up to Mackie, who had by now cut more road in less than an hour than most operators do in a half a day. I felt like I could see his fat heart bulging as he climbed down from Bertha and spat.

"Mackie," said Rick loudly over the dozer noise, "let's finish up later. I've got to check a well so you can leave your flatbed here until after dinner and ride with me. I think we got time to stop and grab a beer."

Mackie looked at Rick and nodded; that idea was always a quick sell for him. He climbed up on the dozer; Rick nudged me, and I looked at him. He motioned with his eyes at Mackie, who had just turned off the dozer and removed the ignition key. He turned and stood in front of the operator's seat without looking at us; he picked up the cushion and deposited the key under it.

"Next question, Rick," I said quietly, "what are you going to tell Mackie about what happened up there today?" Mackie had gone to the flatbed truck to fetch his lunch suitcase.

"If he even thinks about it," Rick began as he walked toward his truck, "I'll just tell him you were playing a joke on him." He smiled and jumped into the driver's seat. Mackie climbed into the passenger side, and as they maneuvered around my truck, I heard Mackie yell, "He did what? That low-life son of a bitch; you just wait until I see him later!" And then they rounded a turn in the old road going down the hollow and were gone. I wondered if I could go with Pracon when he left for home and if it was far enough from Mackie.

I waited about fifteen minutes and then climbed on Bertha. Carefully I slipped the key into the ignition and depressed the clutch; the motor came alive with a loud rush, and I realized that this thing was quite a bit bigger than the one I had driven maybe two times in my life. In what seemed like an eternity, I managed to turn it around, barely hitting my truck once, and started up the hillside. I made better time when I got to the "Mackie" expressway, and soon I was at the location site. I guided the dozer over to Pracon. He informed me that I was doing better than he thought I could and to hurry and uncover part of him. I knew I had to hurry; it was getting dark, and this baby had no headlights that worked anymore. At least that is what I discovered when I tried the switch.

"Just lower the blade and cut down on me," he instructed. "You will not be able to injure me with that thing."

"Pretty sure of yourself, aren't you?" I replied, struggling with the control levers.

"Jim, I have been in asteroid showers, do not worry."

"Yeah, but I'm doing the dozing." *Compare that to an asteroid shower*, I thought.

"Perhaps you're right," returned Pracon. I forgot he could read minds. He laughed.

"Gettin' pretty cocky there," I joked. The dozer skinned up the hillside until the blade would go no farther, then I turned sideways on the hill and cut downward. Pracon seemed to be domed shaped as I cut away the soil and shale layers. As I continued cutting back and forth sideways on the hill, the cliff of the cut grew to a height of ten or twelve feet. With fifteen feet of creature sticking out of the hillside and most of the creature's domed middle uncovered, I cut off the dozer and left it, to walk over to Pracon. I almost tripped on a shale outcropping and realized that I must have been cutting in the dark because it was now pitch-black, and I could barely see Pracon.

"You were trapped pretty good there, Pracon," I said. I wondered how much more of him was still under the hillside. I reached out and touched the front of him. A wave of happiness swept through me as if I was reading his mind. Man, it was intense. It was a rush, if you know what I mean.

"Yes, you are right, Jim," he said through my head, "but not for long."

"You mean reading your mind?" I was confused. I get confused when stuff like this happens; you wouldn't think so, but I do.

"No, I mean trapped, and yes, you can read me by physically touching me, it is a weakness of my kind," he said regretfully. "Now stand back and let me see if I can free myself."

He didn't have to tell me twice. I jumped off to the side of him and waited. Moments later, I actually heard the ground moving and felt a quakelike shaking, and in the dark, I could just make out Pracon's shape as he pulled clear of the bank, and it collapsed behind him into the void where he had been lodged. He looked to be about twenty-five feet long and half as high in the middle. In the dark, I saw him turn to me; I was glad I was on his good side. He was a big guy, all right.

"So how's it feel to be free?" I asked. I knew already. I had felt his happiness, like picking up a puppy; you know it's happy, like that I suppose.

"Wonderful," he yelled, "this is better than summer in the Antares system!"

I didn't have to touch him to tell he was a happy camper, but I walked over and did it anyways; the rush from the contact was incredible if not addicting. It made you feel so full of energy you think you're going to burst. I laughed out loud and realized Pracon was laughing also. Too bad he was leaving; I could learn to like this guy. He must have read me because he sighed and started talking again.

"Yes, I will be leaving at first light, your star will give me enough energy to make deep space where I can find a tasty plasma cloud and feast for the first time in many of your years. I have dreamed of this moment for a long time, I am in your debt, Jim."

"You dream," I said surprised. It must have been the last of the surprises in me for the day.

"All living things do." He had me there.

"Well, what now, big guy?" I asked. I had no idea what time it was, but it had to be close to ten or eleven o'clock by now. By all rights I should be dead on my feet, instead I felt just the opposite, like I had just gotten outa bed.

"I believe you need to rest as is common with your life-form, is it not? These effects you feel will not last long, Jim."

"OK, Dad," I sassed him, "I'll turn in shortly."

"Thank you, Jim," he retorted, "but I don't think I want to be your father, he must be very patient and loving."

"What about your dad," I ignored his sarcasm, "what was he like?" I wondered if he even had a father, but then he had dreams. I could imagine a larger version of Pracon standing over him scolding him for some childish prank. I smiled.

"I never saw my father," he answered, "although I do have his memory line. It was because of that, that I ended up here on your planet."

"Your father's memories made you come?" I asked, "Were you looking for him?" I must be getting tired; I was confused again.

"No, Jim, I came here to hide," he explained. "Some very bad beings were after me."

I have to admit this sounded pretty wild. Looking at him towering over me, able to withstand an asteroid storm and then bury himself in a hillside for a hundred years, made it hard for me to accept. He must have picked up my skepticism.

"Jim," he began, "I had gone to feed with my family in the tail of Perseus, in the outer ring of this galaxy, it was my first time away from my home in the Procyon system, and I was so excited to be there that I wandered away from my mother and two brothers. Just as my sister found me, the Maglarr, who were extracting metals from some nearby planet, attacked us. They hit my sister with a compression beam and she died right next to me. I fled toward the Orion belt and they followed me."

I felt sorry for him, and I reached out to comfort him. The wave of pain that shot through me almost killed me, I'm sure. Not only did I feel his anguish, but also for a brief second, I witnessed his sister's horrible death as the beam hit her, and she turned to her brother and let out the most painful screams I have ever heard. In the next second, she was in pieces; some of them hit Pracon, and I felt his terror as he turned and fled.

"Jim, Jim," Pracon was nudging me with his body. I must have fallen to the ground. I crawled to my feet without touching him. I didn't need another rush like that one.

"I'm fine," I murmured, shaking my head to clear away the vision. I hoped I wouldn't have any nightmares, at least not about this shit, no way.

"Go ahead, Pracon, I want to hear the rest," I said bravely.

"Well, after that," he began reluctantly, "I circled into the Orion belt, spotted the Oort cloud surrounding your star system and hid in it until they passed. My father was here many years ago and I knew from his memory that you had a low gravity where I could recover from the partial hit I had gotten from the beam."

"It hit you too?" I was amazed he was still alive. The memory of the beam was frightening.

"Only slightly, but enough to hurt me if I had returned home where the gravity is many times higher than here. You know the rest."

"Who the hell are these Maglarr beings?" I wanted to go kick some alien ass right now.

"The worst race in the universe," he replied. "I hope you never come in contact with them. No one survives against the Maglarr, no one and nothing can stand in their way for long."

"You did," I said. He seemed so tough.

"No, I ran like a scared qwimmy." He sounded like he was ashamed to be alive.

"A what?" I laughed. "A qwimmy!"

"A very timid creature, hardly anyone has ever seen one. But the Maglarr"—he actually shuddered—"no one wants to see them or even hear that they are in the next star system."

"Is that what happened to your father?" I asked.

"Yes, my last memory line from him is the Tayhest-Maglarrian wars." He came near me now, and I could feel the warmth of the creature. It felt good against the night chill.

I must have fallen asleep. A very restful sleep, because I really don't remember anything until Pracon nudged me.

"Jim," he said quietly, nudging me with this massive trunk that protruded from the front of him.

I was lying on the cold ground. I looked around myself; I was still on the location, and it hadn't been a dream after all. The sun was just coming up over the eastern ridge of the hollow, and the mist of a cold morning was heavy in the air. The sunlight shining through it was quite blinding. I could see my breath, but I certainly hadn't spent the night on the ground; had I been inside Pracon all night?

"Yes," he answered, "but I woke you because we have company coming."

I turned to him and stepped back a few feet to get a good look at him in the daylight. He was grayish in color; his entire body was covered with scales that did not overlap but rather seemed to fit very snuggly together like an elaborate jigsaw puzzle of oddly shaped pieces, some small and some as big as a Stop sign. They meshed together forming a body very similar in shape to a tortoise shell but with no leg openings. The trunk was huge compared to an elephant's, and even though it was connected to the rest of the outer matrix of tiles, it was smooth; the pieces in it were no bigger than a fingernail. The trunk must have been ten or so feet long and slightly whiter in color. All in all, Pracon resembled a turtle with no legs or head. That was OK with me; I liked turtles. In the spring, in West Virginia, when they go to lay their eggs by the streams and rivers, they cross the roads in these hills in large swarms, headed for the water on the other side. It's hard not to hit them with your vehicle; they number so many. One day, I collected about fifty of them and filled Rick's truck that night. Boy was he pissed, but what a riot it was, the next morning when he opened the driver's side door and the turtles began pouring out. I thought he was going to kill me, especially when he saw all the shit they left behind. Someday he'll laugh about it, hopefully. I hoped Pracon wouldn't remind him. I was pulled from my daydream by a truck horn, and I looked down the hill and saw Rick's truck coming up the hollow road. He was alone, which surprised me since he should have had Mackie with him. Maybe he was hiding under the seat, ha!

Rick pulled past my truck following the dozer tread marks, sailed up the half-complete well road, and pulled to a stop a few feet from Pracon and me. He didn't look happy; maybe he had remembered the turtle trick. He jumped outa the truck and walked up to us, looking at Pracon with obvious interest.

"So you got him uncovered," he said to me. "It didn't take you all night, did it?" He looked around at the carnage I had created with the dozer.

"No, I just woke up," I answered, stretching my arms over my head. "He makes a great bed." I pointed to Pracon. I noticed he was now floating about three feet above the ground. It was very impressive to say the least.

"How do you do that?" I asked. Rick was impressed too.

"Let's just call it electromagnetics," he said. "I just wanted to see if I was functioning. I will have to leave shortly."

"Yeah," said Rick, "Mackie's just down the road, eating his second breakfast, on us." He turned to me and nodded.

"How soon before he gets here?" asked Pracon.

"He said he was going to eat till one of us came down to the diner and paid for it." Rick looked at his watch. "He's already been there a good thirty minutes."

I knew this was going to be an expensive well, but this was ridiculous; he ate like a starving man. I checked my wallet; I had a blank check, so I was OK for another thirty minutes or so. Any longer than that, and I would be in deep shit.

By now the sun was over the ridge. Pracon had lightened to an off-white in color; he seemed eager to hit the trail. Humming, almost.

"Well, I guess this is good-bye," I said to him. I felt sad, old-friend sad.

"Yes, I am ready to go." He reached for me with his trunk. "Let me leave you with something, something special, for helping me," he said, touching my forehead very gently.

I felt a flash of energy through my head, and though it wasn't painful like earlier, my head felt like it was going to burst. Strange pictures and sounds filled my conscious thoughts as he withdrew his trunk from my head and rose in the sky.

"I wish you well, Jim," he said, rising higher in the sky, "and you too, Rick."

We both stood there waving to him like he could see us, as he turned and disappeared like a shot.

"You OK?" Rick asked me. "What did he do to you?"

"I'm OK," I answered, but I knew I wasn't because I knew what Pracon had done to me, and I wasn't real keen on the idea. I felt the little hairs on the back of my neck to see if they were standing up. They were, like quills on a porcupine.

"I'm going to get Mackie outa the diner," I said. "You want to wait here or come with me?" He smiled.

"I wouldn't miss it for the world." He laughed.

"Somehow I knew you'd say that," I said to him. I wondered if I should call my bank and check my account balance first. As we started down the hill toward the trucks, I looked up at the sky one more time where Pracon had gone and wondered why he had done what he had done to me. My brain was so incredibly full.

"See you at the diner," I said to Rick. My mouth felt like it had cramps.

He looked at me like I was nuts. I looked back at him as I climbed into my truck and realized that I had just spoken to him in Tharx, a dialect of the Regulus system, and I knew it like it was the English language. As we drove down the hollow, with Rick following a good distance behind me, I realized that while I had found an alien friend, I had probably lost my sanity, if I ever had it to begin with. I laughed out loud . . . at what I had lost and found.

# CHAPTER 2

## Home Sweet Home

Several months had gone by since my discovery of Pracon, and life had gone on as normal as it usually did for me. The well had been drilled on the same spot we found him, and it had been a good one, so we had drilled several others in the hollow. Mackie had never forgiven me for using his dozer, even though he ate twenty-two dollars worth of food that morning, but I didn't care; he wasn't the first dozer operator I had pissed off, and probably not the last. And Rick and I had pooled our resources and bought several choice properties in the same area of the Pracon well, as we named it, and had been quite successful with them. We had become financially independent because of that, so we no longer needed to use investor money, and therefore, we could work when we wanted to and slack off when we felt like it. It was a good feeling. Rick and I never talked about what happened, probably because he knew I was still having nightmares and flashbacks, and talking about the whole thing seemed to make them worse. Sometimes I would just start talking in Tharx or some other alien language without even realizing it. A lot of my friends put up with it, I figure, because I had money now, and when I partied, I partied pretty hard. Rick hung in there because he was my friend and, I think, because he liked crazy people.

When he had told me he was getting married to Samantha, his high school sweetheart, I had decided to throw a huge bachelor party. I planned it for the weekend before the Superbowl so we could recover in time, in time for the game, that is.

It was the day after the party, and I was taking the day off to recuperate. Everyone had drunk too much including me. Besides, it was ten degrees outside and snowing awfully hard for West Virginia. My head was throbbing, and my body was aching. I had taken a dozen aspirin and Tylenol to no avail and was considering going back to bed even though it was one o'clock in the afternoon, and I had just gotten up an hour ago. I was sitting in the living room of my house in north Parkersburg watching my girlfriend, Joan, and my dog, Wolf, in the kitchen. She was bent over looking into the refrigerator for something to feed him, and he was helping her by nosing around the meat drawer trying to get her attention. He finally brought his collie-shepherd nose up into her ample bosom and tried to nuzzle her through her sweatshirt.

"Cut it out, Wolf," she scolded, playfully pushing his nose down. "He's been living with you too long," she said, turning to me. I smiled like a proud father.

He finally got fed up with the nice-guy routine and grabbed the handle on the meat drawer and pulled it out for her. Before she could stop him, he grabbed our dinner steak and marched it over to his dish and dropped it into it. He almost had the Saran Wrap off it by the time she got to him. She grabbed it from him and turned to face me. He never growled at her; he was a smart dog.

"I'm not eating it now," she said, showing me the teeth marks he had put in it. She turned back to him and tossed it in the dish.

"Here, bad dog!" she yelled at him.

He looked at me, and I nodded OK as he ripped at the rest of the wrapping. He knew she wasn't mad at him, but he needed a little encouragement, just a little.

She walked over to me and sank into the couch next to me.

"Now you'll have to take me out to dinner." She pouted.

"Honey," I said looking out the window at the snow falling in a hurry, "if this keeps up, we may have to eat Wolf for dinner." He looked up at me and growled. My head was throbbing.

"Shut up, Wolf," I scolded. He barked at me; it hurt worse. I looked at Joan. She gave me one of those "I don't feel sorry for you" looks and kissed me on the cheek, pressing herself against me teasingly.

"Is the poor baby hungover?" she teased. "Maybe I should put on some music, how about AC/DC?" She got up to go to the stereo, and I missed her as I grabbed for her.

"No please, I'll do anything," I begged, knowing how loud they were, "no tunes."

"Dinner," she answered. She knew she was in a power position. She was right too. She was smart and pretty.

"OK," I gave in, "just some place quiet."

She came back over to me and settled in close to me again.

"Oh, does Jimmy want mommy to make his head stop hurting?" she baby-talked me. She ran her hands up under my flannel shirt and tried to pull my chest hairs playfully. I grabbed at her chest, trying to tweak her nipples as she fought me off. She jumped up from the couch and stood there teasing me with her fingers, motioning me to follow. I knew I couldn't catch her in my condition, so I stood and acted as if I was going to fall from dizziness, which wasn't really too far from the truth. She reached out to catch me, and I had her. I grabbed her around the waist and deposited her on the couch and dove on top of her. My hands went under her sweatshirt, and I felt her warm breasts through her bra. I squeezed them lightly and snipped at her neck with my mouth. She responded and grabbed at my ears, which were one of my weaknesses, and we tumbled about on the couch in serious foreplay. Things were getting a lot warmer, and we were about to move to a more comfortable setting when the doorbell rang in the hallway.

Wolf had already finished his steak and had gone over to check it out for me. He was a quiet dog until he knew who it was, then he would react appropriately. One bark usually meant a friend or one of my well tenders; two barks meant it was Rick who tried to teach him to bark like the Jetson's dog, Astro, when he was a puppy; and three or more barks meant it was a total stranger or one of my relatives, none of whom lived in the area. Sometimes when he was being a pain, he would bark and growl in a weird combination just to mess with me. Today he barked twice, so I climbed up from the couch and went to the steps leading down to my front door, which is halfway down to the basement like most split-foyer homes. Wolf was sitting up, wagging his tail, waiting for me to open the door so he could jump on Rick. Joan had gone into the bedroom to straighten up herself, not real happy with the situation since she knew Rick and I might be up to something that would probably last all day. As I started down the steps to let Rick in, I could see him through the front-door window, a little half-moon with three panes of

Plexiglas I had put in for security; I heard the phone ring. I knew it was cold out, but I was a little pissed that he hadn't called first, so I motioned for him to wait a second and turned to go get the phone in the living room. It stopped ringing, so I figured Joan had grabbed it. I went for the door and was shoving Wolf to the side and reaching for the lock just as Joan said, "Rick's on the phone for you." I felt my neck hairs rising.

I peeked out the window at the figure standing at my front door. It looked like Rick—that is, Rick with a serious look. He was looking straight at me.

"Joan, ask Rick where he is right now." I turned and yelled up the steps. I still hadn't unlocked the door. And he was still standing there motionless.

"He says he's at home," she replied, coming into the living room with the cordless phone from the kitchen.

"Tell him he's also at my front door." I was just a little bit worried now, and Wolf picked up on it and moved away from the door. He was very smart.

"He says you must be crazy," she relayed from the Rick on the phone.

Again I peeked out the door at the other Rick. I turned to Joan and made a gun with my fingers, and she headed for the bedroom to grab my pistol from my nightstand. I love working with smart people.

"Go to Joan," I ordered Wolf. He obeyed at once. He bounded up the steps and came back in a flash with the gun in his mouth, sideways like I had taught him. I took it from his mouth and checked the safety. It was off.

"Wolf, go protect Joan," I whispered, and he ran up the steps to her side. She was still standing in the living room near the steps with the phone in her hand. I motioned to her and Wolf to get back out of the way as I reached for the doorknob and deadbolt. I twisted the deadbolt, and it clicked loudly inside the door and was about to unlock the doorknob lock too. The Rick at the door, however, apparently didn't remember that I had two locks on the door because he started pushing at it, trying to get in, rather desperately I might add.

"Rick," I yelled, "step back from the door, will you!" Now by all rights, he shouldn't have stopped shoving and shouldn't have stepped back as quick as he did because I had yelled at him in Tharx, not English. My "red alert" went off in my brain, and I melted back against the wall as whomever or whatever it was opened fire on the door. It certainly wasn't a gun that he fired. My metal front door could withstand a blow from a .44 Magnum, but whatever he fired melted the middle of the door and put a two-foot sizzling hole in it. I didn't actually hear the weapon go off both times, but a second hole appeared in my door near the knob, and I could almost feel him rushing the door. I dove down the steps leading to the lower level of the house as the door came crashing in against the wall I had been up against a second earlier. I spun on my stomach halfway down the steps and slammed a shot off at the Rick person standing in my foyer. It was really weird shooting at my best friend, but then I have a huge survival instinct, or so I had been told by people who had been in fights with me and against me.

The shot hit him square in the stomach area and should have killed him instantly or at least dropped him. Instead he stood there, with menacing eyes focusing quickly on me, and leveled a weird looking gun at me as I rolled right on the steps. The red beam that came out of the weapon caught me on the side of my ass and stung like a son of a bitch. Through painful tears I pulled the trigger again. This time I hit the asshole right in the neck, and his freakin' head flipped backward off his torso and rolled out the front door and down the steps. I started to get up, but the gun in his hand went off again, this time missing me by a mile as it hit the wall behind me, exposing the inside of my bathroom to me.

"I don't want a window there!" I yelled as I aimed for his gun arm and shot it off with two well-placed shots below the shoulder. The rest of the son of a bitch was still standing as Wolf leaped on him from the living room railing. He knocked him down and proceeded to bite at his other arm as I crawled up the steps and grabbed at the loose arm and weapon. The hand was still wiggling, and I was really hurting, but I wasn't so bad off that I couldn't pull the weapon loose and toss it up the steps toward the landing.

"Get off, Wolf," I commanded. He stepped back from the body lying on my floor and licked at my face in satisfaction. I looked at him and patted his head even though I felt he had been just a tad late in jumping to the rescue. I guess that's why I was the one bleeding all over the foyer's stone floor, and he was the one getting a hug from Joan as she arrived at the scene of the attack on my ass.

"Are you all right?" she cried out suddenly when she saw the blood streaming from the back of my pants and pooling under me. Her sympathetic look made me feel wanted as she rushed from Wolf's side and came over to help me up. I nodded as I struggled to a standing position, hot blood running down my leg. I looked down at the body and quickly decided it wasn't human. In between the exposed neck and shoulder tissue were shiny metallic parts and sinews as well as glowing spots of bulbous tissue. Hollywood would have been proud, very proud.

I lumbered to the doorway and looked down into the yard for the head. It had settled on the bottom step and lay there looking straight ahead eyes wide open.

"Wolf, fetch," I said to him. He jumped through the doorway and grabbed at the head. He tried to pick it up by the hair, but it came loose, revealing a shiny skin-colored covering on the top of the head. But Wolf wasn't giving up; he grabbed it by the nose, picked it up more carefully, and carried it almost to me when it also came loose, revealing a shiny metal surface. Not your typical skull, that was certain.

"This is fuckin' weird," I said turning to Joan. "I do believe I've been attacked by an alien cyborg." She looked very convinced, something she had not been when Rick and I told her about Pracon. I don't blame her; most oilmen are born bullshitters. I stooped and picked up the head with both hands and looked into its open eyes.

"You will die, Guardian," it said to me in Tharx. And then the eyes turned red.

Now, I don't know what you would have done, but I said, "Oh yeah," and dropkicked it through the front doorway, into the snow-covered yard. Barely a second later, it exploded vengefully, throwing Wolf and I down the stairs and Joan up into the steps leading upstairs. Glass went flying everywhere as the front upstairs' windows of my house imploded, tattooing the walls with shards of glass. I landed on my sore ass, and Wolf landed on top of me. We both yelped.

"Joan," I yelled, "are you OK?" I pushed Wolf off me gently and tried to stand up. In the distance, I heard sirens coming this way, and coming fast.

"I'm OK," she cried. She must have stood up because I heard her and then saw her at the top of the landing. She looked beautifully unhurt but a little disheveled. She pushed her hair back as she came down the steps to me and kissed me on the lips.

"Does this mean we're not going to dinner?" she joked. What a comedienne.

"I think so," I answered. The sirens arrived at my driveway and started up it. It was a long one, almost a half a mile from the main road, with a couple of privacy turns built into it. Minutes later, I saw a familiar face. It was the same trooper who gave me a ticket last month for doing a hundred and twenty on the highway out in front of my house. He stared down at the body and then down at me.

"You gonna make it, Mr. Edwards?" he asked, surveying the wreckage in all directions. He glanced out the door at the crater in my yard and fingered the hole in the door before turning back to me. You could tell he was thinking hard.

"Yeah, Carl," I said, "though I'm not too sure about my ass." It was really hurting now although it wasn't bleeding anymore. His name was Carl

Jarrett; his brother was my surveyor, though he hadn't known that when he'd written the damn ticket. Afterward, he had come back to my house to apologize probably so I wouldn't fire his brother, and we had put a serious dent in a bottle of Jim Beam. We also found out we had a mutual fondness for brunettes and fast cars. I liked him; he wasn't Mr. Serious like his brother Bill, unless he was in uniform like now.

"You OK, ma'am?" he asked seriously. I could hear a siren in the background and hoped it was the ambulance; my ass was on fire. I had been shot before, but it had not felt like this.

"Yes, officer," answered Joan politely as she stood and helped me up. I whispered in her ear, and she turned to Carl. He came down the steps and helped her help me up the steps to the landing where I glimpsed the ambulance coming up the driveway.

"Come on, Wolf," she said heading up the stairs, following my whispered instructions to secretly snatch the alien weapon I had tossed there. Wolf looked at me, and I nodded toward Joan. He followed her, and they disappeared into the upstairs. The walls were speckled with glass pieces from the upstairs' windows.

"Jesus, Jim," remarked Carl, "what the hell happened here?" His eyes had followed Joan also, so he had to say something besides "nice ass." I shrugged.

I was filling him in on what had happened as the paramedics arrived at the doorway. In the distance, I spotted Rick's truck coming up the driveway. Joan came down the steps holding a towel and began to dab it on my butt.

"Holy shit!" I yelled in pain. She pulled it away; it was almost blood free. I looked at my ass where I had been shot. It looked burned more than it did shot. Yeah, that's what it felt like, a burn. The medics were still standing there, so I motioned them into the house where it was only slightly warmer. They looked around the house and then back at me.

"Good party, huh?" I said to them. One of them smiled; the other didn't. He looked at Carl and then back at me; he was the serious one.

"Anyone else hurt?" he said to Carl seriously. Carl looked at me. I shrugged.

"Only him," I said, motioning to the body behind us. Carl and I moved aside as they advanced on the body. I could see my injury wasn't good enough for them. They both were close enough now to see the body wasn't complete or human.

"Come on, everybody," I ordered, after a few minutes of standing around watching the gaping paramedics, "let's go up to the living room where it's warmer." Carl had gone out to his cruiser and came back in behind Rick as I started up the steps. They grabbed my arms and helped me up into the living room. There was glass everywhere. The smiling medic had come up with us; his buddy was still examining the body.

"Your partner's really morbid," I said, turning to the one medic. He nodded.

"It's his first day, at least with me," he said, as in "I don't like him either." "Why don't you go lean over the back of your recliner and let me have a look at that wound." I nodded gratefully.

Rick and Joan had been talking in the kitchen while Carl made notes and asked them questions. They kept looking back at me hanging over the chair; Rick said something to Joan, and they laughed.

"Hey, cut it out!" I yelled at them. "I want sympathy."

Wolf barked at me and wagged his tail; he was enjoying the company and the commotion. The medic had pealed away the remains of my Levis and was examining my ass. I felt foolish standing there butt naked, but even my BVDs had been melted by the shot I took in the old butt.

"The bleeding has stopped," he commented, "and I swear it looks like you've been cauterized. Strangest wound I ever saw." His eyes said it all.

"Hey, Kirk!" he yelled while rummaging through his case. "Have you got any large gauze pads with you? I think I can patch you up right here," he said to me, "but you might want to come down to the hospital and have a doctor look at it." He applied an ointment and stood up, apparently waiting for his partner, Kirk, to bring him the gauze.

"Where the hell is he?" he muttered, walking over to the stairs. I'm sure he was about to say something but never got out a word. The sound of gun going off and the shocked look on his face as his chest exploded in red death told me he had found his partner. He fell back against the wall in the hallway as I heard someone rushing the steps.

All hell broke loose at the sound of my gun going off; Carl jumped up from the kitchen chair and flew into the living room, pulling out his police special as he came running. Rick grabbed Joan and pulled her back into the dining area and rushed into the room almost behind Carl. I didn't know what he expected to do, but at least he wasn't standing in the living room with his pants at his ankles, freezing his you-know-what off. As I dove over the front of the recliner, I saw the head of the other medic appear by the railing of the stairs and the barrel of my gun come through between two of the rails.

"Look out!" I yelled from my spot on the floor. I flipped the old Strato lounger on its side and grabbed at what was left of my pants. Carl saw the medic's head and the gun the same time I did and leveled his gun to fire. He wasn't quite quick enough; the bastard was quicker and took a round in the left shoulder. It threw him back against the fireplace, and he fell to the hearth, dropping his gun in the process. The hollow point bullets I had loaded the gun with put the hurts to him. Meanwhile, Rick had realized that even with his knowledge of the martial arts, there was no way he could stop a maniac with a .357 Magnum in his hand; he turned and dove for the kitchen doorway as the maniac medic came into view on the top step. He fired at Rick and missed him. With catlike reflexes, he turned and sprinted to Carl's motionless body. He seemed to sense that he was out of the picture, and he turned toward me with a malevolent look on his face. I felt like I was at a slight disadvantage or I should say, shit outa luck.

Now through all this time, say maybe a good thirty seconds, Wolf had been taking in the whole situation and analyzing it in his doggy brain. As the medic approached me, he decided his time had come, and he hurled himself at the maniac from behind the easy chair, where he had been hiding, in true animal anger. He was a fast dog; I ran with him every morning or rather tried to keep up, and he was not much more than two years old, so he had expected to pounce on this guy before he knew what hit him. So did I. It didn't quite work out that way; the medic was somehow quicker, and as Wolf leapt at him, he turned and clipped the dog on the side of the head with the gun. Wolf went down without a sound and lay in a heap at his feet. He aimed the gun at Wolf and would have shot him had I not thrown the ashtray at him. He spun to deflect the oncoming missile with astounding quickness, like he knew what I was doing before I did it. I had expected as much, what with the luck I seemed to be having; so from my position on the floor, I reached up to the end table and grabbed for anything I could use for a weapon. The only other thing worth throwing was my stereo remote control, so just as he tossed the ashtray aside, I started to throw the remote and climb to my feet for a last ditch attack. I didn't want to die on the floor. Then a loud voice in my head started screaming at me, and suddenly I knew what to do.

At the same time that I stood up, Rick must have decided to try his own assault, being Mr. Black Belt and all. Apparently the medic deduced that he was quicker, therefore more of a threat, and turned toward Rick. At that instant, I hit the button on the stereo that activates the radio tuner, and the medic turned back on me. Somehow he knew what was about to happen, at least it seemed that way to me, plus his expression had changed to one of puzzlement, like all of a sudden things weren't going so good. Rick hit the floor on a roll as the radio station I had been listening to last night—after the bachelor party when I was drunk, stoned, and deaf—came blaring to life. I had hoped for a loud rock-and-roll song, my favorite kind, or a car commercial; they're always too loud too. I should add that I'm pretty damn proud of my Sanyo stereo and the four-hundred-watt speakers that go from floor to ceiling in my living room; they can sure pump it out. And if the truth were known, I had passed out while listening to it, so the volume was still cranked. George Thurgood and the Destroyers never, ever, sounded so good as they wailed out "Bad to the Bone" from the speakers. The effect of the music probably saved my life or Rick's because the music did exactly what I knew it would do. The medic froze like a fucking mannequin or a statue, and as he did, Rick shot a hole clean through him with the alien weapon. I grabbed an AC/DC tape and threw it into the cassette player, made sure it was rewound, and switched the stereo function to cassette. With no loss of sound, the tape began playing, and I motioned Rick it was OK now, as the level of sound was deafening, and speech was out of the question. The medic looked like a cartoon character, froze in midturn with a big hole through his middle; it was freaky.

I walked over to him and removed the gun from his stiff fingers and saw the same guts and wires that had been sticking out of the other Rick. I grabbed the remote and turned off the stereo, and as I did, he sank to the floor. I looked at his face. His eyes were still looking at me though he still didn't look quite so sure of himself now.

Suddenly he spoke, "You must die, Guardian." He fixed me with an angry stare.

"Holy shit!" I yelled. I knew what was coming, and I was getting just a little goddamn tired of the whole mess. I lost it, and I went over the edge. I bent down and picked up the son of a bitch by his belt and neck, screaming at him in some alien dialect as I ran at my front window or rather what was left of the frame. I threw him through it, still screaming, and as I turned, I yelled in English, "Hit the floor!"

As I fell to the floor, I noticed everyone else was already on the floor. Sure enough, the body blew up. The sound and the concussion shook the foundation and blew out few more windows somewhere. The sound of glass breaking and boards snapping finally subsided, and in the distance sirens could be heard again. I later found my front concrete wall had completely cracked and broken, but for right now, all I knew was that I had survived to live another day. My ass might hurt, but I was alive. And my hangover was gone, whoopee, because I could sure use a drink.

Joan came around the corner from the direction of the dining room as Rick came out from behind a chair. They looked at me for answers, which I didn't have, though I had known what to do. Then Joan spotted Carl, groaning in pain, on the hearth, and went looking for something to stop the bleeding. Rick came over to me as I picked up a dazed Wolf and laid him on the couch. I told him to call 911 and went over to Joan. She was pressing on Carl's shoulder with something out of the medic's supply bag and looking at me. Carl was floating in and out of consciousness and managed to come around long enough to say "what happened" and passed out again. I almost wished I could pass out too.

"What is happening?" Joan said, looking up at me, both frightened and angry. "Who did you piss off this time?" She knew I wouldn't answer; I never do, but what she didn't know was I couldn't. Hell, I had no idea what was happening.

I shrugged my shoulders. *Someone who thinks I'm a fucking Guardian*, I thought, *whatever the hell that means.* I didn't like the implications; frankly it scared the hell outa me. And I was pissed at myself for leaving my gun on the floor downstairs; it had resulted in one dead medic, Carl getting shot, and all the rest of us almost dying. It was a stupid mistake that I wouldn't let happen again.

I was giving myself hell when the troops arrived; police types from all jurisdictions and directions converged on us, fire trucks vied for position, and three, count 'em, ambulances also pulled in the driveway. I brushed the glass from the couch and sat down next to Wolf. He was going to be OK; he let me know by licking my hand. I thought about licking Joan's, and I knew that wasn't going to happen today.

"You want to stay with me tonight?" Rick asked me, coming over and dropping onto the couch on the other side of Wolf. He looked worried.G

"No"—I nodded—"I don't know who's after me, I have my suspicions"— boy, did I—"but I don't know what to do about it. Can you handle things around here for me for a while?"

He nodded. He seemed to know what I was going to do, but did I?

Everyone poured upstairs at the same time, asking questions and shouting orders. Even Wolf seemed a bit lost in the confusion. I wondered if there would be more trouble and then suddenly if everyone was human. There was only one way to find out. I stood up and looked for the controller to my stereo. *Here goes*, I thought.

"Quiet everyone!" I yelled, picking up the remote. Most of the people in the room looked at me and quieted down, but some of them were looking at me like I was nuts. The police didn't like me ordering them around and started to come over toward me. I grabbed my gun from my waistband and waved it around the room. Everyone stopped moving. Even the police, thank God.

"We're going to try a little experiment," I said and aimed the stereo controller at the stereo. The resulting music surprised most of them and proved deadly for one officer, who froze like a statue next to his partner who turned and looked at him. Slowly everyone in the room followed my eyes to the frozen officer.

"Don't touch him, he's explosive," I warned. Somehow I knew they would listen this time. I handed Rick the remote and the gun then reached into my stereo cabinet and pulled out my Walkman. I walked over to the statue while shoving another AC/DC tape in its slot and turned the Walkman up full volume as I slipped the headphones onto his head. I wondered if his ears were real. I knew his nose wasn't. I grabbed the nose and ripped it off, exposing the shine-metal finish underneath. Nobody thought I was nuts now as they stared at his face and then back at me. I tossed it aside angrily.

"Rick," I said, pointing at the stereo, "turn it off." He aimed the controller, and the music in the room went off. For once I enjoyed the quiet. All you could hear were the tiny sounds coming from the earphones. The alien remained frozen in place. I let out a sigh of relief.

"Let me guess," I said to his confused partner, "he just started riding with you today."

He nodded a nervous yes. "My regular partner called off today."

"This is the third one, in less than an hour, that came here to kill me. I don't know what the hell is going on, but I'll tell you one thing, don't turn off that Walkman," I explained. I hoped the batteries were still good. The player was capable of auto reverse, so I knew we were safe there.

"If he unfreezes and sees he's in trouble or that his identity has been revealed, he will activate some device inside his head and kill us all," I cautioned them all. They appeared to be listening intently to my every word; I liked that. Finally one of the stunned officers spoke up.

"OK, everyone," ordered the cop, "let's clear the house before something else happens."

I was all for that. I said a silent prayer to myself, not normally something I do, and went over to Joan. She looked dazed, tired, and crabby, but she smiled, sorta.

"We're outta here," I said. "Grab your stuff, it's time for a road trip." I saw Wolf's ears go up and knew he was going to be fine. He loved road trips as much as I did.

Out front they were loading Carl and looking over Joan and Rick. I noticed a medic looking at me, and I nodded a definite no to treatment of any kind. He seemed to understand and turned back to the others. No more medics for me or my ass today.

"What are you going to do with him?" I asked one state policeman, like any of us knew. I pulled my windbreaker off the hook and put it on; it was getting cooler out as night fell.

"We have some Feds coming," one of them answered. "They'll probably want to question you too."

"OK"—I nodded—"I'll wait out here if you don't mind." The cop smiled. I walked over to Rick and Joan standing in the yard looking at the damage. Wolf was prancing around but still had a spot of blood on the side of his head by his ear. I bent down and patted his side, and he licked my face.

"Rick," I said softly, "why don't you take Joan and Wolf up to Charlie's place"—Charlie was an old friend who lived out in the country about a mile past nowhere—"and I'll come a different direction, that way you'll all be safe." Joan didn't look happy with the arrangement, but she knew it was for the best. I pulled her to me and planted a kiss on her trembling lips as Rick nodded and slipped the alien gun into my windbreaker pocket. They walked to his truck, and I watched as they climbed in and started moving. With most everyone pulling out at the same time, Joan didn't noticed my vehicle still sitting in the driveway. I wanted to wave good-bye but turned back toward the house, sighing as I walked. I couldn't stand to lose even one of them. I looked at the front of my house and noticed how utterly destroyed it was; windows were gone, walls were buckled, even the edge of the roof was blown back on itself. It was amazing that we had all survived both attempts.

My ass was getting cold; the melted pants were of little comfort, so I went inside for clean ones, wondering as I walked past the "thing" and his two very nervous bodyguard cops. What was in store for me now? I felt a brain shiver go through me and hoped I wasn't about to have a flashback or something, courtesy of Pracon's touch. I knew that knowing Tharx and also what to do with the remote had kept me alive, but sometimes the visions he had given me were too much for this Homo sapiens to handle, and this felt like one of those times.

I was back in the yard, staying well away from the house, when a huge green step van pulled up the driveway and headed toward the house. *Feds*, I thought, *this is going to be fun*. I lie to myself all the time. I went to the door and yelled in that the Feds had arrived. One of the cops answered me and sounded very relieved. I saw three Feds get out of the step van and walk toward me. They looked kind of old, like they had come out of retirement for this job. They all had gray silver hair and seemed shorter than I had expected them to be, though their outfits had Fed written all over them. I laughed out loud for no damn reason. Then they stopped in front of me. Maybe they were specialists in this kind of thing.

"Are you Jim Edwards?" asked one of them. He seemed to be the boss.

"Yes," I answered, "for the time being, the alien is in the house listening to music." The humor slipped by them; *they must be Feds*, I thought.

They looked at one another, and I had a creepy feeling that something wasn't right. Finally, after a miniconference, the boss went back to the truck and retrieved a large black satchel and went into the house. The other two stayed with me, making me feel like I was being guarded for some reason. A few minutes later, the two deputies came out, got into their cars, and left. One of them nodded to me, but neither said a word. When the deputies had disappeared from sight, the two feds stepped up to me and motioned to me to join them in the house. Actually, they kind of forced me to come with them, if you know what I mean. I felt badly outnumbered and just a little uneasy. I felt for the alien gun in my pocket. I wished Rick had not squirreled my .357 in Joan's bag. It felt more like a real gun; this alien thing felt like a Mattel toy. Well, at least she would be safe.

We entered the upstairs, and I found that they had moved the alien to my dining room table and had removed my Walkman. I grabbed it off the counter and stuffed it into the pocket of my windbreaker to cover the small lump of alien gun. By now, they had attached a big black horseshoelike device to the alien's head. I have never seen anything like it before. One of them reached to it and flicked a switch behind the back of it. The alien's eyes came alive, and I jumped back into the kitchen, ready to run out the back door.

"It's OK," one of them said. I stopped dead in my tracks and went back to the table, more curious than scared. For the moment at least.

"Who sent you?" the Fed closest to the alien said. He said it in Tharx. It registered in my brain, and I was just getting ready to do a Jesse Owens impersonation when the Fed closest to me reached up and put his hand on my shoulder. I must confess, their short stature was not very disarming, and I did tower over them; but I had seen a few little guys whip up on big guys, and I didn't know what kind of fire power they were carrying, so I relaxed my shoulder and casually slipped my hand down to the pocket. I felt confused, but I really wasn't getting any bad vibes, so I relaxed and watched what was going on, on the table. The alien on the table was struggling against an invisible force, trying not to talk; at least it looked like that to me.

"He looks like a Beta android," said the Fed next to me.

"No kidding," I remarked, "and why do you say that?" I didn't want to appear stupid to the little guy. My brain seemed to register the answer before he even gave it; *the size, almost correct, not quite.*

"His size actually," he said, scratching his chest. He looked back up at me and caught me watching him scratch; he pulled his hand down and seemed embarrassed.

"Bojj," said the alien on the table through gritted teeth. The two Feds at the table looked at each other with wide-eyed surprise. I don't think they liked the answer very much. The third one, next to me, made a funny noise and rubbed his chest again.

"He's Beta, all right," he said to me, "Beta Memda."

Again, the name sounded familiar to me. "Out past Rigel?" I asked, my head spinning, mind overloading.

"Yes," he commented, "you've been there?" He seemed impressed.

"Not recently," I joked and was sorry I said it because I'm a firm believer in Murphy's law. It would probably come true. For some reason though, I knew where it was; a star map floated through my thoughts as if to confirm it.

"Must terminate Guardian, Bojj directive," growled the guy on the table; he was clearly more agitated now, and his neck was starting to bulge. None of the Feds seemed to mind that his neck was about to explode; at least they didn't appear to be worried. One of them touched the back of the head device, and the alien on the table stopped moving, and surprisingly, his neck stopped bulging and returned to normal; at least it looked normal to me.

"We won't get anything more from him," said the Fed next to me. "Deactivate him." He said it so casually. One of the other two fiddled with the device, and the body on the table gave its last breath, or whatever, and went dead. One of them picked up the arm and let it fall; it flopped on the table with a confirming thud. The Fed next to me went over to the body and removed the device and handed it to one of the others.

"He was only activated yesterday," he said, turning to me. "He found you quickly." The other two nodded. Like I was supposed to be hard to find?

"I'm in the book," I said, pointing to the phone in the kitchen. The reaction I got was a surprised look from all three. I walked into the kitchen and pulled open the drawer under the phone and removed the phonebook and dropped it on the counter. They walked over and stared at the phonebook like they had seen a ghost. Then they started looking out the windows, and the two who worked over the alien cop began running around the upstairs like the place was on fire, and they couldn't find the door.

"You know," I began, "you guys don't act like Feds. You act like you're from another world." I knew the answer even as though I really didn't want to hear it.

"I am Torgan," said the one who I had been talking to. "We are from the planet Entimall. We should have been here sooner, but we got lost near Alpha Centauri." He kept looking out the windows and listening for something.

"What are you doing?" I asked. I knew that answer too.

"Keeping a watch for more of these Beta droids," he answered, staring out one of my back windows.

"How many more could there be?" I asked. I didn't know that answer.

"Impossible to know," said Torgan, "could be one, could be a thousand." His two buddies heard this and made little noises with their lips. It was comical, almost. But after the day I was having so far, my sense of humor was pretty dull, if not dead.

"So, you can't keep this up forever, what are you going to do?" I asked. I wondered where the real Feds were right now. Now I was starting to creep out.

"We have a ship coming, Melnor has activated the beacon from the vehicle out front. We should have left already." He started making those little lip noises. I almost laughed. Any other day and this would be comedy with a capital *C*.

"Torgan," I said, spinning him around by the shoulders, "what the hell is going on here? Tell me why these fucking aliens are trying to kill me. Who is this Bojj dude and why are you here? To fight them or did you just stop by to say hi?" I wasn't going to let go until I got some answers. He stopped squirming and looked up at me.

"We are the last Guardians of the Tau Ceti system," he answered, pointing to his buddies, "and when we heard the news that there was a new Guardian, an associate of the great Pracon, we decided to come and seek his help. We had no idea you were battling Beta's until we got here and scanned the area, located you and intercepted the call for federal assistance and, um, well, here we are." He stopped to inhale and placed his hand on his chest like he was saying the pledge of allegiance. He pulled it down when he saw me look and damn if his face didn't redden a bit.

"Why did you act so surprised when I showed you the phonebook," I began, "and why do you think I'm a Guardian? Does knowing Pracon make you a Guardian automatically?" I hoped not. I don't think I was the only one confused here.

"Guardians don't usually tell anyone who they are, or where they live, it can be very dangerous, as you can see," said Torgan, "and we are not used to someone like you, you are too daring, Guardian Jim Edwards." Suddenly a light went on in his head; I could tell by the look. I could feel it starting to glow in mine.

"Have you not been before the Order and confirmed as a Guardian for this system?" he asked incredulously. I don't think he wanted me to answer that. I shook my head back and forth, the universal "no," while my brain started fitting pieces together. He appeared to understand the "no," for he suddenly looked as confused as I was about the whole damn thing.

"Then why are they trying to kill you?" asked Torgan. His two buddies had come over to us and were listening to us question and answer each other.

It had gotten darker and darker outside, and in another few minutes, it would be pitch-black. I held up my finger as in "wait a minute" and went around the room, closing curtains and turning up the heater. It was cold in the house even with my jacket on. We couldn't stay here much longer. I motioned them all into the dining room, which was in the back of the house and still had its windows. The bedroom would have been warmer, but I couldn't see myself sitting around the bed with these three goobers. I turned on the light over the table, went to the fridge, and pulled out a six-pack of beer. I brought it back to the table and handed it around until we all had one. They watched me open mine and followed my lead as I took a long swallow. Immediately they all spit their beer straight out their mouths and started gagging and choking. Mine tasted good, and the second would be better. I ignored the mess on my brand-new table and waited until they had calmed down. One of them turned and puked all over the alien on the floor where they had shoved him when I went to get the beer. The final insult no doubt. I grabbed another.

"OK," I began, "let's see if we have this right. Some guy named Bojj thinks I'm a Guardian, whatever that is, and hires these Beta androids to come and kill me. You think I'm a Guardian, so you come all the way here from Tau Ceti to ask me to help you. Right?"

They all nod at me in unison.

"Now," I continued, "we don't know who told this Bojj dude that I was a Guardian nor how many droids he sent after me?"

They nodded again.

Now we were getting somewhere, I hoped. "So who told you I was a Guardian?" He was the son of a bitch I wanted to meet.

"Melnor," answered Torgan quickly. He wasn't taking the rap.

"The guy who signaled for your ship?"

They nodded. Neither were the other two taking the blame.

"Where is he?" I felt like I was making progress finally.

"Out in the vehicle," answered Torgan. Like I should know that!

"Then go get him," I ordered angrily. *So I can wring his little neck*, I thought. *Who knows, maybe the Bojj heard it from him too. Could I be that lucky?*

Torgan sent one of his buddies out to the van, and several minutes later, they returned. I noticed that even though they had only suit coats on, none of them appeared to be cold. I was going to ask and decided not to for the time being. Torgan had a brief private discussion with Melnor, who looked just like the rest of them, a bunch of little old men, and turned to face me.

"Well," I said, "who told Melnor?" I sat back and crossed my arms over my chest. This brought an unexplainable murmur from all of them. I unfolded them quickly and waited. Torgan acted like he was clearing his throat.

"Crouthhamel of Altair, he was at the last meeting of the Order."

I put my hands to the back of my head and rubbed it. I didn't want to ask it, but I did. "Who the hell is Crouthhamel?" I couldn't wait for this.

"I am," said a voice from the living room.

I spit my beer onto the table and turned to the archway not knowing what to expect next. It wasn't a letdown, for in to the room strode a very tall, very wicked-looking creature. His skin was reddish black in color—no, a blackish red—and his features were hard and angular. With a couple of horns, he would have looked just like the devil. Plus he had several belts of weird-looking weapons and ammunition, if that's what it was, crisscrossing his torso and strapped to his waist. Under the belts was a costume of black and silver tunic and pants, and upon the chest area of the tunic appeared to be a family crest of some kind. It was a very sharp outfit to say the least, worn by a person of obvious position, a position I was sure to be made aware of immediately. His manner and sharp features, his uniform and deep voice, together with brilliant green eyes, commanded instant respect, at least from me. I turned to the Entimallians—they had disappeared under the table, although you could still see the tops of their little heads—and shook my head in disgust. I turned back to Crouthhamel and stood up to meet the Altairian.

"I'm Jim Edwards," I said, sticking out my hand in greeting. He hesitated and then stuck his opposite arm out to me. He only had three fingers and a thumb, which appeared normal for him. I clasped his hand in mine and shook it. I'm sure it was his first handshake ever. It was hard as a rock as I'm sure the rest of him was too. His eyes went straight through me and then fell on the little guys under the table. He didn't look like he was happy to see them, although the look on his face changed only slightly.

"Torgan," he barked. I heard those funny little noises coming from under the table, noises that they had made earlier. A moment later, a terrified Torgan came out from under the table. He looked sick.

"Yes, mighty Crouthhamel," he said in a strange dialect; I barely recognized it. My brain said it was Gooide. I didn't think Torgan wanted me to hear this conversation, so I pretended not to understand.

"What are you doing here?" asked Crouthhamel. I swear the table started shaking. I stifled a laugh, but a smile crossed my face. He saw it but chose to ignore it. Maybe his race didn't have humor in its genetic code.

"We . . . a . . . came to help the earthling fight the Betas," he stammered, pointing to the dead Beta by the table. He folded his arms across his chest and tapped his shoulders with his fingers. "We put a Vega collar on him," he said, relaxing a bit.

"And," said Crouthhamel. He was not long on words.

"He was sent by the Bojj," said Torgan proudly, "and he was only activated yesterday." As he brought his arms down to his sides, I saw him give his chest a quick rub. Again I wondered what he was doing but didn't ask.

"Where is your ship?" said the Altairian. His look was one of disgust.

"It should be here any second," offered Torgan. It sounded like a prayer.

As if answering Torgan's prayers, I heard a soft hum from my backyard, and through the window, I could barely make out something settling down softly into the snow. It wasn't very big, whatever was out there.

"Get in it and get out of here," ordered the tall guy, "and tell no one what you have done or seen." Torgan nodded so hard I thought he was going to break his neck.

"If you do," continued Crouthhamel in Gooide dialect, "I will remove the sex organs from your chest and put them on your back." He had stepped closer to Torgan and barely whispered the words. At least it finally answered my question about all the chest rubbing. What a bunch of perverts.

Never have four people left my house quicker than Torgan and his buddies. They flew out my kitchen door like their lives depended on it and took off so fast in their little ship that it took the snow and half my topsoil with it into the air.

"Jim," said Crouthhamel, rather nicely for him, "I'm sure you have many questions."

I nodded and was about to agree when he continued in Tharx, not Gooide.

"But before we begin, I think we should move to a safer location." And then he turned and headed toward the front door. I was still nodding as I jotted a quick note to Rick and Joan, "Gone for a ride, be back soon, Love, Me."

He seemed on a roll, so I let him call the shots. I hurried to catch up.

"Follow me," he semiordered from the front doorway. I had picked up the Vega collar, and he reached out for it. I handed it to him without a word and went out the front door behind him.

His ship was sitting almost on my front steps, so I couldn't get a good look at it, but it was bigger than the other one. The side facing the steps was open, with the door or hatch forming a ramp up into the ship. Crouthhamel had to duck going in, but it was big enough, so I didn't have to, even though I'm slightly over six feet tall. I hesitated at the opening; he turned and looked back at me. I hoped he wasn't going to say, "Trust me." He didn't say anything, so I walked up and into the ship. The door snapped shut behind me. *So much for second thoughts*, I said to myself.

We were standing in a room about ten by ten with walls of blinking lights and control panels that curved up to a rounded ceiling. To my left, or rather the front of the room, was a huge gray screen or window, I couldn't tell which, and in front of the screen was a matched set of chairs. The arms of one were folded up, and Crouthhamel, who had deposited most of his belts and weapons in a large drawer that appeared in the opposite wall, went to this one and sat down, pulling the arms down. He motioned to me to join him. The seat was as comfortable as it looked. He pressed several buttons on the right arm of his chair, and a seatbelt came out of the chair and surrounded his chest and waist. He reached over to my chair; his arms must have been four feet long. With a skill born of repeated movements, his hands touched the appropriate buttons on my chair, and I was instantly surrounded in the same manner. The straps weren't tight, but they sure held you in place. The screen in front of us came alive, and we were looking at my driveway and the land beyond it. I noticed it was snowing again. He began touching the arm of his chair, and I felt the ship start to elevate; in front of me, the landscape disappeared beneath us, and I found myself staring at the tops of the hills and houses around mine, then the entire county bordered by the Ohio river, until I couldn't make out the individual details, just the darkly lit colors and sparkles of light. It was fucking far out.

"Screen forward," he commanded, and the view changed to a cockpit view of night sky and clouds, above which I could see the stars blinking. We continued to rise at what I would consider slow, like he was either letting me adjust to the feeling or just being nice. I decided it was number two.

Crouthhamel looked over at me. I couldn't tell what he was thinking; don't you hate that about some people?

I decided to break the ice and talk first. "So much for 'Home Sweet Home' huh?" I sort of asked, in Tharx, meaning my house or what was left of it.

He repeated the words to himself, obviously thinking about what they meant, then he smiled. It made him look completely different, almost human I decided. Almost.

He looked over at me and nodded. Touching more spots on his chair, the screen or rather the ship tilted up, and a microsecond later, we were in space, heading away from the planet. He directed the screen "aft," and I saw the planet for the first time like I was a freakin' astronaut. It was really cool. Crouthhamel touched my arm and motioned toward the screen.

"That's"—he pointed out—"Home Sweet Home."

# CHAPTER 3

## Dead and Buried

According to the front view screen, we were headed straight for the moon. And though we really were going fast now, and the moon really was approaching us rapidly, the silence between us made it seem like hours. It had probably been two minutes. Finally the tall man spoke.

"How much do you know about the Guardian Projects?" said Crouthhamel the Altairian without taking his eyes off the moon.

"Nothing really," I answered. I searched my mind for some record left behind by Pracon. Nothing, well, nothing I cared to mention right now. I stifled the urge to impress him; it wasn't easy. I found I already liked him for some reason. Chalk it up to Pracon's mindfuck.

He nodded and continued to fly straight at the surface of the moon. I noticed that we appeared to be getting real fucking close, and I wondered if he planned to land on it or just ram it. I began to get a little nervous when the moon filled the whole screen, and I swore I could see little flags on the surface.

Suddenly we were turning hard and flying straight across the surface, oh, say, about a thousand feet or so above it. I realized I was leaving handprints in the arms of the chair and relaxed my grip a little. I glanced over at Crouthhamel. He looked like he was doing more thinking than flying.

"Let me tell you a little bit about the Projects," he began, "and maybe it will answer some of your questions."

# The Guardian Projects

I nodded, jerking my head toward him. He had used English, it had surprised me, but I didn't think he even noticed my amazement.

"Many hundreds of your years ago, in the galaxy known only as Alpha, a race of beings called Alpharians began what we call the Guardian Projects. They began by simply visiting neighboring star systems and sharing their advanced technology with a very select group of beings from each of the various planets in these systems. It was to help create a universe of peace and cooperation, and the rules were simple, with the common good most important of all. Of course they made mistakes, not even the most advanced peoples can be perfect, ourselves included. But the basic goals remained intact over the years. Today, the Projects have even spread as far as your planet, although it was an accident, it has been waiting to happen for over a hundred years, maybe more. The Alpharian Council, which no longer has any Alpharians on it—by the way, they are an extinct race by your standards—still meets to oversee the Guardians and solve the problems of the known universe, that it is capable of solving, I should add. I will explain what I mean by that later. For the moment, it is most important that I explain how you have suddenly come in contact with the Projects and why your life is in jeokardy." His English needed a little work, badly.

"I would imagine that I have Pracon to thank for most of what has already happened to me," I said. I couldn't wait to thank him.

"Yes, you came highly recommended by the honorable Pracon," he answered, ignoring the sarcasm. "He was the last of his kind in the Procyon system." His verbiage caught my attention.

"What the fuck?" I asked. "He's dead!" I couldn't believe it. I had just met him.

"I cannot explain right now," said Crouthhamel sadly. "Let's just say he died like the master Guardian his father was, truly courageous. It is the same reason why I was late getting here."

"The Maglarr?" I said. He looked at me quite shocked. I felt shocked.

"Yes"—he nodded—"they have been more visible lately."

I wanted to ask him about Pracon, but he held up his hand and continued.

"In fact," he continued, "the Council met on Entimall, in an emergency session because of the Maglarrian presence. Pracon was there, and at his urging, they decided now would be a good time to put a Guardian in this Parsec. At Pracon's urging, and a strong second, it was proposed that we contact you, personally, a rare occurrence I must tell you, since your world has not been contacted, yet."

I felt thrilled and a bit suspicious; what can I say, oilmen are like this.

"So that is how Torgan found out about me. He said you told him."

"I did," remarked Crouthhamel nodding, "I am Senior Guardian for this and several other parsecs. It was my duty to call the roll at the Council meeting because of its meeting place, in one of my galaxies. Torgan is one of them, for now anyways. He is going to be severely reprimanded for coming to your star system, without my approval."

*Boy, I'd hate to be in his shoes*, I thought. "Is that why the Betas showed up?" I asked. "They followed him?" It didn't make sense; they were there first, before him.

"No," he answered. He brought the ship to a halt. We were on the dark side of the moon, and believe me, it really is dark here, fucking dark.

"It would appear that his arrival was a coincidence," he offered. "The Bojj were responsible for the Betas being activated, but how they found out about you so quickly is now my problem to solve. The Council meets in secret and all matters are confidential. And all Guardians are sworn to secrecy, on a death oath, if it is violated." He looked over at me, making sure I heard the last part.

"So you've got a traitor in your midst!" I concluded, "and he or whatever it is, told the Bojj and they switched on the Betas." Made sense to me, but were the Maglarr really part of the equation? I didn't ask; why, I can't say.

"Yes, it would appear to be so," he agreed, "for there have been Betas on your planet for many years. Their sudden activation is the real problem. You see, the Bojj were thought to no longer exist; they haven't been heard from in several hundred years."

"Not since the war with Maglarr?" I asked. He again seemed surprised at my knowledge. *Thank you, Pracon*, I thought. I wasn't mad at him anymore.

"Yes"—he nodded—"that is when they disappeared."

"How many Betas are on my planet?" This was a surprise to me. I don't like surprises, never have, not even the good ones, well, maybe the good ones, like sex.

"The Bojj seeded this galaxy centuries ago," he said, "there is no way to tell how many are here, although the way you were attacked makes me think the number is very small."

*Yeah, take two more off it*, I thought. "Why did the Council let them do that?" I asked. "I mean seed this place?"

"The Bojj and the Maglarr were both very bad alliances for the Alpharians, remember I said they made mistakes."

"Big ones, huh?" I added. I knew big ones. Like drilling a crooked well.

"For the Alpharians, they were final ones." He waited for my reaction.

I felt a chill run through me at the thought, but I nodded and tried to look cool. This was heavy duty shit, and I wondered if I was ready for it since I was obviously being asked to enlist as a Guardian by this guy. I wondered if I really had a choice.

"So every time I show my face on earth, the SOBs are going to attack me?" I asked; the idea didn't thrill me, and I couldn't, not go home. I hoped.

"No, once you left with me, they will back off. They were trying to get you, alone, before you joined. The Bojj have never directly confronted the Order, they are too sneaky for that. Plus they knew we would hunt them down for killing a Guardian. They have failed." His last statement sounded more like a question than a fact. I decided to get to the fine print.

"You mean, once I'm a Guardian, they won't touch me?" I felt my choices begin to fade to one. Crouthhamel was looking at me as he had earlier. He nodded to me.

"Once you become a Guardian, they will think you are after them, and the Bojj cannot take the risk of being any more exposed than what has already happened here. They will likely deactivate all the Betas on your planet to cover their tracks. Torgan's Vega collar was really a blessing for us; it confirmed their presence was not something left over from long ago. They may not be aware yet that we know that fact. It may help me expose the traitor."

"So I will be able to go home as a Guardian," I said; it never hurt to ask the same question a different way again.

Crouthhamel nodded. "Yes, of course, we all have homes, as a Guardian, you would be protecting your home star system and the parsec around it." He made it sound easy, too easy. But then my options were rather limited, Guardian or death. It was a no-brainer for this guy.

"So," I asked, "how do I defend the whole parsec from my planet?" I could see myself picking up the old intergalactic hot line and asking for Crouthhamel of Altair and the operator saying, "Which one, I have more than one." I smiled to myself. Or getting a busy signal, that would be a bummer.

He smiled back at me like he had read my mind.

Crouthhamel must have been lowering the ship as we spoke because all of a sudden a ship came up to meet us, head on; the sensation was just like being at a traffic light when the guy next to you rolls backward, and you think you've rolled forward, but you haven't. I sat there staring at the other ship; it had the same coloring as his uniform; the black and silver colors shone back at me illuminated by Crouthhamel's exterior ship lights where utter darkness had been moments ago. It was hypnotic. The crest on the front of the ship was different though from the one on the Altairian's uniform. I noticed this as he came back to his chair with a small case in his hand and sat down without strapping into it. I looked back at the ship; it was sleek, powerful, and menacing. I immediately fell in love with it. I knew it was mine, just like I always knew which presents under the old Christmas tree were mine. I sat back smugly; I was going to raise some major hell in that baby. Oh yeah.

As I sat back, I felt something slip over my head, and suddenly I was paralyzed in my seat. My thoughts went to the Vega collar and the dead Beta, and I felt my blood turn to ice. The old hairs on the back of my neck were probably sticking out like cat whiskers. *How could I be so naive*, I thought. *Here I am, thousands of miles from earth, sitting on the dark side of the moon with an alien who looks like the devil, and daydreaming about flying around the galaxy in that ship.* If I could have hit myself, I probably would have smacked myself right in the head. Boy was I stupid. Then he spoke ever so softly.

"This is not a Vega collar," said the Altairian, as if reading my mind, "it is a T&T collar, training and testing, it will not hurt you, trust me."

I really hate those two words. But I tried to relax anyway.

"The T&T collar was developed back in the old days, when we had to train and test a hundred potential Guardians at a time. I have to use it on you, rather than train you myself, because my time is now critical. I must reach the Council and tell them what has happened here and I can't use a deep space communicator without someone overhearing me. And I can't leave you here untrained. I hope you understand." His voice was awful silky, smooth even for the devil.

"Then why can't I move?" I asked suspiciously. He came around my seat and crouched in front of me. His green eyes were hypnotic but not threatening. Again I tried to relax, but I kept seeing that commercial with the egg frying and the announcer telling you it was your brain on drugs.

"It is a side effect, nothing more," he assured me. Then he reached above my head, and I felt a weird sensation. I don't think I actually heard the facts and figures, but they swam through my mind, and I found myself learning and answering the questions it asked me, out loud. It was as if you were being taught something and then quizzed at the same time. In a steady progression, the thing on my head fed my brain with facts and then asked me about them. The more I answered, the more Crouthhamel nodded and smiled. I felt his enthusiasm and answered the questions even quicker. Suddenly I was answering the questions before they came into my mind. The trainer on my head began to heat up, I could feel it. He told me later that it was actually smoking at that point. I must have passed with Pracon power!

"That's enough for now," he said, snatching the collar from my head. "You seem to have some uncanny abilities. And you seem to know as much about the universe as a forty-year veteran," he rambled, smiling quite happily, "and as much about ship mechanics as a Betelgeuse engine installer. Are you sure you haven't used a trainer like this before?"

"Never," I answered, "my only contact with life beyond my planet was when I met Pracon." I felt I should keep the contact between Pracon and myself confidential. I stood up, tested my legs, and walked to the viewing screen and switched the view through a series of above, below, and rear pictures. I knew how to use it. Cool. I turned to Crouthhamel. He sat silently; perhaps he knew and was honoring my secret. That was cool too.

"Is that mine?" I pointed to the other ship.

He nodded yes. "If you choose to join us, I will make it so."

"What the hell," I said, all pumped up from the testing, "what have I got to lose." *Besides my freakin' life*, I thought. He seemed to accept my answer.

He went to the back of the ship and entered the weapon's room. The ship's capabilities, both weaponry and range, are awesome. One of the cases he brought forward held a remote controller for the other ship. I knew it. He gave it to me while he set the rest of the contents down. I used it to turn my ship sideways to the side of his ship and locked the airlocks together. I would have entered it had he not stopped me.

"Your ship is a modified one," he cautioned. "I will have to show you what they have done to it, there is no training collar for it." He was standing beside several smaller metal cases and a uniform like his, only the crest on the front was different.

"How did you come up with that crest?" I said out loud. King of the dumb questions, that's me.

"This is the crest worn by all of Pracon's family for over a thousand years, he wanted you to wear it, he said it would be an honor for his people if you were to wear it. His family has never allowed anyone to wear it so don't take it lightly." He handed me the uniform. The crest was the same as the crest on the front of my ship. The realization hit me hard, and I felt sadness and anger for Pracon. I vowed to him as I stood there looking at the tunic that his death would not go unanswered. Crouthhamel read my thoughts; he was too good at it.

"He said to tell you," said Crouthhamel, "kick some ass." He smiled.

We both laughed. From the sound he made, I knew he hadn't laughed in a while. I felt very honored, and I hoped I would never let him down. At least not a lot. We entered the other ship and the hatch hissed closed.

I woke up with a start. I had been dreaming about having my own spaceship, a big blackish red-skinned warrior and little men from the FBI. Then I realized I was in a chair not my bed, and I looked around and realized I was on a spaceship.

"Oh God," I said out loud, "it really happened." I fingered a button, and the chair lifted to an upright position, and the arms lowered into place.

"Computer," I said, remembering some of the things that Crouthhamel had shown me before leaving, "give me a quick look around." The view screen did a 360 circle around the ship and then a 360 vertically. I was still on the dark side of the moon, alone now, hovering over the unseen terrain.

"Thanks," I said. It seemed appropriate.

"You're welcome," answered the computer in the same voice I had heard from Pracon. It was spooky, but I liked it. I sat there for a few minutes rethinking the past few days. Friday had been the party, Saturday had been the war at my house, and Sunday I had spent with Crouthhamel on the moon. I wasn't sure, better ask.

"Is it Monday?" I asked.

"No, it's Tuesday," corrected the computer. "You slept through most of Monday after Commander Crouthhamel departed."

I decided right then and there to buy a good watch with a day and date reading on it. Then I remembered space-time was different altogether, oh well.

"What time is it," I asked, "in West Virginia?"

"You should buy a watch."

*You should answer my question, smartass.* I suddenly hoped it didn't read minds too.

"I am known as Crown," stated the computer.

"I like smartass better," I joked. Should I tell it the name Crown was a dog's name? Nah. Maybe later.

"You want me to answer you," it answered almost threateningly.

"Let me think about that," I said sarcastically. I sat for a second and then realized I had better check on Joan, Rick, and Wolf.

"OK, Crown, let's go home." I touched the controls on the arm, and the ship leapt forward and pulled away from the moon easily. I pretty much played with it all the way back to Earth, talking to Crown all the way. It really wasn't a computer as we know it, but rather an artificial life-form capable of its own stubborn directions and opinions. It was like having Pracon as a copilot. Suddenly he spoke up.

"Jim," said Crown, "you have fighter jets from your continent headed for us, do you wish to engage or deceive?"

"Deceive," I answered, "and change course until we've reached five thousand feet and then resume original." I rose from my chair, letting Crown take over, and wandered into my weapons room. By now the ship was invisible to everyone on Earth, which was better for all concerned. I had taken the Guardian oath and studied the Alpharian doctrine, so I didn't want to break any of the rules just yet. I had discarded my clothes and put on the uniform that Crouthhamel had given me. It was probably the most comfortable set of clothes I had ever worn, a little heavy but still comfy. I can't describe the material as anything more than some kind of a woven metal, yet it felt warm like flannel and stayed cool like nylon. I had been told by Crouthhamel that it was indestructible, but I didn't want to test it right now, at least not while it was on me. I rummaged around till I found my weapon's belts and tucked a couple of Zalo Disorganizers in the holsters. They were nasty weapons with no adjustment for power; when you hit something, it was gone. Just what I wanted, a no-bullshit gun.

"Jim," spoke Crown, "I have resumed course and we should arrive in Parkersburg in five minutes."

"Thanks, Crown," I teased. "You know, on Earth, the name Crown is usually given to a canine, certainly not a highly intelligent life-form like yourself. Perhaps a more prestigious name would suit you." Boy, was I playing with the devil.

"Like Columbus or Archimedes or maybe Pegasus." I sat down in the control chair and resumed playing with the ship, dropping to skim the mountaintops and climbing back up to the clouds. I spotted an airline coming out of Charleston airport and flew alongside it as it climbed into the sky and then broke away and headed for Parkersburg following interstate I-77 north. Crown had been quiet all this time, and I figured that I had pissed him off. I had been serious with him; I didn't like the name Crown, at least not for the computer on my ship. I had thought about calling him Pracon, but it brought back too many depressing thoughts, now that he was dead. And it wasn't Earthy enough; maybe Crown would suffice.

I was sitting there mulling over Pracon's death and how I might find out more about whatever had happened to him when Crown spoke up.

"Jim," said Crown, "I have given this name thing some consideration."

I hoped he had not picked Hal for a name.

"Yeah, so what's it going to be?" I asked.

"Merlin."

"Merlin." I rolled the name around on my tongue. "Yeah, I like it. Merlin the magician, yeah, it fits you like a glove."

"Now we need a new name for you," said Merlin smugly.

"Thanks, but I think we'll stick to Jim, but you can call me James, if you wish, Merlin."

"Do you not possess a second name?" said Merlin. He sounded playful.

"Yes, but don't get any ideas, I prefer Jim, OK?" The discussion was over as far as I was concerned. I was about to remind him who was in charge when the city came into view; you couldn't miss the floodwall surrounding it. It was a beautiful sight, and I felt a little more homesick for Joan and, of course, old Wolfie.

I guided the ship over the city; it wasn't very big, no New York or nothing like that, and spotted Route 2 heading north along the Ohio River. I followed it just above the treetops, and my house came into sight within minutes. It looked like a dump, worse than I had imagined it would look. Even the fresh covering of snow on it failed to hide the missing windows, curled up roof, and broken walls. The missing front door left a gaping black hole, and along with the rest of the damage, it made the house look like a Halloween pumpkin carved by the insane, or maybe Jim Walters on acid.

I wondered if my stereo was still there and all my other stuff. Maybe I could get Rick to hire somebody to fix it up. I was going to stop, but I saw no reason; Joan wasn't there, so I headed west into the mountains, steering a course straight for Charlie's house.

I almost flew over it; it's not easy to find even when you're looking for it. And searching from the air was all new to me. Plus Charlie lives in no man's land, on a ridge top that he can barely reach and only then by four-wheel drive. Most of the ridge is tree covered, so I figured I would have to clear a little place to land. I could barely see the two trucks in the yard in front of his house; both were snow covered, but one of them looked like Rick's. I felt like jumping from where the ship hovered, but I controlled myself and spotted a sparse area of trees about thirty yards to the right of his house.

I turned on my ship's Zalo beam, just like the one in my hand weapon, only bigger and rapidly disorganized a half-dozen scrub pines clear down to the top of the snow. The ship settled down into the clearing, and even though I thought I had room, it still snapped off a few adjacent tree limbs as I brought it down to ramp height and jumped from my seat.

"Merlin, look after things, will you," I said. I stopped next to the door and opened a small cubicle and withdrew a wrist sensor. I had to wear one or not leave the ship, Guardian orders.

"No problem, Herbert," remarked Merlin, using my middle name. "I will let you know if anything happens of importance." He sounded so impish, what a shit.

"I'm going to rename you, Shithead, if you ever call me that again!" I yelled, running down the ramp and disappearing into the trees. Then I stopped and turned around. The Shithead had found out my middle name, impressive and sneaky.

The ramp closed, and the ship vanished from sight. You couldn't even tell it was there; there weren't even any footprints, except mine. I decided to approach the house quietly in case any Betas were hanging around, but mostly because Charlie was a trigger-happy old coot and didn't like most people. Hell, he really didn't like anyone, but he did tolerate Rick and I, probably because our well on his property had made him virtually self-sufficient financially and also gave us the right to enter the old fart's property. Otherwise, we'd probably be dead. Did I say he was trigger—happy? I reached the edge of a big pine and could see his front door through the trees; it wasn't easy because the trees were heavy with snow, and the branches of the large pines were hanging down almost to the point of breaking off. I didn't see anything alien going on, so I decided to announce myself. I broke from the trees and walked toward the house.

"Hello in there, anybody home?" I thought they would recognize my voice; I was wrong. That's when I heard the click of the gun and turned to face Charlie.

A single blast from Charlie's old 12-gauge shotgun rang out, echoed across the ridge, reverberated back across the hollow—we don't call them valleys in West Virginia—and knocked me backward into the snow. I felt like a mule had kicked me, but I didn't feel shot. I sat up slowly and found Charlie aiming his shotgun at me again. The look on his face went from amazement to shock as he realized the guy had survived the blast, and that the guy was me. Behind him, from the house, ran Wolf, Joan, and Rick, screaming his name and mine. Wolf was the one barking. I felt my stomach and looked down at the material; not a single mark showed. It hurt, but not like the hurt from a load of buckshot. The uniform was indestructible, holy shit! Charlie just stood there looking at me and then at his gun.

He shook his head apologetically. "I'm right sorry, Jimmy Boy, we figgered you was, well, dead and buried!"

# CHAPTER 4

## Tweedledee and Tweedledum

As Charlie helped me up, Joan and Wolf converged on me and succeeded in knocking me to the snow again, but this time it felt good, especially with Joan on top. I kissed her long and hard as Wolf licked both our faces wildly. Rick and Charlie stood back observing us, and I could tell Rick had spotted the uniform from the look on his face. He was interested, in a Trekkie kind of way. Apparently no one but Charlie saw me get shot, and by now the buckshot had settled deep into the snow.

"Christ, Jim," sputtered Charlie as I sat up again, shoving Wolf aside and rolling Joan to the other, "I couldn't tell who you were—"

"That's OK, Charlie"—I cut him off—"you must have missed me, I'm fine. Come, everyone, let's go inside, I could use a drink." And Charlie owed me a big one. We went inside, but Charlie muttered all the way in about his shotgun and the need to get another one 'cause the one he had couldn't shoot straight. I happily let him think what he was thinking; he wouldn't have believed the truth anyhow.

We had a good old time at Charlie's home. I ate, more like shoveling, for the first time in several days. Everything tasted so good, so I ate almost everything in Charlie's fridge. I made a note to myself to ask Merlin about food, and then drank up all his beer too. In between mouthfuls, I told them what little I could, which wasn't much, and listened to what had happened while I was gone, which wasn't much either. That afternoon, Rick and Charlie went into town for supplies, and Joan and I went to her temporary bedroom to look at the inside of my uniform, if you know what I mean.

"So what happens next?" asked Joan as she lay on the bed next to me, snuggling into my side. Her breasts were nudging me, reminding me of how luscious they were, and how hungry I had been for her nipples. I scooted down, rolling to my side, and suckled them, feeling the nipples harden in my mouth while running my free hand down her side and around to her ass. It was a fine ass; the words round and tight always came to mind. I squeezed her one cheek at a time, kneading the flesh, letting my fingers run down her butt crack, bringing my index finger almost to her womanhood, feeling our wetness. Mr. Happy, our nickname for my penis, began inflating again; he wanted a replay of the last-scoring drive. She felt so good; I wanted to make love to her again, but we knew they would be back soon, and we needed to talk a few things out before then. I scooted back up and smiled. She squeezed me hard, and I felt Happy throb back at her grip. She squeezed again and smiled back at me. Two can play this game.

"I have a meeting to go to in the Aldebaran system," I replied, "then I guess I'll be settling into the routine that I worked out with Crouthhamel." I really shouldn't have used his name. "I am going to try to keep things going here and be a Guardian too." She looked at me like I was nuts. My "OOPS" sensor went off.

"When do we see each other again," she snapped, "the year 2000?" Her hand came loose from Happy quicker than you can say "iceberg," and down he went.

"Come on, Joan"—I didn't like where this was going—"you have to go back on the road in a few days, and you'll be gone three weeks doing your thing all over the tri-state area." She was the Midwest supervisor for a large cosmetics firm, and it put her on the road a lot. She knew I was right but refused to admit it right away. She grabbed her ointment off the nightstand and went after the burn on my butt; it had healed quite a lot already. Finally she slapped the other cheek, ooh!

"I know," she conceded finally, "but that's different. I don't worry when you're running around the hills here, but now you'll be, God only knows where"—she pointed to the ceiling—"and I can't call you when you're out in space, battling bad guys, or take care of your boo-boos." I let her whack me again, double ooh!

I grabbed her and pulled her to me. We were about to heat up the bedroom again when we heard a truck coming up the ridge. We, I did say we, didn't want to be embarrassed, so I, not we, dressed quickly. I was sitting on the couch in the living room playing with Wolf when Rick and Charlie stomped in the door, loaded down with food, beverages, and stuff.

"You look human again," teased Mr. Rick Wisecracker, reaching over and rubbing the top of my head as in "horn check." I swatted at him, and they both laughed. I wondered how he would react to the Entimallian reproductive organ location, but I let it go, Guardian Code secrecy bullshit.

Rick popped me a beer, and as Joan came out of the bedroom looking very human, not to mention sexy, he popped one and handed it to her. God, it was good.

"I think the danger has passed," I said to Rick, who settled on one side of me, "so maybe you could get someone to give you an estimate on fixing up the old homestead while I take another road trip. I should be back in a week, and we can figure out what to do then."

"Sure, Jim"—he nodded—"you want me to look after Wolf while you're gone?"

I nodded and looked at Wolf. He knew something was up and came to me cautiously, giving me those big puppy dog eyes that every dog can do so well. I rubbed him, and he settled at my feet. No way was I taking him along.

We talked about stupid shit and joked with each other until way past midnight. By then I was sitting on the couch, teasing Joan who was falling asleep, sitting up and feeling pretty tired myself, when my sensor went off on my wrist.

"Jim," said Merlin, "we have to go now." He sounded so human; it was freaky.

"It's my computer," I said to a surprised group. Even Wolf was sitting up, cocking his head at my wrist. I felt like Dick Tracy.

"I'm not a computer," said Merlin, "I am Merlin, a life-form."

"OK," I said interrupting Merlin, "I'm on my way." Picky, picky, picky.

"It's my copilot," I corrected myself, standing and reaching to pull Joan up and into my arms for one last smooch. I remembered the Zalos and squeezed her first before putting them on again. I shook hands with Charlie, patted Wolf, and walked out into the night. I turned in the front yard and waved to Joan at the door; she looked so good, so . . . warm. Rick had followed me out the door, and I let him come. He was like a brother, screw the bullshit, he wouldn't see much anyhow.

"I'll take care of everything," he said, and we hugged as Merlin opened the hatch and flooded the field with light. He eyed what he could see in the light.

"I know, I'll be back." I strode up the hatch feeling good about myself for once and sealed the hatch behind me. I dropped the sensor in a small receptacle next to the door and my weapons in a drawer that Merlin opened next to the hatch.

"Thanks," I said.

"Did you have a good time with all your buddies?"

"Yes, what's going on? I thought we didn't have to leave until tomorrow AM." I finished putting away my stuff and headed for my chair; it spun around to meet me. Nice touch, huh! See if Kirk's chair does that.

"Change of plans, is Joan as foxy as she sounds?" Merlin had been listening on my sensor relay.

"Yeah, Merlin, she is an absolute doll." I could have gotten angry, but I needed him, even if he was a voyeur. Plus I would have done the same thing.

The screen came on, and I was looking at Crouthhamel; he must have sent the message while on his way somewhere. He looked pissed.

"Jim, I have a problem in the Altair system and you've got to handle it for me. I know what I said about territories, but something major has come about and I am pulling every Guardian I have out here, to the Rigel system. I need you to go to a planet called Pyritium and find out what the problem is; I have not been able to reach them since I received a distress call from Choric, their leader. He called it a P1 emergency. Check it out for me. I will be back in touch from Rigel." The screen went blank.

"A P1!" I said out loud. "Isn't that the one meaning total planetary destruction is imminent?" I strapped in and gave the screen a quick 360 look both ways.

"Yes, it also means they are unable to stop it on their own," responded Merlin. "It may require a Mothership."

"No shit?"

"No shit!"

"Yeah, well I'm not calling in a Mothership until I know what the problem is on Pyritium, you know the penalty for that." I didn't want to lose my job the first day out.

"Shall I handle this while you're sleeping?" said Merlin. He liked to fly as much as I did, but I didn't think I could sleep, I was pumped. No sleep for me. And I didn't care if it was out of my territory; hell, I was on a mission, my first mission as a Guardian, hot damn. My only regret was not joining the rest of them at Rigel.

"No, I can't sleep." I took the ship straight up and just missed an Allegheny commuter flight. I felt the chill of shock at the near miss but kept on going up.

"Way to go, Lindbergh," remarked Merlin.

Did I hear a giggle? "You could have said something, I forgot about the damn airport." I snapped, imagining the collision of the plane and my spaceship.

"I knew you'd miss it, I just wanted to see what you'd do." He laughed. I didn't find it funny, stupid maybe, but not funny.

"When you're done, Chuckles, set me a course and engage," I ordered, "and give me one parsec per hour, that should put us there in a little over five hours." The ship was set up in PPH, parsecs per hour, in deep space drive, which is what I call it; I can't pronounce Betelgeuse until you get to about 999 PPH, then the Zalo Time drive kicks into gear. This multiplies the DS drive by hundreds or thousands, maybe even more, and would have put us on Pyritium in the same amount of time it takes to slow down from such a high speed, or about five hours! Anyhow, I wanted time to do some studying and maybe even—yawn—some napping. By the way, Zalo is to the universe what Acme is to us earthlings; a lot of my equipment is labeled "Zalo, furnishing the Universe since before time began." Pretty impressive motto; I couldn't wait for the commercials.

"Aye, aye, commander," barked Merlin almost sarcastically.

The ship came out of DS drive as smoothly as it had gone into it. I could barely discern the increase or decrease in motion, except of course if you were watching the screen, then all the objects around you turned into streaks of light like it does in the movies we watch on Earth. We were just outside the Altair system, a binary star system with one big bright sun and a softer white dwarf star. Slowing down just barely woke me up from the nap I hadn't thought I needed but really did after all. I felt good.

"Do you have a fix on Pyritium?" asked Merlin, who apparently liked to tease me.

I decided to ignore him. I took the ship through the solar debris that surrounded the system and headed for the dwarf star. The bigger one was rotating so fast it was almost flat, something to be avoided.

Pyritium was the closest planet to the smaller star; its gravity is lower than Earth and its people taller. I knew via Pracon that they had gills on the sides of their necks, but I still wondered what they looked like, especially the females.

"Gimme orbit," I said to Merlin rather gruffly. I signaled the planet that I had arrived and waited for their reply. I tried to imagine what this Choric guy would look like.

"Orbit locked in," said Merlin. "Nice job getting us here." He said it in a complimentary tone. Score one for the human.

"Thanks, Merlin," I replied. It never hurt to be pleasant, plus I was suddenly nervous.

The screen beeped, and I released the view scene of my orbit around Pyritium and found myself looking at a tall thin woman, pretty but agitated about something; at least I read it that way. Call it view-screen vibes.

She waited for me to say something and finally spoke. "Welcome, Guardian, I am Trayla, daughter of Choric."

Boy, I liked the sound of "Welcome, Guardian"; I let my ego roll it around for a minute and then answered, "Hello, Trayla, I am Jim, son of Herbert." She missed the joke, so I continued more seriously, "Where is your father?" I asked, "And can you give me permission to land?" You always asked; some planets were real picky about that.

"We don't know where he is, and yes, please land at the following coordinates"—she sounded as nervous as I was—"and I will meet you there."

I nodded and fed the coordinates into the computer, signed off, and pulled the ship out of orbit. As we approached the coordinates, a domed city came into view.

"Shall I take us in?" asked Merlin politely. He was learning how to handle me.

"Yeah, man," I said, climbing out of the chair and walking toward the back of the ship. "I want to unload up and clean up." I waited, but he didn't make one smartass remark.

I don't care how clean the ship's laser shower got me; it just wasn't the same as an Earth shower with water and soap, still, you couldn't beat the sixty seconds or so that it took. The toilet was something else though, with its tiny seat and disintegrator plate. I checked and sure enough it was a Zalo. I was just finishing arming myself when Merlin announced we had landed in the city. I grabbed my sensor and snapped it on my wrist as Merlin opened the hatch. I stood there for a second, taking a deep breath, trying not to look nervous. Thank God, the suit absorbed sweat or I'd look like I'd been out in the rain. My family sweats a lot, what can I say.

"Be careful," he mothered, "I don't like the feeling I'm getting."

"I know what you mean and no problem," I replied. "Take care of the ship."

"No problem, Jim." He and I were sure thinking the same way now.

I walked down the ramp; Trayla and several Altairians, two males and another female, all greeted me with the Guardian salute, a left fist to the chest area, and then bowed. Then one of males stepped past the rest and stood in front of me.

"Thank you for coming, I am Gellid, minister of defense," he said to me. He looked down on me, which gave him an excuse to size me up, as they all were doing politely. I tried to see his gills and caught sight of one, high on the back of his neck. This was definitely cool, I decided.

"So fill me in on your P1," I said. I hadn't seen anything threatening yet. I hoped for their sake that it was a P1, or they could lose their Guardian privileges, which would then be giving an invitation to every pirate in the galaxy to visit them.

"Please come with us," said Gellid, turning with Trayla, and walking away from me. Both of them seemed rather uptight, which might be normal for Altairians. The other two, a male and the other female, walked at my sides, still staring at me.

"You are an earthling?" asked the male. I turned to him; his gills were bigger and he looked younger and friendlier.

"Yup, always have been too." I smiled. I thought he was going to laugh, but Trayla and Gellid had turned back to me and tightened up the group. I looked at the female next to me. She was built like a brick shithouse, a very tall one. Besides the gills, the only other outward difference I could politely see—besides their height, that is—was the lack of a nose. There was some kind of an opening there; it wasn't gross, just an opening of skin, like vertical lips, but it wasn't a nose. As I looked further, I also noticed that they didn't have any ears. The thing above their mouths must be their hearing organ; I wondered if I should ask if they could smell. I didn't remember Crouthhamel not having a nose or missing ears, and these people weren't red either. I searched my memory for two places called Altair and came up blank, which was nothing knew for my memory. *Oh well, I'm sure there is an explanation for the difference in these Altairians and the red one*, I thought.

We passed through several very high doorways and finally came to a closed door. I felt like a midget, a fat one. We entered a conference room; the big table in the middle tipped me off, and they seated me at the head of the table. My legs dangled above the floor; the chair legs were so long. I felt like I was stealing Gellid's seat from the look he gave me. I felt under the seat for wires. He realized the look he had given me and tried to explain.

"That is Choric's seat," he said. "He is my father." He seemed a bit more sociable after getting that out on the table, so to speak. He even tried a smile. That meant Trayla and him were brother and sister. No wonder they were so melancholy; I would be too. I smiled back. I could be sociable too, even if I was short.

I noticed a view screen come on at the other end of an otherwise very plain room. Several other Altairians entered the room and quickly took seats, trying to get a look at me without being obvious. They didn't seem all that bad, just stuffy.

Gellid spoke up and the screen came alive. "This is New Choric," he said. The screen showed a city much like the one I was sitting in now. Dome covered, ultra modern by Earth standards, and nestled in an ugly valley of yellow ground. I didn't see any foliage or plants at all, anywhere. "That was two days ago," he continued. "This is New Choric today." The screen showed only the yellow ground; it looked like Mackie had been there. The city was gone. I looked around at them; they all looked serious to me. Same valley, no city.

"OK, I'll bite," I said. "Where did it go? Was it destroyed by someone, stolen or was it just lost in space?" A little humor never hurt.

"Guardian," began one of the older dudes, "the city and all two hundred thousand people in it, just vanished."

"Nobody saw it vanish?" I asked a bit surprised. That's a lotta people to misplace, ouch. All I got was universal "no" nods all around the table.

"The nearest city is over a thousand pics from New Choric," said the same dude.

"Merlin," I whispered. I knew it must be a long way.

"A pic is two of your miles," he whispered back quickly. Several Altairians were giving me the eye. I smiled back at them. I'm glad he didn't shout it.

"We sent an enforcement squad to the city when we lost communication from them," replied Gellid, "and they found no trace of anything or anyone."

"What about satellite recon, did it show anything?" I asked. This was weird.

"We usually have only outward facing recon, we do not need to monitor the planet surface," responded the old dude, "but we did rotate them the mespic we knew there was a problem there."

"Let's look at the recon pictures," I said; I knew a mespic was a very small unit of time, a second or two maybe. This was getting weirder.

The satellite recon pictures came up on the screen, and I had Gellid run through them quickly and then more slowly. It had been a terribly cloudy day, but even still, all you could see was yellow dirt; no city appeared in the pictures whatsoever.

"Did your satellites show any alien presence during the day?" I queried. I had to find something; I was a Guardian. I needed someone or something to shoot at.

"None really, the only vessel in our area that day was a Silmarrion ore transport, which went by long before we lost touch with New Choric," answered Gellid.

"Soil samples?" I challenged. Maybe some kind of Disorganizer hit it.

"Negative, we found only the usual high concentrations of acids and no unusual temperatures," he retorted.

"Seismics?" I asked. I was quickly running out of questions.

"They appeared normal, but we do have a lot of volcanic activity on this planet. Also, most of our sensors are placed to detect the activity in those regions, not around our cities." He seemed ready with answers, too ready.

"We do have an increase in activity in and around the volcanic regions," injected the older Altairian. Gellid gave him a dirty look.

"Who are you?" I asked the old dude.

"I am Nilton. I am the minister of the interior," he stated proudly, straightening his posture and puffing his chest out. He looked at Gellid defiantly. I liked the old buzzard immediately.

"You're in charge of all the state parks, huh," I joked. Humor people, come on.

"We don't have any parks outside the cities," he corrected me. "The acid rain storms on this planet are perpetual, and severe in some areas, like New Choric."

That explained the lack of foliage.

I looked up at Gellid; I just didn't like the dude for some reason. He was so haughty.

"Your father," I said, "he was at New Choric when it disappeared?"

Gellid nodded; the look on his face told me he cared for his old man, even if he was a snob.

"He was going to dedicate the new Aqriport," he said, "it would have been so beneficial to New Choric and the whole planet."

"What's an Agriport?" I asked. *And don't say an airport for vegetables*, I thought.

"It's a molecular transporter, developed to transport food on an interstellar level, along with consumer goods, hover crafts and even water," replied Gellid. "New Choric is, or was our food and material distribution city."

"Please don't mention food," I said; my stomach was just starting to demand my attention. "So what are you going to do until I figure out what happened?"

"If you mean for food and water," he answered, "we have a supply here to last us until more arrives, and all our cities have backup water and food."

I looked at Gellid and wondered if the stupid routine was genuine. I know having a city disappear with thousands of people was horrible, but come on, you don't call the Guardians for that. At least not without some kind of proof that they're needed—you know, like signs of alien destruction, craters, gas clouds, thermal spikes, whatever—it just wasn't there, and that pissed me off.

"I meant about the rest of your cities, goddamnit. If there is no threat to the rest of your planet, why did he call this a P1 emergency and how did your father manage to send out the signal, for that matter, why did he not call you first for help?" I get a little grumpy when I'm hungry. Something wasn't kosher here.

Almost all of the Altairians looked surprised when I said P1, except Gellid and Trayla. I waited for an answer. It had better be a good one. I wondered what the Council would do to them for lying to Crouthhamel. The investigative branch of the Council, which usually decided if and when the Guardians would be called or not called, could have better handled this. They were good at that too.

"I was the one who called it a P1," admitted Trayla. "I used a voice duplicator when I sent out the distress signal." She gave me the "I'm so sorry" look, which I didn't buy. Holy shit.

The rest of the Altairians just sat there in shock. Lying to the Alpharian Council was like cutting your nose off to spite your face. They had better hire some heavy dudes to defend their planet, 'cause when the Council found out they cried wolf, they were liable to throw them out of the cradle of protection, forever.

"What the hell made you do that," I yelled, "are you stupid?" I couldn't believe I was hearing this. Again, something told me there was more to this than what I was hearing. Gellid had risen from his chair when I called his sister stupid. I looked over at him and gave him the mean look I was noted for on Earth, and he promptly sat back down. Yes, I have a mean face, especially when I'm hungry. Too bad, I was already pissed about missing the action on Rigel, and I really didn't know what I could do here. The Council would probably have to send in the Blame squad, sorry, the Investigative branch. By now, Trayla was crying; I noticed her gills were puffing out too. Yes, it was weird.

"I didn't know what to do," she stammered through the tears, "and Gellid wasn't here. He had gone to New Trillion and wasn't back yet." Was I wrong or did I see Nilton's eyebrows go up just a bit.

"What kind of city is that?" I queried. I wondered why they have a New in every name, and then it dawned on me. This planet was a rehabitation by the Altairians about a hundred years ago. Their sun had blown a hydrogen cloud, and they had been forced to stay with their cousins on some other planet. Talk about having relatives over for the holidays; I think they were gone fifty some years before they returned.

"That is the city of Science and Research," said Nilton. He gave Gellid a funny look after he said it.

I was about to question Gellid, which would have been fun, when an Altairian burst in the room. He flew to Gellid, gills puffing, chest heaving, and spoke into his face, or ear I guess you could say. Talk about getting in somebody's face. Gellid looked up at the screen after pushing a button in front of him. All I could see on the screen was more yellow dirt.

"What's going on," I said. Time for more bullshit or what?

"That," he said turning to me, "is what is left of New Hamel. It just vanished like New Choric, without a trace!"

"New Hamel," said Nilton to me, "was a domestic city for Kellic Altairians." He was the only one who looked upset; that bothered me for some reason, but why?

"What's a Kellic?" I asked. Call me Mr. Stupid Question.

"A red Altairian," he said to me. "Like Crouthhamel, your commander," he added quietly.

I think I was starting to get the picture. In all their grand posturing about what an advanced society the Altairians were, they forgot to mention one thing. They had segregated the Kellic Altairians to areas of the planet that were "hot" areas, not the most enjoyable place to be for an upper class Altairian. What a bunch of bigots. I sat there and shook my head at the thought. Racism in space, how quaint.

"Well," I said, rising from my chair, "I think I'll go see what's left of New Hamel." I turned to Nilton, "Care to join me?" I was ready to leave, period.

He nodded, surprised, and we left the rest of them sitting at the table, staring at the screen and us as we walked from the room. I felt like bitch slapping Gellid, but I didn't.

"Merlin," I said from the hallway, "did you hear all that?"

"Yes, not exactly the most compassionate people are they?"

"No, say listen, did you run any scans on the planet yet?"

"Yes."

"Well?" What was he doing, besides pissing me off.

"Would you prefer me to answer now?"

"Yeah," I said, finally picking up on his hesitation, "Nilton's OK."

"I have seismic activity scans showing disturbances all over the planet," he hesitated again. I looked at Nilton.

"What else, Merlin?"

"I believe there is some kind of intelligence behind them."

"No shit, really, like what?" I looked at Nilton again. He raised his eyebrows at me. I noticed they were kind of bushy, like Groucho Marx's. I decided not to mention it. And I kept a straight face too.

"I can't explain it yet, it's really just a feeling."

"That's cool, we're almost there; plot a course to New Hamel, please." I decided to be polite. He did say a feeling, as in, he had feelings? Interesting.

"All set, Jim."

Almost while he was saying that, we approached the ship. The hatch was open, and we quickly seated ourselves. I couldn't reach Nilton's chair, but Merlin activated the straps. I had to remember that; it could come in handy.

I didn't want to rip the dome off the city, so I used plasma drive, which still got us there in under ten minutes, which was pretty fast considering the other side of the planet was about thirty thousand miles away. It was big, but it had a low mass for such a large bugger of a planet.

"Are you sure this is right?" I said to Merlin; there really was nothing there on the viewer, except yellow dirt.

"You bet," he responded. He had already been with me too long; I could tell.

"I want to get out, is it OK?"

"Yes, just don't get your feet wet, the ground is very acidic." Nilton nodded as Merlin answered me. I made a face, hoping Merlin could see me. I went to the clothing locker, put on some space boots, and went out the hatch. The area looked like Mackie had been there; the ground looked like it had been turned over for spring planting as far as you could see in all directions. I clumped around in the heavy boots until I got tired of them, looking for something, anything, but there was nothing to look at. There was not one single damn scrap of material lying on the ground. It made me think though that wherever the city was, it might still be in one piece, hopefully.

"Jim," said Merlin, "can you come in now? I want you to hear something, besides there is a nasty acid cloud headed your way."

"No problemo," I said, walking to the ramp. I kicked the boots off and banged them on the side of the ship and followed Nilton in, wondering what I would be listening too.

"Ready," I said, sitting down. Nilton offered me something that looked like food. I grabbed it. It was like a granola bar in outward appearance. It tasted like chocolate. I think I swallowed it whole. I was about to ask Nilton what it was when Merlin must have activated the sound system. I could barely hear anything.

"Turn it up, will you," I complained, "my ears aren't as good as yours." Actually they were terrible, too many rock concerts and drilling rigs.

The sounds were clearer now; it sounded like people yelling, yelling in Tharx and several other languages. The voices faded away to silence, followed by two huge bangs that almost broke my eardrums. Nilton threw his hands to his face in agony. At least he only had one ear. He looked pained but motioned OK.

"Sorry," said Merlin, "I had it turned way up and forgot to delete your boot banging."

"You forgot!" I exclaimed. That was one for the record books. I looked over at Nilton. He seemed to be recovering poorly. I shook my head; I could still hear my boots banging on the side of the ship, deep in my eardrums.

"Jim, the voices," Merlin said excitedly, "they were coming from underneath us." That would make me forgetful too.

"What?" said Nilton and I together. We both had the same stunned expression; I'm sure.

"The voices were coming from below us, then they just faded away. I scanned the area, but all I can find below us is a large lava flow, moving away from the area. And now it's gone too."

"Are you sure it was lava?" I had an idea it wasn't smart rocks doing this.

"Not positive, no, it was over a thousand meters below us and going deeper." I could tell Merlin didn't like being unsure of anything. I looked over at Nilton; he seemed a little white in the face. I looked at the screen; a light flurry of yellow flakes was coming down on the ground. It was cool looking and deadly too.

"Acid snowfall," I commented to Nilton. Stupid questions sometimes make people talk. He seemed to want to talk about something, or maybe he didn't.

"We call it a rainstorm, what is snow?"

I looked at him in surprise. I needed to take this guy to Colorado quick. "Frozen water, that crystallizes in the atmosphere and falls on the ground, you've never seen snow?" He shook his head. Poor guy. He didn't look good.

"So what is the funny look on your face for, Nilton?" I asked slowly and softly.

"I think we need to go to New Trillion immediately," he said nervously. "I hope it is not what I think it is." You could tell he was hoping about something.

"And what is that?" I asked. I could almost hear the drum roll.

"A nephid," he replied hesitantly. He looked like he had seen a ghost.

"Let me show you when we get to New Trillion," he pronounced before I could ask him. "It is something you have to see for yourself."

"Merlin, do you have a handle on that?" I said.

"Yes," he said as the ship rose, "New Trillion is north of here, ETA in six minutes." And we were gone. I was going to ask Merlin if he knew what a Nephid was but decided to wait. I would know soon enough.

"Nilton, what was I eating earlier?" I said, trying to ward off the primitive urges from my stomach.

"Garf bars, they're very good," he remarked, offering me another one. I hungrily accepted it. I tried to eat it slowly.

"Is this chocolate?" I said with a full mouth. I rose from the chair and went to the food and drink dispenser and got a glass of water for each of us.

"Not quite." He smiled slyly as I swallowed what was left of mine.

"You don't want to know, Jim," said Merlin. He sounded like a cat with a canary in its mouth.

I looked at Nilton; he shook his head in agreement. Maybe I didn't. Just then, a small domed city came into view in front of us. Its dome was closed. The landing port was closed too. I smelled the fish a fryin'.

"Guess they're not expecting us," I said, fingering the transmitter controls. "Knock, knock, anybody home?" I said. The screen remained blank. It didn't make me happy. I think my lack of sleep was making me a little grumpy too.

"Who do we need to talk to in there?" I asked Nilton, pointing my finger.

"The head scientist, Dr. Carber," he answered. "He has final authority on opening the landing port. I don't know why he won't answer." He looked worried.

I smiled slyly too.

"Dr. Carber," I said in my nasty voice, "you have sixty mespics to open the port, or I will open it for you. Merlin, count to sixty in mespics, will you please." I turned to Nilton. "What do you know about this guy?"

"He is a renowned scientist and doctor, I worked with him for years before I was made minister of interior. Together we solved many of the problems that were first encountered when the planet was rehabitated. I consider him a friend and colleague," he rambled on. "Why I spoke with him only yesterday about setting up another agriport, right in New Traylid, the city you landed in first. But we agreed that the difficulties of installing larger holding tanks and storage facilities were too much to overcome, and building a new city would be far more economical.

"New Traylid," I laughed, "don't tell me it's named after Choric's two kiddies, Trayla and Gellid. They should have called it Bigotville, no, New Bigotville." I think Nilton almost laughed. His gills popped open and closed real fast.

"Time's up," announced Merlin and added, "Jim, someone just activated a defense shield." Nilton's eyebrows went up again. I smiled, yeah, slyly.

"Bingo!" I shouted at the screen. I lowered the left arm of my chair, which held all the controls to my armaments and fingered the Disorganizer beam. It bounced off the shield like water off a duck. *OK*, I thought, *you want to play games, try this on for size.* I fingered one of my new "Merlin" weapons, the antimatter gun. A jet-black beam shot out from the front of the ship, hit the shield silently, and just kept right on going. When it hit the wall of the dome, it blew a hole big enough to fly a 747 through. I shut it down, or it would have kept on going. Awesome. Nilton almost jumped out of his seat.

"What was that?" he exclaimed.

I smiled. "Black Death, an experimental weapon," I said proudly. Just then, Merlin moved the screen, and we could see a hovercraft leaving the same city. You could see my hole in the background through the open port the hovercraft was leaving through. Merlin must have tied into the city's security viewer system.

"Whose that?" I asked.

"Can't tell, Jim," Merlin remarked. "It's shielded."

I was just about to pursue the SOB when the screen came on and made both of us jump a little. A badly wounded Dr. Carber, clinging to the desk in front of the screen, looked back at us; he was trying to talk, which is a bit hard to do when your face has been rearranged. I mean it, someone had done something to him; he was a hurtin', dude. It looked like his left arm had been severed at the elbow too. He saw Nilton, and his eyes went from pained to sad, and then he collapsed from view. In the background, I could see a piece of equipment with lights blinking.

"What is that?" I said to Nilton.

He had put his head down after seeing his buddy collapse. He looked up to where I was pointing, and his gills popped wide open. *These guys would make lousy poker players*, I thought.

"My god," he muttered, "someone has set the portable reactor we first brought here, to overload. It will destroy the entire city." He looked panicked.

"How much time do we have?" I asked. I felt the rush of adrenaline coming.

"A few mespics, I'm afraid," he gasped. "We'll never get clear of it."

"Who wants to get clear of it," I stated. "Can you turn it off, if I get you into that room?"

He nodded at the same time I reached for the Disorganizer beam. With his directions and my dumb luck, we cut through the walls in microseconds to the room where Carber was sprawled out. I powered up the ship and drove right into it. I swear I could hear the scraping of metal on metal as we went through wall after wall. The people in these rooms dove for cover as I cruised through, though some of them had already sought cover. *They must be the smart ones*, I thought. I jumped up as we stopped, grabbed Nilton, pulled him out of the ship, and literally threw him in front of the machine; to our left lay Dr. Carber. He looked dead.

Now I had carved out a pretty big hole, and I'm sure I hurt somebody along the way, but as Nilton shut down the reactor, I heard a loud cheer go up from the people who had followed behind the ship and from the hole, or rather trench, I had cut in the ceilings above and behind us. They all seemed to know what that reactor could have done to them. Several of them came through the hole behind us and went to the figure on the floor. I thought he was dead, but I guess Altairians are pretty feisty. He actually moved when they picked him up and placed him on the desk.

"Merlin, how's the ship?" I asked. It looked OK from where I was standing.

"May need a paint job," he answered. I nodded to myself. I knew this bullshit with the reactor was meant for us as well as the good doctor and everyone else in here. It pissed me off. Somebody was going to pay, oh yeah.

Nilton had gone over to his colleague and leaned over him. He backed away quickly and motioned everyone else away too.

"What is it?" I said, walking over to him.

He was shaking and pointing to Carber. The good doctor's head had shriveled up, and as I stood there watching, the rest of the body began to swell and move like there was something inside it. I grabbed a Zalo from my belt and fired it directly at the body. Most of it disintegrated as the crowd around me gasped in horror. They backed away from me like I had the plaque, which was OK with me; I had just about had my fill of Altairians with their damn popping gills.

"What was it? Goddamn it," I said grabbing him. He looked at me and shook his head. I let him go, and he slumped a bit.

"Nephids," he said. The crowd behind us gasped, and I swore I heard their damn gills popping. "Someone put a nephid in his mouth." He was still shaking as he said it. Apparently they make lousy snacks.

"Then it's time to show me," I demanded, trying to cool down. It wouldn't do any good to give him a heart attack. He nodded and turned away from the desk.

He looked around the laboratory where we were standing and spotted a door on the other side of the ship. He started toward it, stepping over bits of wall and ceiling; the crowd murmuring as he walked.

"Merlin," I said, "where did that ship go?"

"New Traylid," he quipped. He was getting tired of the bullshit too.

"I knew it." I nodded and turned to the crowd of Altairians. "Did any of you see who paid the good doctor a visit?" I already had my suspicions. No one said a word. As I looked at them, they all shook their heads and averted their eyes so I wouldn't call on them, like I thought they would answer, hah! I turned back to see what Nilton was up to and found him standing at the door he had discovered.

"It's locked," he said. He stood defeated.

"Locks only keep stupid people out," I said, whipping out a Zalo, "no offense Nilton." I let go a shot at where I thought the locking mechanism should be, and a hole appeared, but the door didn't budge. On the other side of the hole, I saw something move up against the other side of the door. It was so big; all I could see was skin or something pressed over the hole. It looked like elephant hide or something like it.

"What the fuck?" I said to myself. "Merlin, what the hell is on the other side of this door?"

"A very large Nephid, I believe," he said, "and according to my sensors, it will soon be on your side. It is growing at a rapid pace."

Merlin's prediction didn't take long to come true. The door broke a mespic later, and I was looking straight at a Nephid, or rather the part that came through the door at me. Man was it ugly. It looked like a giant fat slug with a huge mouth on the front of it, making gross sucking noises. The inside of the mouth looked like a fucking artichoke after you peel all the leaves off it and get to the center. I jumped back, pulling Nilton with me, and leveled both Zalos at it.

"Don't!" yelled Merlin, Nilton, and most of the people in the place, but it was too late. The twin blasts tore open the front of the ugly shit, and that's when it exploded from the pressure within it. I didn't know it was full of water, nobody told me. It must have swallowed half of Lake Michigan or its Altairian equal. Water and guts blew into the room swamping and knocking everyone off their feet. The room almost filled to the top before it ran out the hole I had cut for the ship. I staggered to my feet and grabbed Nilton up from the floor.

"Yeech," I said, spitting water from my mouth, "so that's a Nephid."

Nilton coughed and spit and nodded. We were all soaked to the gills, so to speak.

"How big do they get?" I asked, and the light came on in my head. "Big enough to swallow a fucking city?" *Wanna bet yes*, I thought.

Nilton regained his breath and nodded. "Yes, I suppose it is possible."

"How fast do they grow?" I really didn't want to know.

"It depends on how much water they can get a hold of," he explained. "Carber and I came into contact with Nephids years ago when we discovered one near a volcano. It was indestructible, but we managed to control it with shocks from a seismic pulsator we were using at the time. Carber convinced me to bring it back to the lab and see what it was made of, with the understanding that we would then kill it. We didn't have Zalos back then, so we brought it back for the research."

"Did you kill it then?" I queried. Why do I ask questions when I know the answers already.

"Carber told me he had killed it. I was called to work for Choric himself and didn't see him for many months. I assumed he had." He didn't look so sure now.

"Hmmm," I muttered. I walked into the large room where the Nephid had been and looked around. I saw a table smashed against a wall and walked over to it. The equipment on it was totaled, but I spotted what I thought might help answer some questions, on the floor behind it. I had to be careful, the place had been smashed up pretty good, and shards of glass or something like it lay in a tangle around it. I bent down and pulled an info disc out of the rubble and walked back into the other room.

"This should answer some questions," I announced. I motioned to Nilton, and we entered the ship the second Merlin lowered the hatch. I was soaked, so I didn't sit down. I walked to the sidewall behind my seat and inserted the disc in the slot provided by Merlin. The screen changed to the face of Dr. Carber.

"I have managed to immobilize the creature," he said, looking more complete than the last time I saw him.

"This must be his early notes, I never saw this," Nilton cut in; he looked worried.

*It's the one he "forgot" to show you,* I thought to myself.

Carber continued, "And after examining the creature, I have decided to deprive it of food and water and see what happens; if I am correct, it should not kill the creature." The disc stopped and began again, "The most amazing thing happened today. As the creature appeared to be dying, it went into gestation, as I had suspected."

Nilton and I looked at each other. The disc began again.

"The offspring ate their way out of the mother and then began to eat each other. I had to separate them in specimen tanks or there will only be one of them alive very shortly." Again it paused briefly. "They are now about as long as my finger, and if you hold them, they try to suck through your skin. I am going to try and feed them."

"I have chosen a name for them; I will call them Nephids. I have discovered that all they require is water to survive, but if you give them too much, they begin to grow immediately. Cell division is even too rapid to allow examination, and so I will have to be extremely careful. I grew one the size of my desk, and now I have even more little ones to take care of now." The disc paused.

"Was this guy nuts?" I said to Nilton. He seemed to be a bit fidgety. I stopped the tape and then it hit me.

"You knew they were called Nephids," I accused him, "so you must have seen this disc before now." I reached for him, and he tried to get away. Merlin was quicker and closed the hatch.

"I tried to stop him," cried Nilton, backing up against the wall, "but he went to Choric and convinced him that we needed these things to control the planet. He told Choric that they could be used to control the Kellics."

"So they made you minister of interior for a planet that has no interior." I spat at him.

"They were going to kill me," he whimpered. I walked over to him and grabbed him by the neck and pulled his face down to mine. Now I was really pissed, and I'm not nice when I'm pissed.

"I want the whole story or I will make you wish a Nephid was inside you." I threw him down on the floor of the ship.

He looked up at me and knew it was over.

"Choric let him breed them although he kept an eye on Carber, because Carber figured out why the planet was so devastated. It was the Nephids.

The Nephids secrete an acid after consuming water, so he knew then what was happening to our beautiful planet."

"Beautiful," I said sarcastically. I was already sick of the color yellow.

"Yes, before the sun lost that hydrogen cloud, our planet was said to be one of the most beautiful in the whole system. We only came back because our temporary home planet became even worse than this. And we hoped to fix this one someday."

"So Carber knew that you two hadn't captured the only one, there had to be one last gigantic son of a bitch out there." I was starting to figure it all out.

"Yes," he whined, "Carber told me that he went to Choric with the news. Choric decided to keep it a secret and use it to keep control over the planet."

"So that's why the Kellics have all the water stored in their cities. Better them than you."

He nodded sickly. I wanted to kill him right there, but I held back. I figured Crouthhamel probably would when I told him.

"So what happened to your little arrangement?" I asked. This oughta be good.

"I don't know, maybe the Kellics tried to take control of the Agriport and Choric decided to teach them a lesson."

"A lesson," I screamed, "by killing hundreds of thousands of people!"

He cowered against a bulkhead. I was contemplating going back to Traylid and leveling the city. Something given to me by Pracon must have stopped me.

"Why did you come with me?" I asked suddenly.

"I may be a coward," he said, "but I couldn't stand by with all those people dying like that. I decided to come with you and see if Carber had gone nuts and released the Nephids in the Kellic cities. I wanted to help you, I . . ."

"But you chickened out, didn't you?"

"I did bring you to New Trillion."

He did do that much, and he must have known I would put it all together, or would I have if I hadn't found that disc, and would I have known he was involved up to his popping gills. I wondered how much help he really wanted to give me.

"Who was that in the other ship, Choric?" I asked.

"I think so, I don't believe he's dead," he reasoned.

"Hmmm," I said to myself, "we have two problems now." I opened the hatch and went out into the room. Several Altairians were busy cleaning up.

I had them give me a hand with the reactor, and we managed to drag it into the ship. I thanked them and closed the hatch in their faces. Nilton hadn't tried to escape. Maybe he did want to help. I really didn't care at this point; one false move, and I would drop him like a bad habit.

"Merlin, plot me a course to the next city in line with the two that disappeared, and make it a Kellic one. It probably is anyways, that bastard Choric is—"

"Aye, aye, sir," he joked, interrupting me before I could really get going.

I didn't appreciate the humor, but calming down was the right move. I backed the ship out of the dome—not an easy task for me, I hate to back up anything—and spun it around and engaged the drive system. I was calm now.

"Do you think this giant nephid is smart enough now to find water on its own?" I said to Nilton. He was sitting in the other chair looking lost.

"Yes," he agreed, "now that it's been shown where the water is, it will go after more, and grow even bigger."

"And easier to find," added Merlin.

"Could those other domes still be in one piece or has this thing crushed them?" I wondered out loud. Nobody answered as we sped over the yellow ground.

We arrived at a small domed city about five minutes later and skidded to an abrupt halt at the entrance; it was already sliding open, so I skipped the screen and pulled on into the dome. Altairians, red like Crouthhamel, were massing around the ship, waving and yelling like the savior of the universe had arrived.

"Boy are they glad to see me," I said smugly.

"I believe they think you're Crouthhamel," Merlin said, destroying my ego trip. He was good at that.

I put the ship in stable hover mode and walked out the hatch almost before it was down all the way. Nilton followed like a whipped puppy. The crowd reaction was comical as I strode into view. The cheering stopped, looks were exchanged, and then as they saw another person behind me, the rejoicing started all over again until they saw Nilton, and it abruptly stopped. They started to walk away in small groups, going back to whatever they had been doing, as letdown as I was too.

"Wait," I yelled, "who is in charge here? We have an emergency on its way!"

That brought the crowd to a quick stop. I had yelled it at them in Kellic, which I knew suddenly like English. A really tall Altairian broke from the crowd and came to me. He was even taller than Crouthhamel; he must have been nine feet tall. He had a nose too. And ears where they should be. I quickly explained the impending Nephid attack, even detailing how Choric and Carber had set the whole catastrophe up, hoping he would believe me. I then laid out my wild plan to stop the Nephid as he stood there listening in disbelief to me. I'm certain if I hadn't been a Guardian and sent by Crouthhamel, he would have either laughed or locked me up. He shook his head at me and gave me the look you give a crazy person. Maybe I had hit him with too much too soon, oh well, to bad, can't be helped, no time left now.

"Let me see if I understand you," said Sethhamel; he had a funny name, related to Crouthhamel no doubt. "You are telling me that Choric has unleashed a gigantic monster that he has known about for years."

I nodded, and Nilton nodded, but he paid no attention to him.

"And now this monster is on its way to devour my city because I have water stored here and that is what it lives on, and the more it gets the bigger it gets!

I nodded again. Nilton was trying to speak; his gills were working overtime.

"And the reason this planet is a barren, acidic wasteland is because the creature, this Nephid, gives off acid when it shits?" I nodded, some words are universal, even in Kellic. Shit is shit.

"I believe," Nilton interjected, "the Nephid's secretions are being blown into the atmosphere by the volcanic fields to the south of you. It has apparently been here since before we returned to the planet. I have always thought that it must have been trapped, possibly in a large pool of water near a volcano, constantly growing, gestating, and growing again, finally set free by the stellar explosion. There may have been hundreds at first, until the water became scarce, then they consumed each other in a desperate attempt to survive." Nilton finished talking and looked over at me. He was standing a little straighter and a little taller. I nodded.

"I always wondered why we held all the water," Sethhamel said, starting to believe me. "They led us to think it was a concession to keep peace, those noseless, one-eared, highballed . . ."

I won't bore you with the remainder of his Kellic curses, suffice to say I wasn't exactly healing the bond between all Altairians on this planet. And then Nilton's gills popped so loud; I thought his head had exploded. I couldn't help but laugh.

"I hate to interrupt," warned Merlin, "but I have detected that strange seismic disturbance about nine hundred pics from here and closing fast." He was such a downer sometimes.

"Thanks, Merlin," I said. Sethhamel had heard Merlin also and started looking around. Merlin enjoyed doing that; I was positive.

"So how much water do you have?" I asked, wondering how fast we could institute my master plan.

"Twelve hundred tubs in storage, we recycle constantly," he stated.

"A tub is a hundred gallons, Jim," said Merlin.

"That's not much, is it?" I said trying to figure it all out. "Merlin what is our lift capacity?" I knew the gravity beam of my ship was strong, but it wasn't a freakin' Silmarrion ore transporter, and I wasn't sure of its limits.

"We can move that much Jim, but I don't think it will be enough to entice the Nephid away from the city."

"Why," I asked, "we can't set off the reactor here?" That was my plan, anyhow.

"New Altair, this city, is the recycling center for the whole planet," answered Sethhamel, before Merlin could tell me.

"Oh, shit," I said. I wasn't even trying to be funny. So much for the master plan.

"Yes," affirmed Merlin, "and chemical waste as well. And we don't have the time to move it all. You need a better idea and quick."

I stood there looking around for a new plan and muttered, "It's too bad we can't pipe all that shit out into the next valley."

"Why don't you use the Agriport? We have to move all the waste in our storage dome. It runs almost a pic back into the hill behind us and holds millions of tubs."

"You have an Agriport!" I exclaimed. I thought there was only one.

"Yes," replied Sethhamel, "but it's not an interstellar model, it's how we bring most of the waste here from all over the planet. The rest is brought here in those." He pointed to several large cylinder shaped hovertrucks. Suddenly a new master plan appeared, right out of nowhere.

"OK," I plotted, "are they programmable or remote controlled?"

"Programmable," he answered, sensing a new master plan.

"Good," I continued plotting, "here's what we' re going to do." I laid out my master plan to Sethhamel and Nilton. Sethhamel would have to send the trucks he had, out to slow the Nephid down, while Nilton pulled the plug on the Agriport. I was going to move it to a new location and hopefully put an end to this menace once and for all. When I finished laying out the plan, we all split and went in different directions. I hoped I could trust Nilton to do what he said he would do.

## The Guardian Projects

A short while later, we were hovering over a large valley about two hundred pics from New Altair. Nilton had joined me with a couple of other Altairians on board, and we had just lowered the Agriport to the floor of the valley using the gravity beam. Nilton had wired up the old reactor to the Agriport and set up a remote control, which he stood holding next to me as we watched the viewing screen. I had split the view in three sections, one with Sethhamel; one on the hovertrucks sitting between the Nephids' projected path and the city; and the final view, on the valley below us.

"Remember, Sethhamel," I said, "the last two or three trucks have to pull the creature away from the city by trailing the waste this way."

He nodded. "I have fifteen hovertrucks filled and waiting, strung out straight at you," he confirmed. He looked tense as a piano wire. He should be; there was no place for his people to run and hide. Talk about up the creek.

"The Nephid has arrived at the first truck's location," announced Merlin.

I signaled Sethhamel to start dumping.

"Jim, it seems to be passing the waste trucks at an alarming rate, it may not stop," warned Merlin.

"Cross your fingers and say a prayer, Merlin," I said to everybody.

"It is enormous, Jim," said Merlin, "according to my sensors, it's over a thousand pics wide and I can't tell how long it is, there seems to be no end to it."

"It should be, it's got almost all of the planet's water in it," I surmised, "and with the low mass of this planet, it probably makes tunnels like cutting through butter with a hot knife."

"Yes, we do absolutely no mining here," confirmed Sethhamel.

"Wait," said Merlin. "Good," he added, "it seems to be slowing down and turning back on the trucks, yes, it's going for them." I smiled. It was going to work after all.

"It's headed your way," confirmed Sethhamel. I nodded to him. "Start the reactor, Nilton," I said, turning to him. He fingered the remote in his hand. I watched him refinger the buttons a second time.

"It's not working!" he exclaimed, looking over at me. He looked scared shitless.

"Try it again!" I yelled. When was I going to learn.

"Jim, look," said Merlin; he had magnified the screen portion that showed the Agriport and the reactor. The connection between the two had come loose from its makeshift setup. It didn't look like sabotage, just the worst possible dumb luck.

"Damn," I muttered, "can you bring it back up?"

"Not enough time, Jim," answered Merlin, "but I can drop the ship a lot faster."

Sethhamel started yelling something on the other screen, but I held up my hand and dropped the ship straight down on top of the agriport. Nilton bravely scrambled out the door and headed for the reactor. Go, Nilton.

"We are receiving a transmission from inside the Nephid!" yelled Sethhamel. "You can't detonate the reactor, there are people in there. They say there are many survivors in the two cities, and they have some air left, and the domes have held up, this is incredible, Jim!" he exclaimed. "You've got to find another way."

By this time, Merlin had tied into the transmissions, and I could hear the conversation going on between Sethhamel and some guy in one of the cities.

"I can hear them," I replied. "We'll hold off on the reactor." Shit, holy shit.

Nilton came back in and grabbed the remote. He listened to me as I explained the situation, then I signaled Sethhamel to let the agriport start doing its thing. Instantly, a layer of liquid and sewage appeared on the pad and began running over the edges. We had skipped the containment vessel, naturally.

"Prepare to be swallowed," I yelled, "and find something to hold on to!" I could see the ground moving in the distance. "Here he comes."

In the next instant, a darkness fell over that part of the view screen, and we became lunch for the big mother. The mouth was so big I never saw the edge of it before it sucked us into it. It tossed us around like a bad pill as it swallowed us. Except for Nilton and I, strapped in our seats, the other two Altairians flew around the control room like tennis balls at a Wimbledon match. Hours seemed to go by, though it was probably only a few minutes, and finally we came to rest. I could feel the ship floating. At least I hoped it was floating.

"Merlin," I said, turning on the exterior ship lights, "how far did we come?" As the lights came on, I drew a sharp breath and gasped along with Nilton. The two Altairians were starting to move on the floor; one of them looked up and gasped also. In front of us, not more than a hundred yards, bobbing in an underground lake, lay the one city, and off in the distance, the second city could be seen, wallowing in the darkness. The tops had been partially cracked open, like an egg missing a tiny portion of its shell, on both cities, yet they had remained intact structurally enough to stay afloat. I knew we were in the belly of the damn thing, and yet I couldn't see the other side of it, nor much of the top, as I gave the screen a quick 360 using my high beams.

"About nine hundred miles," Merlin finally said. I believe he gasped also.

The view screen was buzzing with incoming calls, but I only took one of them, and when Sethhamel appeared on the screen, I said only one thing and then signed off. "Tell everyone to hold on to something real solid 'cause we're all going sailing." I didn't want to yak for twenty minutes about the situation. I raised the ship out of the water and flew toward the two cities. Lights flashed up at us as we flew over them. I hoped everyone below was heeding my advice.

"Merlin, take us up to within one hundred feet of the roof," I ordered. It was time to carve the turkey.

"Are you going to do what I think you're going to do?"

"We are quite deep in the ground you know," warned Merlin when I didn't answer him. He was getting nervous.

"What kind of pressure?" I asked. It was my way of answering.

"Considerable."

"Good, point us down the valley and hold on tight!" I exclaimed. The two Altairians looked at one another. I climbed out of my seat and took them into the weapons room and crammed them into a couple of half-filled lockers. At least they wouldn't be thrown around now. I strapped back in and fingered the controls. Time for some antimatter power, oh baby.

I didn't know that it had not moved from the Agriport site, which was apparently still spewing waste deep into the creature, but then, I didn't care at this point. As the beam hit the side of the Nephid, it made the creature convulse and shake in pain. The ship began to roll, but Merlin took over and stabilized it. I suppose I could have used the Zalo Disorganizer, but this was more precise, and I needed Precise. I cut a huge slice in the Nephid horizontally and nothing happened except more shaking and wiggling. Then I cut a long vertical slice in the damn thing, from top to bottom, and all hell broke loose. As quickly as the ground above us began to pour down into the creature's stomach, the water came gushing up at us slamming into the ship and pushing us ahead of it like a cork in a champagne bottle. The two cities weren't far behind us. As I had hoped, the creature's stomach pressure and volume was greater than the ground pressure above us, and it pushed us quickly to the surface about seven or eight hundred miles from where we had first been swallowed. The sunlight was blinding, but oh so welcoming, as we burst free.

I pulled the ship out of the water and up into the sky above it. Below us, the first city came into sight as it popped loose from the opening like it was alive. It tore past us down the valley, riding the tidal wave of water like a surfboard with no rider. I hoped it landed right side up. As the second city emerged from the belly of the Nephid, I signaled Nilton to detonate the reactor. I was hoping the explosion might send the water up into the atmosphere too. Below us, the first city was already a hundred pics away and floating right along, with the second city chasing it. I pulled the ship twenty thousand feet straight up as Merlin signaled to Nilton and I that the reactor had indeed received the signal from the remote. I swallowed hard and nodded back at Nilton. I tried to look confident.

The reactor exploded deep within the dieing Nephid, yet so large was the creature that it took several seconds for the force to reach the opening and, as we soon learned, every other direction too. The ground buckled in every direction for hundreds of miles, and the two cities we were tracking were pushed even farther away. Nephid guts and water rained upward in every direction, striking the outside of the ship even where we hovered in the sky. The screen showing Sethhamel and his city went into convulsions, and I quickly realized it was the city and not my screen that was jumping up and down as the shock waves passed under it. Luckily these cities had all been constructed to withstand severe seismic disturbances; a city on Earth would have been reduced to rubble in seconds if it were hit by the force now hitting New Altair. Water and whatever else it had eaten continued to explode upward and outward as the valley began to resemble the Gulf of Mexico.

"Holy shit" was all I could say. I thought Nilton was going to faint.

"Incredible how much water that Nephid had consumed," said Merlin. "I can't even give you an approximation as to the actual volume."

"Holy shit," I said again. The water kept coming up and out, and I wondered if I had saved two cities or drowned an entire planet. Not bad for my first mission; I could see the headlines now, "Guardian Kills Millions on Pyritium."

"It's already raining on this side of the planet, Jim," said Merlin, "and if the atmospheric pressure holds, it may snow very soon in the lower latitudes."

Nilton looked at me. "Holy shit," he said. He had been with me too long.

Finally, and I do mean finally, the water began to slow to a stop, and then it reversed direction, running and raining back into the area where the Nephid had been, filling up the immense hole that was instantly created as the surface ground collapsed downward. It looked like a small ocean to me. Oh baby!

"How far does it go?" I said. I couldn't see the end of it even from where we were hovering.

"You don't want to know," said Merlin mysteriously.

"Why?" I asked. *Maybe, I don't want to know*, I thought.

"It will soon reach the volcanic field, if I am correct," he said, "which may damage the mantle of the planet."

I wondered if it was a good time to pray. I could see the new headlines, "Guardian Destroys Planet on First Mission." I was wondering what could be worse when Merlin spoke up.

"Jim," said Merlin. He seemed to be enjoying himself.

"What?" I said angrily. I didn't like his tone of voice.

"Crouthhamel just came into orbit around the planet."

"Fuck me," I said to myself. I was expecting to catch hell in a big way. A short but illustrious career. The screen came on; he was talking a mile a minute with Sethhamel and finished his conversation before looking at me. I knew this because I had Sethhamel on split screen and the new ocean below also.

"Hello, Jim," he said exhaustedly. He looked like shit. I mean, I was tired, but he looked beat to shit. "I hear you've been busy."

"Just a bit," I remarked. I looked at the ocean screen and then back at him. I don't think I was very convincing.

"Sethhamel tells me that you saved his city from a Nephid?"

"Yeah well," I began, "old man Choric set him up big time along with all the other Kellics." I rested my case quickly and folded my arms across my chest.

"I don't think so," said Crouthhamel, "but let's get together at New Choric, before I go any further, there's someone I think you should meet there." The screen went off, and I was looking at Sethhamel. He was smiling, so I smiled.

"You did it!" he exclaimed. "And I've been told by Crouthhamel that what is coming down on the city here is actually snow not acid." I switched screens, and sure enough, it was snowing there. Somewhere in my head the mantle of the planet was cracking and shifting toward absolute destruction, yet nothing was happening. I decided to go along with the party mood and continued smiling.

"Before you leave, please stop by New Altair and see me." The whole screen went back to the ocean as he signed off. The view was indescribable, a huge bluish-green ocean surrounded by yellow sand. A Crayola original.

I pulled into New Choric amidst a huge celebration. At least I didn't see a rope hanging around with a noose on the end. There was just enough room to bring my ship into the entrance and maybe enough to open the hatch. People were everywhere, yelling and laughing, dancing at their good fortune and generally having the time of their lives. When they saw my ship coming, the crowd parted to make room, and a wild cheer went up into the air. I let the two Altairians out of the lockers, I had forgotten earlier, and we all exited the ship. I was the last one out. A wild cheer went up as I appeared at the doorway and didn't stop until a very old Altairian, a white one, with the Altairian I call Crouthhamel, approached me. He looked the same, only older and very tired. He walked up to me and clasped my hand. We exchanged salutes, and he turned to the old Altairian.

"Jim," he began, "I'd like you to meet the honorable Choric, leader of this planet." He noticed my funny look, and his eyes told me to behave myself.

"Choric," I said, "when did you get here?" I still had not accepted the extended hand to shake it. Crouthhamel didn't know me very well. I was still a little cranky, and I wanted some answers. Crouthhamel's look told me to accept the hand, so I did, but the delay in doing so did not escape Choric or Crouthhamel either.

"So this is your new Guardian," he said to Crouthhamel while looking at me and smiling. "I would like to thank you for saving us all from the hands of death. That was quite a ride you gave us." *He had been in the city the whole time*, I thought to myself, *and that didn't make sense. I smelled a rat somewhere.*

"And this is an excellent location for New Choric," he added, sweeping his arms wide, "and Crouthhamel tells me the new Agriport will work great here." The silenced crowd roared their approval and cheered as he clasped my hand once more.

He signaled to Crouthhamel, who nodded me toward his ship, and we walked over to it through the crowd. People were cheering and clapping us on the back. I wondered where the refreshments were, and from the looks of the crowd, what they were, some of the people were already a bit warped. I looked back at the city and the outer surroundings as I entered Crouthhamel's ship; the city had finally come to rest on apiece of ground some twelve hundred pics from the point where it had come out of the creature. As the water had receded into the valley below, one city had settled here and the other one on the other side, looking to me as if it had been built there, just like this one here. I smiled to myself as I walked into the ship.

"Merlin," I spoke softly, "keep an eye on Nilton."

"No problemo, chief," he responded. He was getting crazier hanging around with me too.

"So what's the deal here?" I said to Crouthhamel. "I've been told that Sir Choric here had a hand in this Nephid bullshit."

He motioned me to sit down at the table he had in his ship. It was kind of a war room, with a table and several chairs secured to the deck, placed around it. *His ship must be larger than mine*, I thought. The walls were all covered with view screens; I liked it. I wanted one like this, and then it occurred to me that I might not have my own ship after today. I sat down silently. Choric was still smiling like a politician.

"Jim," said Crouthhamel, "I have been talking with Choric and pieced a few things together with his help. I believe you are blaming the wrong party here." His eyes softened and he continued, "Carber never told Choric about the giant Nephid, he knew only of the ones Carber had in his lab, which he kept his eyes on by placing his own scientists in New Trillion."

"What about the water then? Why did he place all the storage facilities in Kellic cities? Why did he murder Dr. Carber and try to kill me at New Trillion? Or for that matter, why did he try to keep Nilton quiet about the whole affair, if I may ask?" Choric had his head down, but since he was so damn tall, I could still see the darkening sadness in his face. Then it hit me. "Gellid and Trayla," I said. They both nodded and Choric looked up at me. Someone he loved very much had just torn his heart out and stomped on it; that much was certain.

"Gellid tried to kill me at New Choric," he said sadly. "I never knew about the Nephid, Carber had told Gellid, and Gellid must have decided to use the information to gain control of the planet."

"And Trayla thought she was luring you, not me, into a trap," I said to Crouthhamel. He nodded.

"They thought I would show up and figured I would go to the nearest city to warn everyone and get sucked up by the Nephid," reasoned Crouthhamel, "or send me on a wild qwimmy chase to New Hamel. Carber and Gellid had worked out a way to draw that monster to any city they chose."

"And the water storage?" I asked, knowing the answer, but wanting to hear it anyway. Crouthhamel gave me the "too far" look, as in you have gone . . .

"My son convinced me," answered Choric sickly, "that it would be a nice concession to make to the Kellic people, so I ordered the construction of all the facilities to be near or adjacent to their cities."

"I should have guessed then it was Gellid I spotted leaving New Trillion, and Trayla was trying to lure me there when she told me that her brother had been there earlier, when the first city disappeared. They were going to blow the place up with the reactor that Nilton managed to shutdown, after first killing Carber, say, is he in on this?" I asked.

"No," said Crouthhamel, "I think Nilton was only a loyal pawn they knew would talk under pressure, but Gellid had him thinking this was all Choric's doing. They would have killed him too if they had been given the chance."

I shook my head in utter disgust. I had very nearly killed Nilton myself.

"So what now," I asked, "kick some ass?" I didn't think he was up for it. And I was pretty tired myself. I had seen the one sun setting as I boarded his ship, and I wondered if that meant I had been up another day without sleep. I was tempted to ask Merlin what day it was now. Except it didn't matter, not now.

"I think we will leave that to Choric," said Crouthhamel. "I think you've done enough here already." I still couldn't tell if he was angry with me or not. I also didn't care. Choric had risen from his chair and offered me his hand as a parting gesture, and I immediately grabbed it. I felt sorry for him; his own kids had fucked him behind his back. I couldn't imagine what I would do if I were him.

He left with his politician's smile on, and the crowd cheered when he reappeared. The party sounded like it was in full swing now. My stomach was growling, and I wanted to leave, but I had to ask first. I sat down and turned to him.

"Are you angry with me," I blurted out, "'cause I know about P1 and . . ."

"No, Jim," he said, interrupting me; his voice sounded tired, "at first I thought you had overstepped your role as a Guardian."

"You mean because it wasn't a P1, but something the Blame squad should have handled?" I hoped. He smiled at the name I had given the investigative branch of the Order. I love nicknames except my own.

"Yes," he answered, "luckily there really was a crisis, for you and the people in these two cities. Do you know how many lives were at stake? I still can't believe there are people like Gellid out there, even after the years I've spent as a Guardian." He shook his head at the depravity of the two.

"You should live on Earth for a while, it's loaded with people like that." I didn't smile either; it was true.

"Well"—he nodded unbelievingly—"I guess you can grab some food and head back home, your work is done here. You really did a great job for me."

I was going to say something smart, but Merlin spoke from my wrist and interrupted me.

"You have a message coming in, shall I transfer it to Mr. C's screen?"

Crouthhamel gave me a look for the "Mr. C."

I smiled. "Go for it, Merlin."

Gellid and Trayla were standing at the screen; they didn't look like whipped dogs to me. In fact, they looked pretty nasty if you know what I mean.

"Guardian Jim," said Gellid, "you are hereby charged with the willful murder of Dr. Palinkas Carber, the destruction of government property at New Trillion, and the theft of one Cyclon fusion reactor from said city."

I smiled. I wasn't impressed with those two twits.

"And the abduction of Interior Minister Bahrcord Nilton," added Trayla, who was showing her true bitch colors. "You are hereby ordered to New Traylid to surrender yourself and your ship." Boy, were they something or what.

"Is that Gellid and Trayla?" asked Crouthhamel.

"No," I said, "that's Tweedledee and Tweedledum." I smiled at them as I spoke to him, but I wondered though, why Daddy hadn't already slammed their asses in jail or wherever you stick people like that. I knew where I'd put them.

"Gellid and Trayla?" questioned Crouthhamel.

I laughed out loud at him, and he realized I had made up another nickname and began laughing with me; the two of us laughing like when you're tired and you get punchy. I reached over and turned off the screen. The last thing those two saw was my erect middle finger. We left the ship to join the celebration, and the cheering started all over again. What a crazy bunch these Kellics are. Did I mention they're tall?

As Crouthhamel started out the hatch, he turned and looked at me, laughing to himself, shaking his head at me this time, and muttered, "Tweedledee and Tweedledum."

# CHAPTER 5

## Do Not Pass Go

Merlin said I was lucky; I say it's skillful luck. You tell me. The Nephid had dug so many holes around the southern volcano field that the whole thing collapsed inward when the water made contact. A few are still active underwater, but the planet didn't blow up or nothing. My head on the other hand felt like it had.

"What day is it?" I said. My head felt like I had been lying on the train tracks when the Noon Amtrak came through. This had to be the worst hangover I have ever had in my whole life. I could still hear the train in my ears.

"Friday, Earth time," said Merlin. He sounded happy.

I sat up in the subdued light of my ship; I had apparently partied with the Kellics and then racked out on a bed that came out of one of my walls. I think several days had passed. It hurt to sit up, so I lay back down. The train whistle went off again.

"You have a call from New Hamel and you had one earlier from New Traylid, but I couldn't wake you. I told you not to drink the Jillianna, by all rights you should be dead." Boy, was he cheerful. And loud too.

"Who is it?" I really didn't feel like talking to anyone.

"Sethhamel," said Merlin, and then the idiot turned on the screen.

"Jim," said Sethhamel cheerfully and noticed I was lying in bed. His family, wife, and two daughters crowded behind him at the screen. They noticed I was still in bed too.

I opened my eyes a little farther and noticed I was lying there in my underwear, along with the whole family. I snatched the blanket up and felt like passing out.

"I wanted to invite you to join us before you leave today, we are having a celebration in your honor here at New Hamel. Can you come?" he ended, trying to shield his daughters' eyes. I didn't blame him; I had to piss really bad, and you know what that means. Morning wood, oh baby.

I nodded and the screen went gray.

I slid my pants on and stood up; it seemed like an appropriate time to get sick, but I held it back. I headed for the toilet. Don't ever puke on a disintegrator plate; take my word for it. Merlin dispensed a small pill for me as I cleaned up and dressed in a clean outfit and stumbled into the control area. My bed had been put away. I don't like being mothered. I activated the drink cabinet and tossed the pill.

"Merlin," I said, "if you ever turn that screen on again, without my permission, I will do something terrible to you." What, I didn't know, but he didn't either.

"Sorry," he said, "I took a message from Choric earlier; would you like to hear it?" I nodded, and he activated the screen. The pill was working incredibly fast, thank God. I felt very alert and tingly all over.

"Jim," Choric began, "I have returned to New Nilton, formerly New Traylid, and placed my children in custody, all charges against you have been dropped. I would like to invite you to a celebration in your honor later today. Please let me know if you will be able to attend." The screen went off. I wondered if the expression "kill them with kindness" had been invented on this planet. This reminded me of the Thanksgiving Day my family and I celebrated at home, again at my Aunt's, and then finally at my Grandmother's home.

All that turkey and dressing finally caught up with my sister who added her stomach's contents to the dinner table at Grandma's house, as in "projectile you know what." Of course, my cousin immediately got sick after seeing my sister blow dinner through most of her facial openings and followed up with her rendition all over my other cousin. He freaked out; hell, he and I were both eight or nine at the time, and he stood up, knocking his chair sideways into the dog. The dog jumped up from his begging spot—he was always fed from the table—and bit my cousin on the forearm. My uncle whacked the dog with the dressing spoon, and he was out like a light. My dad whacked me because I was sitting there laughing my ass off and couldn't stop. I don't remember the rest, except dinner ended rather quickly, and we all went home in a hurry. The dog was never the same after that, nor would he come near the table ever again. We also never ever celebrated Thanksgiving like that again.

I turned on the screen and did a 360. Crouthhamel's ship had left New choric. I wondered if he was still on the planet.

"Merlin," I asked, "where is Crouthhamel?" Maybe Merlin knew. I was kind of hoping he would join me on the party route. I remembered him there earlier.

"I don't know, his ship left earlier this morning, you had not yet recovered from your debauchery when I observed him departing rather hurriedly."

I was feeling better. "Let's go to New Hamel across the lake and remind me to stay away from Jillianna, would you?" He liked playing mother, so I let the debauchery comment go.

"No problemo," he remarked. The ship rose softly and exited the dome. The opening was already open; workers were passing in and out with materials on floating repair bots fixing the damages to the dome. They stopped and waved to the ship as we flew toward New Hamel. The water looked blue, and the clouds overhead were white now instead of yellow.

"The air quality has improved dramatically in just twenty four hours, Jim," said Merlin. He must have seen me looking around. "You really did save the planet, you know."

"Cut that out," I said, "you want me to get a big head." I was busy explaining what a big head was as we arrived at the other twin city. It was the same as before with the cheering and waving as the ship settled into a stable hover. I joined the crowd and was literally carried to a makeshift podium and given the key to the planet or something like that. I toasted the good people of New Hamel several times and gave a short speech about how lucky I had been and how fortunate we all were to be standing there in one piece. I left the podium and joined Sethhamel and his family at a table set up for the impending feast. I noticed his daughters were identical twins and quite good-looking for Kellic Altairians, as well as his wife, who looked more like an older sister. Oh baby.

"Nice to see you all again," I said exchanging handshakes with all of them. "This time I'm dressed." Did I see his wife blush? The daughters giggled and whispered to each other.

"What happened to Crouthhamel?" asked Sethhamel. "We were hoping he could also attend with you."

"So was I." I shrugged my shoulders. "Merlin said he left early this morning, in a hurry." I saw platters of food coming toward us, and my stomach rejoiced. I don't know what it was, but it tasted good, and it went down smooth. I'm sure I taught them all how to eat that day because I couldn't get enough. Thank God they didn't give me a shovel. I was finished gorging myself and carrying on polite conversation with the family, mostly the daughters, when I saw a man approach the table. He spoke softly with Sethhamel and left.

"Trouble?" I asked; I was a nosy person.

"No," he replied, "they must still be cleaning house at New Traylid, we haven't been in contact with them since Choric left."

"New Nilton," I corrected him. "The message I received from Choric this morning was from New Nilton. I guess they renamed the place. This was obviously news to all of them. I wondered why.

"Well, he certainly deserves it," his wife agreed.

I nodded. He had laid his life on the line reconnecting that reactor, knowing all the time that I or anyone could have plugged the damn thing back together. I wondered what happened to him. I think I had several drinks with him at the last party, but my mind was rather foggy about it. Wonder why! I decided to look him up before leaving.

"Well, I'd better be going now, I still have to see Choric before I head back to Earth," I said, standing up. The twins gave me a hurt look and began pouting.

"Sorry you can't stay longer," said Sethhamel rising also. "We would like to get to know you better, Prill and Dree were going to give you a tour of the city." He motioned to his daughters, who looked up and smiled innocently. I felt the lecher, Mr. Happy, stir in my pants and knew it was time to leave.

"Maybe next time," I answered, shaking his hand and his wife's. The two daughters rose and came around the table to me.

"Can we walk you to your ship?" asked one. She was a little taller than me and used her height and breasts to fence me between her and her sister's budding mounds. Mr. Happy wanted to stay and play. I smiled at Daddy, who waited calmly for my diplomacy to take control. I shook his hand and pried myself free.

"Sure," I answered, "let's go." I grabbed their three fingered hands and marched toward the ship. I had to keep stopping, shaking hands and hugging people, mostly the females, but finally we arrived at the hatch.

"Well girls," I said trying to escape, "take care of yourselves." Somehow I knew they wouldn't have any problem doing that. I broke free after promising to come see them again and gave them each a quick kiss on the cheek, which didn't satisfy them, until our lips met, and they had one more chance to rub up against me. The hatch seemed to take forever to close as I stood and waved good-bye, as a crowd began forming around the twins. *Not today Happy*, I thought.

"Merlin," I said; I felt a bit tipsy, "why don't you take us to New Nilton."

"No problemo, dude," he said. "Were those friends of yours?"

"Barracuda," I replied, "and hungry ones."

"Oh" was all Merlin said. The ship rose as a final cheer from the crowd arose along with it. They were still waving as we disappeared from sight. I sat back and relaxed. *I could do this everyday*, I thought.

"Merlin," I said, straightening up a bit, "have you had any more contact with New Nilton?"

"No," he answered, "why do you ask? Smell something funny?"

"Just wondered, probably nothing," I replied, wondering if I did smell something peculiar, if not rotten.

I had Merlin take the long way slowly around the planet so I could rest my eyes. I wondered if I had drunk more Jillianna; all of a sudden, I was real sleepy.

"New Nilton," said Merlin, waking me from a very strange and erotic dream—use your imagination; it'll come to you.

I tried to sit up straighter and found I was strapped in. I looked at the screen. The dome was open, but only a few Altairians were waiting at the landing zone. It was now nightfall, and the place had shadows that began to bug me right away.

"Where is everybody?" I asked; I still felt a little groggy, but the nap had helped. I got up and drank a large glass of water; at least it looked like water. I felt good.

"Choric's message said to meet him in the Great Hall," said Merlin. He landed the ship and opened the hatch. I had deposited my weapons in the locker drawer earlier, and I didn't see any need to take them out now. One more party and off we go to Earth. I hoped Joan was still in town, so did Mr. Happy.

"Take care of the ship," I said, adding "please." I walked down the hatch and met the Altairians who were waiting for me. They seemed pleasant enough as they escorted me through the city. Still, I could not see anyone else or any signs of partying going on in the city. *Oh well*, I thought, *these people are stuffier than the Kellics, but I'll show them how to loosen up*. We arrived at a large door, and it swung inward to reveal a large crowd of people. I still wondered why they didn't have noses and resolved to ask one of them. Suddenly the room felt chilly. No one had tried to shake my hand, and no one seemed to want to cheer either; in fact they all seemed a bit hostile. I felt my red alert go off in my head, and as I was starting to tense up, the crowd parted, and I was looking directly into the faces of Gellid and Trayla.

They didn't look any more happy to see me than I, them. The crowd pushed me forward toward them. I noticed they were wearing weapons. Oh shit.

"If it isn't the dynamic duo," I quipped. "What are you doing out of jail?" I felt like a piece of bacon on its way to the fry pan.

"If it isn't the mighty Guardian Jim," smarted Gellid, ignoring my question. "Glad you could make our little celebration. Grab him." I knew that last remark wasn't made to me, and my sixth sense told me to start swinging the old fists.

I caught Gellid once in the face before the rest of the room jumped my shit. I think everyone in the room took a shot at me before Trayla restored order and faced me with her bitchy look.

"Put him with the rest," she ordered the ones holding me. I was semiconscious at this point and fading fast.

"Wait," she said. She walked to me and ripped the sensor from my wrist. She dropped it on the floor and crushed it under her foot. She turned and started to walk away as I passed out. I vaguely remember seeing Gellid lying on the floor; I must have tagged him a good one. Happy to be of service, dickhead.

I awoke to more head pain. My eyes were swollen shut, so I couldn't see much; and my nose felt broken, so I couldn't smell anything either. *Least I had a nose*, I thought. I tried to move and almost passed out again. I brought my hand up to my head. Even with my hard head, I still had quite a knot on top of it.

"You got that when they threw you into the opposite wall," said a voice I knew from somewhere.

Who ever it was helped me sit up. Through blurred vision, I recognized the Altairian I had joked with about being an earthling when I first landed. I slowly turned my head around the room. I counted about twenty bodies in various positions. One of them was Choric. I tried to stand and fell back down. That's when I spotted Crouthhamel, laying on his back not far from Choric. As I crawled to him, I noticed he wasn't moving. Gentle hands tried to help me, or were they trying to hold me back. Regardless, I reached his side and tried to tell if he was breathing.

"Is he alive?" I said. I coughed and spit a red wad of blood onto the floor.

"Barely," he answered. He turned his head toward me in obvious pain. "They broke my back," he sputtered. "You don't look so hot yourself." He coughed horribly and continued, "It was a trap, Choric was tortured and killed because he wouldn't give in to them, that's when they started executing people. They faked a message to me but couldn't reach you." He coughed again, struggling to finish. "The message said he needed help, so I came here, and they jumped me. Is he still alive?"

I motioned to Choric, and several Altairians shook their heads.

"No," I said to him. He said something in Kellic; it probably wasn't nice, and it made him cough even worse.

"Lay still," I ordered. I sat back and tried to clear my head. I wondered where Merlin was; he had to have heard what happened in the big room. He could get us out of here, if he could find us, that is. I looked around at the bodies. Most of them looked dead. Choric was dead, but his hand was holding the hand of an elderly woman; it must have been Mrs. Choric. *The kids had even killed their mother*, I thought. *What kind of animals were they? Maybe they were part human.*

I motioned to several Altairians, and they came to me.

"Help me stand up," I whispered as I struggled to rise. I forced back the blinding pain and tried to stand on my own. They let go of me, and I stayed up. *Good*, I thought, *now to move around.* I managed to move a little and finally made the door after much stumbling and cursing. Have I mentioned how stubborn I am at times? The door seemed firmly locked. I sank down in front of it and tried to think of what my next move would be; I knew I had to get help for Crouthhamel, or he would die, and I'm sure there was others in here who needed help too. I wished I had a Zalo Disorganizer with me. I was lying there feeling hopeless when I felt the vibrations of someone walking toward the door from the other side. Whoever it was must have looked through a peephole and missed me sitting there. As the door swung in against me, I crawled to my feet. It must have been a guard checking on us or sent to get one of us. He never saw me coming. I snapped his neck in anger and dropped him to the floor. The door was starting to close, and I couldn't chance it locking, so I grabbed for it and stumbled over the body and fell. Like an idiot, I hit my head again. I fought the blackness away and reached over the body for his weapon as my foot hooked the edge of the door.

This had taken place in probably nanoseconds, yet it seemed like minutes had gone by when suddenly a second guard pushed against the door, opening it all the way. He tried to jump back when he saw me lying atop his partner, holding his weapon. But I wasn't about to let him get away. I depressed the button on the weapon and a beam shot out of the end and smacked him right in the chest. He tumbled backward and fell out of sight in the hallway.

The weapon looked like the ones they used on *Star Trek*, and I wondered if he was dead or stunned shitless. *Who cares*, I thought. Two Altairians came over to me, one I knew, and helped me up. The three of us carefully entered the hallway. It was deserted except for the lone guard. We pulled him back inside and, like idiots, let the door swing shut.

"Fuck!" I exclaimed; there was no doorknob of any kind on our side, so even if it were unlocked, we couldn't get it open. I looked at the weapon in my hand. It had a little chamber with a flip open lid, and inside was a dial.

"Turn it all the way up," instructed the one Altairian.

"Don't mind if I do," I thanked him. I turned it all the way in one direction and hit the button. A beam hit the door; it seemed stronger than before, and the door started to glow and turn black. I shut it off when a hole appeared in the middle and waited for it to stop smoking. With my tunic for padding, I reached out, tripped the latch, grabbed the door, and pulled it open. I was about to go into the hallway when I heard someone coming. *Good*, I thought, *I need a prisoner*. I motioned the others back and flattened myself against the smoking door. It was hotter than hell, and I wiggled as the heat burned my skin from my ass to my shoulders, but I remained silent. I turned the weapon back down and waited.

The guard walked right into the open doorway, and I stunned him quickly. I dragged him into the room and motioned for someone to listen at the door. I knelt over him and slapped his face a few times. It didn't bring him around, but it felt good. Precious minutes ticked by as we waited for him to awaken, and I probably should have left to find Merlin, but I didn't want to leave anyone behind. I couldn't tell what was going on in or out of the city, so I wanted to pump this guy before I did anything. Just as I was about to give up on the guy, the first one started to move. I went over to him and helped him sit up. He came around with a shock when he realized who was helping him. I smiled at him.

"Do you know why you're still alive?" I asked him. He shook his head and appeared frightened. *Let's see how scared he really is*, I thought. "Because I need some information," I whispered, "and if I don't get it, then they get you." I pointed to the others standing behind me. They looked like they could kick some ass, namely, his ass. He nodded rather quickly.

"What happened to Crouthhamel's ship?" They must have hidden it, but I let him tell me.

"Gellid flew it around the planet and brought it back here, it's hidden."

"Where is my ship?" This was the big one, and from the look on his face, he knew it.

"It left, flew away, we tried to stop it with our weapons but it blasted the bay door down and flew away. We thought you were alone." He sounded worried now.

"Then what happened?" I demanded. I hoped Merlin had gone for help.

"We have been fortifying the city for an attack from the Kellics. Gellid said they were trying to take over the planet and you were helping them. Trayla said they were angry over the Nephid because it had destroyed their cities instead of ours, even though they set it free. Fortunately Gellid managed to destroy it and save the planet."

"Very interesting twist," I commented. Old Gellid had brainwashed these high and mighty Altairians, "and did he tell you that it was his fault those cities disappeared in the first place?" The guard looked confused now. "And did he tell you that he personally wasted Dr. Carber before I even arrived at New trillion that day?" Again, the confused look.

"Do you know what a sucker is? It's you, for believing his shit. He killed his own father and mother!" Boy was this guy gullible or what? I pointed to the bodies.

"He said Crouthhamel did that." Then he noticed Crouthhamel.

"Why would Crouthhamel use your weapon when we have Zalo Disorganizers that would not leave a trace of the old man when fired? And why leave his parents' bodies here, with the rest of us criminals?"

He looked a bit enlightened and less confused.

"Crouthhamel could have killed him in New Choric if what you say is true, and no one would have known. Then it would have been a complete surprise when the Kellics arrived, which wasn't going to happen, because Choric was coming back here to arrest his two kids for murder and mayhem, instead they killed him and ambushed Crouthhamel," I concluded, again pointing to the bodies.

He looked even more enlightened. Stupid fuck. I needed to get in touch with either Merlin or Sethhamel and stop them. It would either be a slaughter or start a civil war between the two groups, and these people didn't really want either; they were just stupid for following Gellid and his bitchy sister.

"I need to get to a view screen," I said to him. "Do you know where there is one I can use, and are you willing to help me?"

"Yes," he offered, "I will take you and I will help, I don't like being used."

"Good, I don't either," I said, motioning to the one Altairian I knew and tossing him a weapon. "Defend the door, pile up bodies if you have to, just don't let them get in here." I glanced at the door and saw the sign, which said "Signature Rm. 102"; it had slid sideways, and I noticed a one-way mirror behind it. "What do they use this room for anyways?"

"Banking transactions," answered my prisoner. He looked at what I was looking at and shook his head. "These rooms are supposed to be completely confidential," he explained. "That is Gellid's doing," he said, pointing to the mirror.

"Don't you love a sneak," I scoffed, "still think he's a good guy?"

"I'm with you," he acknowledged, shaking his head in disgust. "Gellid and Trayla will pay dearly for murdering the great Choric and his Queen."

I don't know how many minutes went by; we zigged and zagged through the hallway and finally came to a side hallway and went down it to the end and entered a view screen room. It was empty, which was lucky for my prisoner whose real name, no kidding, was Clemic, can you believe that. He was a Clem all right.

"How do you get this thing on?" I said to him and without waiting began pushing buttons. Trayla's face appeared. She looked quite upset at seeing me.

"How did you get free?" she stammered and turned to someone and started to yell that I was free. I flipped the same button, and she disappeared as quickly as she had appeared when I first started playing with it.

Clem leaned past me and pressed another lever, and a screen in Sethhamel's city appeared with his wife in front of it. She looked quite shocked to see me or maybe it was my bloody face and tunic. I smiled.

"Where is he?" I said quickly.

"They left to rescue you at New Nilton," she said confused. "Are you all right? You look terrible. What's going on there?"

"Get a hold of him, stop him, it's a trap he won't get out of alive," I ordered, without answering her questions. She nodded, quickly realizing the situation, and the screen went blank.

I was just about to ask Clem how to raise my ship when my control room appeared, and I was looking at the empty control chairs.

"You look terrible," said Merlin. "Where are you?"

"View Room 12," chimed in Clem; he was staring at the screen, trying to figure out who was talking. I could tell he was impressed; it was rather unnerving, like talking to the invisible man or something.

"A computer?" he asked finally.

"I should be so lucky," I whispered.

"I heard that," said Merlin.

Damn he had good ears. "Just kidding," I said. "What is your status, where are you, and do you know where Sethhamel is right now?"

"I'm fine, outside the city and almost here," he answered like the smartass life-form he had become since riding with me.

"Did you catch my transmission to his wife?"

"Yes, I relayed it immediately, and he is holding a few hundred pics from here."

"Good, find me, we have some ass to kick"—I turned to Clem—"are you with me?" He nodded and extended his hand. I shook it and gave him a Guardian salute for good measure too.

We had settled into a couple of chairs and were waiting for Merlin when we heard a commotion in the hallway. I only had one shooter, but I gave it to Clem who seemed surprised. *Might as well test him now*, I thought.

"Hold them off, I want to try this screen one more time." He nodded and appeared grateful at the chance to prove himself. Any other reaction from him, and I would have dropped him on the spot. I was playing with the screen when the door turned black, and a hole appeared in it. Clem had turned over the table and was getting ready to gun somebody, anybody, down when I heard Trayla's wonderfully bitchy voice.

"Give it up, Guardian, you'll never get out alive!" she shouted.

I finished with the view screen and turned toward her voice, hoping the controls were correctly set.

"Is that what you told your father before you killed him and your mother?" I shouted back. "You slimy bitch." I loved to goad people into stupid things, and it usually worked.

"He was a weak old man, who wanted to make the Kellics our equal," she ranted. "He put the Agriport in New Choric to keep them happy." I thought she was wrong, but I didn't want to stop her now.

"Is that why Gellid let the giant Nephid loose on those cities?" I goaded her more.

"He told me the time was right to kill two qwimmys with the same shot. Then we could blame the Kellics for his murder and have an excuse to punish them." Boy was she burying herself good. I looked through the opening in the door and spotted a few others with her. This was going to be good.

"Too bad you didn't kill me when Gellid killed Dr. Carber at New Trillion; that reactor Gellid overloaded almost went off." I was finishing her and him with that one. Oh baby.

"We didn't expect you to get there so quick," she admitted, "but we weren't expecting you anyways, we wanted to kill that bastard, Crouthhamel, plus Choric had people there spying on Carber, we wanted them out of the way too."

"Did you expect Nilton to go along with all that killing?"

"Gellid said he'd follow Choric's orders . . ." Her brother showed up and interrupted her. I knew what he was doing; I could hear his nasally voice. He was telling her that she just broadcast the entire scheme to the whole planet from the view screen in the room. I tried to stifle a laugh but didn't succeed.

I turned back to the view screen I had played with and smiled to the people who were watching; no doubt they were feeling just a little used.

"You heard it here first," I said. "Now stop arming yourselves and get some medical help to Signature Room 102. People are in there dying and it's all Gellid and Trayla's fault." Just as I finished, the wall to the outside of the room began to dissolve, and the nose of the ship appeared. Meanwhile, Gellid had heard what I had said and lost his cool completely.

"I'm going to kill you, Guardian!" he screamed, rushing to the door, blasting his weapon wildly. He really was the dumber of the two.

I motioned Clem to the side and turned to my ship. "Merlin," I said, "give that son of a bitch a taste of the Disorganizer cannon." He did have good ears; a mespic later, a beam shot out the front of the ship, just barely missing Clem and I, but not Gellid. He vanished in a mespic along with the rest of the door, part of the wall, and everyone in the hallway, including Trayla, the super bitch. The opposite wall of the hallway smoked slightly from the end of the beam and was cracked open like a blackened eggshell. All of them were gone without a sound. It was cool.

"oops," said Merlin. In the quiet following the shot, his voice was awe inspiring to say the least.

"Merlin," I teased, "you broke the rules of the game; I wanted to waste the bitch."

"Sorry, I guess I got carried away," he pleaded, yet still sounding rather proud of himself.

"No problemo; take us around to the front door." The hatch descended before I finished. As Clem and I left the room and boarded the ship, you could just barely see a wisp of smoke where the people in the hallway had been standing. It was a helluva cannon, I observed as the hatch closed, and we began moving.

Clem still didn't know who I was talking to, and even though it hurt, I laughed out loud at the look on his face. He took it well and laughed with me.

Crouthhamel lived and, by the time I found him, after doing the shower and tunic routine, was already lying in a hospital bed looking bored out of his mind. The doctor, who fixed my head and facial damage with strange scanners, had told me his back was going to heal and that he would be up and around in no time. Medical science is light years ahead out here. I walked in just as Sethhamel and his wife were just arriving. I had already gotten my medical attention and was itching to get the hell off Pyritium while I still could. Crouthhamel looked over at me. I was cleaned up, armed to the teeth, and wearing a spare sensor; I was taking no chances, not anymore.

"Well, once again you succeeded," he said to me and clasped my hand with the same force he had the first time I met him; only this time it hurt.

"Ouch," I joked. I looked at him and Sethhamel. They looked like brothers. I glanced at his wife and then remembered the twins. I quickly looked around the room, prepared to bolt if they were there. Crouthhamel saw me and knew and tried not to laugh. I made a face at him. He laughed anyways.

Sethhamel turned to me.

"Order has been restored," he said, smiling, "and we are in your debt, Jim. They would have massacred us when we got here, instead they welcomed us with open arms and relations with this side of the planet have never been better. I want to thank you on behalf of the entire planet and our newly elected leader." He pointed to the door as Nilton walked in, dressed as Choric had been dressed. He walked up to me, smiling confidently and grabbed my hand. I stood there in shock, actually speechless for once.

"Where did you come from?" I said. "I thought you were dead!"

"I came here with Sethhamel, I was still in New Choric when you left for here."

"Now I remember," I said, thinking the last few days over in my mind, "you were the one who introduced me to . . ."

"Jillianna," he finished for me. I nodded. That shit could kill you. Everyone in the room started laughing, including me. I thought I heard Merlin too.

It seemed like every time I left a city they were busy repairing something I had destroyed and waving happily after me as I left. A strange inconsistency I'm sure, one which I hoped wouldn't happen again real soon. I took the ship to a high orbit and circled the planet a few times admiring the greening process at work. The wind streams of the planet had carried the water over much of the planet, and the industrious Kellics and their noseless counterparts had already sent out hovercraft loaded with seed to establish a planet wide greenhouse of food. The seed had already started to germinate in soil that now appeared to be acid neutral. The sad part was the death of Choric and his wife; he had apparently been a real driving force for the whole planet although Nilton seemed to be settling into the job with a surprising knack for it. The frightening part of the whole affair came to light when they searched Gellid's quarters and found more discs from the old Dr. Carber's lab. He and Gellid were going to export the Nephids to other planets, and then after the Nephids had destroyed the planets, they could move in and take over the planets. Talk about a real estate scam of universal proportions, and with no regard for life either. How they were going to get rid of the Nephids was a question no one could answer, not anymore, Merlin had seen to that.

If Gellid hadn't jumped the gun and tried to kill his father, they might have succeeded. But when Carber found out that the plan had been screwed, he had threatened to take the whole thing public; that was why Gellid had gone to New Trillion and killed him. And the whole scheme might have worked if we had been a few minutes later in arriving there. I shook my head; it all boiled down to what my dad had taught me. People kill for two reasons: love or money. Or sometimes both.

"I have a Zalo supply base on screen," said Merlin cheerfully following my command.

"Why are you so happy?" I asked. Maybe he got whacked during the fighting on the planet. I pulled out of orbit in deep space drive.

"I can't tell you," he teased, "but you'll find out soon enough."

"OK," I said. I really didn't care, as long as it was good news. I quickly forgot as I looked at the base appearing in front of me. Magnified on the screen, it was a huge ball of lights in front of me. It must have been half the size of our moon, and on the top and bottom, a huge lighted letter Z stood out against the space and stars beyond.

"How far to Macy's," I said. I wondered what the magnification of the screen was set on; it looked right next to us.

"Half a parsec," said Merlin. His cheery voice reminded me of Cecil's voice on the old Beanie and Cecil show. Cecil was the seasick sea serpent, remember? I came out of DS drive into plasma drive quickly, so I wouldn't fly right through the place. It really was right next to us. I looked it over, marveling at what I could never tell anyone on Earth, without being committed.

I spotted a docking zone and was about to head for it when an ugly black ship pulled in front of me and grabbed it. I wished I had a horn on my ship;

maybe I could get one put in it. I spun the ship and circled the base trying to find a free zone. The place was like a beehive, and only on the third go round did I finally find a place to pull into and dock. I put the ship on stable hover, and the bay opening closed around me, like a huge mouth. In front of me, two suited bodies waited for the huge overhead light to go from red to green and then signaled me it was OK to depart my ship. One of them met me at the hatch as I walked down the ramp and saluted me Guardian style. I returned the salute and followed him toward a door opening in front of us. Inside his helmet, he looked green. He was about my size, maybe a little smaller, and smiled at me as he turned to me.

"We don't get many Guardians here, it is an honor," he bullshitted. His voice was smooth as ice, even in Tharx.

"Really," I answered. The walls were covered with ads for everything from weapons to ships. From the latest drive systems to food synthesizers. I would have bought one had I not finally found the one on my ship. Merlin failed to mention it to me, the smuck.

"I didn't see any other Guardian ships here," I commented.

"No, sir, not at the moment," he replied, "but they will be here on and off over the next few cycles on their way to Aldebaran for the big meeting."

Shit, I had forgotten all about it; I had better make this a quick stop and head home. I would have one lousy day home and then back on the road again. I wondered if this was always going to be this way.

We entered a lift, and the green guy turned to me.

"Section?" he asked. He had been babbling to me about all the wonderful things they had on sale today, but I had been thinking about Joan and going home and had spaced off.

"Section?" he repeated. He didn't seem the least upset that I wasn't listening. I knew he wasn't human then.

"Do you have an outer ship hardware section?"

"Exterior supply," he said to the lift.

It began to move, but I couldn't tell which direction. A few minutes later, it stopped and the door opened. The room in front of me seemed enormous; a government warehouse is all I can think of to describe it. Pieces of ships hung from robot Hoverpods, and crates and boxes were stacked to the ceiling in between them. More pods were shuffling boxes around, and my escort touched me on the arm as a pod came hurrying by with a ship part of some kind. It missed us by inches. He pointed to the floor.

"Please stay in the white area," he cautioned me. "The Go area is only for the robots."

I nodded OK and stared after the little bugger as it disappeared down a shaft next to the lift. *They must do installations here too*, I thought, *that's great.* My escort turned me over to an old green dude standing behind a huge array of screens and controls. He looked up and spotted my uniform. He must have called for help because another old green dude appeared from around a stack of boxes and took over for him. He walked over to me and extended his hand. He had six or seven fingers on each hand; I couldn't tell and didn't want to stare.

"How can I help you, sir?" he said. His forehead was beating in and out.

The skin looked leathery but smooth. His body was smooth also, but his face was wrinkled from his large eyes, which didn't seem to blink, clear down to the tunic he wore. It was green also. His posture was bent slightly, like he had done all the moving of the boxes way back before they had pods to do it, and he spoke slowly as his eyes darted around the room each in different directions, very bug like.

"How can I help you, sir?" he repeated. It was like talking to a tall thin frog.

"Sorry," I lied, "this place is fantastic." His eyes continued to look in opposite directions until one aimed itself at me.

"I need some stuff." I explained what I wanted, and the look on his face changed from one look of surprise to another. As I detailed what I wanted to put into the front of my ship, he nodded and punched numbers into a small calculator like device in his left hand. At one point, he stopped me and talked into a small round device on the front of his tunic. Finally I finished, and he spoke into the device again.

"We can supply most of the parts from here," he said to me. "The rest will have to be synthesized in another part of the base and transferred to your docking zone for installation, what type of ship are they using now days, I will need the model number."

"Merlin," I said. I hoped he knew.

"Cyclone One, Galaxy Class," he answered through the sensor on my wrist.

The old dude looked at me funny. Now he was staring with one eye.

"What?" I asked him. Both eyes were on me now. Maybe I had a booger on my nose. I checked. None. I much preferred one eye at a time though.

"I didn't know they had those out yet, I had heard only one prototype existed for that model," he said in amazement.

"That is correct," answered Merlin, "and you're talking to it."

"Fascinating," replied the old guy. Both eyes were on the move now. He seemed almost afraid of me. It had shocked me too. I didn't know Merlin was the damn ship; I thought he was like added to it, like you would put a computer in a vehicle or a radio in your car. I tried not to look as flipped out as the old guy and my escort, who had slipped a little closer when the older dude freaked on me.

Behind us, the lift opened, and an ugly huge, fat guy got out. He turned to his escort and shoved him back into the lift.

"I don't need no help!" he shouted at the escort in Hortic. It was a strange dialect for these parts, and I felt the hairs on the back of my neck start to rise in alarm.

"Service," he bellowed in Hortic. It sounded uglier coming from him.

He was really ugly. He put the *U* in ugly, that's for sure. Why he even made Mackie look small and good looking. I would have to tell Rick about this guy for sure. He had little beady eyes, which were covered by an extremely ugly set of brow bones; his nose came straight out with a single hole, and his mouth was part bones and all teeth. The skin on the rest of his face was an ugly purple with warts of liquid-filled skin popping out all over his head. The top of his head had a large ridge of bone going down the middle of it, and the bone stuck through the skin at the peak. Did I forget to say he stunk too? From where I was standing, I could already smell him. The smell was sickening.

"SERVICE!" he screamed. Then he actually looked over at us.

"Well," he said waddling over to us, "what's taking so long?"

As he talked, I could see fluid running out of his mouth and spilling down the front of his outfit, a jacket of some kind, pants that bulged to the point of bursting and boots big enough to put a small child in, without opening them. I also noticed he wasn't carrying any weapons that I could see. I think I remembered reading a sign prohibiting them from the inside of the base. Hell, I had all mine on and nobody said a word to me. *Maybe rank has its privileges*, I thought. Both the old dude and my escort were now behind me for some reason.

"I think I was first," I answered him in Hortic. He turned to me with his beady eyes. Behind him, his tail swished into sight. I caught a look at it out of the corner of my eye. It was big and ugly too.

"We will be done in a mespic," said the old one. He looked uncomfortable. Maybe it was the stink.

"Well, what have we got here?" gurgled the ugly one and then croaked at me. "If it isn't a little Guardian." His breath could stop a train. "Are you lost, little man? Shouldn't you be with your mommy?"

I turned around to the old dude trying to ignore the stench and ugliness.

"I will have these parts sent to your ship and have the rest sent over from the synthesizer section as soon as they are done," said the old guy. I thought he was going to be sick or something.

"Thanks," I said. Out of the corner of my eye, I saw the fat ugly asshole reach for me. I waited until his pawlike hand was just about to reach me and turned toward him and squared off. The smell almost made me pass out.

"I don't think you want to do that," I said as I deflected his hand from me. It felt like it was connected to a tree trunk. He drew his hand back and squinted at me.

The crest on my tunic caught his eye, and he drew back his arm to his side. I could almost see the gears turning in his head. Then he turned and started back toward the lift. His tail whipped back and forth menacingly. He had apparently changed his mind for some reason. I drew a breath of fresh air.

"Merlin," I said.

"Yes, Jim," he said back to me.

"Track him if you can, he's trouble."

"He sure is, that was a Tayhest warrior, and I don't believe I have ever seen one myself, I will try to keep track of him."

"Aren't they buddies with the Maglarr?" I said. Maybe I should go kill him.

"Not for a long time. They claim no allegiance with anyone."

"Who would want too?" I asked. Merlin didn't answer and didn't have to; I knew the answer already.

"Anything else?" asked the old guy.

"No," I said, "how long will that take?"

He looked relieved. "It should be done by the time you finish eating."

"How did you know I was going to eat?" I was puzzled.

"Everyone eats at ZuZu's when they come here," he replied.

"Sounds good to me," I said. Boy, were they fast on installations. I couldn't wait to try out my new toys. I went with my escort to the lift, and we left for ZuZu's.

When the door opened into the restaurant, I was greeted by a scene right out of the movies. Weird creatures and languages I barely recognized filled the room; a smoky haze filled in the spaces between them and must have been a deodorizer too. Some of them were standing and some were seated at tables scattered throughout the room. Some of them saw me enter and then went back to their own conversations, some loud, some whispered. A few of them looked alarmed at my uniform and left the minute I took a seat at the bar.

I wondered where the ugly Tayhest had gone, but I sat down anyway. Next time we met would be the last. I knew that for some reason.

"Can I help you?" said a woman's voice next to me.

I turned toward the voice and found myself talking to a cat. Well, not quite a cat, but she was fur covered and had whiskers. Apparently she wasn't wearing anything except the apron tied around her tiny waist because all I could see was fur, smooth silky fur, golden brown in color covering her entire body. Her ears were turned to me, but rotated, like a cat, different ways every now and then, as I sat staring at her. *Nobody on Earth would believe this*, I thought. She was almost as tall as me sitting on the bar stool, and I could look right into her eyes. They were jet black, like little pits of darkness. You couldn't see anything in them; it was almost unnerving to me.

"You haven't been here before?" she asked. I shook my head. "Then you probably never saw a Nack have you?" She and I hate to say this, purred. She had a sensual way about her, but I think Mr. Happy was as confused as I was; hell, I never lusted for a cat, but her looks made you want to stroke her, and it felt strange.

"I was wondering what kind of food you had here," I said. I looked around for my escort. He was nowhere in sight.

"What system are you from, Guardian?" she asked sweetly.

"Tara," I said in Tharx. I noticed she had fingers because she was holding some kind of electronic order pad in one hand. I also noticed she had clawlike nails on those fingers because she ran the other hand down my arm, and I could feel them through my supposedly indestructible tunic. The first one had gotten pretty messed up on Pyritium, and this was another one just like it. It didn't feel indestructible at the moment.

"So you're the Guardian who was on Pyritium," she said. Her eyes were freaking me out. The room seemed to quiet down when she said that. Maybe it was my imagination. She was trying to get closer to me, and I was beginning to feel a little like a rat in a trap. A little old man, clad totally white from hair to toe, with an almost human face, sitting beside me, nudged me in the back. I turned.

"Better not get her turned on, you'll have to kill her to get her off you," he said to me. He looked familiar. I turned back to her and noticed she was actually purring now. I took his advice, better safe than sorry. Barmaids could be trouble.

"Do I get my food now or what?" I tried to sound nasty. It didn't work.

"Tell her you don't like fur?" said the little guy behind my back.

"I don't like fur in my food either," I said to her. Her purring stopped, and she turned with a huff and walked away from me. I let out a long breath and turned to the little guy.

"Thanks," I sighed. I wondered if I would get my food, and if I should even eat it.

"You must be Jim," he said. He said it in Gooide.

"Yes, who are you? I don't think we've met," I wondered out loud. *How nuts was this conversation*, I thought, *especially here, millions of miles from home.*

"I'm Belgo from Entimall," he said, shaking my hand. "You know my brother, Torgan." He smiled.

"No shit," I said, man it was a small galaxy, "are you working undercover?" I whispered the last part.

"No, I'm here picking up parts, why?" he said puzzled.

"I thought you were in disguise," I said, and then thought "oops" as his look changed from happy to angry.

"You don't have to be abusive," he said and rose and walked away. I watched him leave my sight in the haze of smoke and turned back to the bar. Apparently his brother had been in disguise. Who knew?

"Food," said an electronic voice as a plate floated down the other side of the bar and stopped in front of me. I looked at the plate and laughed. It was a hamburger and French fries. A bottle of what looked like Coke sat on the side of the floater.

"Ketchup," I asked it. It flew off and another floater came by with an assortment of condiments. Some of them were moving in their bowls. I found what I thought was ketchup and picked up the burger. It tasted rather good, plus it went down and stayed down. I really didn't know why I was eating here; I had food on board. I guess I just wanted to see what the place was like. Now that I knew, I figured it was time to leave. Unfamiliar creatures on both sides convinced me it was time.

"Merlin," I said. The creature that had sat down in Belgo's seat looked at me.

"Yes, Jimbo." The other creature was eating with his nose, if you call it that.

"How's it going and don't call me that." I hated that nickname. The other creature, who was drinking normally, nodded too. I almost laughed.

"They should be done in an Earth hour, Boss man."

"OK, I'm going to walk around," I replied. "Let me know when they're done."

"No Problemo." Merlin was on something I was sure of it.

I left the bar and took the lift to an observation deck where you could look down on all the new construction going on and inspect the workmanship close up by using a device very similar to what you might find on top of a skyscraper. You know, you drop a quarter in it, and you can see objects that are far away, close up, whichever way you swing it. I switched one on, it didn't cost anything here, and put my face up to it and started checking out the ships under construction. It really magnified the view; hell, I could see what the workers had in their hands.

One ship was done and it appeared from the distance that it was being loaded with crates, so I swung the scope around to see what was going on board. The Ropod that was loading it was blocking the sides of the crates, but as it swung them into the cargo hold of the ship, I saw the side of one crate. It had "Pafewvtnqlja" written on it. I knew that word from somewhere. I was half looking, half thinking when a shadow crossed the viewer, and I focused in on it. It was the ugly Tayhest warrior and several of his buddies, standing behind the ship, looking very suspicious. Suddenly one of his equally ugly buddies reached into the hold and pulled out a case of whatever the stuff was and walked away like it belonged to him. I followed him in the viewer for a few seconds and turned it back to the ugliest of them. He was looking around to make sure no one saw anything. I tried to turn away as quickly as possible, but it was too late as his gaze turned upward, and he spotted the observation deck with me behind the magnifier. His eyes met mine in the viewer, and his eyes narrowed, as mine got bigger.

I stepped back and glanced down at him. He was saying something to his other two ugly friends and pointing at me.

"Oh shit," I said to myself. They all went in different directions. Why did I have to be so nosy? I ran from the deck and into the lift and commanded it to take me to my loading area. It seemed to be in low gear and telling it to go faster didn't do any good.

"Merlin," I said, "I've got a problem."

"You sure do, that Tayhest warrior is headed straight for you," he answered, "and both lifts are going to stop at the same spot."

"Stop," I said to the lift, "which way Merlin?" The lift came to a stop and started beeping a warning. I really didn't give a shit at this point.

"Go to exterior supply again."

"Exterior supply." I said to the lift. It started moving again. I breathed a sigh of relief and then remembered the other two plus the one, who stole the box of Pafewvtnqlja, were probably looking for me also.

"Merlin, I think there are three more Tayhest warriors also looking for me, check it out one time, won't you." It was no time for joking around, but I found it relieved me, and right about now, I needed a whole bunch of relief.

"Yes, Mon Capitan, you do have three more converging on you. And it looks like they have all changed direction to intercept you. They're following your lift's coordinates."

"Should I change direction again?" This wasn't going well.

"It won't matter and Exterior Supply is a huge room. You should have about ten seconds lead on them when you get to Exterior Supply," he added. I almost wish he hadn't told me.

"Thanks, doesn't this place have security?"

"Yes, but they are busy investigating the theft of a case of artificial sunlight."

That's what the word Pafewvtnqlja meant, sunlight, artificial sunlight.

"Merlin," I shouted for no reason, "these are the guys who stole it!" The lift came to a stop, and I jumped from it and ran past the old guy at the controls and into the Go area. I dodged a bullet fast Ropod on its way to fetch something and dove into a gap between two stacks. I pulled out a Zalo from my belt and aimed it at the opening. Suddenly I smelled one. A stack moved behind me, and I pulled the gun around my waist and blasted into the new opening right behind me. I heard a savage scream and a Tayhest stumbled into view holding less of his left arm than he had started with that day. He must have been moving the stack with his bare hands. These guys were as strong as Superman.

"Shit, shit, shit" was all I could say. And I was in it up to my ass. I stuck the Zalo away and started climbing up the stacks. I had no sooner reached the top and rolled free onto the top of one stack, when the two stacks were jammed together roughly. I rolled to the edge of the moving one and vaporized a very stupid Tayhest warrior. One down, three and a half to go, no two and a half. I hated fractions. The stack started wiggling, and I knew it was going over with me on it. I went to the edge and peered over it. The warrior saw me and stepped out of sight. I looked over at the next row of boxes and crates. It was a good ten or fifteen feet, and I was no Ralph Boston. Just then, I spotted a slow moving Ropod heading down the aisle about ten feet below me.

As the stack I was on began to tip for the last time, I jumped down on the Ropod. I landed in the arms of the thing like a baby in its mother's arms. One of my two Zalos fell from my belt and landed within ten feet of a warrior who came around the stacks from the other direction. He went for it, and I grabbed at my second one. In the position I was in, it took a second to pull it out. As I aimed over the arm of the Ropod, the warrior fired my other one. His shot hit one of the arms, and for a split second, I was airborne until I grabbed the base of the Ropod on my way to the deck about twenty feet below. The armed ugly was about to fire again when I blasted him while hanging by one hand. The shot hit him and the Zalo he was holding, and he disappeared in a puff of smoke along with the gun. I let go of the Ropod as it turned toward the spot and landed with a roll. Damn twenty feet felt like fifty. I jumped up against a stack, and a small pod zipped by me. Then a second one came even closer. The little bastards were trying to hit me. I glanced up and found the control eye and blasted it and a small hole into the ceiling above it. I hoped it wasn't an outer bulkhead. It wasn't, thank God. Instantly, a maintenance pod zipped over to it and started fixing the hole; it began moving back and forth weaving a new metal skin over the hole while a second pod waited with a new control eye. I crept slowly down the side of the stacks. I wouldn't have long before they could see me again.

"Your closing on one," said Merlin. He sounded excited for me.

"Is it the big fucker I met first?"

"No, it's the wounded one and he's armed with something."

"Which way?" I whispered. Then I saw him come around the corner; he had a small remote in his hand. He spotted me and pulled back around the stack quicker than I could shoot him. He was a fast for a fat bastard.

"Where is the first one?" I asked Merlin. A pod came zipping by me and smacked into the stacks to my left. It crumpled to the deck and flopped around like a fish, its two bottom hooks opening and closing menacingly.

"He's working his way around the stack to your left."

"I'm in the middle, right?"

Another pod sailed much to close, over my head and turned for a second shot. *The wounded Tayhest must be trying to keep me busy while his boss sneaks up on me*, I thought. I blasted the pod as it dove at me. He's doing a good job too, I concluded.

"The first one is climbing up the stacks now," said Merlin. A stacker pod came flying around the corner, like the one I had fallen into, headed straight for me with its arms stretched out in front of it. Its warning lights were menacing.

"Merlin, is the equipment installed yet?" I blasted the incoming pod.

"Yes, Jim," he replied, "and Zalo security is now coming up the lift toward you. I have alerted them to the Tayhest theft, and they have confirmed it."

*Great*, I thought, *I hope I'm alive when they get here.*
"Jim," asked Merlin, "why don't you have your suit on?"
"What?" I said. What the hell was he talking about?
"Behind your neck, squeeze the label of your tunic, and do it quickly."

I reached the label and squeezed the thing. Instantly my suit went completely silver in color and seemed to take on more weight. Just what I needed, another fifty pounds to lug around. It seemed to fit better though. I didn't know you could turn the damn thing on and off; good thing it was on when Charlie shot me.

"Above you, Jim!" shouted Merlin. I looked up and saw the Tayhest as he fired a weapon in his hand. A small projectile, much like a bullet hit me right on top of my left shoulder and bounced off without penetrating the material. It suddenly occurred to me that the tunic must have been activated on Pyritium when I was getting the shit beat out of me. That explained why I didn't have any broken ribs because those people with Gellid and Trayla kicked the shit out of me that day. Totally unhurt, I dove to the middle of the aisle as a stacker pod came crashing into the spot I was standing at and demolished the stack. The Tayhest above me had been standing on the stack and tried to jump to the next one as the stack collapsed and crates came tumbling down at me. He must have been trying to reload his weapon at the same time he jumped, and the idiot apparently couldn't do two things at once or just couldn't move his huge body fast enough. He followed the crates as they crashed to the floor, abandoning the weapon in midair. I scrambled away from the cascading crates and managed to back into the opposite side of the aisle and up against the stacks on that side. The suit felt like I had a full body cast engulfing me, yet the crates that tumbled onto me felt like they were filled with marshmallows and not ship parts.

"Merlin," I said, "will the Hogan projector reach me?" It was one of my new toys I just had installed. The Tayhest was on his feet now and searching for his weapon among the crates as he caught sight of me sitting there in front of him. He looked quite pissed at me. I could hear a commotion coming from the place where the other Tayhest had been hiding with the remote control for the pods. I ignored it and leveled my Zalo at the ugly one across from me as he dove behind a large crate. Damn, these guys were fast for their size. His tail was sticking out, so I shot it off for him. The effect was instantaneous; he rose from behind the crate with another crate in his hand, screaming in pain and threw it at me. I had to dive to my left quickly as the crate smashed into the stack I was leaning against, knocking the Zalo from my hand and sending it sliding under the pallet next to me. I jumped to my feet expecting another attack by the Tayhest, but he was running down the aisle away from the commotion coming around the corner at me. I was about to join him when I saw it was the security team, trying to restrain the wounded Tayhest as he fought them off.

"Don't they have weapons?" I asked Merlin. Don't say no, please.

"Nope," he replied, "no one is allowed to be armed on this base except Guardians, and yes the Hogan will work where you are right now."

"Good, what's the location of Mr. Ugly?" Maybe I still had a chance.

"He has gone about fifty yards to your right and is weaving down another aisle right now. He's moving pretty fast for his size. Just follow his trail of body fluids," said Merlin, "but you had better hurry, there is another lift at that end of the warehouse."

I went to my knees looking for my Zalo as the battle by the security force continued to close on me. I saw it, but it was clear under the stack, out of reach. *Shit*, I thought. I stood up and assessed the other Tayhest. He was fighting off about six or seven security men, with one freakin' arm. I was having trouble counting them as the Tayhest continued to fling them all over the aisles. And he was winning too. I noticed something on the floor in front of me and decided to join the fight.

"Heads up!" I yelled as I picked up the flopping pod from the deck by its rear fin and tossed it right into the face of the Tayhest as he was about to hurl another guard. The clawing front hooks grabbed hold and buried themselves in his face. He screamed in pain and fell to the floor, groping at the claws with his one good arm, trying to rip it loose. *Now the battle was even*, I thought, as I turned and ran after the ugly Tayhest warrior. Not that they weren't all ugly, he was just my first encounter, and it had made a big impression. Like a first kiss, only worse. Sure enough, he had left a trail of fluid that was easy to follow. I reached up and flipped my suit off.

"Where is he?" I said as I ran down the aisle with renewed energy. I noticed the traffic of Ropods seemed back to normal; they were moving in various speeds up and down the aisles, staying in the green GO area and, above all, ignoring me. But I had to step carefully in several aisles as there was no white area, and some of those little pods could really move.

"Still ahead of you, go over two more aisles at the next intersection and he should be directly in front of you, the pods have slowed him down too." I noticed the fluid trail was almost gone too.

"Has he found the lift yet?" I gasped; running wasn't a specialty of mine. I turned at the intersection and just missed a very large Hoverpod going the other way. It momentarily turned me around, and I stopped dead.

"The other way, Jim, follow the pod," corrected Merlin.

I ran behind the pod and then turned off at the second aisle. In the distance, I could now see the Tayhest; he was moving slower than before. He turned and spotted me behind him but kept going to the next corner and turned. A pod must have struck him because he stumbled back into view, and I heard the warning beep they give off when their path has been blocked. He let it go by him and disappeared again, but I had closed a lot of the gap between us.

I was beginning to breathe harder now; did I say I loved to run? And I wondered how he could run so far, as big and fat as he was, compared to, say, me.

"He's spotted the lift," Merlin stated, spurring me on faster. I wanted this fucker.

"Use the Hogan on him, that should slow him up," I said to Merlin as I rounded the last corner and saw him ahead of me. In front of him, I could see the pod shaft and the lift next to it. The Hogan came on, and I suddenly appeared in front of him, an image running at him, an image projected by the new machine on my ship. An image that is so real it will even cast a shadow. As I expected, he pulled to a stop in front of the charging image, ready to battle the charging Guardian. He glanced back at me; I was to far away yet for him to worry about, and he saw I was like the guy in front of him, weaponless, and a grim smile crossed his face. He turned back to the image in front of him. The image squared off in front of him. He was I.

"I'm going to kill both of you!" he screamed at the image. He swung his arm out at the image as I came up behind him. The image had feinted and ducked, and his swing went over the image's head. He missed another punch, saw me behind him and jumped at the image and passed right through it, stumbling toward the lift.

Merlin put another one in front of him, but he walked right through it. He wouldn't be fooled again. I ran up behind him, prepared to stop him somehow, but I had to drop into a crouch at the last second, as a pod flew over my head and then turned left. I thought I had missed my chance. He could have reached the lift and gotten away, but as he walked toward it, he crossed the green area, and a fast moving Hoverpod struck him in the back. It tumbled him forward away from the lift to his right and almost knocked him into the pod shaft next to it.

As he stood up, I saw my chance and threw myself into him as he turned toward the lift. It was like hitting a brick wall. I fell backward on the deck, and he turned toward me. I had forgotten to turn on my suit, and the collision knocked the wind out of me. I landed on the green area and lay there gasping for air as he came over to me and looked down at me. His face was a mask of pain, but he forced a cruel smile as he lifted his huge leg to squash me. I couldn't move as I watched it rise above my head.

"I'm going to enjoy this," he growled in Hortic. "It is a great honor, on my planet, to kill a Guardian."

"Wait," I croaked, all I could do was breathe at this point, that and move my head a little. I tried to raise my arm and turn on the suit, but all I could do was breathe. He hesitated for just a split second, which was just long enough for the pod I spotted out of the corner of my eye, to run into him. His leg was in the process of coming down on my head when the pod struck him in the side on its way to the shaft. He tumbled sideways, trying to knock the pod away as it beeped back at him. It continued pushing into him, and just as he managed to free himself from the pod, his foot went over the edge of the shaft. He fell backward and disappeared out of sight, clawing at the air around him.

I sat up and felt my shoulder where I had hit him. It hurt like hell, but nothing felt broken. I turned on the suit again and looked over at the shaft. A paw appeared at the edge of the shaft and then a second one. I couldn't believe it. I stood up, wondering what it was going to take to kill the bastard, and almost joined him in the shaft had Merlin not yelled, "Pod!"

I threw myself to the floor as an equipment-laden pod whizzed over me, the edge of one piece now scraping harmlessly down my back. I crawled over toward the shaft and the two paws still hanging from the edge. Suddenly his head appeared above the edge, and I found myself looking into his eyes. They were ugly too.

"I'm going to tear you apart," he grunted, as he began to pull himself up and out of the shaft.

"No you're not," I answered, as I swung myself around. "You forgot something very important." I popped him right between the eyes with my left foot and followed with my right. His grip wasn't good enough to hold the edge, and he fell backward into the shaft, screaming my name. At least I'd like to think it was my name and not some Hortic obscenity.

"What did he forget?" asked Merlin.

"What else," I exclaimed. "Do not pass Go, do not collect two hundred dollars. Get it? Do not pass Go?" Hmmn, time to play a game of Monopoly with Merlin before he learned all the rules.

"What kind of rule is that?" pondered Merlin, but before I could answer, he exclaimed, "Look out, Jim, he's coming back up. He landed on a Ropod and it's bringing him back up!" Crablike, keeping low, I backed away from the shaft opening, not knowing what to expect.

Sure as shit, the Tayhest warrior appeared, but this time he was firmly embedded on the top of the Ropod. He was impaled from the back, through the spot where his tail had been. I bet it hurt like hell before he died. Poor baby.

His huge body hung down the front of pod, so you could barely see it carrying him, like he was floating in air on his own power. It was a sight straight from hell, had to be, as he passed silently by me and continued, as far as I know, to hang there until the Ropod had made its rounds.

I stood up after crawling into the safe area and was busy dusting myself off when the security dudes showed up. One of them handed me my Zalo, and I quickly holstered the precious piece. I don't know what the hell I was thinking chasing that big son of a bitch with no weapon. One of the security men asked me which way the warrior had gone.

"Thatta way"—I pointed after the Ropod—"but don't worry he's not going to give you any trouble."

They all looked at me skeptically.

As I stepped into the lift, I turned and said, "He forgot the rules of the game."

They looked at me like I was crazy, which I am, and getting crazier by the day.

"Do not pass GO," chimed in Merlin. We both laughed as the lift engaged.

# CHAPTER 6

## Meaty, Beaty, Big, and Bouncy

We left the base, Merlin and I, promising not to return for a while. The artificial sunlight had been recovered, four Tayhest warriors killed, the last one having died from Hook's disease, get it? And compared to what I destroyed on Pyritium, I would have to say a minimum of damage was done to the base. I headed the ship back toward Earth after selling the Tayhest ship back to the Zalo's and clearing up what I owed on the stuff I bought. I had some goodies put into the ship, and now I was enjoying one of them.

"Why does the music have to be so loud?" asked Merlin. I wondered if he knew he was interrupting the best song on AC/DC's *Back in the Black* album. I ignored him until the song finished. My ears were vibrating.

"Why not?" I countered. These Zalo speakers were awesome.

"Doesn't it hurt your ears?" he asked.

"What ears," I said. He obviously wasn't a hard rock life-form. At least not yet.

"Crouthhamel is coming on the screen," he announced, "with your permission, that is."

"Do it," I said. Glad to see he remembered. I killed the stereo for the time being.

"Jim," said a smiling Crouthhamel, "do you raise hell everywhere you stop in this universe?"

"It's beginning to look that way, isn't it?" I replied. He didn't sound very upset, which was a good sign. And he was smiling.

"Do you know who you killed at the base?"

"Nope, should I?"

"Does the name Zordon do anything for you," said Crouthhamel.

"Kinda." I mused; I vaguely remembered it from somewhere. "As in Lord Zordon," I said out loud; it was coming back to me. "Holy shit." I remembered.

"Yes," he answered, "you killed the son of Lord Zordon of the Tayhest Empire, the son of the being who killed Pracon's father during the Maglarrian wars."

"No wonder he freaked when he saw the crest on my tunic," I wondered out loud. "Score one for the good guys, yeah!"

"You had better stay clear of them; they will no doubt put a high price on your head for this," he cautioned.

"Ironic, isn't it?" I commented. Nothing like pissing off an entire race of beings. I wish Pracon had been here to enjoy this.

"Yes," said Crouthhamel, "by the way, do you still have my tre card?"

"Yes," I replied. A tre is the intergalactic unit of exchange, money so to speak. I wondered what he would say when he found out what I had spent; I decided not to bring it up.

"Bring it with you when you come to Aldebaran," he said, "and don't forget, the meeting is in two days, your time."

"OK, no problem," I replied. Shit, I had forgotten all about the meeting again. I nodded as the screen went gray.

"Good thing he didn't ask you about the bill," remarked Merlin.

"No shit," I said. I turned up the music and headed for Earth with a taste for Joan in mind. I hoped she was home; I would hate to have to track her down, but I knew I would if she wasn't.

Merlin hated when I flew the ship. I always came out of Deep Space drive at the last minute, ripping space warps all around us as I literally threw an anchor out the back door and dropped into Plasma drive. This time it was no different. I came so close to Pluto; I could have removed its atmosphere if it had possessed one. A trail of debris from the Oort cloud trailed after us as I swung the ship around toward Earth and activated the deceive mode. Minutes later, I entered the Earth's atmosphere and guided the ship down toward North America and home.

As the ship settled into hover mode in my front yard, I noticed my house had been restored to its original condition, even the front yard had been leveled smooth. I couldn't tell if anyone was home, so I decided to ring the bell from the ship.

"Merlin, tap the bell with a sonic murmur, will you." Another one of my new gadgets.

I knew a delicate murmur would turn into a wall-smashing burst if I tried it. Merlin turned on the ship's speakers, and I heard the doorbell chime. I listened for any little sound. The screen showed the garage door was down, but the absence of snow left no clue whether any one was there. Suddenly I heard the sound of footsteps, little ones, and then I saw the front door open a crack. Joan was standing there in her bathrobe. Oh baby.

"Nice boobs," I said through the ship's speakers.

She heard my voice but couldn't figure out where it was coming from and smiled at my greeting.

"OK," she laughed, "I give up, where are you?" She pulled her bathrobe tighter, not because she was shy but to keep warm in the cold January air.

"Right in front of you," I announced, opening the hatch and jumping down the steps into her arms, which opened to hug me. Now I know why sailors like to come home from the sea. We hugged and kissed as the hatch closed behind me, and as we entered the house, she turned and looked at the invisible ship.

"Just like the movies, huh?" she remarked.

"Only better," replied Merlin. He liked having the last word.

She looked down at my sensor and started to say something and decided not to, and gave me another bear hug. Oh, Mr. Happy liked bear hugs.

"I knew you'd be back in time for the Superbowl," she said.

"You know me, Mr. Nick O. Time," I said. There was no point in telling her I had forgotten and that I just wanted to see her. She would find out soon enough; Mr. Happy would vouch for that.

"Come on," I ordered, "my team's got the ball, and we're about to score. Why don't you show me your goal-line stand." I pulled her up the steps into my arms and carried her the rest of the way into the bedroom. It was an exciting Superbowl to say the least; both sides won even though it went into overtime twice.

I didn't board the ship until late Monday night. I could say I didn't board Merlin, but that sounds kinda queer. Joan had already left that morning for her job, which was in the Columbus, Ohio, area, that week, though she didn't really want to go. It made me feel good about our relationship. The extra time before I left I spent with Rick and Wolf. We spent the day going over business and tossing the Frisbee around in the yard even though it was in the forties and raining lightly—what I call a West Virginia drizzle.

Several times the Frisbee had hit the side of the ship, and once I thought Wolf was going to smack it himself as he jumped for an errant toss. Merlin must have risen up as he jumped at the Frisbee because Wolf had landed and sniffed the air trying to figure out what was wrong with the picture. He seemed to shake his head like a human and then ran back to us. I could tell Rick was dying to see the ship, so just before dinner, I told Merlin to reveal himself for a couple of seconds. I have to admit, sitting in my front yard, it, Merlin, was breathtaking. His paint job was awesome against the surrounding trees and hills. I almost took Rick and Wolf inside and decided not to at the last minute. It would compromise my oath, and I couldn't rationalize that just yet. I was apparently growing up, you know, maturing.

"Well, Merlin," I said as I climbed into my chair and activated the straps, "let's go to Aldebaran. Why don't you drive tonight?"

"My pleasure," he said as the ship rose and left my home below us, "and shall I add, it's nice to see you rested."

"Good, then let me show you some more 'rested,'" I added, as I cranked the seat back and settled in for a nap.

"How fast do you want me to get there?" he added in first person, something new for him.

"Leave me time to shave," I replied. I think he is developing an identity.

"And shit too?" he joked.

"Why not?" I laughed. Nothing more fun than dumping on a disintegrator plate, and yes, I'm being facetious.

"Jim," said Merlin. He may have already said it several times. I pulled myself out of the dream I was having and brought the chair into an upright position. I must have really been under, and I couldn't get the screen in front of me to stop twisting and turning. It reminded me of a demented kaleidoscope.

"Yes," I answered, rubbing my eyes. The screen was still doing its thing.

"Our plans have been changed," he said. "The meeting has been changed to the Chaga Galaxy."

"What?" I asked. *The what galaxy, Chaga? When the fuck did this happen?* I wondered.

"Who, when, and why?" I said. Something smelled in Denmark.

"Crouthhamel programmed my computer when you were zonked out on Pyritium. He ordered me not to access his entry until we left Earth for

Aldebaran and promised to disassemble me if I tried. I believe he has a severe security problem," he concluded, with some degree of convincing. He knew I didn't like secrets kept from me by friends or fellow Guardians.

"He does have a big security problem," I admitted, remembering the Betas and the Bojj, "but you might have told me that he was on my ship and played with my computer. It doesn't matter now anyway, but next time, find a way to talk to me about it, will you please. We are a team, you know." I figured a little guilt might help him decide next time.

"Sure, Jim," he answered, "thanks for not getting pissed at me."

"No problem," I said, pointing to the screen. "Is that what the Time drive looks like?"

"Yes, I am doing in less than four hours, what it would take me two weeks to do in Deep space drive. About a hundred thousand parsecs per hour," he bubbled with enthusiasm.

"No shit," I commented, "how does it feel to you?" It looked like a bazaar kaleidoscope to me. And he could feel it.

"Incredible."

Now I knew why he was so happy on Pyritium. He had accessed his computer, against direct orders from Crouthhamel, and even now wouldn't admit it. He was happy because he knew he was going to have the chance to try out Time drive and couldn't wait to do it. What a sly dog. I smiled to myself. I would have done the same thing; hell, I did it with Christmas gifts sometimes, even when I knew I shouldn't. I didn't blame him a bit, yet I began to wonder if he was part human.

"Couldn't wait, could you?" I said out loud.

"What?"

"Nothing, Merlin," I replied. "How much longer do we have to reach this Chaga galaxy?"

"Another three hours with slowing down added into the time."

"Good, I'm going to eat something and get cleaned up."

"OK," he answered, "thanks again for understanding."

"No problem," I answered from the shower, "I would have done the same thing."

"I thought so," he replied happily.

I sat in the backroom and ate dinner in silence. The screen was making me dizzy and the seating allowed me to stretch out my legs. *I must be getting bored with flying*, I thought. The last thing I remembered was dressing in my uniform and sitting back down to relax before we arrived at Chaga galaxy.

"Jim," announced Merlin, "we're here."

I climbed up from the lounge; I must have fallen back to sleep again. *It must be some kinda jet lag*, I thought.

The screen was stable but full of cloudlike vapors and millions of lights, both blinking and glowing through the clouds of whatever. It was almost like looking into a fog bank with your high beams on and rain hitting your windshield at sixty mph, except the vapors and clouds kept changing colors ever so slowly.

"Where are we, hell?"

"The Casper Nebula of the Chaga Galaxy, Jim," returned Merlin. "I'm waiting for clearance from that buoy straight ahead to proceed into the nebula."

"What's in there?" I thought I could make out a space buoy in front of us. It was damn hard to see.

"A Mothership. *Alpha One*, I think they call it," said Merlin.

"Shit, I thought this meeting was on a planet somewhere," I said. Now you could see ferocious bolts of energy striking the fog in front of us, and flashes of things exploding here and there.

"You're not the only one, there's quite a line of ships behind me," he added, "but we're early, I made sure we were first in line." He sounded like me; I personally think the only place to wait in line is at the front.

"Good," I replied, "I hate to wait in line." I swung the view to the rear of Merlin and saw a line of ships of various shapes and sizes lined up behind us. I settled into the control chair and checked out the Z view above and below us. It was clear of ships as well as I could see through the wisps and vapors of the Casper Nebula.

"I have clearance, Jim," said Merlin eagerly.

"Good, let's get a good seat, OK?"

"No problemo, Boss man."

We glided forward into the thickening haze; the ships behind us started to follow, but I couldn't see them now even as close as they were to us. I was going to exchange words with the one behind me but decided not too. It might compromise the obvious secrecy of our location. The haze cleared up, and the Mothership immediately filled the screen. It was humongous. It was planetary in size.

"Holy shit," I muttered. It must be the size of Earth.

"Big, isn't it?" said Merlin. "I calculate over twenty thousand miles in circumference."

"Probably can't hide this too many places, huh?"

"Nope, good, there is a central landing dock opening up ahead."

I was about to answer him when he shot forward, throwing me back into the seat and then forward almost into the viewer as he came to a fast stop. I was about to curse at him for driving like I do when he turned on the rear view, and I saw a black ship like the one which cut me off at the Zalo base trying to unsuccessfully cut us off. Whoever it was settled for second place and glided off to another open landing bay a short distance away from us. Behind him, the other ships were fanning out to the various landing bays available. It seemed like the center spots were the best.

"Is that guy stupid or what?" I asked.

"I don't know, but he wasn't going to cut us off again like he did at the Zalo base," said Merlin angrily. He was showing more emotion lately.

"Is that the exact same ship?" I wondered out loud. "That's very interesting, I thought that was the Tayhest ship I sold to the Zalo people, no wonder they thought I was crazy." I had argued the selling price of a ship I never saw, cool.

"Yes, its engines are a sure fingerprint to its identity," replied Merlin. "No two are identical, and no, it is not the Tayhest ship; that was far uglier than that thing."

"I thought I was the only Guardian at the base that day," I muttered. "Who are they, can you tell?" Something told me to pay attention.

"No, I only know it's a Darassin ship, at least the design is very similar, but the penetration amplifier you had installed on the screen will not penetrate the ship's hull. Maybe when they open the hatch, yes, I'm getting something now."

The screen came on, showing three extremely black dudes in Guardian uniforms departing the ship. They had really long faces, almost like a collie and black fur or something from the top of their heads right down into the tunic of their uniform. They looked about my size but thinner; hell, everybody looked thinner to me. I wondered if synthesized food was higher in calories than normal food. I made a note to check it out. I caught a glimpse of the hands of one of them. The hands were extremely black and covered with fur on the tops, interesting, with fingers of extraordinary length.

"Are they from the planet 'Lassie,'" I asked.

"No, and they aren't Darassin, they're Lussecans, from a star system at the other end of the Milky Way from your home."

"Where did they get that ship then? Are the Darassin buddies with the Lussecans?" I asked. I vaguely recalled something about the Darassin, but I couldn't remember what it was, which was normal for me.

"I can't answer that, but the Darassin system is on the other side of the Altair system and quite a ways from the Lussecans," said Merlin thoughtfully. "Maybe they picked up the ship at the Galaxy auction near the Zalo base we visited, I heard something about it while we were on Pyritium."

"Maybe they did, I still think it's interesting that they didn't reveal themselves to me at the base. And nobody mentioned it either."

"That is interesting, and they were gone when we left," replied Merlin, "but I'm sure you'll find out everything before it's all over."

"I most certainly will," I said as the hatch opened. "I'll talk to you later." I started through the hatch.

"Jim," warned Merlin, "no weapons are allowed off the ships."

I knew there was no point in arguing, so I dropped my Zalo blasters in the drawer by the door and left. The docking bay had an oxygen field, which flipped me out when I saw the opening to the outside was still open. I walked over to it and bumped into a force field of some kind. I almost walked through it as startled as I was, but a hand reached out and grabbed me from behind. I spun around and almost fell into Crouthhamel.

"It would be a shame to lose you now," he said, extending his hand to mine. "Good to see you again, Jim."

"No shit, Crouthhamel, how are you doing?" I exclaimed in pleasant surprise, grabbing his hand and pumping it like a Texan. He looked pretty good since I had seen him last. He almost looked happy too.

"Fine, let's go inside; I want to go over a few things with you before the meeting begins," he replied, leading me away from the opening as if he expected me to repeat a stunt that almost cost me my life. He looked me up and down, like a dad, not a queer, nodding as we exited the bay. He seemed to walk quite normal, which made me nod also.

We walked down a tube shaped corridor and turned into the first doorway we came to, which opened quietly, revealing a small lounge area with easy chairs and tables scattered around it. We took a couple of chairs in the far corner and settled into them as a side door opened, and a Nack came out of it and walked over to us. She had a Guardian uniform on over her brown fur and strode effortlessly to our table and settled into the chair next to mine. I think Mr. Happy recognized her first.

"Hi again," she purred at me, "remember me?"

I think if anyone had taken my picture just then, they would have seen my mouth hit the floor in amazement. I turned to Crouthhamel and then back to the Nack.

"How could I ever forget," I answered. I could still feel those claws running down my arm. Oh boy. Mr. Happy didn't forget.

"I am Tamee," she said, saluting me and offering her hand to me. I saluted back and shook her soft clawless hand. She looked at Crouthhamel and smiled, which made her whiskers almost jump at me. I couldn't get those black eyes out of my head, so black they appeared bottomless. Being a cat lover didn't help either.

"Call me, Jim," I stuttered. "I had no idea you were a member Guardian; why didn't you tell me? For that matter, why didn't you come help me fight that big ugly Tayhest?" I must have looked pissed, although I couldn't seem to get pissed.

"I did," she admitted coyly. "Don't you remember the pod that knocked him down the shaft?"

"You did that?" I uttered, completely amazed. Did I say mesmerized?

"Of course, I couldn't let your precious little head get squashed, now could I?" she purred. She stroked my arm, and I felt the claws again. Neat trick.

"All right you two," broke in Crouthhamel, "let's get down to business. Jim, you're familiar with the Beta problem we had on Earth."

I nodded.

"Well we had a Beta uprising on the planet Debo, in the Rigel system that almost got out of hand. Luckily we were able to get it under control."

"The Bojj?" I interrupted. It was a bad habit of mine.

"Let me finish, will you," chided Crouthhamel. "We were able to dissect a couple of Betas, and I now think it is someone else directing them, using the old activation codes of the Bojj. I haven't been able to get any farther than that. So I decided to bring Tamee here to mingle with the Council members and the other Guardians and see if she can find out anything. She will be able to find out more than you, and I could ever find out."

"For sure," I said looking over at her. She purred at me.

"Do you suspect a Council member?" she said turning to Crouthhamel. She didn't purr at him; she was all business.

"I'm leaning that way," he began explaining, "because the meeting on Entimall was only a regional meeting, and I know most of the Guardians that were there from previous missions." He held up his hand at me. "I know what you're going to say, Jim, but I have been in some pretty tight spots with most of them and seen them in action. I would really be surprised to find any of them involved in this betrayal and subversion."

"But all the Council members were there, and you don't trust all of them," I interjected.

He nodded. "Exactly, Council members must attend all of the meetings no matter where they take place so they have access to people and places that you and I don't."

"Plus," he continued, "they have the longevity that the person behind this would need to be familiar with the Bojj because they were all Guardians once."

"Why would anyone want to start this kind of trouble?" said Tamee disgustedly.

"I don't know yet," answered Crouthhamel, "but I believe the Betas are only the tip of the asteroid."

"I know," I said. They both looked at me surprised. "Love and/or money," I explained, "are the only two reasons that anyone ever kills anyone else." I smiled grimly.

"What about power? Is that the same as money?" asked Tamee, challenging me.

"Basically, when you have one, you have the other."

They both nodded.

"So what do you want me to do? Sneak around too?" I asked. I liked sneaking.

"No, Jim," said Crouthhamel condescendingly, "I want you to keep an eye on Tamee, but stay away from her, so she can do her job." He gave us both a fatherly look.

"Oh, boo," she whimpered playfully and placed her hand on my leg nearest to her. I think she could raise the blood pressure of a dead man.

"No problem," I said to him as I stood up and straightened myself and relieved an uncomfortable feeling I was getting from Mr. Happy. I took off my sensor and handed it to Tamee.

"Take this," I said, "it will keep you in constant contact with Merlin and me."

She stood up and bent straight over with a cat-like grace and fastened the sensor around her ankle. She looked up at me to see if I was watching. I was guilty.

"I'm going back to my ship and get another one, OK?" I said to Crouthhamel. He nodded as I headed for the door. Tamee had already started for the door she came out of and disappeared with a smile at me. I let out a sigh of relief.

"Jim," said Crouthhamel, "I'll meet you here in ten of your minutes, I have someone to see quickly,"

I nodded.

"And Jim," he cautioned me.

I stopped at the door.

"Be careful with that one," he smiled, "or you will find your hands full."

I smiled at the advice and left the room. I wondered if I would follow it. Without my sensor, I felt a little lost; my partnership with Merlin had grown very strong over the last few days, and I was glad to return to the ship.

"Hey, buddy," I said as I walked into the hatch, "you heard everything?"

"Yes," he said teasingly, "and she sounds like a whole lot of trouble."

"You said a mouthful, Merlin," I answered, strapping on a spare sensor band, "but she has a job to do, so keep an eye on her for me, will you?"

"My pleasure, Jim," he drew out my name in a soft voice, imitating Tamee's voice, and did it pretty good too.

"Learn anything more about the Lussecans?" I ignored his impersonation and went into the back to take a whiz. He continued as I peed.

"They went into the main meeting room, and I lost them, but I can tell you that they talked of meeting with a person at the meeting who was going to help them take care of something important. When they entered the main hall, the crowd ruined my spying on them, sorry, they didn't give a name."

"That's OK, just let me know if they come back to their ship."

"No problem, Jimmy," answered Merlin in Tamee's voice.

"Cut it out, Merlin," I said as I left the ship and hurried back to the meeting room. I think I heard him chuckling softly.

Crouthhamel was waiting in the hallway and appeared anxious or nervous about something. I started to ask him, but he began walking away from me the minute I reached him, and I almost had to run to keep up with him. His strides must have been six feet at a time. Once more, I felt like a midget next to him. Yes, a fat one too. He finally came to a door and it slid open in front of him. He stepped into the horizontal lift and beckoned me to hurry. I jumped through the closing door as the lift began moving forward quickly. At the speed we were moving, I wondered how Merlin tracked the Lussecans as far as he did; we must be doing three hundred miles per hour in this thing. Crouthhamel saw me looking around.

"Actually, about nine hundred miles per hour," he said, reading my mind, "so strap yourself into your seat in case we stop fast." He didn't have to tell me twice.

"Did you talk to whomever you were going to talk too?" I asked finally.

"No, he isn't here yet," he said, "which bothers me."

"Hey, what do you know about the Lussecans?" I asked.

# The Guardian Projects

He looked at me like I was a ghost. His mouth moved but said nothing.

"What . . . what?" I asked. I checked my mouth for my foot.

"How do you manage to get involved in shit that doesn't concern you?" he asked. "Do you look for trouble or does it look for you?"

"A little of both," I joked. He didn't think it was funny.

"Why do you want to know about the Lussecans?" he said with a hint of hostility.

Boy, had I hit a nerve or what! I quickly explained the way they had cut us off at the Zalo base when we were trying to dock and the similar incident here at the Mothership. I didn't tell him that I had Merlin tracking them. I knew better than that.

"Stay away from them, they're trouble, Jim," he ordered, trying to sound more pleasant but not succeeding. I started to ask why they were Guardians and decided not to piss him off further. I sat back quietly and glanced around. Ahead of us, the lift tunnel was brightening, and a minute later, we slowed and emerged into a large terminal where dozens of lifts were arriving and unloading an assortment of odd-looking Guardians. Crouthhamel waved to a few of them, but his mood had deteriorated to shit, and he hurried to the next lift we needed to grab. I had to jog to keep up with him. I almost missed it, and he gave me a look somewhere between nasty and disgusted. I avoided looking back and studied the walls of the tube as we sped by, this time slower than before. We suddenly began passing doors on both sides of us, and he placed his hand over some kind of sensor pad and held it there. The lift slowed, and a door on my side met the lift as it pulled to a stop and slid open. We entered a box seat—like room, and the view was awesome. Our box was right on the fifty-yard line, so to speak, and opened onto a room of immense proportions. It was the Meadowlands stadium only much bigger.

"There must be five thousand boxes here," I said as I walked to the railing of our little balcony. On both sides of us, boxes circled the monstrous stadium. Each box had several seats in it, most of which were filled or filling up with strange creatures as I watched in total amazement. I don't think an LSD trip could have given me the visuals I was seeing here nor can I describe it.

I finally saw several boxes with people in them who looked surprisingly human in appearance, who saw me looking at them and looked back at me with the same surprised look that I must have had on my face. I was about to wave at them when old grumpy Crouthhamel started talking to me.

"This is Annual number 2256," he said almost nicely. He seemed to have brushed off the bad mood.

"These meetings have been going on for over two thousand years?" I said incredulously. He nodded and sat forward in his seat. "How many have you been too?" I asked.

"Too many," he answered with a smile. "My dad even brought me with him when I was just a little red carrot." He smiled. I laughed. I wondered if carrots were universal and smiled at the thought of kids all over the universe making faces as they ate them.

Our box appeared to be halfway up the side of the room and directly across the room from an elevated platform, which protruded from a large box. Obviously very good seats.

*This place is big enough to humble a Texan*, I thought.

Below us, the floor of the room was covered with what looked like slot machines but turned out to be food and beverage synthesizers, surrounded by waiters and waitresses of all sizes and shapes. Some of them were riding small Hoverpads up to the various boxes, carrying trays of multicolored glasses and bowls, while others were in the process of refilling and returning to the various machines on the floor area.

Suddenly our waitress popped up from below on a Hoverpad, loaded down with a tray the size of a semitruck tire. She smiled at us when she recognized us. I couldn't believe it; it was Tamee, back in a tiny little skirt and apron.

"Drinks, Guardians?" she asked. Before we answered, she floated over the balcony and handed each of us a tall mug of clear liquid and then floated back out over the balcony. As she floated up and out of sight, she turned on the pad and raised her skirt on her little waitress outfit so we could see her fur-covered ass cheeks. We looked at each other and laughed. Then Crouthhamel turned away from the balcony, opened the bottom of his glass, and drew out a piece of round black metal and stuck it in his pocket.

*It must be a recorder disc of some kind*, I thought. How clever. I tasted the liquid; it was delicious, hard to describe but delicious. It seemed like every time you took a swig of it, the taste changed, from sweet to nutty and then to salty; each taste was different. I was impressed. I wondered if it came in bottles.

"What is this?" I said turning to Crouthhamel. He was studying the room, looking for someone, not paying attention to his drink or me.

"Huh," he said, "oh, that's Chaga brew." He went back to surveying the room. I went back to drinking. I hoped she would return with a refill soon.

Across from us, the platform had been transformed into a large podium with a dozen or so chairs behind it, nice chairs, big ones, meant for important people, with a long table on each side of the back of the platform. From our box, I could hear the noise of a thousand conversations going on all around us, nonstop, and increasing in volume.

Our little box was quiet, too quiet, and I looked over at Crouthhamel, wondering how I could get the old boy out of his somber mood. I noticed he had placed the metal disc to his ear and seemed intent on listening to whatever was on it. I looked away, out at the proceedings, and quite by accident spotted the Lussecan box below and far to the left of ours. Their jet-black appearance made them stand out from the creatures occupying the adjacent boxes. I wondered if they had met with whomever they were going to meet with here.

"We've got our spy now!" exclaimed Crouthhamel as he put the disc in his side pocket and leaned forward in his chair. In front of him was a small control panel; I noticed one in front of me also, recessed into the side of the balcony below the railing. He pushed a button, and a clear screen came down from the ceiling above the balcony, and suddenly the podium on the other side of the room was right in front of him. You would swear you could touch the damn thing.

"It's a magniscreen," he explained, and fingered the controls making the screen move around the room, stopping at various boxes to examine the Guardians in them.

"No shit," I said. I activated my screen and, after several attempts, managed to aim it at the Lussecan box. They were right in front of me, why I could have smacked them if it was real and not just a magnification. I couldn't have timed it better; they all turned around as if someone had just entered the room. I had to see who it was; it was killing me to know. I also wondered who was watching us and was just about to ask Crouthhamel if you could tell if someone was watching you, when he turned and noticed I was also using my magniscreen.

"Who are you looking at?" asked Crouthhamel as he bent over toward my screen.

"Nobody in particular," I answered, fingering the control so the screen moved away from the box. I didn't want him to see the Lussecan box.

"Stop," he shouted, "that's our man right there!" He just about climbed into my chair with me as he pointed to a booth with two very tall people in it. They were skinny, even skinnier than the Altairians, and their faces were real long and drawn out. They had bug eyes and baldheads with skin the color of brass or maybe gold.

"Which one? Who are they?" I asked as I picked his pocket and slid the disc into my waistband. I hated secrets—that is, secrets kept from me.

"They are Darassin, the one on the right is called Cluver, and his buddy is named Remonl. Cluver is the one, or I should say his father, the Council member, who is probably behind all this," replied Crouthhamel.

In front of us, the platform began to fill up with creatures in bright red gowns, robes that went from neck to toe, with different crests of gold designing the front of each one. Crouthhamel swung the screen around to the platform, and as he did, the rest of the room began to drop their screens and follow suit although I'm sure it was just a coincidence of timing. The Council members were taking their seats as he panned the screen over them and stopped at one resembling the two Darassin. He looked a bit chubbier, but it was hard to tell with the robe he was wearing.

"Roegoss," he hissed out the name. A loud gong almost kept me from hearing what he said as the sound echoed throughout the huge stadium, "Alzador must confirm this before the meeting ends." He settled back in his seat and began watching the proceedings.

The meeting was about to start; at least I figured that was the reason for the ear-blowing gong.

"So Roegoss is responsible for the Beta attacks on Rigel and against me on Earth?" I said to him. He nodded and looked forward to the podium as if to say, pay attention and stop talking. Now he seemed antsy, ready to strike antsy.

"Then who's Alzador?" I asked. I had zeroed in on the Lussecans and found them watching the proceedings also. Whomever they had been talking to was no longer there. *Shit*, I thought, *I missed him.*

"A fellow Guardian," he whispered, like they could hear us, in our box half a mile across the freakin' room.

"This meeting will come to order," a voice boomed into our box.

I jerked my screen around to the podium and found myself looking at a very fat Santa Claus. He continued speaking, "This is the two-thousand fifty-sixth meeting of the Alpharian Council of the . . ."

"He looks just like Santa Claus," I laughed. Crouthhamel about fell out of his chair as my voice echoed across the huge room, interrupting the speaker and causing a flutter of reflections as a thousand or more screens rotated around trying to find the source of the voice. I looked over at Crouthhamel and gave him my retard look. I couldn't tell if he was about to laugh or cry. I started to say something when he made a gesture with his hand across his throat that seemed to be universal for "shut up, stupid". I sat back in my seat, feeling a little stupid. Hell, how was I to know that when your screen is down you can talk directly to another box or the whole damn room. I wondered how red my face was; I could feel the warmth in my cheeks.

Slowly, the screens in the stadium returned to the speaker who continued as if this wasn't the first time it had happened. And I'm sure not the last.

"The Loyal Order of the Guardian. All those in attendance please signify." A light came on below my screen, and I followed Crouthhamel's lead and pressed it. It went out. Suddenly my screen began to resemble the end of a movie. Names of the Guardians in attendance began to parade down the screen in some kind of order, maybe alphabetical; I started to read the list and couldn't keep up. Some of the Guardians had names I couldn't pronounce, and some I couldn't even read. It was fascinating in a weird sort of way.

"This meeting will come to order," said Santa Claus as a loud gong, just like the first one, sounded throughout the room. I noticed how quiet it had become and wondered if I had gone deaf. A couple more gongs, and I probably would be. I turned to Crouthhamel and almost said something but caught myself. He looked at me as if he couldn't believe I would do it a second time. He leaned forward and turned off our screens.

"What?" he asked. His mood had improved slightly from earlier. After listening to me fuck up, he seemed to relax a bit. Now he seemed a bit impatient but not quite as antsy anymore.

"Ahh," I began, "where's the bathroom in this place?" I did have to go a little. The speaker was reading reports from previous meetings, and although his voice wasn't booming into our box, it was coming through the walls and floors above and below us. It was boring shit, like when your accountant goes over your receipts for the whole year, and you sit there waiting for him to tell you how much money you should have set aside to pay the IRS, which is what its all about anyway.

"Why didn't you say something before the meeting started?" asked Crouthhamel like a father. He got out of his chair and showed me a panel next to the door. I refused to answer the question; I had answered it too many times growing up.

"Each symbol you push will bring the appropriate lift to you," he explained, showing me the lift code for various functions like eating, going to the bathroom, returning to your ship, and even communicating with another world from a communication room. I noticed the panel of numbers above it and pointed to them.

"Those will transport you to another box, if you know the code for that box," he explained further, "however, I hope you won't go exploring without checking with me first."

Was that an order I heard in his voice? Nah.

"We are in Box 2231; you will need to remember that to return here after you find the bathroom." He turned and went back to his seat. Enough dad for now.

I hit the shitter button and waited. Crouthhamel seemed absorbed in the meeting, and his screen was back down, so when the lift arrived, I climbed into it and left without saying a word. I felt like a kid in a candy store. I could go anywhere I wanted to, if I wanted to, when I wanted too. The lift came to a stop, and I entered a narrow room with privacy stalls on one side and eliminator tubes on the opposite wall. I really didn't have to go; I just wanted to get out of the meeting for a while. I hate meetings like this one even if it was on a huge ship filled with strange aliens from all over the universe. I chose a stall and closed the privacy door behind me. I pulled out the disc and put it to my ear. Whatever was on it was in some language I couldn't understand. Finally, one dialect the old Pracon didn't know or chose not to put in my cranium.

"Merlin," I whispered.

"Yes, Jim," he answered quickly.

"See if you can figure out this shit." I placed the disc over the sensor band and held it there for a minute.

"Well?" I asked. I had to work on being more patient.

"Put it back," said Merlin, "it appears to be a code of some kind, and I didn't get all of it." I put it back and waited.

"I got all of it," he said through the disc in a muffled voice, "but I don't know what it says, I'll have to run it through my computer; can you wait?" I thought I heard someone else in here, or maybe I felt someone else was in here.

"No," I said quietly, "I'll get back with you." I stuck the disc in my pocket and opened the stall door. I half expected someone to be there, a fear left over from my childhood when some weirdo had tried to molest me in a bathroom at a bus station in Rochester. It had forever made me distrust public restrooms. I looked around, but nobody was in sight. By now, I really did have to go to the bathroom, so I stepped to the tube in front of me and positioned it to my height and pulled out Mr. Happy and began relieving myself. Much to my surprise, I really did have to go. I had just finished giving Mr. Happy the usual shake or two when a stall opened farther down the room, and who should walk out but Cluver the Darassin. He didn't seem to notice me until he had walked to the area where you stick your hands under small individual hoods and a hand-sized shower beam runs over them, cleaning them of everything,

## The Guardian Projects

and I mean everything. It probably takes a layer of skin too. I decided to play it cool and joined him at the hood area. He acted like he was too good to speak to me. Then he noticed the crest on my tunic.

Immediately he stuck out his hand toward me. "Greetings," he said in Tharx, "I am Cluver of the Darassin star system."

"Hi," I returned, shaking his hand, "my name is Jim, and I'm from the Earth star system, Tara." He looked surprised; I wondered why. He saw this register on my poker face and quickly spoke up.

"Your uniform is of the Procyon system, is it not?" he asked.

"Yup, sure is," I answered. That could explain his surprise, or maybe he didn't expect to see me alive.

"Do you represent the honorable Pracon family too?" he asked.

"Bingo," I returned in Tharx, which sounds more like your saying "dildo". He understood me and straightened up a little.

"It is a great honor to meet you," he said sincerely. "You must be the new Guardian we have all heard about." He smiled, and his long face drew up sideways until it looked like the smile of a clown. I almost laughed but managed to control myself and just smiled back. It's so hard to be diplomatic sometimes.

"Say what?" I replied, as what he said registered. I knew Crouthhamel would kill me for talking to him, but I found myself liking him, and I certainly wasn't getting any bad vibes.

"Guardian Jim," he answered, "what you did on Pyritium was reported to the Council by the Altairians; my father is one of them, Council Member Roegoss." He said it proudly. It was fascinating to watch his whole face move up and down as he spoke.

"I hope they don't hold a grudge," I said. He looked down at me and laughed a throaty gurgle of sound.

Then his month slapped shut, and he looked at me again.

"You don't know, do you?" he exclaimed.

"Know what," I said cautiously. Maybe I should leave now before I find out.

"The Altairians have nominated you for the highest award a Guardian can receive, the Medal of Uhlon Bathor. It has been given out only a few times in the last hundred years or so. My father said . . ." He stopped talking and held his hand to his mouth.

"What . . . what?" I pried. Oh, was I good at prying.

"I'm sorry," he groaned, "I was not supposed to tell you . . . I will surely be disciplined for opening my mouth this time." He seemed to whiten in color the more he thought about it. I laughed at him. He was a goof like the rest of my friends.

"Don't worry about it, I won't let anyone know I know," I said, grabbing his arm with my hand. "We'll just make this our little secret." Wow, his arm felt like it was made of bands of steel cable and just as strong. He looked a little relieved.

"Put your eyes back in your head, will you," I joked. I had thought they were going to pop out when he realized what he had told me. He hardly seemed like spy material; I had a feeling Crouthhamel was dead wrong. His face drew into a smile, and his eyes returned to normal bug-eye size.

"Thank you, Jim," he gushed, "my father would kill me. He is always telling me to keep my mouth shut, or he would put me back on the ore ships and take away my Guardian status forever."

"No problem, Cluver," I joked, "just don't say Uhlon Bathor in your sleep, OK?"

We both laughed, and this time I laughed with him.

We both left the bathroom agreeing to meet at mealtime. I sat in the lift and thought over the situation. I had to know what the disc said that Crouthhamel had gotten from Tamee.

"Merlin," I said, "I only have a minute before the lift gets to my box, have you figured out the disc yet?"

"Not entirely," he said thoughtfully. "It is a message from Alzador to Crouthhamel, describing a mission he went on for him. All I have been able to figure out is that it was secret and very important."

"I already knew that," I remarked. The lift began to slow. "I'll talk to you later." I jumped from the lift as the door opened and walked to my waiting chair. Crouthhamel looked at me and switched off his screen.

"Where have you been?" he asked. He looked bored, so I decided to liven up his mood.

"Talking to Cluver, he was in the bathroom." I said it as nonchalantly as I could.

I thought Crouthhamel was going to explode. I leaned forward and turned on my screen and started listening to the meeting. He sat and simmered in his chair for a while and finally gave up and went back to his screen. Another old guy had taken the podium and was detailing something about freighters and intergalactic requirements that were being broken or something like that. I felt myself drifting off to sleep, like I do in church. I hoped I didn't say anything in my sleep.

I came out of my dream to find Crouthhamel shaking me lightly on my arm. I looked up at him, and he smiled. I smiled back.

"Come on, Jim," he said sweetly, "the meeting has been adjourned until the tens pic tomorrow, and I'm hungry, aren't you?"

"Yes," I replied; I could feel my stomach come to life at the mention of food, "I guess I am kinda hungry." I stood up and stretched.

"Good, let's get something to eat," he began almost as sweetly, "and you can tell me what you talked about with Cluver." His voice had turned hard by the time he finished the sentence and his eyes cold.

"I want to eat," I warned him, "not get indigestion."

He ignored me and signaled for a lift. He turned and held up the disc in his hand. He wasn't smiling. *Shit*, I thought, *don't let me touch my waistband.* But my hand had already gone to it searching for the disc. I was fucked for sure.

We climbed into the lift in silence and headed straight for the Cafe Crouthhamel, which happened to be his ship if you didn't catch that. I felt like I was entering a den of lions as I boarded it. He came in behind me and sealed the hatch with a slap of his hand on the panel. He motioned me to grab a chair and threw himself into one across from me. He looked about as happy as my dad did the time he caught me skipping school.

"Why did you lift the disc from my tunic?" he demanded. I had two ways to answer that, the truth or a lie. I lied.

"I didn't," I shot back, deciding to take the offense.

"Then why did you check your pants when I showed it to you?" he countered. He smug smiled back at me.

"Because after you dropped it in my lap, I decided to listen to it. I didn't think we kept secrets from each other as fellow Guardians," I snapped the words back at him angrily, "but you be the judge of that, you know I don't keep secrets and you know damn well I couldn't understand it anyways. And as far as your fucking bad mood goes, I'm getting just a little tired of it"—I was rolling now, Joan would be proud of me—"you know I know about the spy problem and want to help, yet you treat me like a goddamn kid. Maybe if you had taken two fucking minutes to explain how the screens worked I wouldn't have embarrassed both of us in front of the Council, and if you remember . . ."

"Stop a minute," he interrupted my rising voice with an upheld hand. My aggressive offense had made a believer out of him. I used the angry mood I had created in my mind to keep from smiling or laughing. I like winning.

"Jim," he began, "I'm sorry, you deserve better than the way I've been treating you, I should have let you listen to the disc the minute I received it; we are, after all, in this together."

"No shit," I agreed. The damn thing must have fallen out of my pocket while I was sleeping. I made a note to have some real pockets put in these uniforms.

"Again, I'm sorry," he continued. "I was so fucking pissed when we got here that all I wanted to do was find Alzador and learn what he had found out about the spy in the Council and then go kill the asshole. A lot of good people died on Debo." He was picking up my cuss words rather well; I noticed. Go baby.

"So," I said. *Pry on*, I thought. *I had him now.*

"Let me get us some dinner and then you can listen to the disc."

"Disc first," I demanded. Maybe I was going to far. Nah.

"OK," he gave in, "but then dinner, I'm starving." He smiled a genuine smile and leaned over and extended his hand in friendship. I met him halfway and smiled back. He stood up and went to the front of the ship and put the disc inside an audio slot device. It came on immediately.

"CROUTHHAMEL, ALZADOR HERE, TRACKED DARASSIN SHIP FROM DEBO IN RIGEL SYSTEM, LEFT GALAXY THROUGH SHIPPING LINES, FOLLOWED SHIP TO JENN DAR GAMMA, SHIP AVOIDED ALL OTHER SHIPS EXCEPT THE SILMARRION ORE CARRIERS, CONTACT MADE WITH SEVERAL WHILE IN SHIPPING LINES, MET WITH TAYHEST SHIP, REPEAT, MET WITH TAYHEST SHIP AT JENN DAR GAMMA."

This was reminding me of a Western Union telegram, plus the manner and style of Alzador's speech made me imagine an old sailor like maybe Long John Silver behind the controls of his ship, barking into a long-range communicator.

"SHIP ENTERED LINES TO DARASSIN SYSTEM, TRACKED TO DARASSA, HOME OF COUNCILMAN ROEGOSS' PEOPLE, OTHER PLANETS NOT VISITED BY SHIP, SHIP TRANSMITTED FOLLOWING MESSAGE TO PLANET SURFACE, 'ALL SHIPMENTS TO JENN DAR GAMMA ON SCHEDULE, PROGRAMMING EVERY THIRD FREIGHTER AS INSTRUCTED, BETAS ACTIVATED ACCORDING TO SCHEDULE ON TAU CETI, TARA, RIGEL DEBO.'"

*Holy shit*, I thought, *someone's been busy causing trouble all over the galaxy, including my planet, those bastards. I wanted a piece of them too.*

"MEET YOU AT COUNCIL MEETING FOR FURTHER ORDERS, CLUVER OUT."

I think the last two words went through me like a hot knife through butter.

"transmitting message from Darassa, will join you at meeting, end code, end message, Alzador out."

"Now you can see why I was so torqued," said Crouthhamel. "I was worried something happened to Alzador even if he is a tough old bird."

"How did you manage to listen to that at the meeting?" I asked as he walked to the control panel and retrieved the disc.

"I wear a hearing enhancement device, which also has been modified to decode any messages my Guardians send me," he explained, showing me a small device from his right ear that sure looked like a hearing aid, and then pushed it back into his ear. "It helps when I can't get to my ship like today."

"I'm impressed," I said nodding my head, "so where is this guy?"

"He should be here by the next session, he did not learn of the change in meeting places until he had returned to Morkan Jmer, his home star system," replied Crouthhamel.

"Where is Jenn Dar Gamma?" *I should know this*, I thought.

"It's near the Utholok system, in the Kommonsolltyr galaxy," he began. "Well, not quite in it, it's a white cone, sorry, a white hole."

"Why would the Darassin be in cahoots with the Tayhest, and what do they want with the freighters?" I was a bit confused. Situation normal.

"Well, it isn't for love, that's for sure," he laughed, putting a plate of disgustingly gross shit in front of me and sitting down with the same thing in front of him. "It's got to be something to do with the Silmarrite on those ships." He speared a huge glob of red chunks into his mouth and began chewing with enthusiasm. He looked up at me and saw I wasn't eating.

"You're not eating?" he said puzzled. He was certainly stuffing his face.

"What is this?" I asked. I kept an eye on it to see if it was moving while I looked over at Crouthhamel.

"It's a delicacy we eat on Pyritium, we call it Garf. It's the part of the Garf you call . . ."

I held up my hand to stop him before he said any more about eating Garf; I was remembering the Garf bars I had eaten with Nilton. I bit a small piece off and began chewing it as Crouthhamel looked on; he was trying not to laugh. It wasn't bad; I decided to continue eating and looked up at him and smiled. He passed me a glass of purple liquid, and I drank it without asking; hell, I didn't want to know anymore. We ate in hungry silence.

Dinner was followed by Altairian cigars in the aft lounge of the ship. I'm sure I enjoyed my cigar more than Crouthhamel since I was getting as high as a kite from whatever was in it. I wondered if a supply of these jewels wouldn't be in order for my ship. I had just snuffed out the last of mine and was watching the room change color and shape when Merlin said something to me. I looked at my sensor and swore I could see a pair of lips on it moving as he spoke.

"What did you say?" I asked. He sounded so funny.

"Tamee is trying to reach you," he repeated. He sounded annoyed at me.

"Tell her where we are and ask her if she's in any trouble, please," I laughed. Crouthhamel looked over at me; he appeared quite normal, which seemed funny to me, and I smiled at him. When he smiled back, he changed colors again and again.

"She said the only trouble she was in was trying to stay awake while keeping an eye on Cluver and his father, Roegoss. She said they have been gorging themselves ever since the meeting let out. She wants to know if she can stop and take a break," finished Merlin. I don't think he liked being a secretary.

I looked over at Crouthhamel, and he nodded approval; he was three different colors now. He reminded me of a twisted lollipop on two sticks.

"Merlin, tell her to take a break, would you please, and why don't you take one too," I laughed at myself. Crouthhamel came over to me and felt my forehead. It was the first time I had ever been assaulted by a lollipop. I pushed him away playfully, and he gave me a funny look, at least I think he did; any look was funny at this point.

"Merlin," he said, "I don't think Altairian cigars have the same affect on Jim that they have on me. I'm relaxed, he's blotto."

"I am nut," I said, my speech error made me laugh harder. *I really was blotto*, I thought and laughed even more at that thought.

"What a fucking buzz," I gasped as I slowly got the laughter under control, "I thought my stomach was going to rupture." Apparently, the buzz was short-lived; I could feel my sanity coming back as the room and Crouthhamel returned to normal. Suddenly the room felt cold, cold as a freezer, colder than, well you know.

"Feel better?" asked Crouthhamel walking over to me.

"No, but yes," I conceded. He must have turned the temperature in his ship way down; he looked like he was frozen too. He even had the shivers now.

"Turn on the heat, will you," I joked. "I'm going to freeze to death." It really was getting cold in here now. My breath was icing on my mustache. He nodded and left the room momentarily.

"Are you all right?" he asked as the heat returned to the room.

"Yeah, the cold knocked it out of me." I had to remember that. I wondered how long the buzz would last without the cold. Oh boy.

I stood up and stretched, did a few bends, a few twists, and looked over at Crouthhamel as he watched me. He was sitting there in his thinking mode, half watching me.

"You know what we should do," I said, "we should go grab Cluver and talk to him mano a mano." That was the extent of my Spanish.

"Let's wait for Alzador."

"OK, OK, but I want in on this, when it goes down," I commented as I walked up front to get a glass of synthetic water. It was pretty good, not like well water from Parkersburg, but it was cold and went down smooth. I stood there drinking as Crouthhamel entered the room. I still had a nagging doubt about Cluver being a master spy.

"You know," I began, "I still have some doubts about Cluver and his father, I just don't see the motive there."

"What do you mean?" he asked. This time he was paying attention.

"Cluver told me his old man had taken him off the ore ships and made him a Guardian, why do that when he was in a better position as an ore pilot? Plus he just doesn't seem like someone who would or could deal with the Tayhest."

"That's a good point, I had forgotten he had been an Ore captain. The Darassin already control the shipping lanes from Utholok to Altair, it does seem rather stupid to risk losing them for a few tres, selling stolen Silmarrite, but the message from Alzador can't be ignored."

"Where I come from this is called a frame-up, it stinks to high heaven."

"It does," he agreed. "You earthlings are a devious bunch, aren't you?"

I nodded to that fact. "It's second nature to us, which could explain why we're not as advanced as we could be. We should, from what I've seen so far, be establishing a place in the galactic market, not stabbing each other from behind all the time." I hated it when I got philosophic; it was depressing.

"Who else would benefit from a Tayhest alliance?" wondered Crouthhamel out loud.

"What about the Lussecans," I said opening a can of worms.

"What is it with you and the Lussecans? Are you still sore at them for cutting you off at the Zalo outpost?" he scowled at me.

"No, I'm pissed because they never came to my aid when I was knee-deep in Tayhest," I shot back.

"But their system is half across your galaxy on the other side of the Borkkan star group," he observed. "It's just their nature, Jim, to be that way, they are only in it for themselves."

"Well it seems like an awful coincidence that they happened to be at the outpost the same time as the Tayhest and driving a Darassin ship on top of it."

Crouthhamel's eyes registered surprise at that fact. "Why didn't you tell me that earlier?" he asked then nodded before I could jump him. "I know, I wasn't being very receptive was I?"

"Well, Merlin seemed to think they picked it up at the auction," I said; I could have made him feel like shit, but I decided not to rub it in. "Say, is there any waq you could check their registration? Find out where they got the ship?"

"Well, I could ask Councilman Labek, I believe his people ran the auction. Yes, I think it was in the Seltorran system."

"Correct, sir," said Merlin, "on the planet Lhll to be exact."

"Thank you," he said, "yes, let me call up old Labek and see if he can shed some radiant energy on this."

"Shed some light," I corrected him. He was picking up clichés from me and mixing them up with his own terms.

"Right," he answered, heading to the controls. He activated his screen and waited for the one to signal Labek in his chamber. It seemed as if a rather long time went by, and finally, the screen lit up, and we were looking at Labek. I recognized him from the podium; he was the biggest one on it. He was huge. And old. A huge old fat mound, with layers upon layers of skin cascading from his chin into his robe. His arms were layered in fatty skin too. He was gross.

"Ahh, Crouthhamel," he said like he was chewing something, "what a pleasure. How are you my friend?" He sounded so insincere.

"Greetings, Your Honor," said Crouthhamel.

*These people have too much respect for their officials*, I thought.

"I am well," he answered the fat one, "and yourself, sir?"

"At my age who can tell," he said jokingly. He laughed at his own joke, and his whole body shook like Jello.

"Your Honor," said Crouthhamel, "I was wondering if you could help me sort out a little information I'm having?" Questioning the "higher ups" was new to him.

"Problem, sort out a little problem," I whispered. The big guy looked over at me.

"And who do we have here?" he asked. His eyes were set so far back in his fatty head I could hardly see them.

"This is Jim Edwards of Tara system, one of my top Guardians," replied Crouthhamel.

"Ahh," he chewed. His fat turned back to Crouthhamel.

"How can I assist the mighty Crouthhamel?" he smoozed. Now I knew I didn't like him, the old fart.

"I am trying to identify a ship that I believe may have been purchased at the auction on Lhll. A Darassin ship."

*Did I detect a slight reaction to this or was my suspicious nature getting the better of me?* I wondered.

"Ahh, I will have to send a request to Lhll for that," he replied. "Do you have the necessary numbers?"

Was he stalling us?

Crouthhamel looked over at me for help. I turned around and was about to signal Merlin when he spoke up. "Ore Rider, Class One," began Merlin, right on cue; he was good. He gave me the rest of the numbers, and I relayed them to Crouthhamel.

"Ahh," said the obese one, "I will handle this personally for you; anytime I can help out the mighty Crouthhamel, don't hesitate to call me." He gave us a fat smile.

"How long?" I asked.

Crouthhamel looked over at me like I had slapped him or something.

"Will it take you . . . sir?" *You big porker*, I thought.

"Ahh, I will be in contact with them later tonight," he said slowly. "I should be able to answer your demand in the morning." He switched off his screen with a fat hand and vanished.

"Why are you so disrespectful?" asked Crouthhamel sincerely.

"Politicians are one step below Tayhest on my all-time favorites list," I concluded, "and I think the old fat fucker knows more than he let on just then."

"Well I bow to your knack for seeing through people," he replied smiling.

"Someone say Nack," said Tamee, entering the ship through the hatch. I don't remember seeing it open, but then I was kinda gonzo for a little while. She walked over to us and plopped her furry ass down in my lap as I sat lounging in Crouthhamel's second command chair. She put her arm around my neck and settled her head against my chest.

"You're hard," she said punching my pectorals playfully. Her statement was made in innocence, but the double meaning registered on my face, and she looked up at the ceiling of the control room as if she was inspecting it for cracks.

"I don't know how I could be," I answered. "I haven't worked out since I started this Guardian stuff." Her bottom was hot, and I was beginning to get uncomfortable. She decided to behave and jumped off me.

"Nothing unusual about Cluver or his father's routine?" asked Crouthhamel. We went back to the conference table and settled in the chairs.

"No, nothing," she replied.

"Did the old man or Cluver meet with the Lussecans?" I asked.

"No, why?" asked Tamee.

"Merlin said he overheard them talking about meeting with someone here, who was going to take care of something for them," I explained.

"Like what?" asked Crouthhamel.

"I would imagine either a payoff or a double cross," I reasoned. "They would be in it for the money, whoever hired them would be in it for the long run."

"But the message from Alzador confirms a Tayhest alliance is forming with someone, and that someone is Cluver. Hmmn, maybe we should test it."

"A Tayhest alliance?" exclaimed Tamee. Her fur began to straighten with alarm. She obviously didn't like them any more than I did.

"Jim, you have a person approaching the ship," said Merlin.

"Who is it?"

"Cluver," he replied, "what do you want me to do?"

"Shit," I said to Crouthhamel, "I told him I would meet him for a drink tonight."

"You want me to tell him to shit?" said Merlin, hearing my exclamation.

"That's not a good idea," said Crouthhamel, talking to me.

"I agree," said Merlin.

"Wait," I said; this three-way conversation was getting out of hand, "tell him to wait there for me."

"Crouthhamel," I pondered, "could anyone besides you decode your message from Alzador?"

"No, absolutely not," he answered. "Why?"

"Well," I began, "let's assume the spy, or spies, could be anyone at the meeting, even Cluver. Then suppose a rumor circulated that you were going to expose the spy at the meeting tomorrow. What do you think would happen?"

"They would try to stop me," he smiled at me, "and we would have them by the bells."

"Balls," I remarked.

"Yes," he said, "why don't you go have a drink with Cluver, and Tamee, why don't you circulate too." We both nodded and rose from our seats.

"Merlin," I said, "tell Cluver I'm on my way." Turning to Tamee, I said, "And be careful, don't act like you know too much."

She nodded.

"I would never do that, Jim," said Merlin. We all cracked up at him.

"I know, I know," I said to Merlin as I waved to Crouthhamel and strode down the steps of the ship. Tamee ran up behind me and stopped me.

"You be careful too," she said to me, her eyes burning into my head. She stepped up to me and gave me a hug, strong but quick, and was off, heading toward her lift and waving as she went down the corridor. Mr. Happy liked the hug and let me know it.

"Be quiet," I said. I hoped Joan was getting as horny as I was getting.

"I didn't say anything," said Merlin.

"I know," I answered.

"Then who are you talking too?"

"It's a long story," I said as I hustled off down the corridor to the lift that would take me to my ship and big mouth Cluver.

Cluver and I had a great time at the lounge where he and his father had eaten earlier. The Mothership probably had dozens of places like this throughout the ship, as large as it was, but this one had to be the biggest. It was laid out like the meeting room, only the outer rim was wide open and not boxed into sections, so from your table, you could see maybe twenty or thirty tables around you in all directions. Guardians of every planet sat around us, talking and arguing, eating and drinking, and just plain having a good time with each other. It was a company picnic to beat all picnics. Cluver had commandeered a table by the edge of our deck so that we could look out over the crowd below and across from us. His mouth and the crest on my tunic drew many Guardians to us, and we exchanged greetings and, in some cases, just a smile of recognition. I met green Zellens of Zalo fame, Chaga Nuies, the host Guardians of the Chaga galaxy with three arms and three legs and a wonderful sense of humor. I also met a frightening group of Tamir Say, who are exoskeletal with a mouth only a mother could love; several human-like people called Beta Krillines; and Beta Cees whom I had seen from my box.

The procession was damn near endless once the word spread that the Taran Guardian who had taken on an entire Altairian planet was there. I met Igarks, Utholoks, Ecck Shassi, Borkkans, Tyrzx, Betelgeuse, Uuks, Felik

Premns, Ocams, Varoghose, and a ton of other aliens whose names I can't even pronounce. I had told Cluver on the way over from the ship about the spy problem, making no secret of it as far as revealing the culprit tomorrow, and everyone he came in contact with got his version of the story, made behind my back so as not to compromise my integrity. I loved it. The guy was a PA system on the loose. Someone would come over to us and, after meeting me, would talk to Cluver, who would pull him or her aside while I was busy meeting someone else. I even met a few female Guardians, one from Volcon, who had long red feelers on her head; one from Melsonia, whose outfit suggested she had at least a dozen breasts under it and an organ on her neck that looked like you-know-what; as well as several I wasn't too sure about. A Horc came up to me, he looked a lot like a fly, and was surprised when I knew his language and was quite pleasant although creepy in a buggy sort of way. Like I said, it was a real trip. I finally had to call it a night; I had consumed several Chaga brews, and I was beginning to feel them; oh hell, I was drunk. I said my good-byes and headed for the lift area, trying to walk straight.

"Your plan worked," said Merlin. As drunk as I was, I started to ask him what plan.

"What do you mean?" I said, sobering up fast. "Is Crouthhamel OK?"

"Yes, but Councilman Labek isn't quite himself anymore," quipped Merlin. "There was an explosion in his chambers about twenty minutes ago, Mr. has it . . . all on screen." He sounded a bit uptight about something.

"Thanks," I said, "where is Tamee right now?"

"She's with Alzador and Crouthhamel; he arrived about an hour ago."

"Thanks for telling me right away," I said; there was a note of irritation in my voice that I couldn't hide.

"You were having such a good time with Cluver," argued Merlin.

"Like I said, thanks for telling me," I said; *let him worry about how pissed I was*, I thought. I didn't say another word until the lift arrived near Crouthhamel's ship, and I started to get out.

"I'm sorry, Jim," said Merlin. "I don't know why I keep things from you; I really don't."

"You're jealous," I said, "a vile human trait, I might add." I knew first hand.

"Of you?" said Merlin sarcastically. He just wouldn't admit it.

"Yes, you nimrod, that's why you do it, I don't blame you, I'm not perfect either." Boy that would piss him off.

He was quiet as I entered the landing dock where Crouthhamel's ship was sitting and strode up the hatch into the ship. I remember Crouthhamel calling Alzador an old bird, but I really didn't expect him to be one.

"Hey, you must be Alzador!" I exclaimed, saluting him and offering my hand. He had been sitting at the table and looked up at me as I entered the ship. My god, he really was a bird; he had huge wings and a face like an owl. And I liked him instantly.

"You must be Jim from Tara." He looked at me and smiled after a very ceremonious salute. He held out a clawed hand from under his right wing and shook mine rather hard. He had an awesome grip, and I was absolutely sure he could work on his ship without a single wrench. He sat back down and folded his arms. They looked pretty damn big too. I'm glad he was on our side. I nodded to Crouthhamel and looked around for Tamee; I didn't see her in the room. Suddenly I felt arms around my waist, little furry ones.

"Hey," I said turning around; I wondered where she had come from, maybe the bathroom, yeah.

"Hey," she mimicked, "you and Cluver were sure putting away the brews."

"Yeah, I know. I'll pay for it tomorrow," I remarked. She gave me a funny look, like she never had a hangover; maybe she didn't get them.

"Jim," interrupted Crouthhamel, "look at this." He pointed toward the screen while handing me some printouts from the Nuies.

The screen came on and even I, the horror movie king, had to gasp at the destruction. Maybe it was because Labek had been so big or maybe because he was at the center of the explosion, but he was painted all over the room and into the other room where the wall had collapsed from the force of the explosion. It reminded me of the Nephid explosion in the lab back on Pyritium, body pieces were everywhere. It was sobering to say the least. Tamee had joined me in front of the screen. She looked up at me and then the screen, but only quickly.

"He must have been holding the damn bomb in his hand," I remarked, glancing at the Nuies' sheets.

"That's what we thought too," said Crouthhamel. "The Nuies are there now, trying to figure it all out."

"Well, it can't be a coincidence that he was checking on that Darassin ship for us and rumors were flying around about you exposing the spy tomorrow." I turned the screen off and sat down at the table. Tamee behaved and didn't sit on me.

I handed him back the Nuies' sheets.

"I filled Alzador in on what we talked about earlier," began Crouthhamel, "and he brought the discs he made while following the ship from Debo. We ran a voice analysis of Cluver's voice, and you were correct in your assumption; it is not his voice but a simulation, and a good damn one too."

I ignored the goof. "Merlin would you be so kind as to check the engine patterns of both the ship here and the one Alzador followed."

"Don't you need mine?" asked Alzador. "I can go get them."

"No need to do that," said Merlin. "I have already compared the logs from your ship, and they are identical; both ships are one and the same."

Alzador looked happily puzzled.

"That's my partner," I assured him.

"Oh, so now it's partner, is it," said Merlin sarcastically. "What happened to 'he's my computer'?"

"You've been promoted, now quiet down, we're trying to think here," I said back at him. I wasn't up for him right now.

"They argue with each other," remarked Crouthhamel. "Merlin is the new prototype ship, the Cyclone, the one I told you they were building for us."

"I would like to meet this Merlin," stated Alzador with respect, "but first we must find our spy. What do we do about the Lussecans, Crouthhamel? They are obviously diverting ore shipments to the Jenn Dar Gamma, and now it looks like Labek was behind it and learned that we knew it."

"Wait a minute," I interrupted, "do you think he committed suicide? Is it normal for his species to do that out of guilt?"

"I think it's a strong theory," stated Crouthhamel, "and I can't see the Lussecans killing him, they would have no reason to kill the silver goose."

"Maybe he didn't know about the Tayhest, maybe he struck a deal with the Lussecans to divert the freighters throughout the universe in return for money and the shipping rights but didn't know about the Tayhest. If he didn't, then maybe the Lussecans killed him." I was tired and rambling, maybe the goose was silver.

"Didn't happen," corrected Merlin. "The Lussecans never left their ship last night." He was so helpful.

"Then how would he know about the rumor you started?" asked Alzador. "Did someone call him?"

"No," I replied, "the Nuies' printouts don't show any transmissions to or from him after we talked with him. Someone went to see him and either told him the rumor or killed him because . . ."

"Because someone else is calling the shots," injected Merlin. He has a knack for interrupting. He will tell you he learned it from me. It's a lie.

"I believe Merlin is correct," observed Alzador.

"Thank you, sir," said Merlin the Ass Kisser.

"I agree too," I added, "but I think that whomever went to Labek's chambers had a concealed bomb with him, a Candygram, if you know what

I mean." I wondered if they had ever heard the phrase "Candygram for Mongo" or seen the movie *Blazing Saddles*. I highly recommend it, if you like to laugh.

"You believe he was murdered when he opened a box of sweets?" asked Crouthhamel. "Alzador, Jim's people are very devious sometimes."

Alzador nodded as he contemplated a candy box bomb. His tufted feathers on top of his head went straight up into a spiked hairdo.

"Yup," I replied, "which means if we find out who did this, we will have our spy."

"But how do we do that?" asked Tamee, her voice heavy with sleep.

The two warriors looked at me, expecting an answer I couldn't give them.

"Well," I began reasoning, "whoever went to see Labek has to be the same person who met with the Lussecans and has ties with the Tayhest."

"Got any ideas?" said Crouthhamel; he looked like he needed some sleep too. So did all of us. Tamee was curled in her chair, purring to herself.

"No," I said finally, rung out with fatigue.

"What do we do about the Lussecans? We know they are guilty," asked Alzador.

"I wouldn't do anything," I answered for Crouthhamel; his look told me it was OK. "They haven't heard the rumor, if Merlin is correct about them not leaving their ship, so I would let them sit for now, unless you want to grab one and stick a Vega collar on him." I liked that idea and so did Alzador.

"Not an option," said Crouthhamel. "They are still Guardians until we have proof of their involvement. We must keep an eye on them though."

*Catch-22*, I thought, *we can't Vega them until we prove what we would know if we did put a collar on them.* My head was spinning now. I felt like I was missing something.

"Let's meet in the morning and go over this again," ordered Crouthhamel. "I'm too tired to think anymore." We all nodded, except for Tamee, who was curled up sleeping in the chair like a cat. I petted her on the head as I left.

The meeting started way too early for me. Merlin had to wake me up several times before finally blasting me with good old rock-n-roll. Strangely, I did not have a hangover, just a recollection of a very bad dream and a nasty Tayhest.

Anyways, we met at the hatch and proceeded to the meeting in thoughtful silence. Once in our seats I began to roll it all over in my mind. All the conjecture was nothing more than that, con-fucking-jecture. I still couldn't explain the message sent to Darassa, and though it was faked, it did go to someone there, nor could I tell which member of the Alpharian Council was a traitor. I was sitting there flipping my screen back and forth from one member to another when Crouthhamel leaned over and touched my shoulder.

"Yes, sir," I said after turning off the screen. I wanted no mistakes today.

"Figured it out yet?" he asked.

"No, I feel like I'm missing something," I mused. "After all, we really don't know the Lussecans were working with Labek, only that when we inquired about their new ship it resulted in his death. They didn't communicate with him, they sent a message to someone on Darassa. He was only killed to cover up their ship's identity. Thanks to Alzador, we know it was them, but maybe he wasn't involved at all. All I'm sure of is that his killer is our spy, now if I knew that . . ."

"Well, don't go anywhere, formal appointment of Guardians is coming up next," he cut in, "and you will have to stand and be acknowledged. It is a formality, but you are technically not a Guardian until you receive the OK of the Council."

"Did he have Guardians here? Did you notify anyone of his murder?" I said, nodding at what he said.

"No," he answered, "the Seltorrans do not know. I do not want the place crawling with investigators just yet. The Guardians from Seltorr are all new recruits and have much to learn before they could be of any help. Don't forget, you bypassed many steps in becoming a Guardian. I sort of rushed you through since Pracon had been such a big influence on you." I knew what he meant there.

He smiled and sat back in his seat. I sat back in my chair and turned on the screen again. Santa Claus was making announcements, and I decided to pay attention. He was calling names and new Guardians were standing up all over the place. Each time our screens would automatically turn to the proper booth and a spotlight would highlight the individual box. Some of the Guardians I had met last night. I had no idea there would be so many new ones. Suddenly, our screens flipped up, and the spotlight was on our booth.

"Stand up, Jim," said Crouthhamel, "let them see who you are."

I stood and accepted the applause as humbly as I could; I was tempted to put my arms over my head like Rocky but changed my mind and behaved, much to Crouthhamel's pleasure.

"Lotta new guys, huh?" I said. I wondered where the old ones went.

"Yes," he answered as the screens came down, "we can talk freely until the speaker stops making the announcements," he informed me. "The Council only recently began expanding the Guardian Order because of the increased Tayhest activity."

"Good," I said, "now tell me, after the Silmarrion ore passes through the Darassin shipping lines, what happens to it?"

"Well, I think it is sent to the Saesinn system for refining," answered Crouthhamel, "deep in the heart of our galaxy, the Betelgeuse then use some of it, and of course, the Guardian order uses the rest of it to construct the outer hulls of our ships, which is even done on our Mothership, the one we're on now."

"Saesinn," I repeated. Again I felt like I was missing something. "Which one is he?" I said, pointing toward the podium.

"Councilman Pollifex," said Crouthhamel, turning his screen manually to the Council platform, "that's him right there. We have never had any other Guardians from the Saesinn system besides Pollifex."

I looked through his screen at the podium, Pollifex was sitting at one end of the seating, and he was a big one. Not fat like Labek but pretty close. Now that Labek was gone, I was sure he took the "biggest one" prize. And he looked strong too.

Suddenly the announcer sat back down, and another Council member took the podium. "We will now pay tribute to the Guardians who are no longer with us," he began. He was an Igark, a creature closely resembling a bluish tree with feet. His head was topped with what appeared to be young plants. It was almost comical had he not been reading a list of Guardians who had died in the line of duty. I could see why we needed so many new ones now. My mind wandered back to our problem, and I began mulling it over again. I looked over at Crouthhamel; he was using his wrist sensor to talk with Alzador in his box. He turned to me and shook his head, meaning nothing new from the old bird. I looked back at the Council and slowly settled into my usual meeting mode, nap mode.

"Jim," said Crouthhamel, shaking me roughly out of a damn fine dream about Joan, "the meeting has adjourned."

"For the day?" I asked, damn I sure felt like I had slept a long time.

"No, nimrod," said Merlin, jumping into the conversation, "just for lunch."

"Oh," I replied, rubbing the sleep from my eyes. My stomach came to life too.

"Cluver called on the ship's communicator and wants to join you guys for lunch," announced Merlin. He sounded bored.

"He said to meet him at the usual place and hurry up; he's starved."

"Thanks, Merlin," I said, "and don't call me a nimrod, you farthead."

"You go ahead, Jim," said Crouthhamel rising, "I have a few things to go over with Alzador; I haven't seen him in quite a while."

"Merlin," I said, "what are the Lussecans doing? Anything suspicious?"

"Nothing, Jim," he said nicely, "they seem to be behaving themselves; the three of them went to the meeting this morning just like nothing was wrong."

"Yes," I commented, "they don't know we know it's them, do they?"

"Apparently not, but I'll keep my ear out for them."

"Eye, keep your eye out," I corrected him. He was as bad as Crouthhamel.

"Eye, ear, what's the difference, I have neither."

"Will you two stop bickering," said Crouthhamel from the doorway as it opened, and a lift arrived. "You're like a couple of old Kellic women." I stuck my tongue out at him as he left. He smiled and shook his head.

"He's right you know"—I nodded—"we do seem to argue quite a bit."

"I thought you liked it?"

"I do, Merlin," I said as my lift arrived, "I do." I probably didn't have a choice either.

Lunch was a repeat of the night before although I stayed away from the Chaga brew and instead went with a synthesized coffee. I ordered Garf, which tasted better than the synthetic Earth food they made for me the night before.

"So," asked Cluver, "can you slip away from Crouthhamel tonight too?"

"Why?" I asked. Apparently he thought I had slipped away for this lunch.

"I want you to meet someone," he replied quietly, too quietly. He was a lousy sneak.

"Who?" I asked. My alert button was warming up.

"I can't tell you," he answered, then when he saw my "I don't like surprises" look, he nodded and said, "A Beta Cee guardian, she really wants to meet you."

I relaxed and remembered whom I was with. "And does she have a friend for you too?" I smiled slyly. He was using my popularity to get laid, the shithead.

"Why, err, yes," he admitted, "but she really does want to meet you."

"What would your old man think," I teased him along, "if he knew you were with me and we were out shanking female guardians." His goldish color was reddening quite nicely.

"He is stuck with old Pollifex," he replied. "Is shanking what I think it is?" His eyes were starting to bug out even more than normal.

I nodded and laughed, and then the Garf stuck in my throat as my brain actually froze all body motioned. I digested what he had said first. The Garf stayed where it was until I stopped my brain from choking me to death.

"Councilman Pollifex of Saesinn?" Something clicked in the old cranium.

"Pollifex the Pain would be more like it," explained Cluver. "He's been with my dad for a ten cycle now, bitching about the ore shipments being too slow because of our shipping rules, I even had to listen to him all the way here. You'd think the Darkhole would have brought his own ship."

"He wants the Silmarrion ore sent faster?" I pried, wondering if Darkhole was the same as asshole. I gulped at my meal, Cluver didn't notice; hell, he ate that way normally. I knew this meant something; now if I could figure it out. Oh baby.

"Yes, he doesn't care if we lose ships in the Jenn Dar Gamma."

"Have you lost many?" I had to talk to Merlin, privately and fast; the meeting would be starting back up soon.

"Oh yes, almost a third of our last lineup, all ore carriers, without a trace, so Dad put a hold on the next lineup until we can some help, weren't you listening yesterday?"

"Oh, yeah," I lied, "I remember now. That's too bad, good thing you weren't on one of those missing ore carriers. "Listen, let's meet later," I continued, changing the subject, "and we'll meet the Cee women, OK?" I rose and started to leave.

"Great," exclaimed Cluver, "I'll set it up; 'talk to you after the meeting!"

We saluted each other, and I split for the ship. Cluver kept eating.

"Merlin, a ten cycle is about two weeks?" I asked as I boarded.

"Yes, now tell me what has you so excited? Your vital signs are way up."

"I think I know who the spy is . . ."

"Pollifex the Saesinn, also known as Mr. Candygram?" He was into it.

"Yup, the same, he had to be the one who received the message on Darassa, not Roegoss or Cluver." I thought about calling Crouthhamel and decided to wait.

"So he met with the Lussecans, and he's in league with the Tayhest even though he's wealthy and controls almost all the Silmarrion ore in the Guardian territories?" argued Merlin. "What would he have to gain? Where is his motive?"

"I don't know, but he fits the time frame; he was on Darassa, why I'll bet he did take old Labek a box bomb, Labek would have let him in, right?" Then a wicked thought occurred to me. "What if Pollifex isn't Pollifex?"

"Who is he, a Tayhest warrior?" joked Merlin. "Oh, surely you don't think . . ."

"Now you're talking, Merlin." I nodded. *And there is your motive too*, I thought.

Of course, Merlin didn't agree with me completely; he never does, but he did agree to help me with my idea. It was beginning to look like it just might work. Maybe I could hedge my bet. "Why don't you raise old Tamee," I said, "and ask her to drop by and see me."

"No need to," he answered, "she's just getting off the lift now."

"Wonderful," I said. I could use a little confirmation. She pranced in with the same catlike grace she always exhibited and flew into my arms for a hug. I wondered if I should scratch under her chin and make her purr, but with time running out, I couldn't afford to waste it.

"Can you," I began cautiously, after filling her in on some of my idea and what I thought was going down, "bring me a Lussecan to interrogate without anyone knowing?"

"No," she said quickly, "they don't like being around Nacks. We make them nervous. I'm sorry." She began to act like she was pouting. I put my hands under her furry little chin and lifted her face up to mine.

"It's OK," I soothed, thinking, I should have known, dogs and cats don't mix, shit, "I guess I won't snatch a Lussecan." So much for confirmation, screw me.

Tamee sensed a tender moment coming and moved toward me, feeling my disappointment and wanting to feel more than that.

"Jim," interrupted Merlin, "Cluver is on the screen, shall I put him through to you?" He had a knack for interrupting, sometimes at the right moment, like now.

"Yes," I grumped, much too quickly, "let's see what he wants."

I forgot Tamee was there, and Cluver gave me quite a shocked look.

"Sorry to bother you, Jim," he said, eyeballing the Nack next to me with interest.

"No problem," I said. "What can I do for you?" He was one horny dude.

"I just wanted to remind you not to be late for the meeting, the first part of the afternoon session is the awards program." He winked at me, another universal signal no doubt.

"Thanks," I said. I knew what he thought was going on, so I played along by pulling Tamee close to me and signed off with a smile. She didn't mind a bit as her hands began to explore places they shouldn't be exploring.

"Listen," I said detaching myself from her grasp, "I need you to keep a close watch on the Lussecans this afternoon; I have another plan I want to try." I decided to leave it at that.

"OK, Jim," she purred. "Should I leave now?" she added with a little pouting thrown in for good measure. She stepped into me again, searching for a soft spot, if you know what I mean. Maybe I should have introduced her to Cluver.

"I think you both should," chided Merlin. "I just heard the first callback gong. That gives you about fifteen minutes to be in your seat, Jim."

"Go ahead, honey," I said to Tamee; the honey part lifted her spirits, "and be careful watching those Lussecans; keep in touch with Merlin, OK?"

She nodded and disappeared out the door; her apron barely covering her.

I tugged myself back into place, cursing at Mr. Happy.

"Who are you talking to?" asked Merlin. "Certainly not me . . . oh, I know."

"You bet," I said. I went to the equipment locker and rummaged around until I found what I was looking for and stuck it under my tunic.

"Weapons aren't allowed, Jim," cautioned Merlin.

"So sue me," I remarked. He didn't stop me, and I left the ship taking the lift back to the box. Crouthhamel was there with Alzador, who was just leaving to return to his box. I tried not to look excited. I failed miserably.

"I don't think I like the look on your face," said Crouthhamel. "Last time I saw that look you were blasting Tweedledee and Tweedledum. I have seen the screen logs from that day." He waited for my answer, knowing it would be a good one.

"I'm on to something," I said. "I know who the traitor is, and with a little luck, I should be able to expose him." I think a lotta luck was closer to the truth.

That put a surprised look on their faces.

"Who is it?" said Alzador first. His head feathers puffed up instantly.

The Council was just getting seated, and I swung my screen around until I had the fattest Councilman on the screen. I pointed to him and shut off the sound; I was learning. The final gong went off as I did that.

"Pollifex, the Saesinn," said Crouthhamel incredulously.

"Yup," I exclaimed, "that's our traitor!" *He had better be*, I thought.

They both looked at me like I had just smoked an Altairian cigar.

"Are you crazy? How are you going to prove it?" asked Crouthhamel.

"I haven't figured that part out yet," I lied. I knew I had better not include them; if it failed, I wanted to go down alone. And it was only minutes away now.

We settled into our seats after Alzador left, and as I adjusted my screen, I hit the waiter call button. Crouthhamel was watching me out of the corner of his eyes.

"A Brewski would taste good right now," I ordered pleasantly. I stood up and acted like I was stretching and waited for the server to arrive. Tamee had changed places with another server to keep an eye on the Lussecans, so I knew she wasn't going to appear. Thank God the service was fast.

Several long minutes later, a Chaga Nuie popped up over the balcony with the huge drink tray in his three hands. He glided into our box, and I motioned him to set the drink down as I stood in front of my screen watching the meeting start-up, and a speaker walk to the podium. As he set the drink down, I pulled a stunball from my tunic and touched him on the back of the neck. It's not really a ball but rather a stick; it's called a ball after the game you play with it. Don't ask. All of the Chaga's legs and arms went limp and the huge tray almost fell as I caught it and handed it to Crouthhamel. A few of the drinks tipped but nothing hit the floor. I stuck the Nuie in my chair and grabbed the electropad controls from his waist and jumped onto the pad. Crouthhamel looked stunned too.

"Have a drink Crouthhamel," I said as I sailed out over the balcony and headed straight for the floor. I had to hurry; time was running out. Above me, Crouthhamel was sitting in his chair holding the drink tray and looking quite befuddled at the Nuie next to him. I hit the floor and blended in with the throng of servers; I knew I stuck out like a sore thumb, but I hoped that from above, I wouldn't be as noticeable. I set off across the floor as the speaker began explaining the nature of the award, which happened to be the highest award, the Uhlon Bathor Award, just as I remembered Merlin. I looked around, and no one was watching me.

"Merlin," I whispered, "turn on the Hogan Projector as I instructed you earlier." I had almost forgotten, which would have been disastrous.

"Done," he said back to me, "don't forget to get as close as you can."

"Oh, don't worry, I plan on it." Boy, did I.

Next to Crouthhamel, the Chaga Nuie took on my appearance as the Hogan image turned the stunned figure into a sleeping me. I heard the speaker say that for the first time in a long time the award was going to be awarded at this very meeting. The crowd of Guardians began chattering to each other, and the speaker had to gong for silence. When he announced that the award was going to a new Guardian, the whole assembly went wild. It gave me the time I needed to reach the floor area directly under the Councilmen's platform. I jumped back on the pad and started to ascend as he called my name. I could see the screens throughout the room turning toward the box with Crouthhamel and the stunned figure, which would appear to be Jim Edwards, passed out in my chair.

*Crouthhamel must be having a baby,* I thought, as the spotlight lit up the box. The pad was rising slower than I wanted it to, and I cursed it several times. I could now see that I was not moving in the box, but Crouthhamel had risen from his seat. *Come on, Crouthhamel,* I thought, *keep them busy till I reach the platform.*

"I think he had too much Chaga brew for lunch," he joked to the crowd. A roar of laughter went up as I neared the bottom of the platform. As I rose into view of the Council, I turned on the pad and saluted the members. Merlin took the cue and turned off the Hogan image as I stepped onto the platform, climbing over the railing and walking toward the podium. A small amount of confusion broke out as the crowd found themselves staring at a Chaga Nuie laid out in my chair.

"I wanted to accept the award in person," I said to the speaker at the podium, a Beta Krilline, tall, very humanlike, and bald as a cue ball. My voice filled the arena.

Every screen in the place turned toward the podium as the Krilline signaled for silence and looked down at me. The rest of the Council was busy exchanging words except the Saesinn; he was eyeing me suspiciously. The Krilline turned toward his fellow members and then back to me. He gave me a slight smile and held the small bluish medal up in the air for all to see. He motioned me to come forward.

"The Altairians said you were different, and you certainly are," remarked the speaker, still holding the award up for the crowd to view.

The crowd murmured. I wasn't the only one who had never seen the Medal of Uhlon Bathor. It was glowing softly as he came around the podium and hung it around my neck, and as he did so, the medal turned a bright white. I hoped that was what it was supposed to do. The crowd began to cheer. I turned around and saluted the assembly to a huge round of applause and cheering. I was just about ready to put everything on the line, and I felt the applause lift my spirits.

"Thank you, sir," I said taking his hand and giving it a strong shake. He nodded to me, without speaking; I wouldn't have been able to hear him over the crowd noise anyway. I turned from him and walked around the side of the podium and shook hands with the first Councilman I came to and worked my way down the side, grabbing various forms of hands and arms and thanking them each as we shook. Pollifex was on the other side of the podium and clear at the end of the line. I continued to ignore him and worked my way toward him as if nothing was wrong. I do believe he never expected a thing was wrong until I got to him. I should also explain that the handshake as we know it is virtually unknown throughout the galaxy; they just don't know how to do it. So some of them had to be shown, and some of them caught on watching me do it with their fellow members. The Tayhest was no different, and he had watched me take the hand of the Councilman next to him, so he was ready to shake when I got to him. He stuck a huge right hand out to me, not happily mind you, but so as not to arouse suspicion, and waited for me to shake with him. I took a deep breath and stuck out my hand. His hand felt very realistic, and I started to have doubts when Merlin broke through the crowd noise.

"Bingo!" he yelled. His quick analysis of the vital signs, through the sensor on my wrist, of the creature in front of me confirmed that it was not a Saesinn and definitely not Pollifex.

The medal on my chest was glowing brighter and the Tayhest could not take his eyes from it. It gave me the precious time I needed to come up with an opening.

"Lord Zordon!" I exclaimed, looking behind the Tayhest, like someone was there.

The Tayhest, still absorbed in the glowing medal, jumped and then turned, expecting to see his leader there. It was the chance I needed. I reached up to the side of his face and grabbed a huge handful of ear, hair, and skin and yanked as hard as I possibly could, downward. The look on the Councilman's face next to him was priceless. One second I was smiling and joking and acting all happy, and the next second, I was standing in front of a very astonished Tayhest warrior with most of his fake face in my hand. The entire crowd went silent with shock. There he stood, Saesinn from the neck down, Tayhest from the neck up. His eyes went from the mask in my hand to the eyes in my head; the intensity of hatred was the same as what I had encountered at the Zalo base. Another prince I hoped. I let the mask fall.

"Well," I said, "if it isn't another Mr. Meaty, Beaty, Big, and Bouncy."

He didn't give me a chance to say anything else as he lunged forward at me with his big arms, trying to grab me and squash me. It was a move that Rick had taught me many times, how to avoid. I stepped to his right and ducked under his arms as they swept over me in the air. The breeze almost knocked me down. He was clearly the biggest thing I had ever fought. As his arms swept over me, his balance was too far forward of the rest of his body, so he had to step forward to regain his balance. I stepped past him and swept my leg into his, it was like hitting concrete, but it threw him even further off balance, and as he stumbled forward, I swung both arms into his back. His momentum carried him clear into the front railing and almost over the top of it. His weight actually bent the top bar as he regained his balance and turned on me. Suddenly I knew how a bullfighter felt; all this guy needed was horns.

Probably only a few seconds had gone by, in a real fight, it's usually over in only a few seconds, and it certainly isn't choreographed like the fight scenes you see on TV. This was no exception; the Tayhest came at me like a charging rhino as I hopped over the chair he had been sitting in and backed into the area behind the platform. A very elegant buffet had been set up on tables surrounding the inner walls of the oversized box, and my eyes swept over them looking for weapons.

"Turn on your suit, dummy," said Merlin.

"Thanks," I said, reaching up to the back of my tunic. Immediately the suit became heavier, almost too heavy to fight in, yet I knew if the big guy hit me, it might kill me. He came at me slowly this time. The medal lit the room. The Council finally came unthawed and began to surround the two of us as the Tayhest slowed to a stop in front of me. He was no dummy; he wouldn't be caught off balance like that again—he and I both knew that. He moved in closer to me, and I backed into the edge of the table. Suddenly his leg shot out at me with amazing swiftness and just barely caught my side as I attempted to sidestep the kick. It spun me to the side, and I quickly moved with the momentum of the kick toward the side of the box. Behind me, the various Councilmen scrambled out of the way. They began to fight with him then, but I think his size and their age were in his favor. He flung several against the walls and a couple over the chairs and almost over the balcony.

"Leave him alone!" I screamed. "Mr. Big and Bouncy is mine." I didn't want anyone getting killed—that was not part of my plan—and I didn't want that hanging over my head the rest of my life. But the stadium was rocking now, and everyone had an opinion on what to do next, and they were all trying to tell me. But all the Councilmen seemed to understand me and backed off from the furious warrior except one stubborn Councilman, the Igark. He came at the Tayhest from behind, his treelike body ramming into the back of the Tayhest with a loud thud. The Tayhest flew forward at me, arms flailing from imbalance, his feet slipping on the smooth flooring. From the look on his face, I knew he intended to crush me if he could, but I had seen the Igark launch his attack, so I was ready for old fatso to arrive.

As I sidestepped him again, I grabbed his left arm and pushed it backward, away from the direction he was heading, the main buffet table. His body twisted around, and his feet went out from under him as he crashed into the table and sent it to the floor with a huge collision of food, beverage, and Tayhest. The contents of the trays and bowls spilled everywhere; food poured, splashed, and rolled across the floor; and trays overturned and dumped their contents down into the middle of the table where the Tayhest lay wallowing in the mess. As he squirmed about trying to gain leverage to get up on his feet, I took a large bowl of reddish goop and thrust it into his face. He screamed in agony as the goop blinded him, and his huge paws went to his face in obvious agony.

"Good thinking," said the Zellen Councilman, "that's Varughose hot sauce." He was standing beside me smiling at the Tayhest wiggling on the tabletop.

"Thanks," I said, picking up a heavy silverlike platter and crashed it down into the bony part of the Tayhest's mouth. Pieces of teeth and bone flew in every direction. I plucked the platter from his mouth and stood back to admire my handiwork. Just then, the Chaga Nuie security team came charging through the door into the box; they appeared to be armed with something. I suddenly remembered my stunball in my tunic and felt behind myself for it. It was still there, so I tucked it farther into my tunic; I could be in real trouble for stunning the waiter in my box. I decided to blend into the crowd of Councilmen and look inconspicuous.

The Chaga Nuies surrounded the Tayhest and turned their handheld weapons on him as he rose from the mess on the table. He stood sullenly quiet as the Nuies sprayed him up, down, and around with weblike capture ropes, which pinned his arms to his sides. The netlike tendons of ropes quickly expanded from the size of threads until they looked like huge hula hoops tightening across his chest and back. He hissed at the Nuies, spraying them with fluid that seeped down his chin from his broken mouth. His eyes were bleeding fluid also, and I didn't think he could see out of them very well.

"Nice job," said the Igark coming over to me, his branchlike arm settling on my back. His head sprouts looked rather flattened, but he seemed in pretty good spirits. Other Councilmen crowded around me, congratulating me and patting me on the back and shoulder, which is another universal show of affection even if they don't know how to shake hands.

"I couldn't have done it with out the buffet table," I joked. It was closer to the truth than I cared to admit. I wondered how hot the sauce was and let it go.

"Jim," said Merlin, "Tamee said the Lussecans are headed back to their ship, and do you want her to pursue?"

"No, Merlin," I replied, "tell her to come back to the meeting hall and notify the Chaga Nuie security force to hold them until Crouthhamel or I get to them. Tell security that they are in cahoots with the Tayhest here."

"OK," said Merlin, "I'll take care of it, nice job on the Tayhest."

"Thanks, buddy," I answered. Sometimes he seemed almost too human.

The Tayhest had been led away toward the exit, and a crew of Sanipods was busy cleaning up the mess. Some of them reminded me of Wolf in the way they were lapping up the fluids on the floor and table. I turned to the head of the Council, the guy I called Santa Claus earlier. You have to wonder.

"How did you know?" he asked me. "Was it possible for you to see through his disguise? Do you possess telepathic abilities like Pracon of Procyon?"

"No, sir," I answered truthfully. "The secret is good detective work, a good partner, and a little luck too." In my case, it would be a lotta luck.

"And what was it you called him?"

"Oh," I said, "Mr. Meaty, Beaty, Big, and Bouncy." Thank you; guess who.

"Yes, that was it." He smiled and began talking to several other Councilmen who laughed out loud as he translated it to them over and over. I looked toward the exit and spotted the Tayhest and the security team as they waited for the lift. He was staring at me, and it gave me the creeps. I turned away and began examining the brightly glowing medal around my neck. It was so cool in many ways.

"You know," said a small white-haired old Councilman, "they say the Medal of Uhlon Bathor has strong powers in the right hands."

"Like what?" I asked; looking closely, I recognized him as Entimallian and immediately wondered where old Torgan was. I hadn't seen him at the meeting yet.

"Hey, partner," broke in Merlin cheerfully, "the Lussecans have ambushed the Chagas at the lift corridor near their ship and are headed for it right now."

"No one else can reach them in time, I suppose," I said. I knew the answer; old Merlin was spoiling for a fight.

"Just me," he said innocently.

*About as innocent as a fox in a henhouse,* I thought.

"Why don't you stop them then?" I suggested. "I'm sure you already have a plan."

"Sort of, thanks, Jim, I'll let you know what's happening later."

"Who was that?" asked the Entimallian Councilman.

"My partner, Merlin, alias Jesse James."

"Can he stop a group of Lussecans on his own?"

"Oh yeah," I replied; I wondered if I should tell him who Merlin really was and decided not too. He was already starting to rub his chest under his robe.

Just as I was going to take the podium and acknowledge the crowd of cheering Guardians who were screaming for me to say something, into the room burst Crouthhamel with a small battalion of security men behind him.

"Jim," he said, calling me over to him. He didn't look real happy.

"Yes, sir," I said, walking up to him quickly, "what's the matter?"

"Your Mr. Meaty the Tayhest has escaped; they found the lift at the lift station below here with four dead Chagas in it. They were torn apart in pieces." The morbid part of me mentally pictured all those arms and legs lying around the lift station, and I felt myself getting unusually angry, more than I do normally, a lot more.

"Let's go kill that son of a bitch," I said, looking into Crouthhamel's face. "I'm really getting goddamn sick of these fucking Tayhest assholes." I know I had the mean look on my face. It even surprised old Crouthhamel, but what really made him jump back was the intensity of the medal on my chest.

It was blazing with a brightness I can hardly describe. It was like a miniature sun on my chest, and the angrier I got at the Tayhest, the stronger it got. *I liked it a lot, maybe too much*, I thought.

"Come on, Crouthhamel," I said angrily, "let's go find that bastard." I headed for the lift as the Entimallian Councilman ran up beside Crouthhamel and me.

"It would appear that you know how to use the medal," he said, choosing his words very carefully. "Use it wisely, great Guardian, and may the spirit of Uhlon Bathor guide you always." He saluted me, and behind him, the rest of the Council followed his lead.

The lift arrived and we boarded. As the doors closed, I returned the salute even though the medal was blinding them now and yelled back at the Entimallian, "Just as long as it guides me to that motherfucker, Mr. Meaty, Beaty, Big, and Bouncy!"

# CHAPTER 7

## Through the Looking Glass

We had to stop and pick up the Chaga security team before proceeding to the lift station; the lift we were in was built for six maybe, and we had crammed at least twenty of us into it. So consequently, when it stopped, we all kinda burst from it. You have to imagine a dozen or more Chaqa Nuies, all with three arms and three legs, trying to get out of the cramped lift. It would have been comical except for the seriousness of the situation at the station. It was as Crouthhamel had described it; parts of the last Chaga security team were all over the place as well as a fair amount of pink Chaga blood. I had managed to calm down in the lift, and the medal had returned to its original sparkle; now, as I stood surveying the scene, I felt my anger rising again, and the medal began to brighten.

"Merlin," I said, "what is Tamee's location?"

"Give me a minute, Jim," he said quickly. "I'm almost done here."

"So how's it going?" I said. I thought I heard the particle beam being discharged.

"All the Lussecans have been neutralized; I just got the last one."

"What do you mean neutralized?" I said; I thought I knew.

"Out of commission, as well as their ship too." Dead is what he meant.

"Tamee?" I said; I hated to spoil his fun, but I had to warn her.

"Oh," he said, "she should have been back at your box by now, hang on, I'll see where she is now. I can't reach her, Jim," he gasped. "The last sensor reading I got from her was before I left the landing area and went after the Lussecans, I'm sorry, I should have kept in contact with her. I must have been paying more attention to the Lussecans. I hope she's all right."

"Me too, pea-brain," I scolded him. "If she was coming to our box, she would have had to come through this lift station." I concentrated on her image, and the medal started glowing brighter.

"I believe the Entimallian was right when he said it would guide you," said Crouthhamel, pointing to a spot on the floor where the light from the medal seemed to be shining the brightest.

I walked over to the spot and bent down toward a shiny object. "Shit," I said. I held up my sensor band, the one she had on her ankle. "SHIT!" I screamed.

Merlin didn't ask me; Crouthhamel said it for him. "Tamee's?" said Crouthhamel. I nodded. I threw it down on the floor; it was already smashed. She must have run smack dab into the Tayhest on her way back to the meeting. I looked over at Crouthhamel; he knew I was pissed now. I closed my eyes and concentrated on the Tayhest and let my anger and hatred for him boil a little bit. When I opened my eyes, the medal was shining off into the far corridor to the left.

We jumped into the first lift in the line and sped off, leaving the Chaga behind to clean up. I didn't want them with me anyways; hell, I didn't even want Crouthhamel with me. I just wanted to find the Tayhest and show him my new toy; I had a feeling it did more than light my path.

It was a bubble lift, a high-speed one, so it spun rapidly as it tore through the ship, so the force of the gravity it generated didn't kill the occupants. I have no idea how fast it went; all I know is it seemed like it took forever before I felt it slowing. Finally it stopped, and the doors opened. We were in an artificial forest, deep in the heart of the ship, with trees and birds and who knows what else.

I stepped out into the shadows of the trees and looked around for signs of the Tayhest, surely he must have left footprints in the ground somewhere, then I remembered the medal. This time when I concentrated, I kept my eyes open, which isn't easy for me—concentrating, that is, plus the forest was a collection of trees and plants from thousands of planets; it stretched for hundreds, no, thousands of miles through the ship, and it wasn't all forest either. In some places, it was arid desert; and in other places, it was actually mountainous, with controlled environments ranging from snow and ice to bubbling pools and tropical rain forests. Carefully mixed in with the plant life was a mixture of lower life-forms, also from all over the universe. You couldn't help but notice all the strange things around you. So preserving all life was a major part of the Alpharian Code. Hence the name Mothership. I wondered if it included Tayhest.

The medal quickly began to illuminate the direction we had to travel, and we set off into the forest. The lift disappeared behind a miniature Deceiving field. I wondered how you found it when it was time to leave and quickly went back to concentrating as the light from the medallion started to fade. I wondered how long I could concentrate as hard as I was concentrating right now. Above us, the light from the artificial sun began to fade into a level close to dusk; soon we would be picking our way in the darkness. This was one of those times I had to wonder, would anyone from Earth ever believe this had happened to me? Hell, I even wondered if it was really happening. Plus it was a lonely place, only visited occasionally by the equivalent of a botanist or a zoologist; no one else was really allowed in here. Once in a while, we would disturb a small creature or bird, and it would go scurrying off into the brush or rise overhead, squawking at us for disturbing its peace. I wondered what it was like at night and how "wild" the night creatures were compared to the daytime ones.

We had gone only a few yards into the actual forest of trees and undergrowth when Crouthamel touched my shoulder to stop. I stopped and turned to him; I had been trying to concentrate and still look around at all the interesting plants and stuff. The medallion was glowing but not like it had been earlier because I just couldn't maintain a constant level of anger; it's not as easy as it sounds, at least not with my brain. I'm not talking about being mad at your boss or girlfriend for the whole day; hell, I could do that. I'm talking about intense anger and hatred, know what I mean?

"What is it?" I whispered. He didn't answer right away; he was listening to something my ears couldn't hear. I don't have the best hearing in the world, have I mentioned that?

"Let's stop here and wait," he said ever so softly.

"You figure he's going to double back?" I whispered.

"Ssh," he spoke, "he has to, the nearest lift besides the one we used is over a thousand miles away." He settled down into the foliage like an Indian and seemed very much at home. I squatted next to him, wondering about the bugs I knew were here and couldn't see, I hate bugs, but finally I sat down next to him as my knees tired of squatting. I was busy inspecting my surroundings for spider webs and bug signs when he touched my sleeve. My eyes went to his pointing finger and followed it to what he had spotted. I could not believe the size of the animal that crossed through the lift area. It looked like a mouse, but it must have been ten feet long. As it turned toward us, I could see it had two horns in a row on its forehead, and it looked mean as hell. It turned away and plodded out of sight. I started breathing again after it left. As we sat there silently, we began to see little creatures of all shapes and colors scurrying about, sometimes right over the tops of our boots—that is, unless they saw us or smelled us then they quickly ran away into the brush, sometimes squawking at us indignantly. I was noticing the trees and their similarity to Earth's trees when we both heard something coming our way. I tucked the medal into my tunic; its light was noticeable in the growing darkness, and I didn't want to give our position away. I noticed the little creatures had grown silent too. In the fading light, the Tayhest came into view; his legs weren't moving, and he appeared to be floating. Then it hit me; he was using a Hoverpad, and no wonder we couldn't find his footprints in the sand by the lift. He was also very much alone. He floated around the lift area, hunting for the spot that deactivated the D-field, and finally opened the lift door. I started to get up, and Crouthhamel held me back. The lift door opened, and the Tayhest entered the lift and was gone in no time. The D-field came on, and the lift disappeared also.

"Why did you hold me back?" I snarled at him. The medal flared under my tunic.

"He's not going anywhere we can't find him, but right now, you had better crank up that medal and find Tamee real fast," he advised me almost fatherly.

"Oh yeah," I said feeling stupid. "I also didn't want to be in here after dark either."

"Well, what concerns me more is Tamee," he said admonishingly.

"Haven't you seen the claws on that lady?" I asked incredulously. I felt she could take care of herself quite nicely.

"Jim," he said calmly, "the Tayhest bury their prisoners alive."

"Fuck!" I exclaimed, yanking the medallion out of my tunic and jumping to my feet. I freaked at the thought, and the medal sent out a beam of light a blind man could even follow. I didn't care what I ran into as I charged off into the woods. Fuck the spiders and bugs; I wasn't stopping till I found her. I ran over bushes and small trees, paying only attention to the light from the medal, screaming her name and cursing the Tayhest.

"Please find her," said Merlin, breaking in on my solo conversation. Boy, he had been quiet for quite a while.

"Use all your sensors, Merlin," I said, still crashing through the foliage. "Don't let anything sneak up on me. I reached back and felt for the stun weapon. It was gone, damnit, I must have dropped it while running. Sometimes I wondered why I was still alive. Maybe Crouthhamel would find it; he was having a hard time keeping up with me, even with his long legs. I can run fast when I need too.

We had gone several miles into the forest when we heard her start shrieking. The medal was still going strong, but I didn't need it to find her now. I burst into a small clearing, and there she was, sticking out of the ground by her head. Within a foot of her was a large six-legged ferretlike animal. Its fur was greenish in color, and it looked very hungry. It had been digging her up for dinner, which may have kept her alive.

"Hey!" I screamed, trying to frighten it away from her. My voice is loud when I want it to be, and I've been known to frighten people by doing that.

The creature turned toward me and bared its teeth. It apparently wasn't going to share its dinner with anyone. So much for scaring it away, damn.

"Careful, Jim," said Crouthhamel, coming up behind me, "that's a Rango cub, they are nasty things."

I really didn't care at this point; hell, I'm not scared of animals, just bugs and spiders, mostly spiders. I focused on the Rango and stepped forward at it. It apparently wasn't scared of me either, and all six legs went into a crouching position as it prepared to lunge itself at me. I braced myself as it sprang into the air, its mouth wide open and full of razor-sharp teeth. My arms were up in a defensive position when the medal on my chest erupted in a flash of blinding light, and the Rango disappeared in a blazing fury of incandescence. The last thing we saw was an outline of the animal and then nothing. I regained my momentum and stepped up to the head sticking out of the ground. I knelt down in front of her face. She looked up at me, a painful hurt look on her face. A few scratches from the Rango were visible on one side.

"Jim," she said softly, tears began trickling down the sides of her nose from her eyes, which looked like someone had used them for catcher's mitts. I put my hands up to her face and wiped away the dirt and dried blood.

"You OK?" I said. She nodded, and I started digging. I know my hands must have hit her as I dug furiously, but she never said a word. Her arms were pinned at her sides with part of the capture harness that had been around the Tayhest. I decided to use it for leverage and wrapped my fingers around the bands. Slowly the dirt gave way, and she began to emerge from the hole. Crouthhamel, who had been standing behind me keeping watch for the Rango parent—I couldn't imagine the size of that mother—came over to give me a hand. I really didn't need one, my adrenaline level was way above normal, but

I accepted the help, and we pulled her free. She tried to stand and couldn't; the Tayhest had broken her ankle when he pulled the sensor from her. I was about to pick her up when we heard a sound behind us, a crunching of sticks and leaves, a body moving very carefully. I stood and turned to the sound and motioned Crouthhamel behind me. He came and took Tamee from me, supporting her as he helped her wiggle out of the harness. Suddenly it got real damn quiet, and I felt the hair go up on my neck. I tensed up, not knowing what to expect. In front of me, the quiet changed to crunching as whatever it was came closer. I glanced at the Medallion; it wasn't even shining that bright. My mind started to panic, you know, little voices saying, "Run, run, dummy, run for your life." That's when it burst into the clearing. It was Cluver and his fellow Guardian, Remonl. They were busy looking over their shoulders too.

"Someone call for a lift?" said Cluver smiling. "How about you, sir?" he added looking at me. "Our rates are dirt cheap!"

"Cluver," I exclaimed, "where the hell did you come from?"

"Merlin called me, strange fellow, never shows his face."

"Merlin is my s . . . partner, he wants to remain anonymous," I said, catching myself; I did not have the right to tell him. "But how did you find us?"

"Oh, well, we almost didn't," he explained, "but just as the lift came back to us, we saw the flash of your weapon and decided that it was probably you shooting up the forest; you know you're not supposed to have any weapons in here."

"I know"—I nodded—"I'll explain later; right now, we've got to get Tamee to a medical station. I think her ankle is broken."

"No problem," said Remonl, "we brought a Medpad." He had a hand controller, which he used to signal the pad at the lift. It arrived in minutes, and we laid Tamee on it and began walking back through the woods by the light of the small flashlights they had brought. The medallion was only glowing faintly now.

At the lift, I turned to Cluver. He was aiming the light back into the woods.

"Why didn't you have the lights on when you found us?" I asked.

"Remonl thought he saw a female Rango; I didn't want to tangle with one of them. They are one of the most vicious animals on any planet." He said this without fear, only as a fact. He was no qwimmy.

The lift arrived, and we all began to climb into it when Cluver gave a shout. His light was aimed back at the forest where a huge Rango stood, watching the lift door, probably wondering where its cub was and if we had it. Suddenly it came at us, moving with an astounding speed. I pulled Cluver back into the seat and was about to flash the medallion at it when the outer lift door slammed shut. We still heard the thud against the door as the lift began moving and the inner bubble closed. We headed for the nearest medical station and deposited the badly beaten Tamee and took another high-speed bubble back to the docking side of the ship and then changed lifts and headed for Merlin. Crouthhamel had insisted we stop and rest. I for one didn't feel like stopping, but he was the boss.

"Merlin," I said striding into the ship ahead of the others.

"I heard, Jim, I'm glad she's going to be OK!" he said relieved. He sounded so human.

"Good, let's get down to business," I replied. I saw no reason to pick on him.

"Where is he?" said Cluver. "You're not talking to a computer, are you?"

"No, Cluver, Merlin"—I looked over at Crouthhamel, and he nodded—"is my ship."

"Get off the planet," remarked Cluver, "really?"

I nodded.

"So you have the prototype living ship," he whistled. "I knew they were trying to make one, but this is incredible."

"I hate to say this," I began, "but keep it to yourself, will you?"

Remonl looked at me and began laughing; I couldn't help but join him, and finally Crouthhamel began laughing too. I do believe Cluver was embarrassed, but he tried not to show it other than to give Remonl a dirty look.

"OK, OK," admitted Cluver, "I deserved that. My dad told me my big mouth would be the death of me yet." He was good-natured about it, but his expression was so comical you had to laugh, which I did until he punched me in the arm playfully. I tried not to show the surprise I felt when he hit me, but he could really pack a punch.

"All right," commanded Crouthhamel, "let's get down to business, Jim, why don't you set up your table so we can figure out how to help the Chaga find this Tayhest before he causes any more trouble."

I strode to my command chair and pressed a series of buttons that Merlin had finally shown me. I had always wondered why I had a large space behind my command chairs but no table like Crouthhamel had in his ship. Slowly a tabletop rose from the floor in the center of the room, followed by a set of chairs surrounding it. It was a fascinating process for me to watch because the chairs were actually part of Merlin. He had explained to me that a certain amount of him was in constant liquid molecular form, so he was able to form just about anything in the room you could ask him to make, within reason; though standard things like my bed and the table had already been programmed into his computer so he would not have to occupy himself with the tedious task taking place in front of us now. Crouthhamel's ship had a permanent table and chairs, but my chairs would automatically form to fit your ass, which was a very nice touch I thought.

I sat down at the head of the table where a sensor pad had appeared and began running my fingers over the pad. A three dimensional picture of the Mothership appeared in the middle of the table.

"Give me directions, and I will cross-section it," said Merlin.

"Let's look at the parts of the ship that everyone has access too," said Crouthhamel, "then add the lift system also."

The outer hull and some of the inner bulkheads of the model began disappearing until half the ship had vanished from the model as it rotated above the middle of the table. I had to admit; it was fascinating to watch as the internal parts of the ship appeared. It beat the hell out of the transparent V-8 engine I had as a kid. Sorry Mattel. What was left of the ship was still an impressive amount of rooms and departments. The forest was still there as well as the meeting hall, all the restaurants and most of the living quarters. I didn't see how this was going to help.

"Now," said Crouthhamel, correctly interpreting the look on my face, "let's see where the Tayhest went from the meeting hall after you exposed him, Jim."

I nodded to Crouthhamel; I had forgotten that you must use your handprint as well as tell the lift where you wanted to go, or otherwise, it went nowhere. The meeting hall and the lift going to the terminal where we found the dead Chagas was all that was left of the ship as the rest of it disappeared from the model.

"That doesn't even take him to the forest," I said, looking at the lone lift tube and the meeting hall spinning before us, "and we know he went to the forest."

"I know, Jim," replied Crouthhamel, thinking. "Let's see where Tamee went after he grabbed her." A second lift tube appeared, and then the huge forest connected to it. It was truly awesome in size. The detail of the computer-generated model was mind boggling too. The Tayhest had apparently used Tamee's hand to activate the lift that far anyways.

"Now show me where the Tayhest went from the forest," said Crouthhamel.

Nothing appeared. It was as if the big son of a bitch had disappeared in thin air.

"Merlin," asked Crouthhamel, "are you still tied into the Mothership's computer?"

"Yes, I just rechecked with my computer; there is no record of the Tayhest leaving the forest."

"But that's crazy," I added. "We both saw him leave it."

Crouthhamel nodded. He was baffled too.

"Maybe he was using two disguises?" said Cluver. "Chaga security did find a body skin for Labek in his room, so maybe he had another one besides the one they found."

"He wasn't in a disguise when he left the forest," I answered. *I remembered seeing that damn tail whipping behind him, probably how he cut the capture harness*, I thought. The model rotated in front of us as we all sat there in silence. I had a feeling we were going to have a harder time finding him than Crouthhamel had figured. They could deactivate the lifts so no one could use them with Pollifex's handprint, but the Tayhest was obviously using another print to use the lifts. But whose handprint could he be using? Suddenly the remark Cluver made began to make sense.

"Merlin," I exclaimed, "can you contact the Chaga for me?"

"Sure, boss." He knew I was on to something.

I turned toward my view screen; everyone was curious and turned with me. Almost instantly, the screen lit up, and the head of security was looking back at us. The face of the Chaga Nuie on my sidewall screen was not a happy one. In fact he looked pretty damn disgusted and possibly a bit lost. Murder on a Mothership was a bit unusual, and this was a multiple one at that.

"Hello, sir," I said very respectfully, trying to get on his good side if he had one left.

"Hello, Guardian Jim," he answered. He obviously knew me. I wondered if that was good or bad.

"I was wondering if you might be able to answer a quick question for me," I began, "so we can find this Tayhest before he manages to hide himself on this ship forever. Tell me what happened to the bodies of the Chaga Nuies that were killed at the terminal?"

"They were sent to the holding area of the ship for transport back to their home planet, Wrosa Three, why?"

Crouthhamel knew instantly why I had asked.

"Did anyone count all the body parts?" I tried to say it delicately.

"Why yes, now that you mention it, I do believe we put all the pieces back with the bodies," he answered, shuffling through a stack of discs and reports that lay in front of him. He was using all three of his hands to do it. He seemed a bit miffed at my question.

"Yes," he said, picking up a disc of information and sticking it in the terminal at his desk, "this is it. All four Chaga Nuies were sent to Holding Area Seven; why do you want to know that?" He was not a happy camper.

"I'm looking for a missing hand, a hand that could have been used to activate a lift system by the Tayhest."

"Oh," he said, glancing at his terminal. I think he had overlooked the obvious, and I wondered if he would admit it. No Earthly cover-up, please.

"Hark," he said, which means shit in Tharx, "a hand from one of the security team is unaccounted for and not with the rest of the body."

"That's why he tore the bodies up," said Cluver in astonishment, "so we wouldn't notice the missing hand."

"Yes," I replied, "sir, would you transmit that information to me, I believe we can isolate the Tayhest with it."

"Of course," he acquiesced, "and I will immediately deactivate the identification print so it can't be used again on any lift."

"I wouldn't do that," I broke in, "that might result in someone else losing their hand or life."

He thought for a second and quickly nodded in agreement.

"One other thing, sir," I added; I thought about asking him his name and figured I'd forget it anyway, so I decided to stick to sir, "what was the level of accessibility of the missing hand? Could the user of the hand go anywhere on the ship?"

He nodded affirmatively again; I could tell I hadn't cheered him up.

"Don't worry, we'll find the Tayhest," I added, to hopefully make him feel good about the whole thing.

"Good luck, I've got over a thousand men looking right now, not to mention all the Guardians that are already looking, and no one has seen even his shadow yet," he said, and with that, the screen went blank.

"Boy is he a Gloomy Gus," I said to the group. "Merlin, add the data from him and let's see where old Mr. Ugly is right now."

The lift trail began to grow as the model expanded to include the lifts that the Tayhest had taken after leaving the forest. The way I saw it, the last lift stop would give us his present location because traveling almost anywhere on a Mothership required a lift. A Mothership is built from the inside out, so the outer lifts and the diameter lifts that go straight through the ship are very fast. I had directed Merlin to color code the various lifts. It seemed like a good idea at the time. The model was still growing with new lift tubes being added as the computer processed the data and added it to the program we were watching. The individual tubes reminded me of the colorful balloon animals you see at carnivals all twisted into various shapes. From the looks of the number of tubes, the Tayhest had done a good bit of traveling to avoid capture. Finally the model stopped growing, and we all looked to see where the Tayhest should be now. The model now looked like a balloon man's macabre version of Earth, with way too many tubes having been traveled and, unfortunately, as I watched, growing again. Something was wrong, big time. I smacked the table in frustration.

"Too many tubes," said Crouthhamel, echoing my sentiments.

"Merlin," I said thoughtfully, "have the computer check and see if by some odd chance these tubes are traveled by a Ropod on a daily delivery route or whatever. It looks to me like these tubes hit almost every accessible area of the ship."

"I'm already checking," agreed Merlin.

"You think he stuck the hand in something and it's traveling all over with it?" asked Remonl, who until now had been as quiet as a bump on a log.

I nodded; he was catching on quickly, as Merlin spoke up, "Security just intercepted a Garpod, its normal pick up program had been altered and the hand was sticking into the manual override. I think Gloomy Gus must have gotten the idea from seeing your model and decided to beat us to the punch, Jim."

"That's all right, Merlin, he's just doing his job before we do it for him, and at the very least, the poor hand won't end up in the garbage. I hate to admit it but that goddamn Tayhest bastard is smarter than he looks, something we had better not underestimate again." The medallion around my neck brightened as I cursed.

I turned to Crouthhamel. He knew what I was going to say.

"I don't think the medal will work on this large a ship," he said, "but you never can tell, still, I think we need to talk first." He looked over at Cluver and Remonl.

Cluver was smart and took the hint. "We're going to get something to eat, I'll check back with my dad after eating, he's on our ship, so leave him a message if you need me," he said, trying not to look hurt. He motioned for Remonl to come with him. They both looked dejected, which almost made me laugh.

"Cluver," I said, standing and saluting him; he loved it, "I am in your debt; without you, I might have been dinner for that Rango." That was sure true.

"Myself included," said Crouthhamel, who also stood and saluted him.

They left the ship happily then, and we sat back down at the table. The model was still rotating in the center, a giant perfectly round multicolored brain.

"Why don't you want me to use the medal?" I asked; I had wanted to go after the Tayhest after dropping Tamee at the medical station.

He looked at me and gave me his fatherly look, which meant he was about to enlighten me so I wouldn't learn whatever he had to say the hard way. He normally crossed his arms with authority and used a stern voice. This time, however, he sat back and appeared to be reflecting on something. He had me worried now.

"Jim," he began tactfully, "the legend of Uhlon Bathor goes back to the beginning of time as we know it and probably beyond that. Suffice to say, Uhlon Bathor was the greatest warrior who ever lived. His battles and deeds are chronicled throughout the universe, and someday you may want to learn more about him, but that's really not what I want to discuss right now. I want you to know the legend of the medal. How you use it is very important; as you know, I also received the medal of Uhlon Bathor many years ago after the Tayhest-Maglarrian wars, for the small part I played." He was so humble.

I nodded but forced myself not to interrupt. I hoped he would be brief.

"I was strong and full of energy then, I wanted to conquer the universe. When I put the medal on, I also felt invincible. It is truly a wonderful feeling to wear it, and I did, for years after; I wouldn't go into battle without it. I felt like the legend had come true for me. I felt as if I was Uhlon Bathor, that even though others had received the medal, theirs had never shown with such brilliance as mine did, nor terrified the enemy as strongly as mine seemed to do. See, the legend says that someday a warrior would put on the medal and become Uhlon Bathor, and I thought I was the one. Everyone who knew me said I was the one; every time I put it on I expected to become Uhlon Bathor, until I finally refused to take it off at all. You are like that somewhat now, am I right?"

I nodded; he was right. I couldn't imagine taking it off. It was mine, all mine.

"Yet you have not worn it for one whole day," he continued, "plus already you have done, with your medal, things I couldn't do with mine. It really scares me, and I must tell you why, because the legend of Uhlon Bathor had a terrible ending to it. According to the legend, Uhlon's planet was under attack by a terrible enemy, and his people were dying all around him. He had been constantly forced to pull his forces backward, something he had never done before, in order to maintain a force of strength and to keep from being flanked by the enemy. He had never retreated in his life; it was not easy for him. Finally he could retreat no farther, and his forces gathered in the last remaining village, his village, where his family and all his friends' families huddled in fear upon seeing him in retreat. The enemy surrounded him and began to lay siege to the town.

"Here the legend gets a little cloudy, but I will tell it as I was told by my father. The people of the village went to his wife, who was said to have mystical powers, not to mention great beauty, and begged her to save the children, at least the children if none of them could be saved. She had promised Uhlon never to use her powers and until then had never broken the promise. Now she went and spoke to her God, asking that he give Uhlon the power to defeat his enemy; in return, she promised to give herself to her God. When the battle began again, Uhlon, who wielded a sword, was suddenly spitting fire at his enemies with every word he screamed at them, and everything they aimed at him bounced back at them ten times more deadly. The battle did not last long, and none of his enemy survived; he killed them all and would not stop even when they begged for mercy. Such was his anger that he killed them as they begged at his feet, and then there were none left. He went home, victorious. When he got back to the village, he found out what his wife had done, and he was furious. His words sent the same fire to his wife and killed her. Whether he meant to or not has never been resolved, but when he saw what he had done, he took her body and went to the top of the mountain and called for her God, the one who had given him the power and begged for his wife's life even if he had to give her up to the God. Well, this is what the God had wanted all along, so right away, he came to Uhlon and offered him the deal he had wanted—his wife's life in return for his life. No sooner had she come back to life than Uhlon slew the God with his sword. He thought he had won again, but before the God expired, he cast a crystal spell on Uhlon. His wife saw Uhlon start to turn to crystal and begged the God to have mercy, but it was for naught; the God had already died. She went to Uhlon and tried to save him with her powers for he had already turned to stone from his feet to his waist, and his pain was very great. He begged his wife, when she could not stop the curse, to end his torture and slay him with his sword. As the curse inched up his body, it drew screams of pain from him as his insides changed into rock-hard crystal. As it reached his chest, his breath started to leave him, and his wife knew she could not save him. She gave up and reached for the sword. When she grabbed it, she could barely lift the mighty weapon, and she again called upon her powers to help her. But alas, her powers had died with her God. She faced her husband as he stood dying before her, his eyes weeping at their fate. His last words as she kissed his hardening lips were his love for her, and then he started to scream as his head began to crystallize. She summoned all her strength and managed to strike him on the head with the sword but with a poorly aimed blow. His screams stopped then, though the blow probably didn't kill him; he had already died the instant before, but it did knock his body backward off the precipice, and before she could stop the body, it went over the edge. It shattered when it hit, bursting into hundreds of pieces at the foot of the mountain. She was saved from jumping after him by the villagers who had followed them up the mountain, and they brought her back to the village. Later they presented her with a basket filled with the crystal pieces. To make a long story shorter, as you say, years later when the Alpharians came to the planet, they heard the story of Uhlon Bathor and sought out his widow who was old and on her deathbed by that time. She gave them the basket of crystals, and they promised her to use them in his honor in future ceremonies."

"So that's where this medal comes from, and the crystal in the center is actually part of his body?" I couldn't believe it, but I did.

"Yes," replied Crouthhamel, "it is thought that his heart crystals are the strongest, but I believe it doesn't matter what part of the body they are from; I believe the wearer and his own heart give the medal its strength. We will never know for sure, and it really doesn't matter to the wearer"—he paused—"but now you are going to ask me, what all this has to do with wearing or not wearing the medal?"

"Yes," I answered; I really didn't see any reason, from what he had told me, not to wear it. I did feel more strength and very invincible, but hell, I felt that way after about four beers. *Perhaps it affected a person's reasoning*, I thought.

He bent down in front of his chair; the table was in the way, so it kept me from seeing what he was doing. Slowly he straightened up in his chair and drew his bootless right leg up and set it on the table. At first I didn't see what it was he wanted me to see, and then I saw them. His toes had turned to crystal on the ends. I gasped and reached for the medal around my neck. Crystal toes were not on my list of ideal body parts. Even with his foot pointing at me, I still had a hard time taking it off. I set it on the table in front of me and watched as it turned back to a bluish color. I sat there staring at it as he got up and came around the table. He was still only wearing one boot, and even the mighty Crouthhamel looked pretty funny in one boot. I smiled at him, but he had scared me pretty good, and we both knew it.

"I had to tell you, no one should wear the medal until they are told the story behind it. I thought I had plenty of time, but the way it works when you have it on . . . I figured I had better tell you fast," he said, putting a hand on my shoulder.

I looked up at him from the chair and picked up the medal. Slowly I placed it back around my neck; of course, he didn't see me wiggle my toes, and I stood up. He knew I had to do it. It comes with the job.

"Thanks for telling me," I said, returning the pat on the back. "Now let's go find that fucking Tayhest." I looked down, and the medal was already glowing again. I hoped we find the bastard fast; I liked my toes just the way they were, not to mention other body parts.

We were headed down the short corridor to the lift when our little world went upside down. The ship reeled to the right and dumped us on the wall, alarms began sounding, and you could hear and feel the tearing and bending of metal. Interior wall pieces, covering the bulkhead supports and structural metal, bent and fell on us. My mind flashed back to the time my truck rolled off the side of a mountain on a particularly muddy well road and tumbled down the mountainside with me in it. You lose some kind of mental control over direction, like climbers do when they get vertigo and can't tell which way is up. Luckily none of the really heavy stuff came down on us, and we were able to stand on the wall as if it were the floor and walk back to the ship.

Merlin was sitting sideways in the docking bay; it looked weird, but at least he was unhurt and undamaged. The outer door had automatically closed, so the room still had air in it. We had to climb over several sidewall beams to get to him, but he seemed like the safest place to be all things considered. As we reached the hatch, the Mothership began to turn back to level; it figures, doesn't it? We slid down the wall to the floor and quickly boarded Merlin.

"Merlin, are you OK? And what the fuck happened?" I exclaimed. "Did someone screw with the main stabilizers or what?"

"Yes and yes, I believe that is basically correct," said Merlin, "although sabotage might be a better choice of words. From what I can find out from the available computer links, someone just blew up the primary stabilizer room and its controls."

"No shit," exclaimed Crouthhamel; he liked that expression, "anyone know where the security team was at the time. I told them this would happen if they weren't careful. Any damage reports yet?"

"Negative, but communications are a tad screwed," said Merlin. He left off the "up."

"I wonder what he has on his schedule for the rest of the day," I commented. "This Tayhest is sure a handful of turds."

"I don't know, but he certainly wants to keep everyone busy," replied Crouthhamel.

"Why?" I asked, sitting back down at the table. "Why keep everyone busy? To make his escape, maybe? Merlin, let's look at that model of the ship Again, with the outer hulls in place." My brain was working overtime now.

The model appeared, rotating in the middle of the table, and I sat there staring at it. I had an idea that the Tayhest hadn't just decided to sabotage any old part of the ship's power plant; he had a reason for choosing the ship's stabilizers and levelers.

"Merlin, I want to see something; stop the model from rotating and pinpoint the stabilizer control room."

The model stopped, and a light appeared on the outside of the ship above the location of the room.

"Thank you, now tell me where the Tayhest could have gone from there," I said, trying to put into words the idea rolling around in my wasteland of a brain. "To get out of the ship . . . yeah, Crouthhamel, how could this guy get outside the ship, and where could he get a suit or something to survive in, for a little while outside the ship?"

"Probably the easiest place would be the maintenance section; they probably wouldn't have too many guards on that part of the ship, and he could steal a deep space suit from the equipment room, but why would he want to go outside? It would take him days to cross the surface of the ship. Even the Repods with boosters are transported by lifts to the sections they are working on; crossing the surface is very time consuming," argued Crouthhamel.

"Merlin," I said, holding a finger up to Crouthhamel, meaning to hold on for a second, "light up the maintenance section and"—what was I trying to get off the tip of my tongue?—"and Cluver's ship. Yes," I exclaimed, "show me Cluver's ship; that's got to be it!"

"OK," I explained as the two areas lit up on the model, "let's assume this Tayhest is smarter than he looks, and I'm getting that impression"—I looked at the lighted sections; something was missing—"show me all the maintenance ports, Merlin,"—and bingo, there it was, right above the main stabilizer control room—"OK, this will work . . . let's say he climbs into a suit at this port here"—I pointed to a spot, say, where the North Pole would be on Earth—"and proceeds to the control room directly beside the port and deliberately sets the stabilizer controls to blow the ship out of whack, but accurately out of whack"—I was on a roll now—"because it would have to be accurate, watch this"—I held my finger over the North Pole spot—"Merlin, turn the model exactly as the ship turned when it went over on its side."

As the model ship turned and my finger followed, you could see it was covering quite a distance almost instantly. I then commanded Merlin to put the ship back to level and held my finger steady on the spot where it had stopped, which was just about Miami, Florida. Sure enough, my finger was almost right over the dock where Cluver's ship was sitting.

"So he used a Hoverpad once he exited the ship?" asked Merlin, figuring it out.

"Yeah, right, once he was on the pad, he blew the stabilizer, and after the ship moved and came to a stop, he simply stepped off of it, having covered hundreds of miles without moving." *Great way to see Miami if you're an Eskimo*, I thought.

"You mean," said Crouthhamel, "that he set the whole thing up to travel back to the Darassin ship, and he never had to move at all; the ship did it for him as it malfunctioned?"

"Exactly," I said, sitting back in my chair and then jumping up as I realized what I had just figured out, "and he must be very close to Cluver's docking bay by now; he might even be waiting for the outer door to open, then he will just slip into the bay and steal Cluver's ship."

Crouthhamel had me replay the ship's movement as it tipped almost ninety degrees on its side and held his finger as I had done. His finger never moved, but it traveled thousands of miles in relation to the ship.

"Incredible," he muttered, shaking his head. "Merlin, can you raise that Gus guy in security? I want those doors kept closed until we get to the bay where Cluver's ship is docked." He sensed my impatience and knew I wasn't going to wait.

"I'm trying, but things are going crazy up there, and everyone is calling for help or information on the ship's condition."

"Keep trying," I said, as I stood and went to the weapons' drawer. I strapped on a Zalo handgun and turned to Crouthhamel. "I do believe we have a job to do." I tossed him a second Zalo and turned for the hatch. Time to make tracks.

He caught it and followed me as I ran into the corridor; the medallion was already glowing brightly.

Cluver's ship had also flopped over in the stabilizer accident and was still leaning on its side against the wall as we entered the docking bay. The outer doors of the bay were just opening, and we dove for cover behind a main bulkhead support beam and drew our weapons into firing position.

"Merlin, can you stick your nose outside the Mothership and see where the Tayhest is? He's not here yet." At least we weren't playing catch-up anymore.

"Gotcha, boss," said Merlin. He loved violence as much as I did.

"Gotcha?" said Crouthhamel, "remind me to tell you what the team of scientists who built Merlin said about Merlin and you." He smiled and shook his head.

Suddenly the Tayhest came floating around the opening and pushed himself slowly through the force field, like the one I had almost fallen out of when I first landed. He stepped off the Hoverpad and walked toward the Darassin ship. He looked like a sausage in a casing that was too small for it. He abruptly stopped and seemed to be struggling with a small pocket in the suit until he finally extracted a remote control device he must have stolen from one of the Darassin, probably from Cluver. He aimed it at the ship, and the ship began to turn itself into the proper position it had been in before the whole place went sideways. I stepped out from the beam and walked toward him until he saw me out of the corner of his eye. I was off to his left side, almost between him and the outside opening of the docking bay. He smiled a wicked smile through his broken teeth. Boy, was he ugly.

"I was hoping to meet you again, earthling," he pronounced, "so I could break you in half." The hatred in his eyes was intense as he turned to face me.

"I do believe you need to take out a weapon first," I advised him, waving the Zalo in his face, "before you threaten someone." I was tired and not up for any mental games, so I aimed the Zalo at him and fired it. The spacesuit instantly vaporized from his front, exposing another suit I had never seen before. I turned and looked at Crouthhamel as if to say, "What gives?" Something was wrong, big time wrong.

The Tayhest laughed at me; he actually tilted his head back and laughed at me. Meanwhile, Crouthhamel came out of hiding, though I had asked him to stay put, and also blasted him with his Zalo. Nothing happened when his Disorganizer beam hit the Tayhest, who turned and sneered at him.

"Well, what do we have here? If it isn't the mighty Crouthhamel," he growled. "What's the matter, don't you like the new material we developed in our laboratory? Just wait until we cover our ships with it; the universe will be ours then, hahaha hahaha." He laughed over and over. Finally he stopped and looked at us.

The ship was level now, and he turned and hit the hatch button on his controller. It swung down a few feet from him. He looked over at it and quickly back at us. He spotted the medal on my chest and stepped closer to me.

"And a trophy for me too," he sneered. "I thought that was the Uhlon Bathor medal I saw glowing on you. I tried to get a good look at it earlier, but you didn't give me a chance; now I'll take it with me. Hand it over, or I'll rip your head off."

I dropped the Zalo on the deck and brought my hands up to the medal.

"Why don't you come and get it, you ugly son of a bitch," I taunted him. "I don't think you have the balls to even try, but please do. I want to see the look in your eyes when I fry your fat ass." God, I could smell him now, yuck.

"With what," he jeered, "that medal? Hahaha, I've seen them before; you're not the only Guardian with one, you know. Old Crouthhamel's dad had one too. I should know, my family has it now"—again he began laughing at us—"why, it's sitting in our trophy case right now, next to his old man's balls."

Crouthhamel went nuts when he heard that; he threw his Zalo at the Tayhest and ran at him, screaming in anger. He was clearly out of control, yet he managed to execute a beautiful flying-scissors kick toward the side of the Tayhest's head. Unfortunately the Tayhest saw it coming and caught him in his big ugly hands.

"Good-bye, little man," he sneered and tossed Crouthhamel effortlessly toward the dock opening and certain death.

I knew he was a goner; I was too far from him to catch him. I watched him land and slide, knowing his momentum would carry him through the force field and out into space. Suddenly Merlin stuck his nose into the hangar and Crouthhamel bumped up against it and stopped. He lay there motionless, probably only winded, but hurt in a different way. He rolled over and stood up; yup, he was seething.

"Want me to blast him?" asked Merlin the Bloodthirsty.

"No, you got to blast Tweedledee and Tweedledum; he's mine." I hoped.

"I'll take that medal now," snarled the Tayhest as he advanced on me, "then I'll be going, so tell your buddy in that ship to move it, or I'll blast another opening right through him."

"I don't think so, asshole, but I do wish I could show this to your ugly kids." I smiled and concentrated on the anger I felt for the Tayhest. The medallion grew brighter as the Tayhest closed on me. As he reached out to me, it erupted with a much stronger flash than when it had dusted the Rango cub; it was like ten flamethrowers all in one. Hell, it was more than that; it was like a burst of intense radiation. I can't even describe it, except it enveloped the Tayhest and lasted until he was only a mere outline, then he and it were gone. I turned to Crouthhamel and smiled. At the moment, I felt like Uhlon Bathor, and I liked it, a lot.

"I guess that suit of his wasn't as good as he thought it was," I observed.

"Nice job, Jim," said Merlin. "I captured the whole thing on disc, so we can send it to the Tayhest, if you like, and give them something to remember you by."

"Oooh, I like that idea," I answered him cheerfully. *Hated by an entire world, not bad for a day's work*, I thought.

Crouthhamel was still standing next to Merlin's nose, looking every bit like a suicide candidate.

"Come on, Crouthhamel, let's go have a brew," I said, walking up to him.

He looked at me and shook his head in disgust.

"I never knew how my father died, they must have tortured him. I guess I really lost it didn't I?" he muttered, still shaking his head.

"Yeah, you looked just like me when I lose it," I joked. "Come on," I said, grabbing him by the shoulder, which I could barely reach, "let's go have a brew." We walked toward the inner door as a crowd of people came bursting into the room through the door. Chaga Nuies always burst into a room; it must be the extra limb effect.

Gloomy Gus was at the head of the pack of security Chagas, behind them a hoard of Guardians, who knew us, followed; maybe a hundred people altogether crowded around Crouthhamel and myself. They all waited for Gus to speak.

"Where is he, the Tayhest?" demanded Gus. "We know he was near here; the outer hull's security system notified us right after the stabilizer room blew up that someone had left the ship on a course toward this section. We weren't sure which bay until that ship of yours notified us; say, who is in control of that thing anyways? Nobody was on the screen." He gestured toward Merlin.

"Which question do you want me to answer first?" I asked innocently. I decided to play with him, the jerk.

"The Tayhest's location . . . please," he said nicely. He must have sensed my dislike of demands. Or seen my "be nice or else" look.

"He's gone," I pronounced. "Gone forever." I smiled at Crouthhamel.

He smiled back, nodding at my teasing of Gus.

"But where did he go?" pleaded Gus; he was clearly not having a good day.

"Why," I replied, holding up the medal, "through the looking glass!"

# CHAPTER 8

## Doctor Livingston I Presume

The party lasted the rest of the night, and I must have been so drunk and tired that I didn't even remember going back to Merlin and climbing into bed. It seemed like no matter how I tried, I kept getting into the middle of things. Now, I hoped, with the death of the Tayhest, maybe everything would settle down, and I could enjoy a little peace and quiet. I was really getting homesick, and still the fucking meeting had not concluded. And to make things worse, after the discovery of the impostor and his escape, the Council had decided to meet the next day in private, so they canceled the last day of the regular meeting until further notice. Crouthhamel also told me at the party that no one could leave until they were done with their secret meeting. Consequently the party lasted much longer than it should have, and quite a few Guardians celebrated, meaning overdid it, right along with me.

Merlin, Mr. C's savior, had made a spare disc of the final confrontation with the Tayhest, and somehow, I think it was Alzador's doing; it ended up being played over and over on the Guardian communication screens throughout the ship. It was a really good feeling to be so popular; I won't deny enjoying it, but I did get kinda sick of watching the damn fight scene over and over. Each time the Tayhest died, the crowd around me would cheer and drink a toast; hell, every time Merlin saved Crouthhamel's life, everybody would cheer and toast. The only time they didn't toast was when I blasted the Tayhest, and it didn't hurt him. Everybody would view the scene and look at their neighbor grimly, and you could see the concern on their faces and hear it in their voices. It was a preview of things to come, a warning that the Tayhest were not satisfied with their own territory and would very soon want more of the universe than what they already claimed. It haunted the older Guardians who remembered the Maglarr and the Great War; I heard them talking and wondered what it meant to the Earth and me. I did not think it would pass us by the next time, and I wondered how much I had added to the equation by becoming such a well-known hated person among the Tayhest. But as usual, my mind shoved my moral dilemma far back into my consciousness where I could deal with it when the time came, as I knew I would. And that's when the party really got wild; I think everybody else followed my lead. Hell, we are all a bunch of "live for the day" kinda guys. That is the easy part; dying is the hard part. Even the obdurate Crouthhamel joined in the festivities, teaching all of us at the table how to sing Altairian drinking songs as we threw round after round of Chaga brew down our throats; well, most of us used our throats anyway. Some of the Guardians did things with their food and drink that you would only say I made up, and yes it was disgusting. That was the first time in my life I ever got drunk with a tall dark red man, a giant owl, a loud mouthed Darassin, and an assortment other strange but lovable creatures. What a Kodak moment.

"Wake up, Jim," said Merlin; his voice was very cheerful, and it didn't hurt my ears to hear it. Love that Chaga brew. I made a note to stockpile some.

"What time is it?" I said, sitting up and hanging my legs over the edge of my bed. My head felt fine, no body aches, no blurred vision; I was in pretty good shape, except I had to piss like a racehorse. I started to get up, and a little pink arm slithered around my waist and held me in place with considerable strength. I turned around and saw it was coming from underneath my covers. I brushed them back to reveal a pink little woman, with a head of short brown hair atop a cute little pink face. She was very nicely proportioned, I might add. Her face was sorta familiar, and I knew I had seen her somewhere before, if I could just remember. Her little pink fingers closed around Mr. Happy, who was very happy about going to the bathroom immediately if not sooner. He set his own timetable, that was for sure.

"Hi, Jim," she said in a very familiar voice.

I know my face went into shock, followed by my cardiac system, Code Red!

"Tamee?" I said incredulously. Where the hell had her fur gone? For that matter, where the hell were her claws? I quickly examined the hand that had the lock on Mr. Happy; it sure looked clawless to me. I tried to remember last night and came up with a definite blank spot toward the end of the evening.

"Who else were you expecting . . . maybe Joan?"

"What," I exclaimed, looking around the room guiltily. "Merlin, are we still on the Mothership, or did you take me home last night?"

"Jim, we're still on Mother One, and you have a message coming on the screen from Crouthhamel; shall I activate it now?" taunted Merlin. I hoped he was teasing me.

"No, damn it," I said, pulling Mr. Happy away from Tamee's hot little hand and jumping up from the bed. I grabbed the covers and threw them around myself like a toga.

"I don't think that's going to work, boss," said Merlin. I turned to the bed. Tamee was lying there stark naked, smiling up at me and trying to grab at me and the blankets. The brown fur, it could be hair, between her legs looked matted down and sticky. She brought her hands to her breasts and squeezed them at me, laughing, her eyes blazing with blackness. I looked down and saw the tent I had erected in the front of the toga. Then Mr. Happy gave me my last warning, move or mop.

I threw the covers over her and ran into the pisser; Mr. Happy was obviously aching for more than one reason. It must have been a longer night than I thought.

"Tell Crouthhamel I'll call him back!" I yelled from the bathroom as I activated the disintegrator plate and opened fire. After what seemed like an hour, I finished and was giving old Mr. Happy the usual triple shake when a voice behind me startled me from my genital reverie.

"My turn," giggled Tamee, brushing by me to the toilet and settling down on the seat. Before I could turn, she grabbed old Happy and gave him a firm playful squeeze, shook him gently, and then kissed him just under his head. Had I not pulled away to go call Crouthhamel, I'm sure she would have gone further. I walked into the main room, shaking my head in disbelief; I must have been really tanked up. I couldn't even remember bringing her back to the ship. I slipped into the uniform I had thrown on the floor and walked to the command chairs, and Merlin rang up Crouthhamel. He appeared on the screen, smiling slightly, like he knew what was going on, on the Merlin love boat.

"Good morning," he said. "I wanted to see if you were alive and let you know the meeting starts in one of your hours, oh, hello, Tamee," he said, looking past me. I turned, hoping she was dressed and of course she wasn't, but she had thrown the covers around herself. Well, almost over herself. I turned to her and pulled the cover a little farther up over her chest. Like I said, she was a tiny thing but very well proportioned. She reminded me of a smaller version of Joan, which reminded me. "How do you know about Joan?" I asked cautiously, forgetting about Crouthhamel being on screen.

"That's what you called me last night, silly," she announced. "Don't you remember, when you were about to—"

"I'll see you at the meeting, Jim, you too, Tamee, remember, one hour, in the booth," cut in Crouthhamel. The screen went blank as he looked at us and shook his head, smiling paternally.

"Oh good," she bubbled as she dropped the covers from herself and grabbed my hand and started pulling me toward the bed. I knew I could have resisted, but her innocuous passion was captivating, and I let her pull me to the bed. Then I let her undress me, and when I was totally naked, I let her devour me as I stood there in front of her, looking down at her petite but full breasts, as she looked up at me with those eyes of pure blackness. She eyed Happy as he again rose to greet her and then leaned forward and ran her tongue around his head. It felt like a real cat's tongue, and the raspy feeling was incredibly stimulating. A few torturous moments later, she stopped and stuffed Happy farther in her mouth than I thought Nackly possible, all the time massaging my already aching balls. I would have given her my load right then, but she wouldn't let me, stopping every time my balls tightened up, letting Happy's throbbing head pop out of her mouth, and always at the last second. I finally took my hands from the back of her head down to her shoulders and forced her back down on the bed, wanting to grab her ass and pull her womanhood to Mr. Happy's hardness, wanting to impale her, seeking to release my load. My balls were so tight they could have made a lump of coal into a diamond.

But she wouldn't have it that way; she scooted back on the bed and motioned me to lie down. Happy and I obeyed without hesitating, though I'm not sure which one of us was in control; her lust was intoxicating and overpowering as she crawled on top of me. She positioned the head and, without hesitating, sank slowly down my shaft, not stopping until she had all of me inside her. How she managed I'll never know, but it was a slice of Nack heaven to be sure. She insisted on remaining on top where she could control the rhythm and tempo of our copulation, though I didn't put up much of a fight. It was a position, I must admit, that I was quite fond of with Joan, though it gave me very little control over Mr. Happy and how fast he reached the point of no control and no return. And no apologies, I might add.

She shuddered and gasped, finally relaxing her inner muscles, the ones that were clamped around him, and let him loose, but only after he had reached a blinding climax that drained my fluids until I felt like I was shooting my very balls into her. Then she settled down upon me with a satisfied purr, squashing herself to me. I looked at her pink body lying on top of me, felt her purring softly, and again wondered where her fur had gone. I also wondered if I had just made love to a female werewolf or something like that. Nothing surprised me anymore, and yet everything did, know what I mean? I closed my eyes and tried to imagine it was Joan on top, purring playfully, but it wasn't, was it?

"Jim," Joan was calling me.

"Jim," again she called me; where was she?

"JIM!" this time Merlin called me quite loudly. And he didn't sound like Joan.

"What?" I said, rolling over in the bed. I must have dozed off after the lovemaking. I stretched out and found I was alone.

"You have ten minutes to get to the meeting . . . don't you remember? Crouthhamel called you earlier, come on, get moving, you've been sleeping since yesterday morning when you got back from the, and I quote, "one wild fucking party."

I bolted into the particle shower—I'd kill for a real one—and threw on my uniform. I was half out the door when I stopped.

"What happened to Tamee?" I inquired.

"I don't know what you mean; did something happen at the party?" answered Merlin. He was obviously following instructions and probably thought I was testing him to see what he would say.

"No really, Merlin, did she leave already?" He was good, that one.

"I don't know what you're talking about, Jim." God, he could lie like a rug.

"OK, I give up," I said, running down the hatch steps and out of the ship. I wondered if anything had happened; maybe I had dreamt the whole thing, maybe she had never been on the ship last night? Maybe I had a colossal wet dream. Maybe I was nuts. Or *D*, all of the above?

I was still trying to remember what really happened when the lift arrived at the booth location. I noticed the lift door was open and climbed out absentmindedly. I was halfway up a corridor when I noticed I wasn't in the booth but heading instead into a stadium tunnel. I turned around and checked the lift number by the door, and it was correctly numbered 2231. I was standing there looking stupid when a shout rang out.

"Jim, come on, the meeting is about to start!"

I looked up ahead to the voice and saw Crouthhamel standing at the other end of the tunnel, waving for me. I hustled toward him as a meeting gong went off, and I heard the crowd noise immediately die down. It was funny how I hadn't heard it until it became quiet, but I'm like that sometimes, especially when I'm concentrating on something, like sex.

Before us, the entire arena had been transformed into a real stadium. All the boxes were gone including the platform of the Councilmen, replaced by seats, and the seats were full, as in SRO.

"Is this the same place we met at earlier?" I asked as I followed Crouthhamel to our seats in the front row of our level. I spotted Tamee and Alzador, next to them was Cluver and Inrew, a Zellen I remembered from the party. Crouthhamel grabbed the first seat, and I sat between him and Tamee.

"The Council decided to open the meeting to everyone on the ship," said Crouthhamel. "This seating is done just like shipping something on an Agriport; they just rearranged the molecular structure of the room."

"No shit," I was impressed. What would a stadium like this be worth on Earth?

"Hi, Jim," said Tamee, sexy but fur covered as usual I might add. She gave my arm a squeeze and then a playful scrape with her claws. She looked up at me and smiled affectionately. I smiled and looked down at her hand on my arm. It must have been a dream. I started to say something, and Crouthhamel gave us a nasty look, which meant, shut up, both of you.

The synthesizers had been removed from the central area, the field area so to speak, and a circular platform, filled with Council members, had been erected. The one I call Santa Claus stood up and walked to a spot in the middle and began talking to the assembly.

"People of the Alliance," began Santa Claus. I had learned his real name was Phayton. His people were a race of people who are absolutely identical to humans, called Jurda, who live in the Milky Way. I made a note to check them out at a later date.

"The Alpharian Council has called this meeting with the greatest of urgency," he continued. "After what happened here two cycles ago. We are now convinced that the Tayhest may pose a much greater threat than ever before; please watch the screens." He pointed above himself as an array of screens floated down into view, positioning themselves so everyone in the stadium could see the picture clearly. Instantly the battle between the Tayhest and myself came on the screen as I was in the process of blasting him with my Zalo. The crowd noise rose and quickly died down as they witnessed the

Tayhest standing his ground and laughing. His remark about the covering of his ships in the same indestructible material brought gasps from the crowd.

"As you can see," he began again, cutting off the screen before I wasted the Tayhest with my medallion, "the Tayhest are preparing for a future invasion of the Alliance, where and when, we do not yet know. It was decided that you should all be aware of the danger of an encounter with the Tayhest until at such time a suitable defense can be formed and implemented throughout the Alpharian Alliance. Therefore, we are hereby canceling all exploratory missions as well as any intergalactic shipping currently under our control. This includes all commercial and military shipments within one cycle of this meeting."

Crowd noise began rising as he signaled for silence.

"Also, we are asking that communications between galaxies be kept to a minimum until we notify the leaders of all planets and systems in the Alliance as to acceptable and warranted communiqué. Each and every planet will be placed on P1 status until further notice or until we determine what the Tayhest are planning." He stopped and the screens came back on, frozen on the face of the Tayhest. The mood of the crowd turned nasty, some of the crowd began shouting at the screens. Others simply made gestures that made no sense to me, though some were quite obvious.

"As you will see, not all is lost; it was possible for the Guardian to destroy the Tayhest warrior." The screen came on as I fingered the medallion, and it burst upon the Tayhest; a roar of approval rose up from the crowd as he vanished in front of my figure on the screen. Phayton waited for the crowd to quiet and began again.

"We are already studying the medal of Uhlon Bathor to see if we can duplicate the same results with a weapons system, and we hereby acknowledge the bravery of the Guardian"—he paused—"will James Herbert Edwards please stand up and come to the Council circle at once."

I felt Tamee and Alzador helping me up out of my chair and heard Merlin congratulate me over the roar of the crowd. I knew I was blushing from the recognition, but I couldn't help it; my legs felt a bit wobbly too. Probably because my life hasn't exactly been a carrousel of awards' banquets, unless you count my bowling trophies.

I stood up and gave the entire place a Rocky salute and then gave the Council members a Guardian salute. I could learn to enjoy this.

"Go down the tunnel," said Crouthhamel. "They will send a special lift for you; you earned it." He shoved me down the aisle with a pat on the back, and I headed for the lift, saluting people as I went until I finally left my arms crossed over my chest and entered the tunnel. Above me and to my sides, they were still yelling my name. Ahead of me, a lift car sat waiting.

"Merlin, who told them my middle name?" I asked. I knew who.

"I know nothing," he joked.

"Oh yeah, I'm not so sure, maybe I should change your name to Cluver."

"Ouch, I had that coming, I promise, I won't tell another soul your middle name, OK?"

"Big deal, you fucker, I don't think there is anyone else left to tell!"

I climbed into the open car, and it whisked me straight down a tube and out onto the stadium floor. More cheers went up as I emerged from the tube and finally climbed out of the car. I walked to the raised platform and climbed the steps and walked to the podium and accepted Phayton's hand. He remembered the handshake and appeared to enjoy it. I wondered if I should show him a high five and decided now wouldn't be the right time.

"James," he began.

"Call me Jim, please," I cut in. He really did look like Santa. He smiled and started again. The rest of the Council looked shocked that I had interrupted him. It was probably a major fuck-up, but I didn't care; I wasn't about to hear Herbert again.

"Jim, on behalf of the Alpharian Council and myself, I hereby bestow upon you the highest Medal of Valor for your bravery and courage in both finding and destroying the Tayhest impostor who dared to enter this ship and spy upon the Alliance." The crowd went wild; you would have thought I had won the Superbowl single-handedly. He looped a clawlike gold-banded object around my neck; the chain it was on felt very heavy. Mr. T would have been salivating over this one. I was glad I had left the other medal with Merlin; otherwise, I would have been walking stoop shouldered with both of them around my neck. I wondered, looking down at it, if they called this one the "Golden Claw" award.

"Thank you, thank you all," I said, looking to the Councilmen circling me. "It is a great honor to serve you; I know I haven't been around here too long, but I hope to continue serving you for a long time to come. I would also like to, if I may"—Phayton nodded—"thank everyone who helped me, particularly Crouthhamel of Altair"—I pointed to him—"the Guardians, Tamee, Cluver, Remonl, and Alzador,"—more cheers rang out—"as well as my partner, Merlin, for without these people my ass wouldn't be here now." Crude but effective, and the cheering crowd loved it.

"I think everyone should know," continued Phayton, "that Jim has already, in the short half-of-a-star cycle that he has been a Guardian, fought and killed a total of five Tayhest including the son of Lord Zordon." He said this while looking over at me.

I nodded. The crowd had oohed and then hushed at the name Zordon; apparently he was persona non grata everywhere in the Alliance. Just another bad guy, yeah.

"Now," said Phayton, "after I dismiss this meeting, I want all non-essential personnel to debark for home, you will have one cycle to use Time Drive, after that we will monitor and enforce any violation of today's directives, as we see fit. All of you, go home and stay home, guard your sectors night and day, be ever vigilant for a Tayhest presence and do not engage, alert your Guardian commander and stay away from them. Remember, we are stronger together than alone and apart. We will be meeting immediately after this meeting with the sector commanders, everyone else is dismissed." A huge gong sounded, and the meeting came to an abrupt end. It was shorter than I had expected, and I wondered why Phayton had brought up the number of Tayhest I had killed. I figured I would find out soon enough. Then he turned toward me again.

"Jim," said Phayton, "the Council is in your debt for exposing the Tayhest spy, we want you to know this, we won't forget what you did for us." He shook my hand with a kind of finality, which gave me a creepy feeling. It must feel like this before they blindfold you in front of a firing squad, I thought, it was that creepy.

"No problem, glad I could help," I was actually real fucking glad I was right about Pollifex; otherwise, I don't know what they would have done with me.

"The Claw of Catau is as sacred as your other medal, guard it wisely, and fly swiftly and safely on your journey home." Phayton said this while I was standing there waiting to get off the platform. It was like the end of a football game.

Crouthhamel and other sector commanders were debarking from numerous tubes that had come into view around the edge of the field and walking toward the central platform, meeting as they converged and forming into small groups. It was an interesting cross section of life in the universe. Crouthhamel broke from his little group and headed for me; his strides quickly separated him from the group, and I walked toward him. Phayton and the rest of the Councilmen were huddled up and seemed to have lost interest in me. I left the platform and met him almost immediately.

"Way to go," he said, grabbing me and actually hugging me. It was a huge show of affection for him, and I finally felt like I had earned his respect. He stepped back and eyeballed the claw around my neck.

"You need to talk to Alzador. I think the Catau race is from a star system near the Morkan Jmer system; he could probably tell you all about it. I have never seen one up close. Very impressive, Jim."

"Thanks, but you deserve one too, you know."

"Well that's debatable, but thanks for the offer, listen, I don't think this will take long, why don't we meet in your lounge area, the place you guys trashed the other night and have a brew before you leave?"

"Sounds good to me, catch you later." That phrase was catching on real well. I turned and headed for the first covered lift I could find; as I walked across the field, I looked back at the platform. Several Councilmen were watching me, and I felt the hairs go straight on the back of my neck. I turned back around and walked faster.

"OK, partner, let's go home," I said walking into Merlin and hanging the new medal next to the other one on the wall of the main room. I let out a raunchy burp—Chaga brew does make you burp—and strolled to my command chair. I was aching to see Earth and everyone on it, especially a particular lady.

"No problem, you have a lady trying to reach you first though."

"Tamee?" I had hoped she was busy leaving.

"Yes, she just called me and asked me to wait until she could get here."

"But I just said good-bye at the lounge to everyone; she was there, hell, she almost burned a hole in my lap sitting on me, to congratulate me on the medal." Damn near burnt Mr. Happy too. What a hot bottom.

"Well, she apparently wanted to say good-bye again."

"OK, then I want to get going." I could taste it, I really could—home, that is.

"No problemo." He sounded charged up for some reason.

"Hey, Merlin, are these people award-happy or what?" I needed a little input.

"As far as I could tell, giving you two medals was highly unusual, Jim, although you certainly deserved them both. And thanks for the compliment, by the way."

"Yeah, yeah, thanks buddy, I just thought it was a little strange, Phayton gave me the creeps when he thanked me, I would almost say I didn't trust him, but that's not true, yet something is up, I can tell you that much, I feel it."

"What?" Merlin liked his answers fast too.

"I don't know, it's just a feeling I get once in a while, so be on guard, will you?"

Before he could answer, a furry arm came around my chair and tweaked my chest, obviously going for a nipple twister. I grabbed the arm and pulled her around the chair easily, or should I say, she let me pull her easily. Watch the claws, please.

"Hey!" I always greeted people like that, especially pinchers with claws.

"I don't want to leave you," she stammered, pushing into me in the chair and causing it to recline. I didn't hit the switch; maybe the recliner part was broke.

"Thank you, Merlin," she murmured. She brought her face up to mine and stared at me with those black pools. I gave her a quick peck on her catlike lips.

Her whiskers tickled my face, and I made a face like I was going to sneeze.

"I'm going to miss you too, really I am, but we have our orders," I commented. Thank God.

"Well, in that case, let's say good-bye like we do on my planet." She stood up and unzipped her uniform and, before I could say a word, stepped out of it.

Suddenly she began to change in front of me. I don't mean change clothes either. Her fur actually disappeared under her skin; her body was pink all right. So much for the dream theory. As I sat there totally stunned, her body began to take on the shape of the pink dream lady, swelling in all the right places, shrinking somewhat around her waist and shoulders. Her face also changed a little, and her head became hair covered. Or maybe the fur changed to resemble hair; I don't know. Hell, however long it took, and it didn't take long, there she stood, naked and pink. The dream was not a dream, and I was no longer in Kansas, Dorothy.

"Neat trick." I couldn't think of anything else to say. Call it tongue-tied.

"Come on," she coaxed, pulling at me in the chair, "and I'll show you some more tricks." She played with her breasts, enjoying them as much as I was watching them. I leaned, the chair came upright, and she was in my arms. Oh baby.

Merlin already had the bed waiting, and I felt Mr. Happy gaining control. A stiff prick has no conscience I've been told. How true, how true.

"Now, can we go?" I said settling into the chair once more, watching Tamee scamper through the inner door and turn to wave. The screen went off as the door closed, and I felt Merlin turn toward the opening.

"Righto, buddy boy." He could sound like a Cheshire cat looks sometimes.

The screen came back on as we cruised out the outer door and turned on a course toward the space buoy.

Several other ships, that I knew were Milky Way people, left with us. One of the things we had discussed over a few Chaga brews was traveling in groups, so as we neared the space buoy, we had quite a procession behind us. I fingered the screen behind us. Cluver was immediately behind me, followed by several Rigellian ships, Inrew's toad mobile ship; probably the ugliest thing in the alliance came next, then the Entimallian Councilman's ship. Torgan, I found out, the Guardian from Entimall was punished for coming to Earth and was not allowed to attend the meeting according to Crouthhamel, so the Councilman was alone in his ship. Behind him was the Seltorran Guardians minus Labek, the Councilman who bought the big one. The Lussecans were missing also; Merlin had killed them all when they tried to escape and then permanently disabled their ship, which was stupid since we could have used it. He said it was an accident, and I believed him, sorta. I could barely see the little black ship of Tamee's, which resembled a teardrop, and was considered one of the fastest ships in the alliance. Behind her was a procession of Betas, Krillines, Taus, and Cees, but I couldn't see all of them; I knew there was more ships behind them, probably a total of twenty or more, all headed for the Milky Way and their respective star systems. I thought I saw Alzador's birdlike ship, way in the back, but Merlin turned the screen forward as he readied himself for Time drive and wanted me to see it. It gave me a headache, so I wasn't thrilled. Of course, he loved it.

"How fast can we get home?" I was definitely homesick now.

"About a day, Jim, I can't go faster than the speed I used coming here, or we might run into ourselves, going back. That would be freaky, wouldn't it?" With that, Merlin surged forward; at first, the stars became streaks of light and then the demented kaleidoscope effect began, and I had to turn away, or risk losing lunch.

"Getting sick?" asked Merlin. He was trying to sound concerned and not happy.

"Sort of, I never could ride a Tilt-A-Whirl, I looked like a Zellen when I got off it, the last time I tried one." This was a Tilt-A-Whirl of unearthly proportions.

"You should have your ears done over, the Jurdas are very advanced in the medical field and not very far from Earth you know."

"I know, I just don't like the idea of having artificial ear parts put in my head."

"Neither does Crouthhamel."

"Yeah, I noticed that . . . say, shouldn't we be using the deceive mode in case we run into a Tayhest ship?"

"Can't do that in Time drive."

"Oh." I wondered if that was important.

"Hey, Jim, want to see something cool?"

He didn't wait for an answer. The screen flipped to the rear. Behind us, all of space looked like a bunch of huge waves lapping at Merlin, with holes in them, and directly behind us was the hole we were making. I noticed the holes shrank and then disappeared into the waves.

"Is that how Time drive works? Where did the folds come from in the universe? Are you making them?" The holes continued to open and close behind us.

"Yes and no, we eliminate the actual distance by not following the surface of the universe, we are actually in the dimension of Time, not space, the folds are part of the fabric of the universe that you can only perceive in Time drive, keep watching, I think a ship is catching up with us."

As I watched, I thought I saw a point of light in the wave behind us, slowly gaining on us, and then it was gone from the screen. I moved the screen to the "Z" position and looked above and below us, several other points of light were moving around us. They continued to disappear every once in a while.

"Why do they keep disappearing?" It was really freaky to watch.

"Different time planes, Jim, they would have to be perfectly aligned with our spot in time for us to even communicate with them. And that's not a good idea."

"Why not?" I always felt stupid asking questions, but it never stopped me.

"Well, even though I am only making tiny holes in the universe compared to the whole, the turbulence of two ships might damage both ships or throw us off course, which would put us in another part of the universe, almost instantly. Remember also that time is affected by gravity, so it changes quite rapidly in some areas of the known universe."

"Known?" Now he had me. I thought somebody might know it all.

"Sure, nobody's ever come back from a journey to the outer universe; it is simply too far to travel, or so we surmise."

"That far, huh?"

"Immeasurable and probably infinite, even in Time drive."

"Because it's linear?" I meant the Time Drive.

"Yes, very good, Jim, I believe you're catching on; maybe someday they will perfect a point to point drive system, but don't look for it to happen in our lifetime."

"Why, how long will you live? I kinda thought you would live forever." Hell, with substitution surgery, I could probably live five, six hundred years according to Cluver the Darassin, Mouth All Mighty.

"Forever is a long time, let's just say a long time, for now."

"Sounds good to me." I yawned. Learning made me sleepy, and I had some catching up to do on my sleep time, that was for sure.

"Why don't you kick back for a while? I'll wake you if something needs your attention or when I start slowing down." He reclined my seat as he had done earlier when Tamee jumped on me.

I like to think of it as Nack attacked, and I didn't argue any more now than I did earlier. I fell asleep almost at once; even my brain felt tired.

I was having a dream about being back on Earth, and in the dream, a huge black cloud had descended upon the planet. It was rampaging the entire planet, terrifying and killing everyone it came in contact with, and calling itself "Jim's Cloud." I seemed to be stuck in the middle of it or else somewhere equally black, and all the souls of all the people it had murdered were floating around me, screaming my name, screaming it in anger, at me.

"JIM, JIM, JIM, JIM . . ."

I woke from the nightmare in a cold sweat, gasping for breath. It was still with me somehow and in real life; nightmares are very fucking scary. I was still sitting in my command seat, strapped in by Merlin no doubt but surrounded by blackness, yet still in the ship, at least it seemed that way. Yes, I was in the ship, I was aware of it, and we were tumbling sideways because, as the screen floated in blackness in front of me, the kaleidoscope effect on it was going sideways. Merlin's voice sounded as if it was a million miles away from me, like the rest of the ship, and yet all around me.

"Merlin, what's going on?" I screamed as I tumbled through the blackness. I must be tumbling; I was getting really nauseous, and I was having more and more trouble breathing. Something was terribly wrong.

"JIM . . . TIME DRIVE . . . REWED UP . . . CAN'T . . . SSSST . . . PIT."

His voice was breaking up now and sounded even farther away, like he was in a box. At least I knew the Time drive was screwed up for some reason and reached for the controls on the arm of my chair. In the time it took me to move my arm, the controls and the chair arm seemed to change position; they just weren't there when my hand got there. No matter how quickly I stabbed at the arm, I was too late to connect with it, and my hand just slipped into the blackness. I brought my hands up to my head, placing my fingers to my temples, and tried to close my eyes to the dizziness that was taking over control of me. My left hand hit the side of my head almost as I raised my arm, yet my right hand traveled much too far to reach the same spot on the other side of my head. I tried it again, and again the same thing happened. Suddenly I knew what was wrong. Almost every molecule on the ship was in a different time and, therefore, in a different place, and from the sound of Merlin's voice, it was getting worse by the second. I had to do something quick, or I was dead meat, literally. I dizzily wondered how I could figure out where the controls would be at a certain time and place and realized I had no time left for thinking out a solution. I had to get lucky and quick; there was no time for anything else. I threw my arms directly over my head in a parallel line with the controls of the chair and felt my finger hit something solid. I knew it wasn't the ceiling, too low, and without taking my hand away, I hit every button I could reach. I hoped one of them was part of the drive system and not the recline button. My arms suddenly felt heavy as lead and I had to let them drop to my side. As I felt myself start to pass out, I closed my eyes again, fighting the nausea and sudden fatigue from lack of oxygen. Almost immediately, I felt the arms of the chair under my arms and opened my eyes to find the ship solidifying around me. The screen in front of me was still doing the kaleidoscope trick, but it wasn't going sideways anymore. A moment later, it turned into the straight-line effect of Deep Space drive, and I heard Merlin as I normally hear him. Only this time he was very agitated.

"Holy shit, fuck," he cursed, "I thought we were dead meat there for a minute. I don't know how you figured out how to pull us out of Time drive, but I sure am glad you did." He took the words right out of my mouth.

"What the fuck happened, Merlin?" Man, was I dizzy. I had just had the ultimate Tilt-A-Whirl ride. I really hate those damn things too.

"I think I know what happened, and I don't like it; let me activate the deceive mode and get us out of here, then I can show you what happened. I believe we were attacked."

He put himself in deceive mode and moments later came to a stop. The lines became stars again. I noticed several star clusters in front of me that I had never seen before today. Suddenly Merlin spun himself around; I saw flashes on the screen and felt my stomach turn over, one more time.

"If you do that again I will throw up on you," I warned him as my stomach turned over again, and I gagged softly. The Jurda system might be my next stop.

"Sorry, my aft weapons and shields are limited, and we have so many good ones on my front. I just wanted to be ready in case we needed them."

"Maybe you should tell me what the fuck is going on then."

"I was attacked in Time drive; someone took a wild shot at us about halfway home from the Chaga galaxy. I think they used an Antimuon launcher because the damn thing went off almost in front of us, throwing us into a time slide that would have crashed us into that cluster galaxy behind us if you hadn't stopped us. Whoever it was knew even if they missed there was a good chance we would collide with something sooner or later. Then they followed us to make sure that if we did manage to come out of Time drive in one piece, they would be there to finish us off."

"So they're firing at our last location?" My head was clearing up.

"Yes, those flashes were more antimuon balls going off; they're quite powerful."

"Antimatter balls, right?" I thought I had them put into Merlin at the Zalo base.

"Yeah, subatomic particles of antimatter; here, let me show you the one that exploded in front of us." I should have stopped him. The screen changed to the kaleidoscope effect as if we were back in Time drive and then flashed brightly; immediately the screen started to roll, and then it went black. The pain was instantaneous, and I knew I should have stopped him.

"Man, what are you trying to do, blind me?" I shrieked, rubbing my eyes. I could feel the sandy sensation you get when your eyeballs blister. I had watched a welder once, which you should never do, and the welding flashes had caused my eyes to blister; it feels like broken glass on your eyeball when you blink. This felt worse. My eyes began to water, and red tears streamed down my face.

"Jim, I'm sorry, I had a strong filter on the screen replay. I didn't think it would hurt you; are your eyes OK?"

I wanted to tell him how fucking stupid he was, but I knew he didn't mean it. The feeling of glass was worsening along with the pain level.

"I need to get some water or something in them, I'll be OK, let's just get the hell out of here, I can barely see, my eyeballs have blisters on them."

"Sure, sorry again, Jim." He sounded as pitiful as I felt.

"No problem." I climbed from the chair and stumbled to the drink synthesizer and retrieved a glass of water. A bottle of Visine would have been real nice right about now.

I sat back down, cursing myself for not having a first-aid kit and squinted at the screen. We weren't moving, or if we were, it wasn't very fast.

"Plasma drive?"

"Yes, I'm trying to figure something out."

"What?"

Silence. He didn't answer me. It didn't seem like a tough question to me.

"Merlin, is there something you're not telling me?"

"Yes."

"WHAT, damn it?" I was not in the best of moods.

"I have no idea where we are."

"So where are we going in Plasma drive? Are you going in circles?"

"No, I'm headed away from the ships behind us, the ones that are trying to locate us, and I don't think they are from the Alliance."

"Neither do I, unless we just signed a treaty with the Tayhest." My brain was back to normal, and I didn't want to hear what it had to say.

"How do you know they're Tayhest ships? We're too far away to identify them."

"Let's just say I'm real good at puzzles. I think I just figured out why Phayton gave me the creeps. He knew the Tayhest were gunning for me and let me leave knowing I would draw their fire and pull them away from the rest of the pack of Guardians. Maybe the SOB even knew they were waiting for me to show up outside the galaxy. What a cocksucker. What a motherfucking cocksucker."

We headed into the cluster galaxy at maximum plasma drive and pulled into a thick cloud of stellar debris. It would make a good shield for now. We shut down.

"Hoping they go by us?" So was I.

"Yes, here they come." I held my breath.

Several ships passed us as I splashed water in my eyes. It felt like acid.

You really couldn't see the ships at the speed they were traveling, but with Merlin helping me, I could make out the sounds of their engines going by us. He had enhanced the sensor readings from their engines but didn't dare run a sensor probe on them. I'm sure he even had the deceive mode off too. It was a ballsy move, and I admired him for doing it. Of course, I didn't tell him that I was still a bit pissed about the eyes.

"What now, Merlin, got any ideas?"

"No, but be quiet. I think one of them is coming back toward us." He had whispered the last part, so I clamped the old mouth shut tight. I knew I was imagining things, but the hair on my neck started to rise. Merlin had shut everything down, even the screen and my air supply. I sat motionless, holding my breath. I had enough air to last a little while, but his actions had spooked me so bad I didn't even want to take the chance of them hearing me breathe. I held it as long as I could and slowly exhaled and inhaled again. I lost count how many times I did that until, finally, I heard him whisper again.

"I know where we are." He must have been eavesdropping.

"Where?" I whispered back.

"The Aktagara galaxy."

"Is that good?" I thought I had a bad Pracon memory about that galaxy.

"No." He didn't sound real shot in the ass either.

"Why not?"

"It's the home galaxy of the Tayhest." I knew I was right.

"Fuck me, I think we should run away very quickly, don't you?"

"Yes, I'm going to, any second now." He was thinking, I could tell.

"Good, I feel like a sitting duck in the middle of hunting season."

"I'm going to give them a taste of their own medicine, don't turn on the screen."

"Are you sure . . ." I didn't get a chance to finish my question. We came out of that cloud of debris somewhere between Plasma Drive and DS Drive, scattering our entire load of crystalline antimuon balls behind us as a present to the Tayhest ship that was still lurking about the entrance to the galaxy. The resultant blasts actually scorched the back of the Merlin, even though we were traveling directly away from the galaxy in maximum DS Drive. We didn't dare go into Time drive so close to the Tayhest home galaxy; it would give our position away. And they might be able to catch us if they could find us. In DS Drive, we could remain invisible to any sensor they used, and even visual surveillance.

"What were you going to ask me back there?" said Merlin. It had been several hours since we left Aktagara galaxy, and my eyes were feeling pretty bad, so I had not been doing a whole lot of talking. Or thinking for that matter.

I sat up and pulled the towel off my eyes; it had splotches of blood on it. A mammoth headache was forming on the other side of my eyeballs too.

"I don't remember, why?" I really couldn't.

"Just wondering, that's all." He sounded like a whipped puppy.

"Don't worry, Merlin, I'll live, just get me home, I can't even see the screen now." It was true; everything was a painful blur.

"I'm planning on it; maybe tomorrow we can engage Time drive."

"What? Somebody say there was a turd in the punch bowl?" I smelled one.

"I still don't have a fix on where we are; no one has been to the Aktagara galaxy in two hundred years, and none of that information is even in my computer."

Now that was interesting, and deliberate no doubt. I made a note to punch someone in the face when I got back to the Alliance.

"I do show a very small star cluster about a day's journey from here; it could quite possibly be the smallest galaxy I've ever seen."

"Let's head for it, maybe there will be someone who can give us directions although this close to Tayhest country makes me suspicious of anyone we run into right about now." Talk about up the creek with no paddle.

"Your right about that, Jim, it is relatively close to Aktagara, less than a hundred thousand light years, but at this point, we must investigate any possibility."

"You mean in case we're going the wrong way?" There's a no-brainer.

"Right."

"Aren't you picking up any interstellar communication at all?"

"Only Tayhest transmissions from their ships back to Aktagara."

"What are they saying to each other? I am nosy, remember."

"I don't know, it's in code I think."

"Well fuck, then how did you find out where we were?"

"I was listening to the conversation on the ship that circled the plasma cloud we were hiding inside."

"What else did they say? Were they looking for us?"

"Oh you bet, you're public enemy number 1 on Tayhest planets. I couldn't be sure but I think they know you were the one who eliminated the spy too."

"How would they know that so soon, no, don't tell me; the fucking Council decided to broadcast the open meeting throughout the Alliance?" Those pricks.

"Bingo, boss."

"Fuck me." I couldn't wait to get back and thank Phayton personally.

"No thanks, I don't do requests," he joked, trying to cheer me up.

"Smartass, I'm going to eat something and get some sleep, you have the controls."

We were almost to the minigalaxy when I awoke from a semiunconscious sleep; my eyes felt better although I had to soak them to get them open. I finally got up the courage to look in the mirror in the bathroom. They looked like a AAA trip planner had gone crazy with a red marker on a road map to hell, but at least I could see out of them. I ate, cleaned up, and went for my chair as we approached the outer edge of the galaxy.

"Tell me what we've got here, Merlin old buddy."

"You sound better, how's the eyes?"

"I don't feel like Ray Charles anymore."

"OK, well, this is an older elliptical galaxy about twenty thousand light years long and only a few light years thick, which should make it easy for us to examine a few hundred stars at a glance; it's pretty loose too."

"Yeah, I can see that; most of the stars look to be in the center area of it. Looks pretty nascent too; how old are the stars?"

"From what I can tell, they are low in mass, so probably pretty old; the inner star systems are younger though, so we might find some help there."

"What do you figure, about a day to go from one end to the other?"

"Yes, maybe a little longer if we stop at habitable planets."

"What do you recommend, professor?"

"Well, Jim, I think we should go check out the planets that are Earth class, but a quick run over the top of the galaxy might pick up subspace communications."

"Go for it, Merlin, let's find some help ASAP!"

We sailed along the top of the disc-shaped galaxy for several hours before Merlin picked up a beacon of some kind coming from inside the galaxy. I told him to investigate it, and down we went into the inner part of the galaxy, following a signal and hoping it was friendly. If my eyes hadn't hurt, and I hadn't been so homesick, I'm sure I would have enjoyed exploring this galaxy; it was exciting, all things considered, zipping down into a strange galaxy.

"Any idea what that signal means?"

"No, it's just a loud noise, want to hear it?"

"As long as you don't break my ear drums, bring up the volume slowly."

We had slowed down upon entering the galaxy and were now cruising by star system after star system; the corona from the stars was quite bright from space, so I had put on my sunglasses. I heard the sound as Merlin increased the volume and didn't say anything until it was well over 90 dB, which is pretty fucking loud.

"Sounds like a huge generator running; hear the hum in it?"

"Yes, it's coming from that binary system straight ahead."

"From a planet? God, what luck, huh?"

"Yes, and maybe, huh?" he mimicked me playfully.

We worked our way through the ring of debris surrounding the two stars and came into the system. It looked like a half a dozen planets to me and made me homesick immediately in its likeness to our solar system. Except for the two stars, that is, and the bright blue planet directly in front of us. OK, so it didn't look a whole lot like our solar system; maybe it was just nice to be out of deep space. I think I had cabin fever. I needed to walk on solid ground.

"I think we will have to look elsewhere, Jim, my sensors are picking up a message mixed in with the hum we're hearing."

"Can you filter it?" I didn't hear it but then, well you know.

"Yes, by the way, the blue we're seeing is a toxic curtain."

"A what? Toxic what?" Great.

"A toxic curtain. I've never seen one, but my computer has an old record of them. It seems years ago, before we had the capabilities to reverse planetary pollution caused by a species destroying their own eco-system, the Alliance would move the people to another inhabitable planet and put a toxic curtain over the old one."

"That's damn convenient. So we can't go through the curtain?"

"No reason too, there is nothing left of the planet's life-forms, every living thing is dead, right down to the simplest of life-forms."

"A whole planet destroyed by pollution? Incredible." Armageddon on you.

"Yes, but it used to happen all the time, all over the universe. They used to think there was an endless supply of planets to support the kind of lifestyle they lived back then, which of course wasn't true; now they can clean up their own planets, so it's no longer a problem."

"Except for the life-forms that no longer exist."

"Exactly, that's why every Mothership has and will have a living world in the middle of it, to sustain the species that can't survive alongside other dominant species or, in this case, on their own planet."

"Maybe I should tell them about Earth before it's too late." I hoped.

"They know already; someday they will begin taking plants and animals from Earth and save them from extinction. They may have already started; I just don't have a record of it."

"Let's hope so, what about the message, anything worth listening too?"

"Not really, a standard warning not to attempt to land due to high levels of radiation and toxic gases, wait, yes, good, they left a galactic map telling anyone who came here where they went."

"So what are we waiting for?"

"Nothing, it sounds good to me, but remember, this curtain may have been put up a thousand years ago."

"Well, maybe we'll get lucky."

We pulled out of the system and began following the directions Merlin had deciphered from the warning. He seemed to think that the curtain was very old and starting to wear out from the volume of the hum, and he predicted it wouldn't last much longer. Then the planet would probably tear itself apart.

His sensors picked up quite a bit of heat and thermal activity increasing on the surface and also below the surface of the planet. What a waste, what an incredible waste. I sincerely hoped that when we found these people that they weren't trashing another planet. I was a fine one to talk wasn't I. Mr. Oilfield, Mr. Poke the Earth full of Holes, Mr. Fossil Fuels. Shit, I hated litterbugs, and I was one of the Litterkings.

I was giving myself a hard time for being in the business I was in, or at least used to be involved with, when I was actually home, when Merlin announced our arrival at the coordinates of the message.

"Is this the right system?" I asked as he came through a tiny ring of debris and into a system, which looked like it had only two planets and one small star.

"Yes, Jim." He took us down toward the closest planet to the sun, and I could see the colors of the surface as we neared it.

"Looks better than the last one." Of course, anything would, even a dumpster.

"Yes, and I'm picking up life-forms on the surface."

"Great, any radio or television signals?"

"No, Jim, no signs of any communications, whatsoever, sorry."

"Hell, take me down and let's have a look at the people, it's an Earth-type planet, isn't it?"

"Yes."

"Maybe they can help me with my eyes?"

"Better be careful."

"I plan on it."

The planet began to enlarge on the screen until only a land mass filled the screen. Slowly the mountains and rivers came into view, and finally I could make out the forests and fields through my blurry eyes. I still didn't see any buildings or roads. That wasn't real good.

"Where's the buildings?" From the tops of the trees I could see nothing.

"Under the trees, very primitive dwellings according to sensor readings."

We settled down into a clearing in a huge forest; the trees looked like they had Christmas ornament bulbs on them, hanging down from the branches. I swung the viewer slowly around us, examining the humongous trees, trying to figure out what was hanging from them. The trees looked a lot like a cross between an oak tree and a weeping willow tree. Suddenly my question was answered as a creature appeared on the screen, standing under one of the trees, picking at the red bulbs, and eating them as fast as it picked them. It

## The Guardian Projects

was a child, a very fat child, a very fat humanlike child, wearing an outfit that looked like it was made from the tree and its leaves.

"God is he fat, look at that porker will you." I've seen fat kids but this one, holy canned ham.

"Close to a hundred kilograms."

"No shit, over two hundred pounds? God, he looks to be only about ten years old." I couldn't wait to meet the parents. Somebody say Jolly Green Giant?

The large child was standing there stuffing his face with whatever was growing on the tree. He finished stripping the one bough and began on the next nearest one, barely taking time to finish chewing before jamming another handful of red things in his mouth. Suddenly a girl about the same age came into view on the other side of the tree, imitating the same actions as the boy. She might have been just a little bigger than the boy, if that was possible.

"Where are we, the planet of the Obese? Talk about Fat City!"

"It would certainly appear that way, I'm picking up more of these beings scattered throughout the forest."

"These are children, Merlin, really fat children."

"Well, whatever they're eating is loaded with simple sugars and a narcotic I can't identify, plus a bunch of other compounds that resemble animal fats."

"I can believe that." I was hungry till I saw them. I looked down at my waist and checked my uniform for tightness. In front of me, the two children finished eating and lay down under the tree. Their faces were stained red from the food they had eaten.

"I wonder what the green and blue fruits are for; they didn't touch them, did they?"

"No, why don't you go ask them?"

"Let's inspect the planet a little bit further; this all seems a tiny bit strange and way too innocent as close as they are to the Tayhest." We left the two sleeping heifers and lifted out of the trees silently. Other spots in the great forest that seemed to cover most of the planet yielded the same results, heavy children and, in some cases, very crude shelters made from the branches of the trees.

"This is getting us nowhere, Merlin."

"I know. Maybe you should go and talk to them; maybe they are smarter than they look."

"That was cruel," I remarked. It was true though.

"And Fat City?"

"OK, OK, you're not the only cruel one." We laughed.

We had set down in another clearing, around which a large, and I do mean large, group of children were grazing, along with a few crude huts. They seemed to be concentrating on only the red fruits and avoiding the blue and green ones; I couldn't stand it anymore. Curiosity killed the cat; hopefully not I.

"OK, open the hatch, I'm going to find out what I can from them."

"Sure, hey, some of those females are carrying embryos."

"Why doesn't that surprise me," I said, strapping on a Zalo and an extra sensor, one for each wrist. I changed my mind and put one around my ankle. Call me paranoid. The hatch opened quietly, and a sweet smell of air entered the cabin of the ship. It smelled wonderful, almost too wonderful.

"Is this air OK?"

"Yes, unless you have hay fever."

"I do." Almost on cue, I sneezed. Of course, Merlin had no tissues.

"Gesundheit," said Merlin in German, laughing at my predicament.

I let him have the last word and went out the hatchway. Several of the children had seen the hatch as it materialized and had waddled over to observe more closely, exhibiting no fear whatsoever. Almost like they were expecting me. They looked at me as I stepped to the ground, and one of them came over to me, a boy of about ten or eleven maybe, still stuffing his face with red fruit.

He began talking with his mouth full, but the Hortic syllables were quite distinct. "Who are you?" he managed to ask.

"I'm Jim," I said, sneezing several times. He turned to the nearest tree and went and pulled a blue fruit from the bough and handed it to me.

"Eat this, it will stop your nose." It was about the size of a golf ball and had the appearance of a strawberry, only it was round. I accepted the fruit and ran it over my wrist sensor.

"What is it?" I was talking to Merlin.

"A healer fruit," said the little porker.

"It does appear to have some kind of medicinal compound in it; I need more time to analysis it though," replied Merlin.

I started sneezing a long string of sneezes and decided it was the lesser of two evils. It tasted like cough medicine as it instantly dissolved in my mouth. Whatever it was, it was in me now.

"Who are you talking to?" asked the boy. He accepted a few red ones from a fat little girl who came up to us and began eating them like he was starved.

"A friend," I answered. I wanted to keep it simple

"Is he on your ship?" said the girl. She didn't miss a beat, inserting the fruit in her mouth.

"Yes," I said. Maybe they were smarter than they looked. My head began to clear up, and my nose unstuffed as I stopped sneezing. I made a mental note to pick a few of the blue ones before I left.

"Do the healer's work on eyes too?" I asked.

"Yes," said another little waddler. He came up to me from the growing circle of children around me and handed me two blue ones.

I accepted them from him and put them both up to my blistered eyes. Almost instantly, the pain and scratchy feeling began to disappear, and I took my hands away. The children began laughing and pointing at me. I realized I must look pretty funny with two blue eyes and laughed along with them.

"What a Kodak moment," said Merlin. He was clearly watching too much television whenever we go back to Earth, that was for sure.

"My eyes feel excellent." They really did feel good.

"Want a red one, Mr. Jim?" said the first boy, offering one to me.

"No, thanks," I said, "I'm trying to watch my weight." I said it without thinking; it would have offended a heavy adult, but it only made the children laugh again. I faked a laugh too.

"Our parents like us to eat," said one of the children.

"Really," I replied, "where are your parents?" This was interesting.

"They will be here soon; they always come this time of the cycle."

"When they come, how do they get here?" Would they even know?

"In a spaceship, silly," said one of the children, "and then they take the older ones away with them."

"Where do they go?" They leave the little ones here alone? How shitty.

"Where parents live, silly."

"Oh, why don't they live here with you?" And take care of you, the bastards.

This brought a puzzled look to the face of several children, the first puzzled look I had seen so far. They were large but not ugly, really kind of cute in a way.

"They don't want to eat up all the fruit; it is our fruit, only for the children, they told us so," answered one of them.

I detected a little uncertainty in her voice, and it worried me.

"So they are going to be here soon?"

"Yes, we thought you were them now; we can't see their ship either."

Why use deceive mode, I thought, and why only the older ones? I smelled a rat, a big fucking rat. I could feel the hairs on my neck go up. Maybe I should wait and meet these parents and find out what was really going on. Then again . . .

"I'd like to meet your parents when they come, can I stay?"

"Sure," said several of the children, "will you tell us where you came from?"

"OK," I said. It must be story time. The children had really gathered around me now; there must have been a hundred of them in the clearing. All of them were grossly overweight but happy and healthy. You couldn't help but like them as they sat down around me, smiling at me with their pudgy faces all red from the fruit they were still eating.

"JIM!" shouted Merlin. I felt a rush of air above me, and I knew Merlin had suddenly moved. I turned around, trying to see what he was shouting about, and a hatchway ramp almost came down on me as I jumped backward and tripped over the children. I fell among them, narrowly missing two of them as I tumbled between them. I rolled onto my ass and was about to stand up when a huge hand grabbed me by the throat and pulled me to my feet. The children closest to me screamed and backed away from me, pushing into each other like a frightened herd of cattle.

"What are you doing here?" said the voice connected to the face, connected to the arm that was holding me about a foot off the ground and slowly strangling me. The face was an older version of the children and, from what I could see, so was the body.

"I'm lost," I squeaked. "I just landed to get directions."

"Don't hurt him, Daddy," cried one of the children. "He wasn't hurting us . . . We were just talking to him." Tears began to run down the chubby cheeks.

I felt the hand loosen around my throat, but the eyes told me not to move. They were evil eyes, eyes of a very bad creature, certainly not Daddy eyes. I felt my feet touch the ground, and I drew a breath into my lungs with relief.

"Where is your ship?" said the huge creature. He was a real butterball but strong as an ox too. The kind of strength a crazy person possesses.

"It was here a minute ago," I replied, rubbing my neck. Another minute and I would probably have been unconscious. I turned around to the children and smiled to show them I was OK. The bigger ones had removed their outfits and were standing there naked. They looked like cherubs. I suddenly felt sorry for them.

"Come, children," said the big guy, "it is time for you to go with your father; your mothers are waiting for you." He didn't sound evil now though, weird.

This brought smiles to the faces of the naked ones around me—they were the oldest ones; the rest had backed away toward the forest, clutching the older ones' clothing and appeared to be sulking. I turned back to the one who called himself father.

"Where are you taking the children?" I asked politely and carefully.

"Why, to their mothers," he said, smiling at me. "Why don't you come too?"

I shook my head as I began to back away from him; that smile had not fooled me. I didn't for one minute think they were going to their mothers.

"Run for your lives!" I screamed to the children behind me. "Hide from them!" As I turned to run, a stun-weapon blast from inside the ship hit me, and I fell to the ground unconscious. The last thing I heard was the children screaming.

Waking up from a stun blast is like waking up after being anesthetized; the first thing you do is throw up, which is what I did almost immediately. I was vaguely aware of being in a dark musty room, and the floor on which I sat retching was stony wet and cold. I finished regurgitating and tried out the old legs. They lifted me up but wobbled a bit as I tried my first step. My eyes adjusted to the darkness, and the walls of the room began to appear, giving the room dimension. I walked to the nearest wall and felt the surface. It was a mirror image of the floor, stony cold and damp with a moldy sweat on it. I sank to the floor, my back to the wall, and let myself become depressed. By God, I certainly had earned the right to do that. I should be home right now, snuggling with Joan and playing with Wolf, or was it the other way around? Instead I was sitting in a fucking dungeon, somewhere in a part of the fucking universe unknown to Merlin or his damn computer. I wondered what had happened to him after he yelled my name . . . Had he been captured too, or had he split for parts unknown? I couldn't blame him for that; sometimes you had to run away. Part of me knew he wouldn't leave me here, especially if he knew where I was, and I felt for my sensors. They were both gone. Shit, so much for that idea. As my eyes grew more accustomed to the small cell I was in, I noticed there wasn't even a bed or chair to sit on or lay down upon. I told myself reality is a prison cell with no bed and slumped farther down the wall to the floor.

"This sure the fuck isn't the Holiday Inn," I said out loud to myself. Almost instantly, I felt a heavy sadness come over me, an intense melancholy. The walls seemed to converge on me, and I began to experience the feeling of being buried alive. My breathing became more difficult, and a violent need to panic crept into my mind. It was like a nightmare while being awake. It frightened me so badly that I started screaming, and kept screaming, until I finally realized it was I doing the screaming. Then I pushed myself up from the floor. As quickly as the feelings had come, they vanished, leaving me gasping for air and wondering what happened. I knew I had imagined all of it. I wasn't in a box under the ground; I was in my dungeon suite, waiting for who knows what to happen to me next. I knew I had let myself become depressed but not that depressed. I walked back to the spot by the wall and sunk down to my knees, placing my hands against the wall where I had been leaning. Did I feel something, I couldn't tell; now it could be my imagination at work.

"Bullshit," I said. I felt a tingling in my hands, and the same images of being trapped alive sprang forcefully into my mind. I pulled my hands from the wall and jumped back. I felt a rush go through my body. I stood there and let the chilling tingle run its course and knelt back down to the wall. The last time I had felt anything like this had been when I had touched Pracon by mistake, not knowing the horror he had in his memory line. No, it couldn't be, he was dead; Crouthhamel had all but said he had died fighting the Maglarr after leaving Earth.

I put my hands against the wall again, a glutton for punishment, and concentrated on a mental image of Pracon. Suddenly the image of Pracon buried in a stone chamber far below me came into my mind. I pulled my hands away again; only this time I felt a feeling of exhilaration. He was alive; Pracon was alive, holy shit! Holy shit! He hadn't died; he had been caught and brought here, wherever here was. DAMN! I felt along the wall, talking to myself about stupid shit, babbling about what had happened to me as a Guardian so far. I was feeling for the spot on the wall where the feelings were the strongest. I circled the room, talking and feeling, talking and waiting for the return sensation, mentally calculating the point where it was the strongest. I didn't yet know if he knew I was here; he could just be radiating the feeling through his surroundings as a cry for help, like when prisoners bang on the walls or pipes in their cells. In which case, he was in for the surprise of his life—if he was listening, that is, or if he was able to receive images. I finally found a spot not far from where I had first felt the nightmarish images; it figures, doesn't it? I knelt down next to the wall and sat for a moment concentrating on an image of myself standing at the well site, watching Pracon rise into the sky above me as he left Earth. Then I slapped my hands against the wall and slowly lowered my head against it. I felt the images I had felt earlier and forced myself to concentrate on my own images. My emotions soared as I felt the images from the wall stop, and I continued to mentally force my images into the stone. I tried to picture them traveling through the wall like electricity and imagined them surrounding Pracon as he lay trapped beneath me. I don't know how long I held myself there, but finally I had to stop; my brain felt exhausted and drained. I turned and sat down against the wall and leaned back against it and closed my eyes. The wall was as silent as the quiet in the room around me. For a while, nothing happened, then I thought I saw an image of Pracon in my mind. I tried to blank out all my thoughts, and then I heard him in my head.

"Jim, is that you? JIM, JIM, JIM." The voice grew stronger, the feelings more pleasant, then happy. I could literally feel him rejoicing, both for me and for himself.

I smiled to myself and felt tears running down my face, and I didn't care. Finally he stopped calling my name and seemed to be waiting for me to say something, so I closed my eyes and said, "Doctor Livingston, I presume?"

# CHAPTER 9

## Somebody Call a Cab

While I was sitting on the floor, feeling both sad for Pracon and happy at our reunion, my cell door flew open, and a rather large Daddy version of the children stood in the doorway. He looked neither angry nor annoyed but rather indifferent to my situation and me.

"Come with me," he said and turned to walk away.

I remained on the floor; I was in no hurry to die.

"Come with me, they will stun," he warned, turning back to the doorway and sighing at my insolence. A real Harvard graduate, no doubt.

I walked toward him, trying to analyze how I could overpower him and wondering how he could be so blasé. As I approached him, he turned and began walking down the corridor. I stepped up my pace; he was taking huge strides. I had to catch up to him before I could even attempt to overpower him. Finally I managed to get close enough to him to jump him from behind, and I leapt on his back and brought my arms around his throat. He kept on walking as if nothing had happened even though I was trying like hell to strangle him to death. I wasn't having much luck at it either. We came to a set of stairs, and he stopped walking. He seemed to be waiting for me to get off. I looked up and noticed the ceiling was lower than our combined height and realized he had stopped so I wouldn't smash my head on the ceiling as we climbed the stairs. I slid off him and looked around behind me for something loose to hit him with. The corridor behind us was barren, even the doors that all appeared to be half open held nothing but empty rooms. I had the whole place to myself it seemed. He began climbing the stairs, and I followed; what else could I do?

We continued down another corridor and up another flight of stairs. This time the stairs were no longer stone but metal or something, and I noticed the walls were more like normal building walls. As we reached the top, the corridor looked just like any other hallway, smooth walls, artificial lighting in the ceiling, increasing in intensity as we reached the other end, lined on both sides with doors of normal building materials only much larger in size to accommodate these giants. I tried several mechanisms next to the doors, but nothing happened, so I gave up and hurried to catch up with Mr. Excitement. I felt like a kid on my way to the ultimate Principal's office for the ultimate punishment. Finally we arrived at a door, and my guide stood aside as it opened on cue.

"Enter," he said impassively.

"Nice knowing you, Einstein," I said to him as I entered. Ahead of me sat a threesome of daddies at a table covered with, as far as I could see, all kinds of controls and screens. These people were so big that the top of the table was almost as high as I was tall, standing there in front of them. One of them motioned me to a group of chairs lined up in front of them; I chose the middle one and sat down gingerly. I looked up at them as they stared down at me and the top of the table, which I could no longer see. I actually had a better view of their legs and crotches but ignored them and glanced around the room. From the screens on the walls to the rows of strange machines on each side of me, I deduced I was either in a control room of some kind or a Nazi torture chamber about to be dissected or drugged into mating with a gorilla or something.

I heard one of them laugh and looked up at him quizzically. He turned to the one in the middle and said something, and they both laughed.

"Who are you?" said the one in the middle, growing serious as he looked down at me. He reminded me of an oversized version of Jackie Gleason and even sounded a little like him.

"James Edwards," I replied. I wasn't about to include Herbert.

"A Guardian of the Alpharian Alliance?"

"Yes." Hell, I couldn't deny it; I was wearing the uniform.

"What were you doing on the children's planet?"

"I was lost and stopped to ask directions."

"Why were you lost?"

"A malfunction in my Time drive threw me into this area of the universe, which is not in my ship's computer." I wondered if I should tell them I was chased here by Tayhest warriors who want me very badly and not for a good time.

"What happened to your ship?"

"I have no idea." An excruciating pain shot through my body; the fucking chair must have been wired because now I was too. Man, that hurt.

"Another incorrect statement and we will increase the energy level."

Now what do I say; how do I tell them that my ship has a mind of its own?

"My ship has a mind of its own." What else could I say?

I looked at the other chairs and decided to move; maybe I should stand. As if they could read my mind, a set of straps quickly slithered around my waist and arms, holding me ever so snugly in the chair but exerting very little pressure.

"Where is your ship right now?"

Hell, I didn't know the answer to that; Merlin could be halfway across the universe right now or circling this place about to attack it.

Again I saw smiles cross their faces, and I knew then they had some kind of mind-reading equipment on that table. Had to.

"I have nothing to hide, so feel free to pick my brain apart if that's how you get your kicks; you must know I meant the children no harm as well as the fact that I am lost bigger than shit." Shock or not, I didn't deserve this.

"Yes, we know that you are lost or else we would have already erased you for invading our territory; you do know what the penalty is for entering Tayhest territory, don't you?"

"Let's see, how about death?" Was that a good guess or what?

"Only if you were lucky, Guardian, and in your case, I doubt they would kill you very quickly; you seem to be on the top of their most-wanted list, why is that?"

"We had some disagreements in the past over who should live and who should die." That was certainly true. And this isn't Tayhest Territory. Yeah!

"Well put, so have we. Do you know where you are?"

"No, but I'd wager it's not the Aktagara galaxy, and those children aren't the property of the Tayhest. At first I thought they might be using the children for something horrible, you aren't, are you?" God, I wish I could block my thoughts.

"You mean like breeding them as a source of food?"

"Yeah, I mean they certainly looked well fed."

"Do you think the Tayhest eat their young?"

"I would certainly hope someone would, I mean I love kids but not full grown Tayhest; those bastards are cruel and savage."

That drew smiles from all of them and a recognition that we did have a common enemy, a fact that gave me new hope that I might be able to get myself and Pracon out of this mess.

"So who are you guys?" They didn't seem all that bad; I was still alive.

"We are the Pheren; who is Pracon?" They all seemed very eager to hear my answer.

"The silicon creature you have in your basement." Clearly I was at a disadvantage in the question department. At least this had turned into an information-gathering session for both of us instead of an electrocution session for yours truly.

"And you know this creature, Pracon? How are you able to withstand his mind projections? He has been driving everyone in the building crazy."

"It helps to be a little crazy to start with, which is what I am, although my friends think I'm a lot crazier." Fucking nuts!

"Can you control him?"

I knew this was a very important question, dealing with freedom for both of us, yet I couldn't let myself be caught in a lie. "In what way?"

"I think you know what we mean."

"In that case, yes and no, Pracon is highly intelligent, so I can reason with him."

"Look, Guardian, we would just as soon let you go; we have no hostility nor animosity to the Alliance. Things that happened long ago are just that. However, we have come in contact with these silicon creatures before and will not let this one loose if it means dealing with him at a later date."

"I can understand that; I certainly wouldn't want to be on his bad side"—I nodded—"nor yours, I might add." and I did quickly.

"Any suggestions?"

"I could go and talk to him. I'm sure that if he gives you his word that he will not return, then he will not return. I believe he is very honorable, but I cannot speak for him now, not until I talk to him. Can you tell me one thing first; how did he come to be imprisoned here?" I had to know; if he had come looking for trouble, then he probably wouldn't listen to me. Ooh, why didn't I think of something else?

"We found him floating in space, our space, so we brought him here; we confined him because we have had so much trouble with his kind in the past." That was the part I didn't understand. "I will talk with him if you like."

"Yes, we must do something with him; the lower floors are virtually uninhabitable while he is down there."

Poor Pracon, he must be fit to be tied.

The straps released me from the chair, and I stood up and stretched. The huge fellow, the same escort I had earlier, came in the room, and I turned to follow him when the one in the middle spoke up.

"Guardian, we want no quarrel with the Alliance; the conflicts of long ago need to be put aside once and for all. This could be the time to do just that."

"I'm all for peace, that's for sure." Especially when it's my peace we're talking about. I gave them a Guardian salute and left the room.

We set off down the corridor, heading back the way we had come earlier, passing by the cell I had been incarcerated in, and down the corridor to another flight of steps. I was wondering if my buddy would follow me all the way to Pracon; he appeared to be a little more cautious than when he had escorted me the first time.

"Do you have a name?" I was feeling quite happy; I was still alive at this point.

"Tarr," he answered. He appeared to be concentrating on the steps as we descended them, but it could have been my question.

"Good, I'm Jim." I think the ice broke a little; I wasn't sure yet. We passed through another long corridor of cells and down another flight of stairs in silence, and I was beginning to think this place was bottomless until we came to a large set of doors. Stone doors, big heavy doors made of rock. I almost mistook them for a wall, and then Tarr leaned into them, and they slid open. There was absolutely no light down here; the light crystals that had been sparsely scattered throughout the ceiling on my floor were nonexistent down here. I stepped through the doors first and groped about for a wall or something.

"Steps," said Tarr as he attempted to grab me.

I heard him, but my feet weren't listening; I lost my balance and tumbled to the bottom after bouncing down about ten of them. I lay there wondering what I had broken, hearing different parts of my body complain to my brain that they were hurt, really hurt, as in "stay down, dummy."

"Jim," said Tarr from the top of the steps. He didn't seem to want to come down.

"Yeah," I groaned; I cursed myself for not having my suit on and tried to sit up. A pain shot up to the old brain from somewhere in my left leg, and my head was throbbing where it had connected with the floor. I wondered if my leg was broken.

"You good or bad?" said Tarr. He wasn't long on words.

"I don't know, give me a minute." I tried to straighten my leg and gasped at the painful response it gave me back. I can be a real klutz sometimes.

"JIM, IS THAT YOU?" Pracon seemed to be yelling.

"YES, I THINK SO!" Why was I yelling? He must be close; I didn't think he was communicating through my ass on the floor.

"YOU ARE IN PAIN, WHAT HAVE THEY DONE TO YOU?"

Nothing, I fell down the steps; I had a klutz attack. I hoped he heard me and understood; I didn't know what condition he was in, except he was screaming.

"I CAN HEAR YOUR THOUGHTS, I AM STRAIGHT AHEAD, WHY DID YOU COME DOWN HERE?"

To talk with you. They want to let us go, but only if you agree to behave when we leave and promise not to return here again.

"IS THAT WHAT THEY TOLD YOU? DO YOU KNOW WHO THEY ARE?"

"Yeah, the Pheren. I do know they don't like Tayhest, so they can't be all that bad."

"JIM, THE PHEREN ARE CALLED A DIFFERENT NAME BY THE ALLIANCE; WE CALL THEM THE MAGLARR."

No shit! I was floored. I should have picked up on that with all that talk about past conflicts; boy was I naive or what? Holy Moses, the Maglarr!

"Jim," said Tarr; he was right behind me, and it spooked me kinda.

"Tarr, I think my leg is broken." I could swear it was bleeding too.

"JIM, HE'S TRYING TO GRAB YOU, BE CAREFUL."

He picked me up like a baby. I screamed at the pain in my leg and almost blacked out from it. Suddenly, Tarr screamed at something; he didn't drop me, but I could tell he was frozen in fear. Pracon must be playing with his mind.

"STOP IT, PRACON, HE'S NOT HURTING ME, HE'S TRYING TO HELP ME; DO YOU WANT HIM TO DROP ME? WHAT THE HELL IS WRONG WITH YOU?" This time I was screaming mentally. Almost immediately I felt him relax a little, and I knew Pracon had stopped whatever he was doing to him; man, what the fuck had crawled up his pant leg.

"JIM, DO NOT TRUST THEM, THEY WILL GAIN CONTROL OF YOUR MIND!"

"Come on, Pracon, this is Jim talking, nobody is trying to take control of my mind; I fell down the damn steps, and he came down here to help me.

Get a grip, will you. I want to get out of here, not spend the rest of my life in a cell. They're offering to let us go; if they wanted to kill me, they could have already and maybe you too. They're real worried about letting you go, so I offered to come and talk to you about the situation. I will not leave here without you, you know that, but you have to give me your word that you'll behave or it's no deal, understand?"

Silence.

Man, he was wired up about something; maybe he was fucked up from something they did to him, or maybe he was hurt so bad from something else that he couldn't calm down and think it out. This wasn't like him at all.

More silence.

"Tarr, can you help me get upstairs? Can they treat my leg?"

"Yes." He turned and began climbing the steps. His arm strength was incredible; he carried me like I was a bag of marshmallows.

"JIM." He still sounded wacky. Then, "Jim, oh Jim, I . . ."

"What? What are you acting like this for? Are you hurt?" He had stopped yelling.

"I must be hurt worse than I thought; it is hard to think. Tell them I will not cause any more trouble."

For the first time, he sounded like the Pracon I knew, but now, I didn't know whether to believe him or not.

"Stop, Tarr, he's still talking to me, please."

He stopped but continued to cradle me. I felt like a baby; it was not an unpleasant feeling at this point. I could learn to like this.

"I was attacked, Jim. I did not see who it was; I must have assumed it was the Maglarr. When I regained my senses, I found out I was here, and that's when I guess I went crazy. I guess I did lose my grip on things." Now he was talking normal, at least to my mind anyways.

"Are you OK now?" Boy, I sure hope so.

"Yes, when you came down here I wasn't, but I feel better now, now that I've had a chance to concentrate on your thoughts; why don't you see if they will repair your leg, and I will control myself until you return."

"Now you're you talking, Pracon, what do you need me to bring you?"

"A plasma cloud would be nice." His thoughts felt comforting now.

"Funny, real funny. Let's get ourselves out of here, and I'll take you to the tail of Perseus; I hear the plasma is thick as honey."

"I can not wait. Jim, are they really sincere about letting us go?"

"I think so; the way I see it, our choices are rather limited, so what have we got to lose that we haven't already lost?"

"Hurry back."

"I will, stay cool, old buddy. Let's go, Tarrman," I said out loud.

Tarr took me to the medical wing, and they found my leg was fractured below the knee, and the bone had pierced the skin. I also had a concussion, but I didn't tell them about my head. Tarr stayed with me as they pushed the bone back in place; I don't know if he had too, but he did. I must have blacked out right after that, but I came around quickly as the Bonemender device reconnected the bone to its original position, and the pain subsided. I made a note to myself to pick up one of those Bonemenders for my ship at the first Zalo base I came to; they worked quicker than a faith healer's hands. If I hadn't seen the guy run it down my leg and up again, I never would have believed it was the real thing. Even the gash was almost healed now. Man, one of these Bonemenders would be worth a fortune on Earth. I didn't have any idea of the actual time it took, but it seemed like I was back on my feet within an hour after Tarr brought me up here. I walked about the room, smiling and thanking the technicians; my leg felt brand new.

"Come on, Tarr, let's get back to the room and work out a deal!" I exclaimed; I could almost taste my freedom.

"Good, Jim, we go now." He wasn't really Einstein, but I liked him anyways.

The three daddies were back in their seats when we entered the room.

"We are sorry for the unfortunate accident; we were not able to put up lights where the creature was placed. He kept driving our people out of their minds," said the middle one, who was still doing all the talking.

"No problem, I have spoken with him. He will behave himself and not return here ever again." I hoped they knew I was telling the truth; I did believe what I was saying. I just hoped Pracon was Pracon when I went back to see him. I sat down in the middle chair to show them I was being truthful.

"What assurance do we have that he will abide by these terms?"

Oh boy, that was a tough one. "None, to be sure, only my word."

The three of them conferred for a few minutes, and then the guy in the middle handed me my wrist sensors from a drawer in the table.

"You may call me Allao Tommot," he said. "This is my brother, Ellus, on my right"—he nodded—"and this is Crasler Tommot on my left." Crasler nodded also. They all seemed suddenly relieved about the whole situation. I wasn't sitting down, so I figured they couldn't access my brain, and I wondered again about the kids.

"Once we have set your friend free, we will be glad to show you our little school here," said Crasler, as if he was still reading my mind.

"How did you know what I was thinking?" I had been thinking of the children. Maybe it was the spot I was standing on?

"You had asked Allao earlier about what we do with the children, so I thought you would like to know we don't eat them." He smiled just slightly.

"I know you don't, but I was a little worried there for a while." Whew. They exchanged smiles with each other, and then Allao spoke to me. I had not missed what Crasler said about this place being a school; I just wanted to get Pracon out of here before I put my foot in my mouth. Things seemed pretty pleasant at the moment.

"You will see to releasing your friend now?"

"Yes, of course; how do I get the chamber open?" I was too busy falling down the steps to notice earlier.

"Tarr will go with you; he can open the chamber," said Allao. "Tarr, go with Jim and let the creature out of the chamber from the back, use the big room doors, and don't stay down there, come back here."

"Good, Tarr go," said Tarr, man of a million words.

I found myself staring at him as Allao spoke to me again.

"Jim, Tarr was one of our most gifted and talented defenders until he ran into a Tayhest patrol about a star cycle ago; by the time we rescued him, they had already done this to him. Someday we will return the same to the Tayhest."

Now I was really staring at Tarr, who had listened and nodded as if it was someone else they were talking about, and I felt tremendous sympathy for him.

"Let me know, I'd love to help." Why had I said that, damn, I was always committing myself to helping other people even when they didn't ask me. I looked down at my feet to see if one of them hadn't got stuck in my mouth.

"We may just do that," said Ellus smiling.

These huge dudes didn't need me to help them; I believe they could handle the Tayhest by themselves. But maybe I should pass along a little information; hell, Phayton had broadcast it all over the fucking universe anyway.

"As close as you are to the Aktagara galaxy, I feel I should tell you what we have just learned about the Tayhest; it is not a secret, just common knowledge for the common good." So what if I include them in the common good.

They looked at me and appeared to be very interested. Quickly I explained the new fabric the Tayhest were covering their ships with and how we had found out about it. They seemed to be listening to my every word, Ellus in particular.

"That is very interesting," he said when I had finished. "I would very much like to see the record of the battle you had with the Tayhest, and congratulations on your victory; they are strong and calculating adversaries." He seemed surprised that I had won, and I wondered if I should mention the former Lord Zordon Jr.

"No problemo, Ellus," I replied, my mouth running with diarrhea. "Let me find my ship, and I will gladly show you the fight scene."

"First, free your friend," said Allao, "then find your ship." He wanted old Pracon out of here, that was for sure.

"Right," I said quickly, "come on, Tarr, let's go set old Pracon loose."

"Tarr, go with Jim."

Tarr led me a different way this time; he seemed to be enjoying me, his newfound friend. I had to admit, I kinda liked the simple giant, and I know I'd hate to be on his bad side. His plain blue outfit was stretched to the point of bursting at the arms and legs, and his frame was a lot leaner than the other three Pheren. I'll bet he could lift a couple of thousand pounds easy, no shit, maybe more.

We finally left the inside of the building and walked along a huge balcony. Below us, the grassy fields changed shades of green as the wind blew it back and forth. I almost asked if I could go down and run in the grass among the boulders that were scattered among the trees and fields like a giant billiards game was in progress. We left the balcony and descended an outside set of steps and came to a huge set of doors. The handles were as high as my head. Tarr grabbed one, pulled it open easily, and turned and watched me struggle with the other one until he finally smiled and put his huge hands next to mine, and together we threw that mother open. He entered first, and I stood looking back at the fields, trees, and boulders; it was very Earthlike, and I became homesick standing there.

"Jim, Tarr go."

Yessiree, really talking my ear off, that Tarr.

I turned to enter the room and found myself staring at a room full of boulders, and as I walked closer to them, the less they looked like rocks. I wanted to investigate them, but Tarr grabbed my arm and pulled me past them. They weren't perfectly round, but they were all about the same size, and that's what made it so strange. Like somebody had collected a whole bunch of boulders about the size of a small weather balloon. Boy, was my curiosity getting the better of me; it was killing me.

We left the big room, went through another set of doors and entered a huge corridor, even bigger than the normal corridors they had here, and stopped in front of another set of double doors like the first ones. Tarr motioned me back and seemed to strain a bit as he pulled at them. I tried to help him, but he brushed me back and continued pulling. Suddenly I felt a rush of air and smelled a foul, rank odor filling up the room. I choked, and my eyes began to tear up as he pulled the doors open farther. I backed away from the opening, trying to find the good air I had been breathing. Tarr turned and motioned for me to come to the doorway and pointed into the sky. I held my breath and joined him.

The doors opened on the edge of a cliff, which dropped thousands of feet to something ugly below; I couldn't tell if it was land or water. I stepped back a little and followed his finger into the sky. Above us, the sky was a bright blue, but farther off in the distance, it was a horrible mixture of dark colors and clouds, ugly clouds, clouds with lightning in them, and God knows what else.

"Tarr go," he said, pointing skyward. I nodded and turned away. I walked back to the other end of the corridor, away from the big room, and took a breath. It was cleaner air but wouldn't be for long with those doors open.

"Come on, Tarr, let's go," I gasped.

He left them open and walked toward me. I was going to say something to him, but he walked past me and went to the very wall behind me and stood there looking at it. Suddenly he reached out and pushed one of the rock bricks that made up the wall, and the whole thing split open and began to spread apart. The light from the doorway revealed the back end of Pracon, and I rushed forward to let him know I was there.

*Pracon, it's me, Jim,* I said in my thoughts.

"Jim." He sounded normal.

"Pracon, can you back out of there? I forgot to ask you before, can you travel?"

"Yes, is there a Maglarr with you?"

"Yes." I instantly worried; was he going to try something?

"He is not strong mentally, is he?"

"No, thanks to the Tayhest; he used to be pretty smart though according to Allao."

"Allao, another Maglarr?"

"Yes, now come on, back out of there, OK?" His questions were making me nervous.

"Yes, it feels good to move, apparently most of my damage was to my intelligence, my brain." He began to move backward, and I turned to Tarr. He wasn't behind me. I turned to the open doorway to the outside and saw him standing there, looking up at the sky. He was like a child watching something interesting. I walked over to him and touched his arm, signaling him to move aside as Pracon floated behind me. I had an image of Pracon trying to push him out the door, and I couldn't tell if it was my imagination or Pracon's intentions.

"Pracon, your OK, right?"

"Yes, I won't hurt him; you like him, don't you?"

"Yes, I do."

"Are you going to leave now too?"

"I have to locate Merlin, and I also want to meet with Allao one more time; things have happened since we last met. Do you want to know them?"

He had reached the door and turned back to me as he hovered just off the edge of the cliff. The air quality had improved to the point where I could tolerate the smells, probably because the good air was now going out the doorway. I stood next to Tarr and watched Pracon extend his trunk like appendage toward me.

"Let me touch you."

"No problem." I leaned into the trunk as he gently touched my face and felt him mixing with me. It was not unpleasant, just weird, thoughts mixed with thoughts, until finally he pulled away.

"You have been busy, haven't you?"

"You know me, I seem to have an uncanny ability to get right in the middle of things."

"Yes, I had perceived that the first time we met. But medalled twice already; that is very impressive, although I detect a hint of unhappiness with your second medal, the Catau, why is that?"

"I think it was given to me to agitate the Tayhest even more; I think they, the Council, were trying to make my head a little more valuable, if you know what I mean."

"Yes, we must talk further about this, but for now, let me touch your friend here."

"No, Pracon, I don't want you to hurt him."

"I don't want to either." Before I could object further, he extended his trunk toward Tarr and connected with his face. Immediately Tarr grabbed at the trunk, and for a minute, I was worried that Pracon might lose it! Then Tarr began to relax, and his arms slid from the trunk of Pracon and fell to his side. Minutes passed and the air must have reversed direction as I began to gasp and choke again. I wanted to step back, but something told me to stay put.

"Jim, hold on to him, he is weak from what I just did to him."

I grabbed hold of Tarr's arm and tried to pull him back from Pracon as they separated; it was almost impossible to do, and he fell backward toward me. I didn't want him to fall to the hard floor; his head didn't need any more abuse at this point, so I braced myself behind him hoping to hold him up. It was like having a king-size mattress weighing five hundred pounds slowly sagging over on you.

"Jim, I am leaving now; he will be all right, I think. I have restored some of his brain to him; tell the other Maglarr I appreciate my freedom, and I will see you in space."

"OK." That was all I could say as Pracon lifted into the air and started to leave. I started losing ground with the old Tarr mattress and felt my knees starting to buckle. "Pracon, help, close, doors." It was all I could manage to say.

For a minute, I didn't think he heard me, then I noticed the room was getting darker, and the air seemed to get cleaner. Slowly I sank to the floor, my strength giving up to the huge weight of Tarr. I tried to get out from under him, but his body was dead weight at this point, and he squashed me down to the ground under him. In a last ditch effort to keep from being crushed, I remembered my suit and managed to reach the activation switch in the collar. It saved me from being crushed, but I was still trapped under his body, waiting for him to come around. The room was quite dark, so I couldn't see his arm as it started to move. I couldn't feel him breathing; maybe he didn't anyways, but I felt his body begin to wiggle on top of me.

"Tarr," I said, "can you hear me?" Please say yes.

Silence.

I heard something behind me, doors opening maybe, and suddenly I felt the weight of his huge body shifting and easing from me. I noticed it was considerably lighter in here, and suddenly I was looking into the agitated face of Ellus. I smiled up at him and rose to my feet. Tarr was leaning against the wall, supported by Crasler and another Pheren I had seen somewhere before. Oh yeah, that was the one from the ship that almost strangled me. He was still looking at me with those mean eyes of his.

"I knew we shouldn't have let that Procyon creature loose!" yelled Ellus at me. "Look what he has done to Tarr!"

I started to tell him everything was all right, but he continued to rant and rave, so I let him. Apparently everyone's feet fit in his or her mouth from time to time.

"I warned Allao not to trust you, Alliance people, but no, he didn't listen to me, now look at Tarr." He grabbed my face and turned my head to show me the figure of Tarr leaning against the wall.

"You're going back in that cell if I have to put you there myself."

I figured about five more minutes and Tarr would come out of it, but as I watched him leaning against the wall, I thought I saw him coming around already. Crasler came over to me and looked down at me. He didn't look too happy either. Come on Tarr, snap out of it. I stepped backward as the two of them advanced on me, glaring at me with murder in their eyes. I was about to run into Pracon's chamber when they grabbed me by the arms and lifted me up off the floor. I felt like I was being pulled apart as they started to walk toward the big room past Tarr. I looked over at him as we went by him; he was starting to move and shake his head.

"Look," I said. We stopped moving.

Tarr stood up, and his buddy released his hold on him.

He looked right at us and smiled, not a goofy smile but an intelligent one, an enlightened one, above all, a happy one.

"I think you should let Jim down now," he said and then laughed at the look on all our faces.

"So much for the village idiot, huh, Tarr?" I said smiling at him.

"Boy, your creature sure unscrambled my head. I still feel a little foggy, but compared to the way I was, this is excellent."

I wasn't the first to reach him and congratulate him, but he reserved a huge hug for me, and I was glad my suit was still on and running. Oh yeah.

"Let's get back upstairs," said Ellus, "so I can apologize to you in front of everybody for what I said earlier."

"Don't worry about it," I replied. "I would have probably done the same thing." I felt my arms to see if they were still attached. Ellus watched me and laughed at my antics.

We crossed back through the big room and headed up the outside stairs toward the upper floors. I noticed that some of the boulders seemed to have moved, and I swore I saw a couple of them moving as I watched. By the time we reached the control room, a crowd of maybe a dozen Pheren had materialized from somewhere and joined us to greet and congratulate Tarr on his recovery. I secretly thought it was the smartest thing Pracon ever did, and Allao must have sensed what I was feeling.

"This is a prime example of what has happened over the years to create such a huge wall between my people and yours. We thought the Procyon creature was a death machine for years, and even when we encountered them, we never expected them to have compassion, let alone feelings and their own intelligence. It's incredible." Allao was a happy dude.

"Yeah, well don't feel like the Lone Ranger there, Allao; I can't even describe the ill feelings that many of my Guardian members have for the Maglarr." *That's it, see if you can piss him off,* I thought to myself.

"I understand, many of my people feel the same way. If I took you to the home planet, there's no telling what they would do to you, and I'm sure it will take many cycles to change that . . . but what your friend has done here today will not go unnoticed nor untold."

"Well, don't get yourself in trouble over it," I cautioned. "I will be happy to be home soon, but I too will spread the word about what happened here."

"Good, unfortunately I have to ask you not to say anything about this to anyone. I know you want to," he added as I tried to interrupt, "but for now, I must ask you to swear an oath of silence."

"I swear," I said grudgingly. I kinda knew what he meant.

"It is for the best; let them go on hating us a while longer. Say, let me show you the school." He smiled suddenly.

"OK," I agreed; it was time to change the subject anyways.

We left everyone in the control room and walked back down toward the cell area where I had been held briefly and came down the last stairs in a strange and confusing scene. Several Pheren were hustling up and down the corridor, pushing the boulders I had seen earlier, into the cells and slamming the doors as other Pheren rolled more boulders up to them.

"Come over here," motioned Allao toward a closed cell.

I walked over to the door as Allao touched a rock on the wall, and a small viewing window appeared that I could just see through on my tiptoes. Inside I saw a boulder, and as I watched the boulder, it began to wiggle and roll back and forth like it was alive. Suddenly it stopped and appeared to be rising from the floor until I saw the damn thing had legs; almost at the same time, arms began to appear as the boulder shrunk in roundness.

"The children?" I asked, totally amazed at the head appearing out of the roundness.

"Yes, they should have been here sooner, but we couldn't risk them going crazy,"

"With Pracon," I said, finishing the thought.

"Yes, they must stay here for some time yet, until they learn how to control their changing abilities."

"You're a shape-changer?" I was fried.

"Of course, did you not know that the word Maglarr is a very old Alpharian word meaning 'one who changes'?"

"No, I didn't!" I exclaimed. By now, the child was looking like a child, a lost one.

"Why the cell?" I didn't understand that either. The child looked harmless to me.

"Now that the child has reached the start of adulthood, the fruit from the trees will no longer suppress his urges to change and change he will. We need to increase our numbers, so it is necessary to interrupt the normal survival patterns and make sure all the children live long enough to reach this age. Watch and you will see; he is not ready to control his urges."

As if he was on cue, the child suddenly began to change into something else—a hideous looking creature that galloped around the cell, screaming and roaring at the walls. He ran past the window, and I backed away. Allao had backed away also. The creature caught the movement and turned, baring its teeth and gums in anger.

We looked at each other and laughed at ourselves for backing up. I looked back into the room, and the child was gone.

"He is probably part of the wall now, he will continue to do this for many day cycles until he finally outgrows the urges and learns to use them wisely. Then we will educate and train him to fit into our society."

I could see now why they wouldn't want one these older kids going into fits around the younger children, man, that would be a fucking nightmare.

"What about the girls?" I had to ask.

"They are even worse, especially the ones who are already bearing children, although they snap out of it quicker than the boys do."

"It figures," I said. It was the same everywhere.

"Is it the same on your planet too?" he asked amazed.

"Only with maturity, Allao, although I've seen some women get pretty nasty at me from time to time."

"I too," he said smiling, "I too." We watched the other children change several more times and headed back upstairs. I could feel my stomach growling and hoped we were going to dinner, or was it breakfast; I had lost all sense of time and day, but my stomach hadn't lost track.

"Is that your stomach making those noises?" he asked.

"Yes, I think it has a mind of its own," I joked. He looked so shocked when I said it that I smiled to show him it was a joke.

"There are species that have double and triple minds in their bodies, you know," he informed me.

"No, I didn't." We passed by the control room and entered another room farther down the hallway. As we walked in, I smelled food, and my stomach rejoiced.

The room was a clear domed cafeteria, and the few Pheren that were already seated at the tables stopped eating and turned to watch us as we headed toward the sidewall. The wall had three-dimensional pictures of various dishes and Pheren writing underneath them; the way it was arranged reminded me of the old Automats I used to eat at in New York. I remembered that I had once, as a small child, tried to reach through the little food window and grab another sandwich from the counter behind the rows of glass doors, and someone behind it had yelled at me and smacked my wrist with something. It hurt for days, although at the time I thought my hand had been severed, and I was too scared to pull it out of the door. I stood there crying until an attendant came over to help, and then she threw me out when she learned what I had done. I was standing there daydreaming about it when Allao caught my attention. We picked our selections by touching the various pictures and went back toward the tables. Along the way, I told him the story.

"What did I order?" I asked.

"Klebsnak, a dish similar to Garf, or so I've been told; at least it's made from the same part of the . . ."

"Don't tell me, please!" I said laughing.

Our food arrived on floating trays like the ones at Zuzu's, and we quickly scooped it off the trays and began eating silently. The pile of food on my plate was humongous and tasted delicious. I suppose I should have been more cautious, but I felt this was no longer a life-threatening situation and gave in to my stomach's reasoning and ate like a pig.

"What is this drink?" I asked, tipping the huge mug to my face for another taste. It was as smooth as Chaga brew, but the taste was totally unique and refreshing.

"Bivy," said Allao between mouthfuls. He was a heavy hitter at the dinner table, that was for sure; his plate was almost empty while mine was still almost full of Klebsnak or whatever you call it. I was going to ask him what Bivy was but decided not too, better not to know. I offered him some of the food on my plate and scooped him off half of it before he could answer; I was already getting packed much to quickly and enjoying the feeling of being full.

"Ever tasted Chaga brew?" I asked as he dug into the rest of my plate that I'd given him. I made a note never to invite him for a barbecue unless I was having the whole cow.

"Never, although I've heard of it." He seemed quite excited at the mention of the words. "It was forbidden in our galaxy years ago because of its intoxicating qualities, so it is a precious commodity now."

"So you can get it here?"

"Not on this planet, but I'm sure there are people in our system that have access to it, even though the penalty for selling it is very steep; there is no longer any law forbidding its consumption."

"That sounds like my planet!" I exclaimed. Things weren't much different on the other side of the universe when it comes to idiotic laws, that was for sure. I sat back, enjoying the feeling of being very full, and studied the bright blue sky directly above the dome; the clouds seemed to be nasty off on the horizon, but here it was a beautiful blue day. Climate controlled.

"Does it ever get dark on this planet?" I asked. I couldn't remember how long I had been here, but I had not yet seen nighttime.

"Not with the blue shield around the planet," said Allao nonchalantly, finishing the rest of his food.

"This is the planet with the toxic curtain around it?" I exclaimed.

He nodded. "We returned here after the Alliance put it up; it has been here a thousand cycles. Then we surrounded the school with a minor force field to keep the rest of the planet's gases and radiation away from us.

"Yeah, but," I responded, "my computer shows an eminent breakdown of the curtain at any time."

"Yes, it would, the field we are using sends out almost an identical sort of hum." He smiled devilishly.

"So you can operate here and nobody knows a damn thing is going on here."

"Exactly, we have no choice, the breeding planet is the only one of its kind that we know of, and we must be near it to harvest the older children and separate them before they go into their changing cycle."

"Aren't you worried about me telling someone about this place?" I had to ask; if they didn't trust me, I was never going to get out of here.

"No, even if you did, the Alliance has no desire to come calling, and I doubt you would tell the Tayhest," he said calmly, "so don't worry, you will be allowed to leave."

"That's a relief," I replied. Now if I could only find Merlin. I glanced down at my sensors on my wrists and wondered why Merlin hadn't located me yet.

"Perhaps your ship is no longer in the area?" he said, noticing my apprehension as I played with the sensor bands.

"I wish I knew, hey, Merlin, are you listening?"

Silence. The kind that makes you worry.

We were sitting there half waiting for him to answer and half enjoying the rest when Ellus came hustling into the room and headed directly for our table. He slid gracefully, which isn't easy for a creature of a thousand pounds or more, into the seat next to Allao and quickly whispered into his ear. Allao's look turned dark and brooding, the relaxed expression turned to one of agitation. Ellus left, and I watched Allao as he rolled the news he had received around in his head. He turned to me, no longer a happy camper.

"The Tayhest have just entered the galaxy, a squadron of six ships, fanning out as if they are searching for someone."

I gulped; I knew, so did he.

"What will you do?" I felt myself shrinking from blame.

"We are safe here, but the children's planet may be discovered; we will monitor them and deal with them only if they get close to it."

"How many ships do you have here?"

"Several, but two are basically transporters for bringing the children here. We really only have one fighting vessel, and I have just ordered him to the children's planet as a precaution."

"Can he handle six Tayhest ships?" Must be a badass ship.

"I would have said yes earlier, but after what you told us, I have to wonder if their new fabric might withstand our weapons too."

"What can I do to help?" I felt totally responsible and just about as helpless.

"Find your ship!" He knew his one ship wasn't enough, not even close.

"How?" I must be missing something here.

"This force field may be blanking your sensors."

"Yeah, it's time to go outside." Out in the shit, yup, that was me all right. The thought didn't thrill me, but at this point, it didn't scare me either.

"Yes, leaving the force field confines may allow your sensors to reach your ship."

"Suppose it's the curtain." Shit, Merlin would never find me then.

"You could go up with the next transport ship and try to contact your ship that way."

"But that won't be for a while, will it?"

"Not until after the Tayhest leave and the ten cycle passes."

Shit, two weeks or more. "OK, where do I find a suit?"

"That's going to be a problem; the new suits are on the ship that just left, but we might have an old one or two here somewhere." He rose from the table and spoke to a nearby Pheren, who looked over at me and took off out of the room.

"He's going to check and see if we have one."

"Swell." I wasn't looking forward to going out onto the planet's surface, especially in an old suit. I didn't like that word, not when it came to protecting me; new and improved sounded better, know what I mean? I felt someone behind me and turned around as Tarr was about to reach for me. He had a funny look on his face; I hoped he hadn't had a relapse.

"Hey!" I greeted him.

"Hey," he returned, "I hear your going exploring, care if I join you?"

"No, love the company." These guys could revolutionize the bodyguard business. Not to mention the NFL, the NBA, and a half dozen other sports franchises.

"Good, come on then, I found us a couple of suits we can use."

"I thought the other guy was looking?"

"He was," he explained as we headed down a corridor; he walked, and I ran to catch up with him, "and I found them first because I was the one who stashed them away the last time I went into space."

"So you know what kind of condition they're in?" Hope, hope, hope.

"Yeah," he replied, "but you don't want to know."

"Yes, I do."

"No, you don't!"

We argued all the way down the corridor and up the stairs to the top floor, which had an observation room, equipment room, launch room, COM room, etc. It was Tarr's domain that was for sure; he was like a little kid in a candy shop. This must have been the first time up here since his encounter with the Tayhest. We had to inspect every room; he wouldn't have it any other way until we finally got to the equipment room. Getting into it was another problem since it looked to me like nobody had been in it for a hundred years except to stack more stuff in it, clear up to the doorway. Need I say, Tarr was absolutely thrilled to find his toys again.

We started moving stuff around, pushing it out into the hallway, restacking it, examining it, and squeezing it into a smaller space until we came to another door off to the side of the room. Slowly Tarr entered the room, motioning me to wait. Several minutes passed as I heard a series of grunts, curses, and equipment either falling down or being thrown down.

"Tarr," I called out after an especially long silence, "Tarr, are you still alive?"

Suddenly I heard something coming toward me from inside the room. I stood there, ready to run, as a metallic thudding drew closer. Ducking under the top of the doorway, Tarr emerged in a metal suit that looked very much like a full-size transformer with a man's eyes and mouth; the toy that turns into a car and then back into a robot, you know? He was looking at me and grinning.

"Come on." He waved. "The other one is all set up."

I followed him back into the room and found a huge machine on which hung various parts of another suit connected to the machine with tubes and wires. He motioned me to stand in a spot among the pieces and hit a switch behind the machine. Instantly the parts began to move into a position surrounding me, and a seat came up from the floor, connected with the seat of my uniform, and lifted me straight up until my head was sticking into a helmet. As I fought the growing claustrophobic feeling of being canned, the arms and legs joined a two-piece torso, and I could both hear and feel the thing being locked into one giant suit.

"Don't move just yet," cautioned Tarr.

A minute later, I heard things popping around me and saw him motion me forward. My feet were halfway up the legs of the thing as I sat into the ass of the suit. I looked at him like he was nuts, which he is by the way.

"My feet are clear up in the knee joints." My voice echoed around in the helmet, and a series of lights came on inside the faceplate surrounding the clear window piece.

"Try to walk," he ordered. "I've made some modifications to the inside."

I decided to see what would happen if I stood up and found my feet were on solid metal. I stepped forward, the suit moving in unison with my body. I stopped, and the suit kept on going by itself, running me smack dab into Tarr. He caught me and stopped the suit.

I looked into his face as he laughed at me. At least we were the same height now.

"I'm glad you think this is funny," I bitched at him. I looked down at the floor and was amazed at how high I was; it felt like I was on the second floor.

"It has been sitting for a while; you need to work it a little," he stated while trying not to laugh anymore.

"How long has it been sitting?" I don't think I wanted to know.

"You don't want to know."

"Yes, I do." Here we go again.

"A hundred cycles."

"Shit, I thought you said you used it last?"

"I did."

"Shit." I tried walking around and found it quite easy unless you had to stop.

"I trained in these suits, Jim, they are very dependable; our new suits are much lighter and not half as much fun to walk around in. These actually increase your body strength about twice what it is, so stop worrying."

"Good thing, I'll need the extra strength just to move this thing."

"You mean to stop it," he laughed. A real comedian, considering he was a blithering idiot an hour ago.

*Funny, real funny*, I said to myself as I tried to follow him from the room. Of course, I forgot to duck at the doorway, and the clang of my helmet brought the sound of laughter to my earpiece. I was so happy I could amuse him.

Since we were on the top floor, and since we weren't boarding a ship on the roof, we had to walk all the way down through the building to even reach the first set of exit doors. We crossed the same wide balcony I had earlier but headed toward the field instead of the big room. The field was empty of boulders, thank God, and we made faster progress than I thought we would, and I could stop too, which I did as I felt like passing out.

"Hold on a minute, Tarr," I gasped. I was sweating like a pig.

"What are you stopping for?" said Tarr, trotting back to me. He seemed to be having the time of his life; he wasn't sweating. His body wasn't drenched clear down into his boots with perspiration. I felt like smacking him; he had no right to be having so much fun.

He looked in my headpiece, at my face closely, and smiled.

"Go ahead, laugh," I panted. "It won't help me to find my ship if I'm dead when I find it."

He walked around behind me as I stood there panting. I tried to turn with him, but his left hand held me in place, so I stood and waited for him to come back around; I could hear him chuckling to himself.

"There you go, I had forgotten to turn on the temperature controls, you were really heating up in there, weren't you?" he said, smirking at me.

I could feel a cool breeze on my body from a thousand little air holes throughout the suit. It felt so good I thought I was having sex. I looked him in the eyes.

He looked back at me, obviously not sorry, rather amused if I do say so, and it really pissed me off.

"You son of a bitch," I screamed, "you're enjoying this, aren't you?"

He smiled, turned around, and began trotting away from me, laughing as he went. I raced after him, screaming at him through the helmet communicators. The more I screamed at him the more he laughed and the harder I tried to catch up to him. I almost caught up to him as we reached the top of a small rise, and I would have gladly kicked him in the ass, but the sound of his voice became very serious.

"Hold up, Jim, we've got trouble."

I managed to bring myself to a stop, although Tarr's outstretched arm helped a little. I could hear myself breathing and feel my heart pounding in my head. We had run a good half a mile, maybe more, if you want to call it running; stampeding would be a better word. I heard Tarr whisper something, but I was breathing so hard I couldn't hear him. He brought his arm up and pointed out across the field in front of us. I followed his arm and finally saw what he was looking at. It was floating about two hundred yards from us, just on the other side of the force field. You could tell the field ended there because the gases and clouds of whatever deadly chemicals seemed to form a wall there.

"That's trouble all right," I commented. Crouthhamel had been the first one to show me a Tayhest ship, way back when he first visited me; I remembered now. Just like their crew, they are ugly things. I can best describe a Tayhest ship by offering this explanation: take a handful of black mud, make a ball in your hand, and then squeeze the ball until the mud squirts out in little bulges between your fingers—that's the front of the ship; add a big belly on the bottom, a horse's ass on the back, and a shark fin on top, and bingo, you got a Tayhest ship. They're supposed to be jet black in color, and usually, you don't see them at all because they run in a deceive mode of some kind, all the time, the sneaky bastards. This one was obviously in trouble, or having some kind of trouble; the parts of the ship—front, one side, and the top fin—that you could see were badly burned and visible to us. The rest of the ship seemed to be flashing in and out of deceive mode, which made the whole thing look like a Salvador Dali painting, especially when you add in the swirling gases and clouds of shit.

"I don't think they have seen us yet," repeated Tarr.

"I don't think they can see the force field either," I added, breathing normally.

"You are probably right, Jim" he agreed, his helmet nodding up and down.

"Can they get through the force field?"

"Oh yes, we were going to walk through it, remember?"

This time it was my helmet nodding up and down. "What do you want to do?" I asked. "Do these suits have any weapons in them?"

"No," he answered, watching the ship intently, "they are worker suits." He raised his right hand and showed me the four circular hooks that served as a hand. I looked down at mine and saw the same thing. Funny, I hadn't noticed it earlier. I looked at my left hand and saw that the things I thought were fingers were actually wrenches and cutting tools arranged like fingers. Call me Mr. Observant.

"We need to alert Ellus and get a security team out here. They may be trying to sneak up on the school."

"You're faster, why don't you leave your suit here and go back and get some help?" I suggested innocently. I wanted to keep my eyes on the Tayhest ship; they weren't here to invade, they were damaged, and I think I knew why.

"OK, but wait until I get back before you go any closer," he remarked as his suit came apart like a pile of tin cans, no, more like industrial drums.

"No problem, I'll just stay here and watch them." I knew that even as big as the ship was, probably three times the size of Merlin, the crew was small, maybe four at the most, according to Crouthhamel. I sure hoped he was right.

I watched Tarr trot off toward the school and turned back to the ship. I knew this must be the ship that had been looking for me in that cloud I hid in, back in the Aktagara galaxy, and those burns on the hull were from Merlin's discharge of the antimuon balls. I decided to take a closer look at the damage; the gas clouds were thicker now, and I could barely see the ship through the crap floating in the air. But before I crept any closer, I wrestled Tarr's suit into a standing position and set it up on the rise of the hill so it could be seen if anyone came through the field. A silent sentry standing guard couldn't hurt.

I circled off to the side of the area we had headed for and jogged into a small stand of trees. They were really not sufficient cover considering how big the damn suit was, but directly on the other side of them was the edge of the force field and an extremely dense wall of polluted air. That would be great cover, and it would bring me to the back of the ship. I was in the process of stepping through the field when the side hatch of the ship began to swing open, so I jumped quickly into the fog.

I suppose Tarr knew about the steep hill, but I sure didn't. I fell halfway down the damn thing, and then I must have somersaulted a dozen times more before coming to a stop against an outcropping of rocks. I sat there dizzy for a second, watching the lights in my helmet for signs of leaks; they turn red when a leak develops, or so Tarr had said they were supposed to, but all of them were still blue. Then I followed my tracks back up the hill almost to the top and began working my way around, just below the top, until it began to level out near the ship. The gas clouds were thick here too, but every once in a while, the wind would blow them in a different direction, and the ship would appear. I spotted a Tayhest walking around the ship, examining the outer hull. He had a helmet of some kind on his head, which came down over his shoulders, and on his upper back was strapped a small air tank with a hose running back into the helmet.

*Good*, I thought, *they can't breathe this shit either*. I needed anything that gave me an edge or evened the score.

He stopped at some damage on the side away from the force field, the side I had worked my way over to, and began examining the hull. He had some kind of a hand torch or something; I could see the flash from it, and he appeared to be fixing a crack in a side seam. I snuck up behind him in the fog. I hoped Tarr was right that my strength was doubled. He turned at the last second, but it was too late for the bad boy. I brought my left arm down on the side of his helmet and smashed him to the ground, and before he could get back up, I snip the hose on the back of his helmet with a snipper tool. I liked the feeling of added strength; now I was as strong as they were, which only made me more cocksure of what I was doing.

I dragged him into the fog, hitting him again as he tried to fight me, and gave him a few more blows to the head after removing his helmet and throwing it off into the direction of the hill. Then I walked back to the ship and picked up his particle welder and slipped back into the fog. I didn't have to wait long before a second Tayhest came out of the ship and began walking around, obviously looking for his buddy. He stopped at the spot where he had been welding and examined the area. I waited for him to wise up; something told me he wouldn't be as easy as the first one. As I figured, he came upright with a whip of his body and stood there looking into the fog, almost directly at me. It gave me the creeps, so I stepped sideways away from the spot where he was looking. Suddenly the left hand of the suit triggered the welder by accident. It wasn't my hand's fault, really; the suit was designed to be highly reactive to any body movement, but not when it came to fighting, and my blows on the Tayhest must have damaged the hand sensors. It gave me a good idea anyway, and right about now, I needed one. The hill and the pool of bubbling liquids at the bottom, which I had barely missed, would make a good home for this ugly bastard.

The flash from the welder must have been visible to the Tayhest because he started into the foggy gases after the source of the flash. His actions made me think he was a warrior and not a regular crewman, so I knew I had to be especially careful with him. As he was approaching the spot where I had inadvertently flashed the welder, I was backing away in the direction I had come from, only this time, I didn't fall backward down the hill; well, I almost fell down the damn thing. I got a little klutz in me. I finally backed up to the edge of the hill and turned on the welder and set it down on the ground. I stepped back away from the edge and far enough away until I could barely see the welder flashing away at the ground. Now I was sweating, even though the suit was working properly. Standing perfectly still, I waited.

"Come on, pick it up, you asshole," I said to myself.

I have no patience for fishing; if the damn fish don't jump on my hook right away then I move to another spot and try again. It used to drive my old man crazy; he was one of those people who could put his pole in the water and sit there for five hours waiting for a bite or a nibble. Not me. So I was about to go pick up the welder and move it closer to the Tayhest when I saw it moving, rising from its location as if he had picked it up. Now was my chance. I advanced on the spot, knowing I might run into him any second when the welder went out. I hadn't figured on that. I turned quickly around and started back toward the ship hoping to catch him by surprise as he came out of the mist. It was a stupid plan, not my best one, that was for sure. Now, instead of pushing the Tayhest over the hill, I had a suspicious warrior running around in the fog looking for me! And he was armed too. Sometimes I wondered how I was still breathing. And I had to go past his ship to get back inside the force field before anyone could help me fight the bastard.

Coming out of the fog of deadly gases, I ran right into him. If I had been ready, I could have smashed him a good one, his back was to me. As it was, I managed to knock him forward as I stumbled to a stop. The suit was responding, but it could have stopped faster, and I wondered if it was going to break down on me, right in the middle of a fight no less. The Tayhest sprang up and turned on me; even through his helmet, I could see his ugly face smirking at me. He came at me quickly, and I swung my left hand into his helmet as he dove under it and knocked me backward into the fog. I didn't know if I had hit him, but I sure knew he had hit me. The lights around my facial plate had blinked red momentarily before changing back to blue. I was on my feet in what seemed like the longest of minutes when he came out of the nearby fog and charged me again. I thought I saw a piece of my left hand stuck in the top of his helmet as he closed on me. This time I stepped sideways and dropped to my knees, actually the knees of the suit, and swung my right arm into his midsection as he came over the top of me, throwing him over the top of me with incredible strength. "Thank you, suit," I said to myself as I rose to my feet and began to run back toward where I thought the school should be, keeping the Tayhest ship on my right as I passed it. I looked over and saw another Tayhest emerging from the ship's hatch and picked up my pace as he looked over and saw me go charging by him. He didn't look like crew either; in fact, he looked like one of the biggest Tayhest I had ever had the pleasure to run from, so I didn't stop to chat.

Just as I reached the edge of the force field, someone hit me from behind and knocked me to the ground. My head passed through the field, but I was caught around the ankles by a Tayhest. He had my legs in a deathlike grip, and I quickly concluded that the other Tayhest must be close at hand. I had to roll over and free myself somehow, or I was about to take a dirt nap. I struggled against the grip and twisted as hard as I could; the strength of the suit proved to be greater than the Tayhest's grip, and I rolled onto my back, kicking at the head of the Tayhest, knocking him backward and sending his helmet flying off into the fog. I planted both feet and threw myself backward through the field and right into the arms of the second Tayhest, the one with the welder. He must have found the field and gone after the second suit that I had left standing where he could see it. Then my head must have become a better target, so he had been in the process of coming back at me for the kill. Boy, that good idea hadn't worked real well either.

He couldn't hold on to me; the suit was too powerful, and I pushed him back away from me easily. But not before he brought the welder up and sliced it across my left shoulder, almost severing the arm of the suit and burning me badly enough to make me scream out loud. He saw the expression of pain in my eyes and let out a roar of satisfaction. He reached up and pulled off his helmet; his confidence was at an all-time high. He knew he had me; I couldn't go back into the fog without risking exposure to whatever gases were there, and I didn't have the quickness to get past him. And now I had to look at his ugly face too.

*Where the hell is the security team*, I wondered. I looked past him, hoping to see the Cavalry charging over the hill and noticed that Tarr's suit was no longer where I had left it. I didn't think the Tayhest had reached it yet, so that meant someone else had moved it or, maybe with any luck, put it on? I didn't feel real lucky right at the moment. I decided to move sideways and protect my back in case the other Tayhest, the one I booted, had survived the fog, managed to find his helmet, and came looking for me. He might have even gone back to his ship for a weapon or two, in which case, I was a dead duck. I wasn't sure if this old suit I was wearing could handle a blast from a Disorganizer.

I took a couple of steps to my right, protecting the damaged left arm of the suit. The lights in my helmet had turned red immediately when he had cut the suit, but I decided to leave it on for the strength it gave me. He blocked me from going any farther and swept the welder in front of me, trying to catch me in the stomach. I jumped backward and moved down the wall of the field, hoping I could somehow get around him. He knew what I had in mind and kept him between the school and me. I decided he just might want me to move in that direction, so I waited for him to swat at me once more, and as he did, I stepped forward and caught his forearm with my right hand and watched as the four hooks bit down into it. This time the expression of pain was in his eyes, and I smiled at him in satisfaction. He grabbed for the welder with his left hand as I raised my left arm to batter him with it. I'm sure I would have hit him before he could cut me with the welder except for one little problem. The other Tayhest had apparently survived and managed to find us through the fog and was now putting a deathlike grip on my left hand. He was trying to pull me back into the fog, back through the force field, as the other Tayhest brought the welder down to my wrist and began slicing through the wrist collar. I let go of the controls in the right hand of the suit and managed to curl my hand backward up into the arm of the suit as he severed the right hand, yanking it from the suit arm, smirking at me and wondering why I wasn't screaming in pain.

Had I been the same size as Tarr, I would be missing my left arm and my right hand by now, but thanks to my small size I was still in one piece. I never thought I'd be saying that! As quickly as I released the right-hand controls, I also released my left hand from the controls inside the suit, and as I felt the Tayhest behind me yank on the left arm of the suit, I pulled away from him as hard as I could, throwing myself into the startled Tayhest with the welder. As I had hoped, the left arm of the suit tore loose and sent the other Tayhest tumbling backward into the fog. Meanwhile, we tumbled over each other, both of us trying to gain the upper hand. This time I was at a disadvantage; my human arm strength in my left arm was no match for the Tayhest, and my right hand couldn't hold onto the welder as he clobbered me with his right hand and whipped me across the back with his reptilian tail. Using the right arm of the suit, I managed to push myself away from him and rolled away from his grasp. His tail must have crushed something on the back of my suit because suddenly the only air I was getting was coming through the hole in my left shoulder and up my right sleeve, which wasn't enough for this guy. I had to get away from him if I could, but he wouldn't let me and dove on me as I tried to stand. He knocked me down, flat on my back, and ripped the helmet from my suit like it was a paper bag. At least I could breathe now, for the moment.

The look on his face was one of complete surprise. He must have been expecting a much bigger person; I'm sure my head looked tiny, sticking out of the neck of the Pheren-size suit.

"Surprise!" I yelled, bringing my legs up and smashing him in the back and tail, hurtling him over the top of me. Now was my chance to get away.

He was on his feet with the agility of a Russian gymnast, coming at me as I struggled to my feet and turned my right side toward him, preparing to counter his charge. Then he stopped dead in his tracks and looked past me, smiling. I didn't like the smile part and turned to see what he was so damn happy about.

Another Tayhest was standing there, having just walked out of the fog and through the force field. He was dragging the other suit by its legs and dropped it facedown in the grass and dirt. His other hand held a weapon that looked a lot like a Disorganizer. I couldn't believe he had gotten the better of Tarr, but the proof lay in front of me. Where the fuck was the security team? Damn it.

He walked toward me and raised the weapon to a firing position.

"I suppose it's too late to work out a deal?" I asked. Maybe if I stalled, someone would show up and save my ass.

He continued to approach me, keeping the weapon aimed at my stomach.

"How about if I leave and never come back?" I asked. Man, he must be an awfully lousy shot; he was almost in my face as I finished the question. Maybe I could get in one good punch, snag the weapon, and dust them both. Yeah, right.

He was at arm's length from me when I threw my final punch, using my right, and with the help of the suit, it hit him squarely in the face. It felt like I had hit a pillow, and my hand bounced off his rubbery cheek without fazing him in the least. He grabbed my right arm as I swung again and let my momentum carry me to the left, helping me by shoving with the hand he was gripping me by, and I tumbled to the ground for the umpteenth time. I made a note to ask Rick for more fighting lessons.

"Hey," I screamed, "at least let me die standing up!" I spit dirt from my mouth and prepared to be Disorganized, wondering how painful it was going to be.

He looked down at me and smiled, not a vicious smile but a goofy smile, a smile I knew from somewhere, from someone. Then he looked back at the other Tayhest and pulled the trigger. I twisted around on the ground, in time to see the horrified look on the other Tayhest as he disappeared into a vaporous cloud and finally vanished. I turned back toward him.

"Are you really that bad a shot?" I commented. If he was, I might just get away after all.

He looked at me and started to laugh and change shape. Almost immediately, I recognized him, and I struggled once more to my feet.

"Tarr!" I shouted. He was still laughing. It was him all right.

He finished changing shape and stepped up to me.

"Are you OK?" he inquired mischievously, smiling down at me.

"Yeah, you sneaky bastard," I answered, incredibly relieved it was him, "so what happened to the security team? Did you come back without them?"

"No," he replied, sweeping his hand around in the air, "they are right here next to us."

I turned to the ground behind us and watched as they emerged from the ground, changing from what I had thought was ripples and mounds in the terrain into their real shapes, huge Pheren giant dads.

"Oh," I said, chiding them good-naturedly, "so you guys have been laying here while I was getting the shit beat out of me. Real nice." Bunch of shitheads.

I loved the smiles they gave me for an answer. I shook my head and turned to Tarr. He was smiling at me, enjoying the whole thing, no doubt about it.

"Is anyone else on board the ship?" I asked, trying to be serious and not smile.

But before Tarr could answer me, the whole area on the other side of the force field erupted in a huge bluish flash followed by an intense white light. The fog and clouds blew off in every direction, billowing up the side of the force field, clearing momentarily and revealing a deserted area of barren rock and dirt where the Tayhest ship had been sitting.

They gathered, looking at the edge of the force field and then at each other.

"What the hell was that?" said one of the security guys, sounding a bit unnerved.

"I think I know," I answered smiling, which made them all look at me rather strangely. "Help me get out of this suit, please." Now it was my turn to smile.

Tarr came over and touched the front of it and stepped back. Instantly the connections in the suit popped apart, and I probably would have fallen down again had he not caught me as the leg pieces fell apart, and I found myself momentarily suspended in the air.

"Thanks," I said, as he let me go, and I stood on the ground. It felt funny at first, like after you take off roller skates and it feels like you still have them on. I bounced on my real feet, glad now to be out of the huge suit.

"So what was that flash?" asked Tarr. His seriousness made me laugh.

"I think we are about to find out," I replied. Call it a sixth sense, but I had a feeling that something had just passed through the force field in front of us and was now hovering above us, listening to me. I felt so relieved in knowing that. Hallelujah!

Immediately they all became suspicious and apprehensive. I must admit I was enjoying this. A little nervousness never hurt anybody, right?

"Merlin," I said calmly to the air above me, turning toward the school, "have you been naughty again?"

They looked at me like I was nuts; little did they know how close to the truth they were, as I began walking back toward the school, leading them all.

After a moment, a voice from above answered me right out of thin air.

"Just a bit," replied Merlin the Destroyer. Then he materialized out of deceive mode, covering us with his shadow, making the Pheren jump a bit in surprise. Enjoying their surprise and my happiness, he asked mischievously, "Somebody call a cab?"

# CHAPTER 10

## The Black Spot's Gone

The ensuing confusion, from Merlin materializing right above to us—which probably prompted several of the Pheren to go and change their shorts, if you know what I mean, to the Pheren warrior ship landing next to the school, triumphantly and undamaged—kept me from concentrating on what I needed to do most of all, sleep. I couldn't remember the last time I had slept, really slept; it seemed like days. And it didn't seem like it was going to happen real soon, especially when the pilot of the Pheren ship reached our little group as we walked back toward the school with Merlin hovering behind us. Merlin looked in fine condition except for the burn marks on the back of him, a result of his own firing of antimatter balls back in the Aktagara galaxy. I also noticed he was rather quiet, and as I know him pretty well, I knew there had to be a good reason for it. I let the pack of rejoicing Pherens out stride me, and when they were a comfortable distance ahead of me, I dropped back and walked alongside him.

"It's good to see you, Merlin," I said, reaching up to touch his exterior hull. I knew the sentimental touch would be lost on him, but I did it anyway.

"Yes, Jim, I thought you were history for a while," he replied with more feeling than I had expected. "It is good to see you and feel your touch."

That floored me; I didn't think he was capable of that. "You can feel my hand on your exterior?"

"Oh, yes, of course, I mean, sure, with my sensors." His reply was less than perfect and delivered haltingly.

Merlin stunk at keeping most secrets from me, and I could tell, now that I knew him as well as I did, when he was not quite telling me everything.

"That's interesting, Merlin, I didn't think your sensors could read emotion?"

Silence. What was he hiding?

"I have a confession to make, Jim."

Here it comes.

"Yeah, let's hear it." This ought to be interesting.

"Well, come around to the front of me, and I'll show you." He lowered himself to hover height as I walked out from under him.

"OK," I agreed, walking ahead of him and around to his front, a noselike projection of aerodynamic perfection.

That's when I saw the crystal emerge from beneath one of his weapon's fluid covers and sparkle in the light. That certainly explained the blue flash we saw; he had somehow installed the Uhlon Bathor crystal into his forward systems display, and because he was a living entity, with plenty of emotion, he was obviously able to make it work like I had.

"Holy shit," I murmured. The whole idea of what he had done was mind-boggling. He was as sneaky as a raccoon at a campsite.

"I hope you're not mad," he said, ever so softly.

"Angry."

"You are?" he asked, not expecting that answer.

"No, people get angry, dogs get mad," I instructed him as I had been instructed as a child. "No, I'm not angry. I flipped out, that's all." Totally flipped, well, almost.

"You're not angry at me for doing that to your medal without asking you."

"Fuck no," I assured him seriously, "I had planned on letting it hang on my, your wall forever. The idea of turning my feet into stone doesn't quite agree with me."

"Really," he said stunned, "I mean about not being angry?"

"Fucking A," I said again; he could have it, damn Alliance bullshit.

"So I can keep it there?"

"Sure, as long as it doesn't fuck you up, agreed?"

"Yes, yes, of course, just say the word and I'll take it off, I mean give it back to you!" He sounded so happy; I half expected him to jump up and down like Wolf does when he sees me come home. Suddenly I wished I hadn't thought about home. Or Wolf.

"So give it to me now." I said, seeing what he would do. I know when I had it on, I didn't want to take it off.

"You're testing me, right?" He wasn't quite sure.

"I'm waiting."

Seconds went by, then he let go of it, and it fell to the ground. I stooped down, picked it up, and looked at him, rolling it around in my hands.

"See how hard it was to let go!" I said wisely.

"I hate to admit it, but now I know how you felt when you had it on. It really does affect you, doesn't it?" He had just learned a valuable lesson.

"Yeah, can you handle it?"

"Yes," he began slowly, "if I make adjustments to my computer and my fluid body molecules, yes, I believe I can control myself and the medal."

"Good, then take it back; I was just wondering where the chain was," I said, feeling the medal's influence. Damn, I hope he can control himself; I knew I couldn't. I reached up and touched it to the spot where he had placed it, and he absorbed it into his nose like a hungry animal.

"Come on," I said, "we better catch up with the rest of the pack."

"I'm right behind you, buddy."

And he was too. Nothing wrong with having him cover my back.

The Pheren, like every other race, knew how to enjoy a good victory and had begun setting up a huge banquet on the balcony area as I climbed the steps to join them. They had decided to celebrate outside so they could include Merlin, a fact that did not escape me. I think they also knew that I was not about to let him out of my sight either. A fact that didn't escape Merlin either.

"Here you go, Jim," said Allao, handing me a huge mug of Bivy, "it's not Chaga brew, but it's the best we have to offer here."

I looked down at the liquid and back up at Allao. "I think I can do a little bit better than Bivy," I said, smiling at him and handing him back the mug. I turned toward Merlin, who was hovering at the edge of the balcony, talking to the pilot of the Pheren ship, who had told all of us several times about the run-in with the Tayhest and how Merlin had come out of nowhere and dusted them with his blue beam. I really hadn't got the whole story yet, but with a long journey ahead of us, back to earth, I knew I would hear it at least once on the way back. He turned as I approached and saluted me as a Guardian would, and I returned the salute with surprise.

"I am Yodgar," he said, "and I owe my life to your friend here. I have never seen this beam of his before, but I am sure glad he showed up when he did."

"Glad to meet you, Yodgar," I said sincerely. "Tell me, how did your weapons work against the Tayhest?" Would he even tell me?

"I have to admit," he began, looking around cautiously, "they didn't seem to be as powerful against the Tayhest as they normally are; it had me worried, I can tell that."

"They had the new fabric covering them, Jim," interjected Merlin.

"I was afraid of that," I answered, "say, how about dropping the hatch for me? I need to get something from the storeroom." I knew if I hung around the two of them much longer, I was going to get the story all over again. The hatch opened, and I went on board and came out carrying a tub of Chaga brew from my personal inventory and left the two of them to their war story and walked back to Allao, whose face lit up like a kid at Christmas.

"Here," I said, dropping the tub on the table next to him and activating the pneumatic pouring spout. I touched an empty mug to the edge of it, and it quickly filled the mug and stopped. I handed it to Allao and watched the reaction on his face as he sniffed at what it was in the mug.

"Is this what I think it is?" he exclaimed, placing the mug to his lips.

I nodded and smiled. Several Pheren had gathered around us to see what we were doing.

"Chaga brew!" he exclaimed, pulling the mug down from his lips and holding it up in the air.

Suddenly the balcony was all elbows and assholes as they stampeded toward the tub and us. I dove under the table to keep from being crushed and rolled out the other side, feeling like a mouse in a crowd of elephants.

"They certainly like Chaga brew," said Merlin through the wrist sensor. "I hope you brought enough."

"Yeah, me too," I joked. They devoured the first tub on the first go round, and when it was empty, a huge moan went through the crowd. I decided another tub was in order and walked back toward the ship as they began to shout my name and Chaga brew at the same time. I wondered if I had started something I couldn't finish. Probably.

I had settled on the balcony wall between Tarr and Merlin, enjoying the drink and the company, wondering what my friends would think if they could see me now. I hadn't really been paying much attention to the celebration going on around me. Tarr and I had been discussing football, and I was trying to talk him into getting a game started. Merlin had said he could synthesize a ball from my food synthesizer, which had me worried, and I had told him to do it. The only problem would be the goal posts, so I was looking around the party on the balcony at the tables, trying to see if they could be taken apart somehow, when I noticed that some of the Pheren had breasts, large breasts. I didn't remember seeing any women since I landed here; now all of a sudden, it seemed like the crowd was an even mix of male and females. They weren't smaller in size, just built different, just like women on Earth, only bigger, lots bigger. We're talking Amazon to the $n$th power.

"Tarr," I said, turning to him with a puzzled look on my face, "where did these women come from?" One of them smiled at me, and I snuggled closer to Merlin.

"They've always been here, just shaped as men," he answered, looking around at the crowd of half-blitzed Pherens. "Those two women over there"—he pointed to two extremely large ones—"are the two men you know as Allao and Ellus."

"No shit!" I exclaimed. They did kind of look like the men they had been. Sorta.

"No shit," said Merlin.

"You knew?" I asked him.

"No, not really, I've just been keeping an eye on the crowd for you, especially after I noticed them changing shapes."

"It must be the Chaga," ventured Tarr, "which means, if you bring them any more of it, they may start free changing!"

"You mean like the kids in the cells?"

"Well not quite as bad, yeah, come to think of it, yeah, like the kids do," he replied. He finished his mug of brew and turned to me and smiled. His entire face became a huge Cheshire grin and then returned to normal. He laughed at my surprise and tagged me playfully on the shoulder, which would have thrown me from the balcony had not Merlin been behind me.

I knew I had brought three tubs from the ship, and I wondered how much was left in the last one. Maybe it was a good time to leave.

"Merlin," I said softly, "are you ready for a road trip?"

"You bet."

As if I had made a prediction or something, I saw a Pheren melt into a puddle and then reform into a huge furry creature very much like a giant rabbit. He looked quite cute until he turned around, and I saw the huge incisors in his mouth. Definitely not a Disney creation.

"Well, Tarr," I said, standing; my ass was numb from sitting on the hard wall, "I guess my work is finished here." Merlin laughed once and then stifled himself as I turned to him reproachfully.

"Yes, I believe we will have to play football some other time," suggested Tarr, as several more Pherens began to change shape, and the final tub of Chaga flew over the balcony to join its two other empty friends on the ground below.

"Let me get you that disc of the fight I had with the Tayhest," I said to him, "so you can give it to Ellus when she sobers up." I jumped to the ledge of the balcony and walked up the hatch steps and into Merlin. I was busy rummaging around for the disc when I heard Tarr shout through the door.

"Jim, get going, we've got a crisis here."

I walked back to the hatch, not knowing what to expect. Tarr was almost inside the ship, reaching toward me as I held the disc out to him.

"What is it?" I couldn't see past his huge bulk. He did make a better door.

"A ship of Nobles from our capitol planet just notified us of their intent to land here in a few moments; it would not be advisable for you to be here when that happens."

"I think I catch your meaning," I said. They are going to arrive and find the entire school stoned on their asses, thanks to me.

"I'll see you again," said Tarr prophetically. "Take care of yourself."

"You too!" I yelled after his disappearing head. Merlin slammed the hatch and immediately put us into deceive mode. I hustled forward and threw myself into my seat and flipped on the exterior screens. We had timed it perfectly.

In the distance, just coming through the force field, I could see a huge ship starting to settle down on the lawn in front of the school. It had trouble written all over it. I turned the screen toward the school, and as we floated slowly upward, I saw that the party had degenerated into a mass of weird-shaped animals, some fighting each other and some copulating, in every imaginable way, all with a wild abandon.

"Looks like we left at the appropriate time," said Merlin, laughing.

"Yes," I agreed. I watched as a huge robed Pheren approached the steps to the school, below the balcony, leading an entourage of more robed Pherens. He probably would have made it all the way to the balcony if that table that was thrown over the ledge hadn't hit him on the head. The last scene I remember seeing was the crowd of Pherens going crazy on the balcony as the Pherens from the ship encircled the downed one. And Tarr waving as he smartly melted into part of the balcony.

I was beginning to think of Merlin as nothing more than a floating interstellar motel room. It seemed like all I ever did was sleep from one planet to another, mostly because I never got any sleep once I got there. Which was probably my own fault too. And I never seemed to be the one who got to blow up the bad guy; so far, it seemed that Merlin had been the one who got to do all the shooting—first the Lussecan ship and then a half a dozen Tayhest ships, battle wagons no less. And now, as I lay back in my command chair, what a contradiction that was, wanting very much to go to sleep; I had to hear the entire story and watch the video replay of Merlin the Magnificent as he used my medal to destroy the Tayhest as they swooped down into the Pheren galaxy. God, I get bitchy when I'm tired. I decided a bit of food might make me feel better and went for the food processor to see what I could concoct from the molecular chamber that held every atom I would ever need to construct a healthy meal. What a bunch of Zalo bullshit.

I get bitchy when I'm hungry too. And I hadn't eaten anything at the banquet, partly because some of it was still moving and mostly because it looked like something you had already eaten at least once. I played with the buttons, and nothing happened, unless you count the red chamber light, which meant the chamber had something in it already. The door flipped open to reveal a crude but identifiable football. The one I had requested for the game we almost played at the school. I pulled it out and rolled it around in my hand, thinking about the last time I had actually thrown one. I spun around and tossed it across the room, not really caring if it hit anything or not; hell, there wasn't much to hit anyways. Except the other medal I had received, the Claw of Catau, which was hanging there by itself. So of course that's where the ball headed, and you know, it hit the damn thing.

The ball stuck to it, like it had been caught, probably stuck on one of the claws no doubt. I turned back to the synthesizer and began mixing up the old molecules. What came out looked almost as bad as what they were serving at the banquet, but I wolfed it down anyway along with a tumbler of Merlin's version of diet Pepsi. I didn't tell him it tasted like chemical waste, but it did, and still does, but I still drink it. I felt a little better after eating but still sort of grumpy, so I decided not to say much as I sat back down in my chair.

"So what do you think?" said Merlin, concluding his story and switching the screen back to actual forward mode. We were going Max deep space drive since leaving the little Pheren galaxy, maintaining deceive mode until we were into Alliance territory.

"I think you did a super job of saving Yodgar's life and wiping out the Tayhest," I answered almost thoughtfully, yawning as I finished.

"You don't sound to happy, Jim." Merlin was getting good at reading me too.

"Don't pay any attention to me, I'm just tired and grumpy."

"Why, did I do something wrong?"

"No, I'm just homesick. I'm not mad at you, really."

"Angry."

"No, damn it," I grumped and then realized I had said the wrong word. "Yes, no, OK, I am not mad nor angry at Merlin."

"Then what?" God, he could pry the lid off an old paint can.

"I'm jealous, if you must know; you had all the fun while I was getting electrocuted and thrown around by angry Tayhest . . . and marooned on a strange planet with a silicon creature who was temporarily insane."

"Mad."

"What?"

"Tayhest get mad not angry," joked Merlin. He laughed at his own joke, and his laugh made me laugh too.

"Yeah, I guess you're right there." My jealousy seemed to melt away. I yawned again and started to close my eyes.

"I wonder what will happen when the Tayhest go looking for their missing comrades; think they will?" He apparently wanted to yak.

"I don't know, Merlin, they may not want to go back there once they find out it is the Pheren who occupy that little galaxy. I thought at first that they were looking for me, but now I really think they were looking for their missing ship."

"You may be right. Yodgar told me that was only a spy ship, which put down on their planet; that's why they didn't have any weapons on them."

"And I thought it was their ego, when they came off the ship unarmed." That Disorganizer was Pheren then. It wasn't a Zalo.

"No, Yodgar said that they are not given weapons unless they are sent on an attack mission."

"You mean they don't trust their warriors with weapons?" That was crazy, crazy enough to be true.

"Yup," replied Merlin.

"All must not be right in Tayhest land," I commented.

"That is an excellent conclusion, which has not gone unnoticed by the Pheren either."

He had picked old Yodgar's brain, that was for sure. Way to go, Merlin

I sat back in my chair, digesting the conversation, wondering what the Pheren knew about the Alliance, probably things I didn't know, yet.

"So," I said, settling back into the chair and dimming the interior lights ever so slightly, "do we know where we're going? In this case, do we know which way is home?"

"Yup," slanged Merlin, "I didn't tell you earlier, but I ran into a silicon creature and had an interesting conversation with him."

"Oh really." Merlin had a bad habit of doing that, something I had to cure him of real soon. Loose ships sink lips, I thought, in this case, mine. I chuckled to myself.

"Yes, he was able to feed my computer the coordinates I needed to get us home."

"Oh really?" If that was all he fed him, I'll be surprised.

"He also told me where I could find you; I believe he called himself . . ."

"Pracon," I finished. "So you just happened to run into him, in deep space, stopped to chat, then stopped on your way to get me and destroyed six Tayhest battle wagons?"

"Yes, that about covers it."

"Why didn't you pick me up first, before you went after the Tayhest?"

"I was headed for the planet with the toxic curtain when I saw the Pheren ship break through the curtain."

"And you figured I was on it?"

"Of course, but I lost him right away, deceive mode, you know."

"Yeah, go on . . ." Maybe I should put on my boots; it was getting deep in here.

"So I figured he might be headed back to the other planet, and sure enough, when I got there, he was already surrounded by the Tayhest, well, you know the rest."

"Yes, in detail, thank you"—I yawned—"but tell me, what else did Pracon tell you?"

"He really showed me very little about himself, which was fine with me; his memory is very powerful and not real pleasant if you know what I mean."

"I do," remembering my first encounter with old Pracon.

"He also loaded the computer with some very interesting information."

"Like what, Holmes?"

"Everything that's in the computers at the school."

"No fucking shit." Merlin's computer probably had more information in it about the Pheren than the Alliance would ever have access to, or could ever find out.

"Yes, fucking shit," answered Merlin. "I now have the most complete map of the universe anyone has ever not seen." He sounded very proud of himself.

"I'll bet you do," I commented, "and even though I want to see it, I don't want you to ever tell anyone that you have that kind of information; it will shorten your life cycle considerably."

"Oh, I won't, Jim, you have my word."

"Good, now show me the way home."

"On screen, old buddy."

"Don't call me that." I was still a little crabby.

"Sorry."

"No problem."

He was right; he had one helluva map stored in his computer. The upside of it was that it would probably save our asses someday. The downside of it was that we were so fucking far from home, so incredibly far from home, that the screen could not project the whole route at one time, only pieces, each piece being millions of light years long. We argued about why it was going to take so long to get home, when it took such a short time to get here, until I finally got a headache and Merlin put me to bed. I slept like a dead person; I don't even remember dreaming. Knowing how long we had to travel made me tired just thinking about it, and the problems we had to overcome in order to get home had given me the headache. Needless to say, but I will, when I awoke, I knew I had plenty of time to kill and very little to kill it with. I couldn't use any excess energy like accessing the computer, showering, or using the interior lights. Because, and here was the bigger problem, unlike TV spaceships, Merlin used a set amount of fuel while cruising in Deep Space drive. We would eventually have to refuel somewhere if we continued very much longer in this drive; only if we went into Time drive, then we could collect enough energy from the universe around us. Unfortunately, in Time drive, we would be traceable; we would have no deceive mode to hide us from the bad guys, who could be waiting for us to do just that so they could attack us, destroy us, or send us skidding through time again. We were safe in DS drive, but it would take us over a year to get home, or longer, even if we did have the fuel, which we did not. Not only that, but by the time we did get home, I would only be a year older compared to, say, Joan, who would be a hundred and four, give or take ten years. I could almost feel my brain short-circuiting as I tried to understand the distance and time concepts involved in traveling almost from one end of the universe to the other. To sum up my mood about all this, don't ask!

It became a real thrill to make my one meal of the day. Merlin would turn on the lights, and I would make a plateful of nutritious but totally disgusting gray matter. We would talk for a while as I ate at the table, and then the lights would go out again, and I would return to my chair and sit in the dark. I felt like a fucking mole.

Even the screen was blank to conserve energy. We had decided to run for a solid week, ten thousand and eighty minutes, I forget how many pics, with absolutely no extra energy being used. I stunk as bad as the toilet, which we weren't turning on either. The floor around my chair was littered with fingernails and skin that I had picked off my hands the first couple of days of boredom, and my new beard was driving me crazy. I felt like I was losing my mind; while sleeping, I dreamed I was awake, and when I was awake, I felt like I was sleeping.

Suddenly the lights came on; it hurt my eyes, and I squinted at the chair controls, waiting to hear Merlin announce it was mealtime again. It didn't seem like it should be though; I hadn't shit yet, and I always did that just before every mealtime. Plus I really wasn't hungry yet; my appetite was zero after eating gray shit for this long. Hell, my tunic was getting looser every day. I tried to stand up and almost fell over; my balance was even screwed up after sitting in the dark so long.

"Whatsamatter," I mumbled. It occurred to me that I had been mumbling something to myself already.

"It's time." Even Merlin sounded a bit sluggish.

"Huh? Time for what? What was it time for, more time?" I blubbered.

"It's time, seven days have elapsed. Now we must decide what to do."

"Really?" I could have cried; I was so happy.

"No shit, Sherlock," replied Merlin. He was as glad as I was that it was over. He was probably sick of hearing me sing and talk to myself too. I know I was.

"Any company?" I shook my head, trying to clear it.

"No, I turned on my sensors about an hour ago, nothing."

"How far are we from the Aktagara galaxy?"

"You don't want to know."

"Yes, I do."

"Not far."

"How fucking not far?"

"Half a fucking million light years not far."

"Only a hundred and fifty thousand parsecs, Jesus Christ, why did we torture ourselves for a fucking week, goddamn, shit and piss"—I stopped swearing and tried to imagine what the hell we were thinking when we decided to do this—"so we've gone about the same distance we could've gone in two hours using Time drive?"

"Yup. And we're still alive too, in case you've forgotten."

"How far is it to that damn plasma cloud?" I said, remembering part of our plan was to fuel up without going off course too much. I ignored his remark too.

"An hour in Time drive."

"Good, let's do it," I said, flipping off the screen. I didn't need to watch the damn thing twist and turn in T drive. I was about to head for the shower when it occurred to me to sit and watch the aft view, so I sat back down and flipped on the rear view as Merlin powered into T drive. It gave me a headache, but I watched it.

A half an hour later, Merlin woke me up. "Jim, wake up and take a shower."

The screen behind us was filled with a bright glowing light, which I discovered were all around us when I flipped the screen forward. "Plasma cloud?"

"Yes, very rich in fuel too. I've been through it once already."

"How can that be, I only just fell asleep."

"Well, we got lucky, I found a small anomy, and it brought us here quicker."

"A what?"

"An anomy, a deep space anomy, a black spot in the universe."

"Don't they call them wormholes?"

"Maybe on your planet, anomies don't worm at all, in fact, they really only have one dimension, time," corrected Professor Merlin.

"So, Professor, this black spot, you knew it would bring us here quicker?"

"Well, I was hoping it would; I analyzed its size and apparent direction and decided it was worth the risk." He didn't sound too sure of himself.

"I'm sure you took a chance without asking me," I huffed, "but I'm not sure that you're too sure of what you did, so before you give me a headache explaining it all to me, I'm going to take a shower and flush the damn toilet; please synthesize me a big juicy steak and a tall glass of something cold."

"Aye, aye, Chieffy," replied Merlin. He sounded relieved that I wasn't going to grill him about the anomy.

"And don't call me that!" I shouted as I walked into the bathroom. No laser shower has ever felt better to me than that one. Likewise, no steak has ever tasted better nor any drink more refreshing, well, maybe Chaga brew, but that's the exception. The synthetic potato blew, but it was a nice touch on Merlin's part, old Mr. Suckup. He even let me drive most of the way to the edge of the Alliance territory. It took us another five fucking days, and that's five days in full-blown, wide-open Time drive to get there. It was almost like coming home. The screen map actually had galaxies on it that I recognized, but I wasn't up for sightseeing, so we kept on going right through the main shipping lanes and space stops until the Milky Way came into view, and we pulled out of T drive so I could identify myself and let everyone whom I considered a friend know I was back in town. I had hoped to make this a quick "Hi, I'm back, call me if you need me"; I couldn't wait to see good old Parkersburg and everyone in it. The nearest galaxy to us, even though the Milky Way was straight ahead so to speak, was the Temon Gavol star cluster, home of the Zellen and half a dozen other races. I was hoping I would run into Inrew, a Zellen Guardian I knew from the meeting, and do some catching up.

We had sat impatiently for about two hours. I could raise no one on the screen, nor could Merlin spot anyone with his sensors. It was creepy. Even in this area, we should have made contact with someone by now.

"Do you think it's the directive from Phayton and the Council that is keeping them from answering us?" asked Merlin.

"I don't know, it seems way too quiet." I barely finished saying that when Merlin's alert system suddenly came to life.

"Company?" Maybe it was a welcoming committee.

"Yes, coming fast behind us, three maybe more . . ." He turned the screen aft.

"Let's not waste a second, go to deceive and give me a positive Z of fifty thousand miles," I interrupted. I didn't like the looks of the aft screen; it was no welcoming committee. And even though they were still too far behind us to identify, I wasn't taking any more chances at this point. I felt us rising straight up and the slight Ferris wheel sensation as we pulled to a stop. Merlin had been quick about it. I centered the screen on the sensor activity and watched as the ships came into range. I was pretty sure they hadn't seen us because ever since Merlin had begun using the crystal, all his systems seemed amplified. Plus they hadn't changed course nor slowed down from a high-speed Deep Space drive.

"Identity?" I already sensed the answer.

"Tayhest Battle wagons, five total, no seven, running in a diamond formation."

"Plot a parallel course and stay up with them, come on, let's move it."

"Why don't I just blast them as they pass us, Jim?" He was already following my instructions. Even as they passed under us, we were already matching their speed.

"Because then we wouldn't know where they are headed, would we?" I answered him nicely; he deserved an answer after following instructions so quickly.

"True, they don't seem to be out for a Saturday drive."

"Sunday, close though."

"Thanks so much, shall we eavesdrop while we follow?"

"Oh do, please do," I laughed; he could say things with the funniest of accents sometimes; in this case, he was either Chip or Dale or some other chipmunk. Maybe Alvin.

We listened in as we cruised directly above them, discovering several interesting tidbits. First, they have awful communication equipment; second, there had been a battle, while we were lost in Pheren land, near the Kommonsolltyr galaxy, and the Alliance had come out a little ahead, though both sides had lost ships; and third, that's where they were now headed, hopefully to surprise what was left of the Alliance.

"Think they have the new fabric?" I asked reluctantly.

"Yup," said Merlin. He liked that word a lot.

"Christ, they're not even running in deceive mode; they don't even care whether or not they are detected. How long until we get to the battle coordinates?"

"We'll never get there; a Mothership has just transmitted a coded message to someone, to clear an area in front of us, up ahead. Whatever they have planned for these guys, I don't think we want to be part of it."

"Show me where, Merlin."

"Here," said Merlin, activating the screen map.

"The Jenn Dar Gamma; that's where we found out the Tayhest were stealing Silmarrite with the help of the Lussecans."

"Yup."

"What do you think they have planned?" I didn't have a single clue.

"I don't know; shall we open up the gap between us a little and tag along?"

"Good idea, Chip." Again he mimicked a chipmunk.

"I think so too."

Maybe we were suffering from space funk, I don't know, but it sure makes you giggle like hell once you get started, and we got started.

"Is it the same Mothership they used for the meeting?" I finally asked, trying to get serious. My face hurt from laughing.

"I don't think so, my sensors are picking up a large presence near the Jenn Dar Gamma, but not near as big as *Alpha One*; also, this one is running in deceive mode."

"Then how do you know where it is?" He had me confused now.

"The Bathor crystal seems to be having a very positive effect on my sensors, more and more."

"You had better keep an eye on its affections," I advised him, though secretly I was thrilled to be able to overcome other ship's deceive mode.

"So do you want to see it?" Merlin spoke quietly.

"Yes."

Merlin activated the screen amplification for the area almost in front of us, although many light years ahead of us yet, and I could make out the outline of a huge round ship.

"Why am I seeing only the outline of it?" It looked to me like you could see right through the middle of it.

"Well, I hate to bring this up, but it looks to me like an anomy is right in front of it."

"A black hole? How could a black hole be right in front of it?"

"I can only surmise that they put it there."

"That's pretty neat, a secret weapon?" I was beginning to wonder if we had been caught in it once already; maybe we ran into an anomy that had been put there on purpose. Maybe we weren't attacked after all.

"I can't tell if it's natural or not, but if it's not, then it's a helluva secret weapon. I'm going to open us up a little farther so we don't get caught in it with the Tayhest." He had gotten real serious now, no more Alvin the Chipmunk.

"That's nice. I've had just about all the anomies I can stand for one lifetime." I agreed, although somehow I didn't think I was correct in my predictions.

We separated ourselves even farther from the Tayhest ships as we flew closer and closer to the Mothership and the anomy. We concluded that the ship was controlling the anomy since it moved with the ship as the ship corrected its position, staying directly in front of the Tayhest. The Tayhest had no idea it was there and continued to head straight at it, neither slowing nor changing direction. When they finally came in contact with it, it was sort of an anti-TV climax—nothing happened, and they just disappeared. Gone, vanished. Then the anomy disappeared too. The Mothership came out of deceive mode, and several ships that must have been in it or behind it appeared on the screen. Merlin brought us to a stop, and I flipped on the communication monitors and sent out a greeting.

Remembering we were in deceive mode, I also switched it off too. Immediately, the screen was filled with the face of a wrinkled-up old green Zellen, who had all the pleasantness of a person who gets woken up in the middle of the night. I knew most Zellens had the personality of a cold piece of shit, so I didn't let it bother me.

"We have you on our screens, please identify yourself," spoke the green dude. A person of few words and little warmth.

"Nice to see you too," I shot back at him. "This is Jim Edwards from the Milky Way galaxy, planet Earth."

"Who is your immediate superior officer?" he asked impatiently.

"Crouthhamel of Altair," I answered smiling. If he knew him, he certainly didn't react like he knew him. By the way, Zellens make excellent poker players when it comes to facial expressions, but they can't bluff worth a shit.

"Please hold your position," he said. The screen went blank.

"I don't like the feeling I'm getting," I said to Merlin, "and I don't like to hold."

"What do you mean? He's just following procedures."

"I don't like procedures, either; that's why I never joined the army." Vietnam was a better reason, but I didn't want to get into that at the moment.

Suddenly the screen lit up, and I was looking at Inrew's smiling face; the background was the interior of a ship, so I knew he must be in one of the ships circling the Mothership. Maybe now I could get some news.

"Jim, where have you been and why are you here?" he asked.

He looked happy enough to see me, but his questions were rather rehearsed as if someone had fed him the questions first. My neck hairs raised slightly in alarm.

"Well, Inrew, I've been to the other side of the universe, not by my choice, and on the way back, I spotted the Tayhest ships that just disappeared near that Mothership. I was following them to see where they were headed and what they were up to, but I'm really on my way back home for some rest and relaxation. How's it hanging?" I had taught that greeting to several Guardians.

"Good." He smiled and relaxed. "Did you hear about the battle at Jenn Dar?"

"Only what I could hear from listening to the Tayhest; how many ships did we lose?" He did seem more relaxed; these must be his own questions.

"Only a few, right at the start, because of that new fabric, then we got some help from the Chagas coming from *Alpha One* with artificial crystal weapons on their ships and that turned the tide—"

"Anybody I know get hurt?" I cut in. I hated to interrupt someone in midbabble, but I had to know.

"I don't think so; it was mostly Guardians from the Kommonsolltyr and Chaga galaxies, oh, did you know Palph, the Utholok?" He seemed to be listening to someone beside him, who was not visible to me.

"Yeah, did he get wasted?" I frowned. I liked him. Ugly sucker, but a real friendly guy who drank like a fish, probably was one, come to think of it.

Inrew only had time to nod when the screen flipped back to the Zellen from the Mothership, apparently overriding my conversation with Inrew's ship.

"You have been ordered to dock at Bay 72, follow the traffic sensor, you will be met by—"

"Why?" I interrupted. I knew something was up, and I didn't like it.

He looked flustered that he wasn't able to finish his speech. "It is an order," he stammered, trying to regain his haughtiness.

"From who?" I shot back. I could tell from his reaction that he could not or did not want to tell me, and I wasn't about to spend another minute away from Earth. My bad temper began to claw its way out of its subconscious cage.

"You will proceed to Bay 72, without further delay," he snapped.

The screen went blank, so I rang him up again, and before he could answer me, I gave him a message to tell his superior. "Fuck you, and the fucking cocksucker you work for, I only take orders from Crouthhamel." He looked like he was going to faint. I snapped off the screen and, without a word to Merlin, put us in deceive mode and headed us backward in DS Drive. Maximum drive, I might add.

"Jim," said Inrew, coming on screen, "you must report at once." He looked worried for me. Now he would see the bad side of me.

"Inrew, I'm bitchin' tired and I don't want to be fucked around with anymore. I'm tired of being dicked around by Phayton and his bunch of cronies. Tell them, if they want me, to come to Earth after me, because that's where I'll be." I smiled and flipped the screen to space view and left a puzzled Inrew behind me.

I must have caught them by surprise because no one came after me. Good thing for them, I was in no mood for any bullshit. We traveled all the way to the Milky Way before anyone communicated with me, except Merlin, who seemed hurt. I didn't consult him before ramming us into DS Drive. But after I told him that I didn't want him to be any part of my insubordination, he understood and even thanked me, which then had me worried. I was so tired though that I really didn't care if they fired me as a fucking Guardian. I was going home and that was that. I was asleep when Merlin woke me to say we had a message coming on screen. He boosted my chair and waited for me. Good man. Or whatever.

"Where are we?" I said, shaking the sleep from my eyes.

"Just entering the Milky Way, near the Seltorr system; do you want to take the message?"

"Sure, put it on screen." I didn't feel near as grumpy as I did earlier.

"Hello, Jim," said Crouthhamel, sitting in his ship, looking far more refreshed than I.

"Hi, Crouthhamel, how's it hanging?" My customary salutation when it came to superior officers, by the way.

"More importantly," he answered, "how are you hanging?"

"I'll be better when I get home and walk on solid ground, no offense, Merlin," I returned.

"None taken," said Merlin.

"What happened to you when you left the meeting? Where did you go?" He didn't look angry nor did he act like the Zellens, so I told him, briefly, how I ended up in the Aktagara galaxy and then the Pheren territory. He seemed to understand, even looked indignant, when I told him that I thought Phayton had set me up.

"I can't believe he would do that!" he exclaimed.

"Believe it, boss," I retorted. "I ought to stop off at the Jurda system and shove that claw up his ass sideways." Damn, this whole thing was making me angry again.

He smiled. "I think you had better just go straight home until I can figure out how to clear you of the trouble you've gotten into now."

"For what?" I screamed, "for not docking at Bay 72? After what they put me through?"

He nodded. "That was a direct order from Smorr, the Councilman from Anadac, and you saw a new weapon being tested."

"Smorr?" I laughed; I wondered if he knew what his name meant on Earth.

Crouthhamel nodded.

"Whoopee shit," I replied, "they know who I am, shit, have they forgotten who the hell is flying their new prototype or is Merlin old news?" I exhaled.

He nodded.

"Anyways, do you know what it is?" I hoped he caught the irony behind my question. He smiled; he caught it.

"No, and I don't want to know. It's only a giant experiment at this point; they don't even know if it works." He was talking by rote now.

"Really, well, don't ask the seven Tayhest ships that ran into it because you can't, they're gone." I gave him a smug smile. I can argue; Joan taught me well.

He gave me the old "I'm getting a headache" look, and I knew he was almost done talking to me. I smiled back at him.

"Look, just go home and get some rest, after I straighten things out for you with the Council. I'll come see you, and you can tell me all about your run-in with the Maglarr."

"Pheren." Calling them Maglarr was like calling a black person a "nigger."

"Right," replied Crouthhamel, "I'll see you again on Earth; now get going."

"Aye, Aye, Mon Capeeton," I said with a French accent; I gave him a salute, and the screen went dead, or rather back to the view of the Milky Way. I sat back into the chair and placed my hands behind my head.

"Home James," I commanded, happily.

"You mean, Home Merlin," he replied, "or am I just the worn-out prototype?"

"Right, old buddy, old pal, full steam ahead." He had been listening.

"Aye, Aye, Mon Capeeton," joked Merlin, with a very nice Parisian accent.

"I do believe," I said rising from my chair, "that this calls for a brew."

"I couldn't agree more," said Merlin. "Have one for me too."

The rest of the trip lasted about an hour; we had not come into the Milky Way from the end, but rather the middle, so we didn't have far to go once we passed the Darassin system. We passed the Altairian system and several others, but I didn't want to stop or even communicate with them; all I wanted to do was go home. Plus, we weren't supposed to use our communication equipment any more than necessary, and since I was already in hot water, I decided not to attract any more attention. By running in deceive mode, nobody knew I even went by, although I'm sure Crouthhamel told everybody I was back. He had been happy to see me, even though he didn't show it. I was his returning "problem child"; that was the look he had given me when the screen had first come on, almost the same look my father used to give me—I knew that one by heart. Hell, today I even felt like a "problem child."

"Do you want me to take us through the Oort cloud," he said as we approached the debris surrounding the solar system, "or do you want to blast your way through it like you normally do?"

"No, you can take us through, just don't take too long, OK?" I had to stop doing that; it might attract attention from the planet. We popped through the cloud and slowed as we passed the outer planets—two of them are still a mystery on Earth—to just over plasma speed until we came to Earth and looped it a couple of times.

"Happy?" asked Merlin, sensing my mood had improved.

"You bet, you bet," I murmured, enjoying the view of the continents and oceans as we completed a second loop, "so let's find Parkersburg."

"My pleasure, Jimbo," replied Merlin, dropping into the atmosphere and matching the velocity of the air. "OOPS, sorry, Jim."

"Forgotten already," I replied, thinking of Joan, well, OK, Joan's body.

With a little work and a lotta luck, I pinpointed Parkersburg on the viewer screen, foregoing the gradual enlarging of the continent, and magnified the screen until I could see my front yard. My heart stopped. There was Joan and Wolf, apparently in the middle of a Frisbee game. I was magnifying the screen to see if I could see down the front of Joan's halter top when I saw her stop and straighten up, looking toward something by the road. I adjusted the screen and saw a carload of rednecks that must have seen her and pulled over to yell something foul at her. Immediately, my blood pressure shot up.

"How close are we?" I grimaced.

"About a hundred miles or so, why?" Merlin knew something was wrong.

"Joan's in the front yard and some assholes are hassling her."

"Won't the subspecies, Wolf, protect her?"

"Yeah, probably," I muttered. I brought the screen back until I could see the whole scene and noticed that three of the rednecks had gotten out of the car. Wolf was standing his ground and holding them back in the field by their battered-up old car.

"Good boy," I said. I could almost hear his snarl. He could be a badass dog.

"Ten miles," Merlin announced.

Suddenly, one of them pulled a rifle out of the car and pointed it at Wolf.

"Fucking asshole!" I yelled. I looked down at my chair arm's weapons.

"I see it," replied Merlin. He was quicker than I was, probably a good thing.

At two, maybe three miles away, Merlin's aim was perfect. He let go a short blast from the forward particle beam, and I watched as the rifle turned white-hot in the hands of the redneck, who dropped it, screaming in pain, and then stood there frozen in fear.

"Shall I disorganize him?" asked Merlin, clearly enjoying himself.

"No," I answered quickly, "Joan hates violence. Let's just fuck with their minds. Project the image of several angry Tayhest warriors all around them on the front lawn." God, this was really going to be fun; I loved this shit.

"Oh yeah, that'll make'um shit," agreed Merlin.

By now, we were hovering about ten yards above Joan and Wolf, who seemed to sense we were there. The Hogan projector quickly sent the requested projections to the ground in front of the startled redneck and his two buddies. The driver, who had not gotten out of his car, was so frightened that he screeched the tires as he pulled out, almost smashing into the side of a loaded coal truck and leaving his buddies behind. The look on their faces said it all.

"Get off my land!" I screamed through the exterior speakers on the ship. The Zalo concert-level sound system almost knocked the hurt one to the ground. The other two took off running after their ride, one of them clearly wet from pissing down his legs. The hurt one, hands bleeding from the sizzling weapon at his feet, turned and followed his buddies, not looking back for fear the Tayhest images were chasing him. I turned off the Hogan and spoke through the speakers real softly.

"Nice tits."

Joan watched the images disappear and looked around for me. The sight of the rednecks, running out of sight up the road, had made her laugh.

"I know you're here!" she yelled. Wolf was jumping up and down after hearing my voice. "So you better not play any more games, or else!"

"Or else, what?" I said, coming down the visible hatch ramp right behind her. She turned, and I scooped her up into my arms. I never dreamt it would feel so fucking good to hold her, almost indescribable if you know what I mean.

Of course, I had to give Wolf a big hug too, but I didn't kiss him. I could have held her in my arms forever, but the hatch was still open, and Merlin couldn't close it because we were still standing on it.

"Jim." No chip and Dale around Joan.

"Oh, sorry," I said, stepping off the hatch steps. The hatch closed and disappeared. But not before Wolf jumped on it, trying to get at me.

"That is so cool," said Joan. "How do you make your ship disappear like that?"

"It's difficult to explain," I bullshitted. "Hey, where's Wolf?"

"Getting the tour." Merlin sounded a bit worried.

"Don't worry, he's trained." I laughed and enjoyed the sound of Joan laughing too. I had forgotten how much I missed everything, especially that sound.

The hatch came down slowly, and Wolf jumped off it before it was completely down and into my arms. He looked a little shook. Just as the hatch went back up, into the driveway pulled Rick with his wife, Samantha. He looked like he'd seen a ghost. I waved at him, and he broke into a huge smile and waved back. He stopped the car—his pride and joy, a Porsche 911—and jumped out.

"Jim!" he yelled, walking quickly over to me, excited to see me and not trying too hard to escape one of my bear hugs. He doesn't like to show a lot of emotion.

"Rick," I said, holding him as he tried to escape; he hates emotional bullshit between men. Somehow he managed to return the hug. It was progress for him.

"We thought we'd never see you again," he began, looking me over and shaking his head. Joan and Samantha almost nodded in unison. That's when I noticed Joan's hair was longer, and she looked a little thinner too.

"Why?" I asked startled, then it occurred to me. "How long have I been gone?" I looked from Rick to Joan. They acted like I was suffering from a mental disorder.

"It's May; you've been gone two months," replied Joan softly. She acted like I was a patient in a mental ward.

"I wondered why it felt so warm and everything looked so summery."

"Didn't you know?" she asked.

"No," I said honestly, "I mean, I should have figured it out, what with all the traveling I've been doing, yeah, I can believe it, man, two months, hell, to me, it's only been a couple of weeks." I began counting days on my fingers, and Joan reached over and grabbed my hands.

"It doesn't matter, Jim," she comforted me. "What matters is that your back now; you are back for a while, aren't you?" She had a tone in her voice that meant trouble if I answered wrong. Thank God I had the right answer.

"Oh yeah," I said quickly, "after the trouble I've gotten myself into, I may be done being a Guardian." I tried the innocent look.

"What could you have possibly done wrong?" Rick laughed. He knew me pretty good. I laughed, and it made Joan laugh. Samantha gave us all a left-out look, and Rick turned to her to explain.

"He's a Guardian," he began, looking over at me for my nod, which I gave him, "and his job is to guard our solar system."

Samantha laughed. She knew we were big bullshitters sometimes, and she figured this was one of those times. She was a thin; hell, a skinny yet pretty blond, but her laugh must have been borrowed from her father. It was a real hearty laugh for a person like her. It always made other people laugh when they heard her. She noticed we weren't laughing and quickly stopped.

"You have got to be kidding," she said, searching our faces for that telltale smile you give someone to let them know they've just been bullshitted. None of us gave it to her.

"OK, guys, where is your ship, Jim?" She thought she had me.

"Merlin," I said to her.

Nothing.

"Merlin!"

"Sorry, Jim, I was watching a special on HBO; what can I do for you?" His voice came from over our heads; and Samantha, Rick, Joan, and Wolf all looked upward at the source.

"HBO?"

"Yeah, there's nothing on regular television."

I laughed and shook my head. "Why don't you turn off the D-mode for just a split second or two, if the coast is clear, and show us what you look like, please."

"His ship talks?" said Samantha to Rick. He nodded but wouldn't look at her. He wanted to see Merlin again.

"OK," said Merlin. Suddenly he appeared over us. As close as he was, all you really could see was his underside, but it was very impressive nonetheless. His silver and black design was both alien and a bit frightening. His rear still had the burn mark from the antimatter balls, but only a small portion showed underneath. Then he disappeared again.

Samantha looked like she was going to faint. Rick grabbed her by the arm to steady her, but she recovered quickly.

"Oh my god," she murmured. She looked at me like I was an alien. Rick should have told her or rather could have told her, but he kept a secret better than anyone I ever met, with no exceptions. Sometimes it drove me nuts too.

"Let's all go in the house," suggested Joan wisely. "I think we could all use a cold drink."

I know I was up for it. I smiled and grabbed her to me. Hopefully Rick and Samantha wouldn't stay long; I could feel Mr. Happy start to come alive.

"Can I come too?" sassed Merlin.

"I don't think the door's big enough, smartass," I returned.

"Wait a minute, Jim," said Rick, "you're forgetting, it's been a while since you and I talked, remember what you asked me to check into?"

I couldn't remember; my head was so full of spaceshit that I'm surprised I could remember my own name. "No," I began, "we talked about production figures, and our next project, the Pritchard lease, and—"

"Right," cut in Rick, "and I sank a shale well on it"—he continued as we walked toward the house—"which turned out to be one of the best gas wells we ever drilled. It came in at five million cubic feet a day and is still doing well over a million."

"That's great!" I exclaimed, wondering where this was headed.

"So I took some of your profits and fixed up your garage like we had talked about, remember?"

"Yeah, OK," I said, finally remembering, "a big parking space for Merlin, so he can shut down when he needs too." We had almost walked to the front of my garage, which, when I had built the house, had been made large enough for three vehicles—a car, a truck, and a place to repair a truck, because one or the other was always broke down or in need of something done to it.

I had put a two-door garage door on it, and as I stood there now, I noticed that the door looked larger than the one that I remembered installing. So much for being observant; I blame it on space lag.

"Watch this," said Rick proudly, fingering a remote that he must have been pocketing up until then.

I turned around and noticed Joan and Samantha had disappeared into the house. But Wolf was still at my side, slobbering up at me, begging for attention. I rubbed his back as I looked over at Rick and followed his line of sight to the garage.

"I had three speeds put into the opener," he explained as the giant door swung slowly downward. "This is the slowest," he said again, showing me the controller and its buttons. "But don't use the high-speed button unless it's an emergency. The door will probably never come back up!"

I laughed, and he didn't. He was into it; there was no stopping him.

"Fast huh?" I commented.

"Fucking fast, I had a special motor put in, just in case you were in a hurry." He laughed then. By now, the door was fully horizontal on the driveway, and the front of the garage wall above the door began splitting into pie pieces, until they were completely apart, like spreading your fingers. It created a huge opening for Merlin.

"The hydraulics came off a dozer-blade assembly and part of a backhoe. We had to move the right wall a bit and raise the front of the garage without making it noticeable from the road," continued Rick proudly, obviously enjoying himself, "but the fun part was extending the back of the garage into the hillside." He looked way too pleased with himself, and I smiled gratefully at him. Then it hit me.

"You dug out the hillside?" The basement of my house and back garage wall were built into the side of the hill. That was pretty common in West Virginia.

"Had too," countered Rick, seeing the look of dollar signs on my face. "I had to guess at the size of your ship, remember, I only saw Merlin once, and I didn't want to do all this and be on the short end. We had to put steel beams into the roof also because we layered the ceiling with lead like you wanted done."

"Holy shit!" I exclaimed, walking into the garage. It was thirty yards deep and ten yards high, probably higher in the middle. It looked like it was almost the same width as it was high. Now I noticed that the front wall next to the door had swung open too. It was big enough all right. Merlin was only fifty or so feet long and maybe twenty or so feet wide most of the time, unless we were traveling fast.

"Holy shit," I said again, turning to Rick, who was still standing at the doorway to my personal stadium.

"Like it?" he was puffed with pride like a new father.

"It's fantastic!" I exclaimed. I certainly got what I had asked for and then some.

"Good, here, this controller is yours." He handed me the remote and waited for me to ask something.

Then it dawned on me. "Where are my trucks and my Trans Am?"

"At my house, I'll bring the Am over later or tomorrow. My neighbor thinks I'm opening a used-car lot." He knew I still hadn't asked the question and waited patiently for me too. He watched me look around, and then I turned back.

"How much?" There, I had said it. It didn't hurt as much as I thought it would.

"You don't want to know."

Merlin's laughter boomed behind us. "It doesn't matter, 'cause I'm worth it!"

"Yes, I do." I didn't, but I did. Merlin continued to snicker. "Shut up, Merlin."

"Nah, Merlin's right," argued Rick, "so let's go join the ladies. I'm parched."

He guided me toward the door that led to a summer porch that I had built between the garage and house. It was the only part of the garage that was original. I opened it, and it felt very solid and heavy. So much for original.

"Steel?" I asked.

"Lead lined too," he answered nodding.

I had told him that lead was a great way to prevent unwanted guests from seeing into the room with scanning equipment. Plus it was the only thing on Earth to work with, except copper maybe.

"Did you use any copper?" I shouldn't have asked.

"Some," he replied, thinking, "in the ceiling and front door."

We had reached the door leading into the porch, and I noticed Wolf was getting worked up over something. I forgot to ask Rick how much was "some" copper when I noticed the door and walls were closing by themselves, yet the remote was in my hand, and I hadn't pushed any buttons.

"What the hell?" I said, bewildered. I looked at Rick. Then I knew who did it.

"How's the room, Merlin."

"Great, may I shutdown now?" Like he had to ask.

Rick looked like a kid at Christmas, seeing his toys for the first time, or Merlin.

"Sure, knock yourself out." Like I had to give my OK.

As the door and walls came to a close, Merlin turned off his deceive mode and settled down onto the floor with a gentle smoothness that belied his mass.

"Special floor too," said Rick, "almost two feet thick with steel-reinforced rods. I didn't know how much Merlin weighed either."

"Am I broke yet?" I was joking, but I studied his face for a serious reply. All this work must have cost thousands of buckaroos.

"You don't want to know."

"Yes, I do." This time I was serious, yet I liked seeing Merlin at rest.

"Let's just say, you're close." Then he laughed at my serious look.

"How close?" I asked. Just then the girls came out onto the porch.

"You don't . . . ," began Joan.

"I know, I know," I interrupted, "I don't want to know!"

Everyone laughed but me. Joan gave me a big hug and a peck on the cheek. We had been at the doorway when they joined us, and now we moved back into the dark garage, which Rick flooded with light from ceiling-mounted halogen beams. Samantha went over to Rick, and the two of them studied Merlin as he lay quietly on the floor. His black and silver colors were no longer pulsating, but he still looked frightening. Wolf had still not left my side but was no longer acting like he was going to piss himself. I grabbed Joan, and we joined Rick and Samantha.

"Where's the legs?" asked Samantha.

"I don't need them," answered Merlin, "besides, they might make holes in Jim's expensive floor." He laughed at his own joke.

"Oh," replied Samantha. She still wasn't used to the whole thing.

"You know," I said walking up to Merlin, "you look bigger in here than you did outside." It was true. Like a piece of furniture in a store that looks bigger when you get it home. He damn near filled up the room. He must be all engine 'cause he wasn't that big inside.

Wolf had crept closer to Merlin, wanting to sniff the huge object when Merlin let out a loud groan.

Wolf bolted through the open doorway, and Samantha jumped with a shocked look on her face. Rick only smiled and stood enthralled at the front of Merlin.

I laughed this time. Joan punched me in the arm. She hadn't jumped though; I made a note of that.

"I'm probably settling a bit, you know," he apologized. "The liquid molecules and all that. I haven't shut down since they made me on *Alpha One*, oops, sorry." He had a such a big mouth sometimes.

Wolf appeared a the doorway again; this time he looked even more worried, and I felt sorry for him, so I called him to me and began rubbing him behind the ears.

"What's a matter, boy? Don't let old Merlin scare you."

"Old Merlin?" said Merlin.

"It's a term of affection, don't let it bother you."

"It's not, we've got company." His voice went from light to dead fucking serious.

Suddenly all eyes went to me, puzzled eyes, frightened eyes.

I looked down at my weaponless belt and swore. The hatch was off limits.

"Who or what is it?" I asked, wondering if I should run for my rifle.

"A Guardian-class ship landed in your front yard, probably Crouthhamel coming to bust your ass," joked Merlin. He knew he couldn't open the hatch, rules.

Rick giggled. His giggle broke the tension.

"Don't worry, honey," soothed Joan. "I'll protect you."

"Who's Kraut whatever?" asked Samantha. She was halfway between totally frightened and nervously giggling when a voice from the doorway attracted our attention.

"Good idea, Jim," said Crouthhamel, looking around as he bent down to enter the room. His height seemed exaggerated in the confines of the garage.

Samantha fainted at the sight of the tall red warrior. In her defense, I will add that he was dressed to the teeth in Guardian silver and black. Wolf barked and hid behind me. Joan seemed to be shocked but still recovered quickly. Rick just stood there with his mouth open.

"What's a good idea," I said, helping Rick pick Samantha up off the floor. She felt like a deadweight ton. I noticed a bump appearing on her head. That was going to hurt.

"Here, let me help," said Crouthhamel, striding toward us.

Wolf began to growl and show some teeth finally.

"Silence, dog," commanded Crouthhamel. Wolf stopped immediately.

He crossed quickly to Samantha; his giant strides together with our surprise at seeing him left us all standing there dumbfounded. He reached to the back of his belt and withdrew a device I had seen before in a larger version. Rick's apprehension made him come alive, and he grabbed at Crouthhamel's arm as he brought the device toward Samantha's face as she lay cradled in Rick's other arm and mine.

"It's OK, Rick," I assured him, moving between Crouthhamel and Rick. "It's a Bonemender." I didn't need any kung fu shit from Rick right about now.

Crouthhamel looked at me with as much surprise as Rick.

"The Pheren," I said to Crouthhamel, "used it on my leg." I tapped my leg where the bone had broken through and smiled at him.

"What?" said Rick. He didn't recognize the Altairian dialect I spoke.

"It will repair any damage done by the fall," said Crouthhamel to him, using a soothing voice I had heard only once before. His tone seemed to work on Rick, who relaxed and allowed Crouthhamel to reach Samantha more easily.

Crouthhamel moved the device over Samantha's head, and she immediately started to wiggle her body parts; her eyes began to open, and I could feel her body come back to life from her unconsciousness, so I removed my hands from under her shoulders and stepped back to Joan and Wolf who had gathered behind me.

Now Bonemenders are like most all the other equipment out there in the universe. It didn't beep or have little lights on it, so you really couldn't tell if it was working, unlike the stuff we have on Earth with all our bells and buttons; but from Samantha's reaction to the device passing over her forehead, we could all see it was, in fact, working like a charm. I had questioned Crouthhamel once about the absence of switches, beeps, and lights, and his answer was frank and truthful.

He said earthlings need instant gratification all the time, no matter what we're doing, even when it isn't necessary—a fault, he said, he hoped we would outgrow someday. I hoped he would never see the toys I owned; I loved buttons and lights. I even had a thirty-two-speed blender in my kitchen. Oh baby.

Samantha had awoken from her faint and was clinging to Rick as she sat on the floor inspecting Crouthhamel's face up close. He must have put on his pleasant look because she finally smiled as he helped Rick pull her to her feet.

"This is my boss," I said, introducing him to everyone.

"Pleased to meet all of you," he said, turning from Rick and Samantha and looking at Joan, smiling the whole while, trying to put everyone at ease.

"She's quite lovely," he said, turning to me.

"What was a good idea?" I ignored the compliment but nodded anyway.

"This room, I couldn't raise you on the communicator."

So that's why he decided to reveal himself, I realized, this must be important.

"Rick had it built." I could tell Rick was digging on Crouthhamel.

"Nice work," said Crouthhamel, turning to Rick.

"Thanks." Rick sounded tongue-tied; who wouldn't be?

All of a sudden, we all seemed to run out of things to say, and an uncomfortable silence fell over the room.

"How about a cold drink?" I said to no one in particular, looking around at everyone. "Merlin."

Silence.

"Merlin!" He could be very stubborn, and he didn't learn it from me.

"Yes, Commander, what do you wish of your slave now?"

"Open the hatch and stop being so sarcastic." God, he was so bad.

"I'm trying to watch a movie." He sounded petulant now.

Even Crouthhamel laughed with everybody else at Merlin's reply. The hatch came down, and I went into Merlin to fetch one of my remaining tubs of Chaga brew.

"You know, you could show a little respect for me when Crouthhamel's around," I said to him while closing up a storage locker in the rear quarters. The tone in my voice was down right pissy.

"Sorry, it's a good movie."

"What is it, and can you say couch potato?"

"*Raiders of the Lost Ark*, and can you say good-bye?"

"Yeah," I said nodding as I walked down the hatch steps, "that is a great flick. I would have ignored me too."

"You have to try this," I said to my friends as I stepped toward the side door, almost falling over Wolf. I made a note to spend some time with him.

Joan caught my arm and helped me steady the tub, inspecting its strange construction as Rick, Samantha, and Crouthhamel followed us.

"It doesn't feel cold," she said to me. She was very observant as well as cute.

"It will be," I said, climbing the steps from the garage into the summer porch where I spent many an evening. I set the tub on a small table between two Adirondack chairs and went into the kitchen to grab a handful of mugs. Joan let Wolf out the door before he got stepped on and followed him outside. I entered the kitchen and opened the cabinet; I noticed all my glasses were clean, excellent. I had two sizes of glasses—mugs and shot glasses.

"Jim," said Rick, sticking his head into the kitchen. The urgency in his voice made me almost drop the mugs. I wondered if I had space lag or was just being clumsy, well, more clumsy than usual.

"What?" I replied, coming down the steps from the kitchen. I immediately smelled a burning smell and saw that Rick and Samantha had gone out on the front porch of the summer room and were gathered around Crouthhamel and Joan, who were bent over Wolf. I lowered the mugs into a chair and stepped through the screen door to the porch. I slipped around Rick and Samantha, which wasn't hard to do, they were both skinny, and found myself looking down at a very badly burned Wolf.

"What the fuck?" I exclaimed, kneeling down next to him. He was lying on his side, breathing weird and whining the most pathetic whine. His fur from under his chin clear down to his own Mr. Happy had been burned completely off, and in some places, his skin was blackened too.

"I just tossed him the Frisbee," began Joan, tears dripping from her onto Wolf as she looked up at me, "and there was a flash as he jumped up to catch it." She had a huge heart for any animal, let alone Wolf. Me too.

Crouthhamel was busy running the device I called the Bonemender over the really bad spots, peeling off the blackened skin and shaking his head in a way that I knew wasn't good.

"Shouldn't we get him to a vet?" asked Rick.

I didn't answer; I just stood there dumbfounded, watching pink skin appear where Crouthhamel's fingers moved. He was moving the mender so quickly you could hardly see his other hand.

"Jim," said Crouthhamel without looking up, "get a covering for him, he may go into shock."

Joan was on her feet before I could move, running into the house.

"Hold his mouth open," commanded Crouthhamel. He had stopped going over Wolf's stomach, which was now a healthy bright pink color, but the skin was so thin you could see the veins and body organs underneath. As he finished going over Wolf's chin, he motioned for me to open his mouth. The sight almost made me gag. Behind me, I could hear Samantha gagging, and I fought the feeling back as I inspected the shattered teeth inside. Crouthhamel carefully cleared the pieces from Wolf's throat and mouth and began running the mender around the gums. I noticed he was humming or something, almost talking to Wolf, as the bleeding subsided and the gums turned baby pink.

"What happened?" I asked. "Did he collide with the engine of your ship or something?" It didn't seem possible, but what else could it be?

"My ship isn't here," replied Crouthhamel in Tharx, without taking his eyes from Wolf. "It's circling in your ionosphere, collecting electrons."

Wolf began shivering. I looked up, and Joan was coming through the door with a blanket in hand. She tossed it to me, and I swept it over him as if we had practiced the maneuver a hundred times.

"How is he?" she asked, settling down on her legs and smoothing the blanket over Wolf's back.

"He'll live," said Crouthhamel, looking up at her, "but he's going to need some corrective surgery that will require a short trip . . ."

"To the Jurda system," I said in Tharx, finishing his sentence.

He turned and nodded to me. Joan's red eyes started dripping tears again, and I reached over to her with my free hand and wiped a tear from the cheek below her closest eye. "He'll be okay, baby," I mouthed, and I knew it.

Just then a bird swooped down into the yard from above us. I caught Crouthhamel's eye movement and followed his line of sight as the bird flew into the center of the yard. Suddenly there was a flash, and it was gone. A few feathers fluttered in the air, settling to the ground with a chilling finality. I heard Samantha gasp and saw the look on Rick's face. I turned back to Joan.

"Did you see that?" exclaimed Rick.

"Was that the bird?" asked Joan, looking at the feathers.

"Uh huh"—Samantha trembled—"I want to go home now," she said, turning to Rick. She was close to crying; she was so scared.

He looked at her and caught the nod I gave him out of the corner of his eye. I believe he would have loved to stay, but he gathered her to his side and walked toward his car, staying well away from the yard. I turned back to Crouthhamel. I wanted a fucking explanation, and I wanted it now. Joan caught the look on my face and looked to him also. She didn't appear to be scared, only confused like I was, and neither of us liked that feeling. And we both knew this was no accident. We all heard Rick's car start, and I turned and waved quickly.

"Well," I said, waiting.

"Well what," replied Crouthhamel. He looked suddenly very tired.

"What the hell is in my front yard? How did it get there, and who put it there?" I demanded. That pretty much covered all the bases.

He stood up and walked into the yard and stood facing the spot where the feathers lay. I motioned for Joan to stay with Wolf and joined him. The look on his face made the hair on my neck stand up. He almost looked frightened.

"It's a Black Nallie." That was all he said. He pulled up his ship's communicator and began to recall his ship.

"A Black Nallie?" I said it like a question, yet I still asked, "What the fuck is a Black Nallie?" I wondered if it was still there, and I picked up a rock from my imperfect yard and was about to toss it when he grabbed my arm and made me drop it.

"Don't, you'll only make it mad."

I was so shocked that I just stood there for a second, rolling his words around in my head.

"What is it doing here?" asked Crouthhamel.

He couldn't be talking to me, I thought, probably talking out loud to himself.

"Did it follow us?" The voice was Merlin's, coming from my wrist sensor.

"It is a possibility," answered Crouthhamel.

"Merlin," I queried, "perhaps you could enlighten me about this Black Nallie."

"It's actually called a Bleck Nall, but over the years the name has taken on a slight change," he began. "This is a very old creature, from a place far away from here."

Suddenly a thin stream of energy of some kind began to thread its way from Crouthhamel's invisible ship straight down to the invisible creature. When the energy reached the spot, a wiggling mass of black appeared. It looked like a floating black Jell-O, like Jell-O in a weightless environment, bulging and shrinking, turning blacker as we watched.

"What are you doing to it?" I asked. Destroying it, I hoped.

"Feeding it," replied Crouthhamel.

"What?" I exclaimed. Hell, I wanted to kill it for what it had done to Wolf. Yet part of me knew it was really not at fault. Now what?

"The Nallie is a creature, at least we think so, that survived the separation of matter into matter positive and matter negative," began Crouthhamel, trying to get me to settle down, "or as you would put it, back when the known universe was formed." He let that sink in and continued, "The Nallie became trapped in our matter positive universe, or I should say the Nallies since there used to be many of them long ago."

"What happened to them, and how can that one survive here with all this positive energy around it?" I had settled down, but now I had a few questions that needed answering.

"I don't know how this one is surviving; the rest of them perished when they came into contact with the positive matter in the universe, that's why I'm feeding this one antimatter from my ship's drive. If this one perishes, so do all of us and the planet we're standing on right now."

"No bullshit?" Only because of what I had seen in space could I believe him.

"No bullshit. I don't know how Wolf survived, except maybe, this thing somehow controlled the contact Wolf made with it."

I heard Joan gasp behind me and turned to her. She was holding Wolf's head and crying again. I walked back to her, leaving Crouthhamel to ponder Earth's dilemma, hoping to comfort both of them. It wasn't going to be easy; I needed a stiff drink or something myself. Time for an Altairian cigar, I thought.

"His eyes are gone," she sobbed to me as I settled next to her.

"It's OK, honey," I consoled her, "I'm going to get him new ones."

She looked at me, and I wiped the tears from her face and gave her a little kiss on her cheek. "You can do that?" she stammered.

I nodded and looked back at Crouthhamel. He was still pondering the situation.

"Merlin," I asked, "assuming this thing followed us back from the part of the universe where we were flung into, why do you think it followed us?"

"Maybe it wants something we have," he offered.

"Did you bring something back with you?" asked Joan. Man, her eyes were red and swollen from crying. I had only seen her like this once before when we had our first fight. I decided not to mention it.

"Not that I know of," I answered. "Just a couple kegs of Chaga brew and nothing else, honestly." She knew I had a habit of stealing hotel towels.

"Well, it seems to want something, and it doesn't appear that it's going to leave until it gets it."

I looked up at Crouthhamel as he said that. He looked truly worried.

"Can we communicate with it?" I asked; hell, he was the expert.

"I have no idea, I have never seen one of these Black Nallies before today. It seems to be holding its own with a dose of antimatter from my ship, but that won't last forever."

"Let me have Merlin take over for a while."

"That might not be a bad idea," replied Crouthhamel. "That way I can go aboard and try and reach Alzador; maybe he can shed some radiant energy on this."

Merlin already had the garage door swinging down as Crouthhamel finished saying that. I hoped he had listened to Rick explain the speed controls. I didn't need to buy another door right about now. Then the situation got worse.

All of a sudden, a state trooper car turned into the driveway, lights flashing, siren blaring. Wolf whined and jumped at the sound, at least his ears were working. I jumped to my feet, waving at the figure in the car to turn off his shit and recognized who it was behind the wheel. The car pulled to a stop in the driveway, and Carl Jarret climbed out, looking at the energy stream and the Black Nallie before walking over to us. Then he caught sight of Crouthhamel for the first time, and his eyes almost popped out of their sockets.

I could tell part of him wanted to draw his weapon.

"He's OK, Carl!" I yelled. This was all I needed.

He didn't relax, but he did continue to walk toward us, keeping an eye on the Nallie and Crouthhamel, all at the same time. It was almost funny. Then he spotted the garage splitting open and stopped dead in his tracks. He began walking again, partly I think, so he could get out of between all the action and close enough to Crouthhamel to put a bullet in him if he had too. He walked up to us and spotted the blanket-covered Wolf. His stone-cold eyes immediately turned soft with sympathy. "Wolf?" he asked. He was a good guy, but he liked simple things.

"Yeah, but he'll be OK," I answered. "How's the shoulder doing?"

"OK," he replied, automatically reaching up to rub it where the Bojj had shot him last time he was here.

He turned to Crouthhamel who was now between him and the Nallie.

"Who's he?" he asked in a policeman-like fashion.

"Oh, he's the devil; don't you recognize him?" I just couldn't resist it.

Crouthhamel looked over at me as if to say cut the shit, but I could just barely see a hint of amusement on his red face.

Carl looked totally confused; he couldn't tell if I was kidding or not, though I'm sure he knew I was or hoped I was anyways.

"What's that?" he said, pointing to the Nallie in the yard.

"You really want to know?" I asked. I was going to tell him it was the gateway to hell, but I didn't want to tempt fate, so I didn't.

"It's a Black Nallie," explained Crouthhamel.

Carl looked unhappy with the answer, or maybe it was the person speaking.

"Some kind of space creature," I told him. My explanation was more acceptable to him, I could tell. Kiss, if you know what I mean.

"Is it dangerous?"

"Yes, Carl," returned Crouthhamel, "we're trying to control it so it doesn't destroy your planet."

Carl looked at me. "Is he kidding?"

I shook my head negatively. "He never kids around," I said.

"Holy shit," Carl blurted out, "what's that stuff dripping on it?"

"Liquid energy," I explained very simply. I didn't think Carl was a sci-fi nut like the rest of us. Again, the old KISS, Keep it simple, stupid.

"Where's it coming from?" A man of a thousand questions.

"My ship," scoffed Crouthhamel. I could tell he was tired of the questions, and Carl didn't work for him, so he didn't have to be polite either.

Just then, the energy began to drop to the ground from under the creature, exploding in miniature flashes. Quickly, l Crouthhamel signaled his ship, and the stream abruptly stopped. Almost immediately, the Nallie began to move toward the house, more in the direction of the open garage door. Carl started to draw his gun, but I gestured to him to reholster it.

"You don't want to do that," I suggested. He trusted my experience and reholstered it. Thank God.

"Think it's full or something?" I asked Crouthhamel.

He didn't answer but followed the creature's movement, watching the Nallie as the leading edge of the thing flashed as it moved slowly in the direction of the driveway now, muttering, "I don't know why it's not affected more by the air molecules."

"Merlin," I remarked, "it appears to be headed for you."

"Yes, I know, what do you think I should do?"

"Whose he talking to?" asked Carl, turning finally to Joan as Crouthhamel and I ignored him.

"His ship, he calls it Merlin," she answered, keeping it simple too.

He didn't know whether to believe her either, but by now, he seemed content to study the situation as a helpless bystander like the rest of us.

"Hold your position; if you have to, you can always take it into space with you. It apparently likes you more than me." I would almost trade the planet for him.

"It seems to be headed to my aft sections; should I prepare my exterior thrusters or wait?" Merlin was as confused as we were, and that gave me no comfort.

"Give me a visual on your position; I don't care who sees you right about now."

Crouthhamel didn't say anything as Merlin materialized. And I must add, when he did, he was right over Carl's cruiser too.

"Lord Jesus," exclaimed Carl, "is that your ship?" Welcome to reality was written all over his face.

"Yup," I answered proudly.

"What is that black stuff on him?" asked Crouthhamel.

"I think that happened when he set off a bunch of antimatter balls back in the Aktagara galaxy."

By now, the Nallie was hovering almost within inches of Merlin's ass.

"That wouldn't do that to the hull," stated Crouthhamel.

"Then what do you think it is?" asked Merlin. He sounded worried. I would be too with a Nallie almost up my ass.

"Maybe you guys ran over a Nallie in space?" commented Joan.

That's when it hit me. Maybe we hadn't run over one; maybe we had picked up a hitchhiker.

"Merlin," I shouted; I didn't have to shout, but I did, "go to a deep space configuration; see what happens when your DS drive ports are visible."

"I'll have to cancel Plasma drive," he answered, "and set down."

"Do it," I ordered. I knew what it meant; it meant Carl's car was toast.

Merlin shut down his drive systems to reconfigure and instantly dropped down onto Carl's cruiser. His weight, probably in the tons, smashed the cruiser until it was about a foot thick. The Nallie followed Merlin, maintaining a few inches of clearance behind him. Of course, the drop didn't damage Merlin.

"Holy Mother of God," gasped Carl, "look what that thing did to my vehicle."

I thought he was going to cry, so I put my hand on his shoulder and tried to console him. "Don't worry, I'll get you another one." It didn't quite satisfy him, but I was to busy for any more sympathy.

Merlin's shape changed to his normal space configuration, his smooth body bulging as equipment and parts moved around to their proper position, finally exposing the massive drive ports at his rear. This was usually pretty much an instantaneous process, but he had slowed it down because of the Nallie. He looked about twice the size he had been and also quite menacing.

"Skip the collectors," I advised him, "there's no room here and I don't think the Nallie is interested in them." I walked toward the back of him with Crouthhamel right alongside me. Joan stayed by Wolf. Carl followed behind us for a few steps and then stopped. I didn't blame him; he was pretty freaked out and had begun muttering to himself about his car.

"There it is," said Crouthhamel, who had realized what I was doing the same time I did, pointing up at Merlin's drive ports.

"Where?" I asked, and then I spotted it too. Inside the right exit port was another Nallie, or at least that was what it looked like. A trail of black shit led from it to the underside of Merlin. The first Nallie entered the port very carefully until it came in contact with the one in the tube. Sparks began to fly, and you could hear something sizzling, then the black on the outside of Merlin slowly melted back into the port.

"Give it a little antimatter," ordered Crouthhamel, taking the words right out of my mouth.

Merlin must have been thinking the same thing because both ports began leaking tiny streams of precious antimatter. The Nallie, or I should say Nallies, began to join together inside the one port. Several minutes passed by as the combined Nallies grew in size until they almost filled the port completely. Merlin had quickly shut down the other port but not before it burned the asphalt driveway clear down to the ground for twenty or so feet behind him. I had hoped he could have done this in space, but now we had to chance it here because he couldn't reconfigure into Plasma drive without closing them up inside him. Something told me not to order him to do that.

"What now, I hope you don't want me to change over to Plasma drive," he said, reading my mind.

"No, just keep pouring on the antimatter." I looked at Crouthhamel, and he nodded at me in agreement.

"I have pressure building." Merlin sounded very worried.

"Hang in there." I turned to Crouthhamel. "Can your ship tilt him on end so the back of him is pointed skyward?" Maybe they would take the hint.

He nodded and began communicating with his ship. Merlin began to experience the pull of the gravity beam from Crouthhamel's ship and began to tilt upward until his nose was the only thing touching Carl's cruiser, who groaned at the sight.

Crouthhamel and I began backing up toward Joan, Carl, and Wolf, knowing the increasing pressure would soon have an affect on the Nallies. What kind of effect, we didn't know. I think we were both hoping they would take the hint and leave.

Just then, another cruiser pulled into the driveway, lights blazing, sirens screaming, probably following up on Carl's lack of radio signal.

"Carl," I screamed, "have him kill the Christmas tree, and why don't the two of you block off Route 2 until we know what's going to happen here, OK?"

Carl saw a good deal when it appeared and took off through the yard, signaling to his buddy and motioning toward the road. I noticed one car had already pulled off to the side, and an entire family was enjoying the spectacle. I hoped nobody in the car had a camera.

"Can your ship lift him?" Maybe we could take him straight up.

"Not in D-mode," replied Crouthhamel, "and we can't risk putting him up in the air like that, we'll have every defense system in your world on alert."

"Shit, I was hoping you wouldn't say that. I wanted to tell Merlin to pressure up until he blew the Nallies out, but not here, in space maybe, but not here. Damn."

"What do you want me to do, Jim?" asked Merlin. "I have already reached maximum pressure, any longer and I risk complete system failure."

What was I thinking? Those Nallies would hang on until there was nothing left of him. If they didn't have enough energy now, they never would. Screw it. Time to play or pay.

"Shut down everything, Merlin," I ordered. "They've had enough free lunch."

Crouthhamel started to say something and then shut off his gravity beam. Merlin slowly settled back down on the cruiser, crushing it even flatter. Seconds ticked by, and I waited for the ground to disappear under us. The world remained whole.

As if answering my prayers, the two combined Nallies came floating out of his port exit tube, absorbing the final bath of antimatter and letting none of it escape.

"Get out of there right now," I shouted again, without needing to, "and use D-mode, Merlin!"

Carl's cruiser moaned as Merlin raised up, quickly reconfiguring and continued to groan as he disappeared into the air. The Nallies remained floating in the same spot and appeared to be waiting on something.

"Send your ship away also," I said to Crouthhamel, trying not to make it sound like an order. He hated orders too.

"Already done," he announced to me.

"Now what?" I asked him. The Nallies were still floating in front of us. Maybe our ships were safe, but the planet wasn't. Why wouldn't they leave?

"Give them a minute, I don't think they will stick around here much longer, it will only hurt them when the energy we fed them wears off." He said it to me while nodding to himself in agreement.

"I hope you're right." I no sooner said that then the Nallies began to split apart and vanish. Another anticlimax. I was getting used to them. It was so much unlike television. I stood there watching the two masses disappear, totally absorbed by the insane thought that they seemed to be glad it was over too. I shook it off.

"That's it," asked Joan, coming over to me, "they just vanished?"

They were gone or so it seemed. I nodded to her.

"That's it, but let me check to make sure. Hey, Merlin, can you tell if they're gone?"

"Yes and yes," he answered happily, "I now know what to look for with my sensors, and yes, the Nallies are no longer here. I'm shutting back down now."

"That's great," said Crouthhamel, walking back up to me, "now maybe we can do something about your Wolf." He never forgot things, even in the heat of the moment.

"Where did everything go, your ship, his ship, the creature?" asked Carl, striding up to us from the road, looking all around, obviously not used to the lack of a big finale, or any finale for that matter.

"Everything is fine," said Crouthhamel to him.

"Really, Carl, everything's OK," I said to him, "so you can let the traffic flow."

"What?" he said, still not pleased with the results. "How am I going to explain all this?"

"You'll figure out something," replied Crouthhamel. He must have signaled his ship because the hatch appeared behind him. He turned and strode up into it quickly. As it closed, he nodded to me, and then he vanished also. Carl's mouth was wide open as he stared at the spot where Crouthhamel had been standing only a moment ago.

"It's OK," I said to him, turning toward where Wolf and Joan had been standing; they were gone too. The sneaky devil must have absconded with them also. I hoped Joan liked her first spaceship ride. Then I heard the screen door to the porch open, and out she came with two cans of soft drinks in her hands. I wondered if he had taken Wolf. Joan read the look on my face and nodded while looking upward. She looked like I felt, relieved, for a lot of reasons.

"I'll make arrangements to get you another cruiser; we'll get one loaded," I began, wanting to end this conversation.

"What am I going to say about that black spot and my cruiser?" said Carl, wanting to write something in his little notebook. He turned and accepted the drink offered by Joan, smiling as if understood her predicament of being my girlfriend. She handed me the other one and winked at me, heading back for the house. I knew what she had in mind. We do think alike, that's for sure. I watched her tight ass walk back to the house; I was about to follow her to confirm our mutual thoughts and show her that Mr. Happy was in complete agreement too.

To my right, the front of the garage began closing upward; the rising garage door as well as the small wedges above it, closing inward too, were highly unusual to say the least. Merlin probably had a movie on already; he told me he copied all the film libraries he could access and said he wasn't done looking or accessing.

Carl watched it snap shut and knew that wasn't the only thing that was closed. He took a drink while snapping his book shut and then shook his head in absolute submission. He was waving the white flag. He waited, knowing my answer wasn't going to work, and not caring anymore. His mind was on overload too; this was not what a West Virginia state police officer would call, well, normal. Then again, this time he didn't get shot.

"What else," I said, turning back toward Carl and smiling, "tell them, the black spot's gone."

# CHAPTER 11

## The Last Word

I left Carl to catch a ride with his buddy after promising to pay all the damages, although I wondered where the money was going to come from; I had still not found out how badly my checkbook had been ravaged. And I really didn't care at this point because I had a beautiful woman waiting for me in my bedroom; as far as I was concerned, the rest of the world could go to hell. Merlin had closed himself into the garage, and as I walked to the front door, I briefly explained to him that I did not want to be disturbed unless the Ohio River overflowed into my front yard or the planet stopped turning. He got the message and promised to watch TV like a good spaceship. The front door was locked when I got there. I knew I should have gone in through the porch. I hate locked doors, especially my own.

I was still cursing as I walked into the bedroom; that is, until I spotted Joan laid out on the bed in a black teddy, her bare butt facing me.

"Why don't you stop playing Guardian and show me your purpose in life," joked Joan suggestively. She had been laying with her feet at the head of the bed and rolled over onto her stomach so she could prop herself up on her elbows and show off her breasts through the thin film of the teddy. They looked more full than I had remembered, and I worked harder at getting my uniform onto the floor. She wiggled her butt at me as I struggled with the tunic. Mind you, I'm not a butt man but rather a breast man, so to speak, but with Joan, it was whatever was showing at the time.

"One purpose, coming up," I joked, pulling one of my boots off as I stood in front of her. Mr. Happy was now proudly standing at attention, waiting for orders.

She reached out and pulled me toward her, firmly but not too hard. Thank God she didn't know how hard I pulled on Mr. Happy. I still had one boot on, but I wobbled over toward her open mouth and felt her lips surround the head. She sucked him into her mouth, alternating between biting the ridge of skin around the head and sucking him halfway down her throat, never taking her eyes off him as he continued to expand even more between her lips. It is truly the second greatest feeling on this planet, and from what I had experienced so far, all the rest too. I could feel him throbbing prematurely and tried to pull him out, but as I tried to back away, she grabbed my ass and pulled me back into her wet mouth.

"Careful, baby," I moaned. "I've been in space way too long." I knew she could feel me throbbing, yet she wasn't letting go, which made it even harder to control myself. The edge of no turning back was right in front of me, and I tried to struggle free, but only halfheartedly. She dug her nails into my butt and acted as if she wasn't going to let go until she tasted my load. Then she must have changed her mind, suddenly pulling her head away from my cock with a startling quickness. She watched my cock bounce and jerk in front of her and looked up at my face as I moaned from the "edge." Then as I stood there dripping slippery fluid onto the carpet and the lone boot, she jackknifed her legs out from behind her and presented them to me as she lay back into the covers. I grabbed them by the ankles and opened them, exposing her slice of heaven to Mr. Happy. He throbbed in agreement as I bent down slightly and guided him forward. I felt him touch her rose petal lips; they were already wet with desire. Then he started his descent, rubbing the muscles in the walls of her vagina, feeling them pull and contract, drawing him farther and farther into her. I could feel myself grit my teeth, and I heard Joan gasp from somewhere on the bed. Again the edge appeared, the point of no control, and I knew it wasn't going to go away this time.

Slowly I drew him out, that's the hard part you know, and plunged him back in, timing it to the throbs, knowing she could feel him swell a little more with each throb, repeating the whole process again, quickly, and then once more, only this time slowly, agonizingly slowly. It was too much; I wasn't going to get away with it again. I knew it, she knew it, and Happy knew it. I slid my hands down the outside of her legs and cupped them under her ass cheeks and lifted her by them and drove him down into her as hard as I could push, feeling him releasing spurts of come with each throbbing rush of blood. Gasping, I felt her coming, like hot oil; her come splashed back over him, hurrying toward the other end of him, dripping out onto my balls and running down my legs. Still holding her ass up in the air, I started to stroke him back and forth into and out of her, almost without any control, unable to stop, until at last he finished pumping and became intensely sensitive, causing me to stop and lower her gently back onto the bed. I collapsed to a push-up position above her, my grimace changing to a nutty, happy smile, a giggle escaping from me. She looked up at me, and the same crazy smile and uncontrolled laugh escaped from her also. Slowly I withdrew from her and stood up, weak-kneed, sweating from the lovemaking, and breathing hard from the orgasm we had just shared. Happy was still hard from the workout and was awash with our fluids, the rest of which were flowing from between her shining pink lips. What a feeling. I turned around and flopped down onto the bed beside her.

She turned into me, pressing her breasts against my chest as our lips found each other and our tongues battled for control over each other.

"Holy God, that was intense," I said, separating our mouths. I slid up the bed, leaving only my leg with the lone boot hanging off it, and pulled her with me. I kicked off the boot on the edge of the mattress and flopped next to her.

"What a purpose," she whispered, hugging herself to me, rubbing her breasts against my chest even tighter, squashing them into me, making my eyes travel to her cleavage and beyond. I brought my hands to the bottom of her negligee and began pulling at it as she squirmed, until it reached the lower edge of her bosoms. I could feel them slowly escape, and I let them out slowly, savoring the feel, enjoying the sight of them, impatiently wanting to see the nipples; and finally they appeared, popping out from under the edge of the teddy, erect and begging to be sucked. She finished pulling the teddy over her head as I lowered my mouth and sucked a nipple into my mouth, biting softly around its base before circling it with my tongue. I brought my hands to the side of each breast and began squeezing them together, kneading them with my fingers as I alternated my head from one nipple to another. Every once in a while I would stop and draw her face down to my mouth and bury my tongue into her lips, until finally she began moaning again, and her eyelids closed and opened in a pleasurable loss of control.

Of course, her moaning and groaning only served to turn me on again too. I felt Happy starting to grow a second time, not something he normally does, and silently thanked him for his cooperation. I rolled her onto her back and climbed over her, sliding Happy into her slippery opening and began stroking him in and out. With each motion, he swelled a little more until he again resembled a miniature bodybuilder, all muscle and veins, hard as a rock, only this time, much more in control of the situation. It felt so good to be back in heaven again that I felt myself moaning right along with Joan. We looked into each other's eyes, watching the pleasure build and spread across our faces. I stopped moving in and out and held him deep inside her, feeling her tighten around him as he throbbed to new heights. Again I felt the edge coming at both of us, only this time, I didn't want it to end as quickly as it had before, and I withdrew my cock and held it back from the entrance, brushing it lightly over her vaginal lips.

"No," she protested, "no, no, don't stop!"

Easy for her to say; I thought, now, for a little torture. I ran Happy up between her pink lips, not into her aching tunnel, but instead, over her clitoris, feeling the button of flesh bumping into the ridge of Happy's head and then down the shaft until he stuck out between us, glistening hard and taut. Slowly I ran him up and down over her button, watching her glance at him as he popped up between us, feeling her button again and again as it hit the nerves under his head that seemed to control all the rest. Finally I could stand it no more, and I thrust him back into her, feeling her come splashing over him again and again. Denying the edge rushing up at me, I decided it was time to suck her beautiful breasts. I stopped plunging and swooped my arm under her back and rolled us both over without removing Happy from his heaven. Now she was on top, jammed to the hilt on my cock, rocking back and forth, screaming lightly about the pain of his fullness. My eyes began to follow the nipples of her full breasts as they swung down into my face when she rocked forward. I hugged her to a stop, vacuumed one into my mouth and began to pump him in and out as I held her motionless. I went for the other nipple and began to bite and suck on it as we both made sounds you can only make when you're about to climax violently. Then I let her go, and she rocked back onto Happy and began to shudder in orgasmic pleasure. I found myself arching my back to match her grinding, and we both exploded together, grinding our teeth, making the most painful of expressions as the pleasure washed over us, wave after wave, like it was never going to end, wanting it to kill us with pleasure, not sure that it wouldn't, until finally it ended. She collapsed onto me and we panted and gasped in unison. Catching our breath, we laughed again, like before, feeling giddy as the after rush came over us and then subsided into exhaustion, complete and total exhaustion. There was no need to ask, that would have been foolish; we both knew how good it had been, so we laid there and fell asleep, together, I think.

It was a good sleep; you know that when you wake up, it's the first thing you think to yourself, almost before you're awake enough to think at all. And then you remember what made you sleep like that to start with, and you groan again in pleasant memory. I felt around for Joan and realized she had already risen. I listened for the shower and didn't hear it. Suddenly my nose came to life, and I smelled something cooking. It was food, real food, fucking all-American food. I felt my stomach growl and knew I had to find it quickly or die from the smell. I rolled to the edge of the bed and sat up; all my senses were working now. If only my legs would work faster and more efficiently, I could already be eating. I stood up and remembered what always came first, Mr. Happy, who needed to be drained or else.

"What is that delicious smell?" I asked, strolling into the kitchen from the hallway, looking around at the rest of the house. Something was different; what was it? I walked up behind Joan, who was standing at the stove, a JennAir, the kind with the built-in charcoal grill in the top, and noticed a big sirloin turning into a zebra of charcoal lines as I grabbed her ass, still naked, just begging to be bitten.

"Hey, sleepy, finally decided to get up, huh?" she wiggled her butt against my hand and half-turned for a smooch. One of her breasts came into view, so I gave it a playful squeeze and rolled the nipple around with my fingers, feeling it swell and harden. She playfully felt for Mr. Happy and gave him a conciliatory squeeze.

"Better cut that out or your steak will go to waste this time."

Meaning she wouldn't let me off so easily if we ended up in the bedroom again. I can live with that, but my stomach couldn't and let me know by growling loudly.

"I don't think that's Mr. Happy making that noise now, is it?" she commented, turning to me and pulling the waistband of my looms out to inspect him. She let the band snap back playfully.

"Not hardly," I joked. "I can't begin to tell you how good that smells." I turned and inspected the micro, yup, potatoes were twirling themselves to death inside it.

"How about a beer?" she asked, heading for the refrigerator, trying to anticipate my every need.

"I got that covered," I stopped her and grabbed a couple of mugs from the counter where she had set them out earlier. I stepped down the stairs onto the summer porch and began fiddling with the tub of Chaga brew. I can't explain how it works, but almost instantly, I was pouring the mugs full of brew, so cold it frosted the outside of them.

"Steak's done!" yelled Joan from the kitchen. She was headed for the table as I came up the steps and joined her. The potatoes were waiting along with a couple of bowls of salad, which must have been hiding in the fridge. I handed her a mug and picked up my knife and fork, savoring the smell and the sizzle in front of me. She had cut herself off a small piece from the sirloin, and I could see the red inside of it calling to me. I cut off a chunk and slammed it into my mouth as she delicately forked one into hers, watching me eat, enjoying my barbarism. I chewed one piece and cut another, an assembly line of food starting at my plate and ending somewhere inside me. God, it was incredible. I made a note to have my food synthesizer overhauled the next time I hit a Zalo base or a Mothership; either that or I was going to install a JennAir and a Deepfreeze in Merlin. I laughed to myself as I thought about flying through space grilling steaks, an imaginary smokestack billowing steak fumes from the top of Merlin's control room.

"What?" she asked curiously.

I told her. We both laughed, then I told her about my food machine and the shit I had to eat. I thought she was going to choke on her food.

"This beer is incredible," Joan commented, finishing her mug before me, which was as rare as my steak. She was the sipper; I was the guzzler.

"Let me get you another," I said, jumping up from the table, picking up my mug and finishing it quickly. I noticed I was a little buzzed already.

"Okee dokee," answered Joan. She was buzzed too.

"Have you noticed," she said, when I returned, and she went after the second mug hungrily, "how the taste changes as you drink it?"

I nodded from behind a mouthful of food. My plate was looking more and more like I hadn't eaten from it as I finished my last piece of steak and began wiping it clean with a slab of Texas toast from the basket in front of me. When that was gone, I sat back and surveyed my stomach to see if it was going to bust or not. I wondered if I could get up from the table.

Joan was still working on her mug, slower this time and watching me watch her. I smiled back at her like a contented cow. She knew the look and laughed.

"This is really great, you know?" I asked without wanting an answer. I knew from her smile. I reached for her hand and almost knocked the platter off the table. It was nice to see my klutziness hadn't gotten any better.

"Let's go into the living room," suggested Joan, "and catch the evening news; I can clean this up later." She offered me her empty mug, and after running for another refill, I found her planted on the couch, flipping the channel controller to the right news station. That is, the one she liked to listen to. I could never figure out why she liked that station better than the rest. I mentioned it as I sat down next to her on the sofa. As she answered me, I looked around the room and noticed it looked very lived in, not like she had been stopping by to water the plants.

"I don't know," she began, "I just think they do a better job of reporting."

I looked back at her and worked on my brew. "So it has nothing to do with how cute that guy is, the one who's talking now?" She didn't look at me right away. A little shook of jealousy ran through me, and I immediately dismissed it. I had no hold on her or she on me. I always thought we agreed on that, but the brew was affecting my brain, and I let it take control of my mouth.

"I just like the way the news is reported," she replied, "plus it let's me know what's going on in Ohio, which is still part of my territory." She looked up at me to see how well I bought it.

Now that made sense. It certainly explained why we were watching a Columbus station and not a Parkersburg station. But I didn't buy it.

"Is he that cute in person?" I wondered, letting the thought out through my mouth like a vaporous leak of deadly gas at a chemical factory. Oh boy, I needed to put this beer down right fucking now; my mouth was a jealous cesspool of trouble tonight. And it appeared to be unstoppable.

"Yup," she answered, catching herself from saying any more. She looked over at me and knew I had caught her; she looked like the cat that ate the canary.

I should have let it drop; hell, it was none of my business what she did when she was on the road. I thought of Tamee, told myself that I should also feel guilty, and then heard myself talking. "So how well do you know him?" I almost bit my tongue off trying not to say it. I was going to ruin a perfect evening with my freakin' mouth. It wasn't the first time either, no sirree.

"I'm sorry," I confessed, seeing the look on her face. "It's none of my business how well you know him." My apology was about as effective as putting a finger over the end of a fire hose. I looked down into her face and saw the tears welling up in the bottom of her eyes until they finally reached the full point and dribbled out the corners and down her cheeks. She turned her face back toward her beer and studied it. I felt myself shrinking down to the size of a jerk, about as big as my you-know-what.

"I met him the last time I was in the Columbus office," she confessed before I could apologize again.

"Oh well, is he a nice guy in person?" I said it like you would ask somebody who had met a real star, not some bozo from the news. Maybe she would take the bait and let it drop. She didn't take the bait or see the trap.

"We slept together," she stated, putting her brew on the coffee table and started to climb up off the couch. The Chaga brew was really fucking with her physically too, and I thought she was going to fall over, so I grabbed for her. She must have thought I was going to do something weird, not that I had ever hurt her or hit her or anything. I don't stomach men who hit women. It must be the Chaga.

She pulled away from me and ran down the hallway to the bedroom and slammed the door about two seconds before I got there.

"Look, I'm not going to hurt you. I thought you were going to fall over; I was trying to catch you," I said to the door loudly.

Silence. Yet I could still hear her saying "We slept together."

"Look, honey," I argued logically, "we are not married, or even engaged to be. I don't care who you sleep with." That wasn't what I meant, but that's what slipped through the old lips.

Silence.

Now what do I say. I tried to reason what she wanted to hear, but the Chaga brew wouldn't let me. I turned around and stared into the bathroom. Her stockings were hanging over the shower rod, and her makeup was scattered around the sink. The toilet looked like it needed watering, so I walked in and began relieving myself. When all else fails, take a piss. I finished and turned back toward the bedroom door. I knew I could break it open, but I didn't feel like that would accomplish anything except piss her off further. I smiled to myself. Just like a woman. She was in the bedroom angry at me for bringing it up, and I was standing in the hallway feeling like a shit heel. I was the one who should have been mad, not her.

"So what if you slept with him," I yelled, "you're here with me now, that's all that matters to me!"

"Oh sure, until I open this door. I don't need you to show me how much you love me by beating me up." Her voice sounded a bit fearful, like it had happened to her before or something.

I searched my brain for inappropriate moments and got zip, at least in the cruelty department; I'm really not into that shit.

"Come on, Joan," I yelled back, "when have I ever hit you?"

"Not you, not yet, and not ever again."

"What?" She had me confused on that one. "What?" I yelled again. At least we had a dialogue going.

"Don't you remember Alex?" came her voice through the door.

"Alex?" I asked; I tried like hell to get my memory to work, but it was off for the evening. Not a bad idea either.

"The guy I was seeing when I met you." The voice was approaching normal.

"Oh, the skinny guy!" I remembered. "The one who tried to cut in on me at the Christmas party I took you to, at the Holiday Inn, when we first started dating." Now it was coming back to me. He had been tall and skinny, well, skinnier than me anyways. We had been having a great time dancing and rubbing up against each other at the party when this tall goon had come up to us and tried to cut in; that is, until I told him to you-know-what. He had almost tried me and decided not to after I gave him my mean look. I would have torn him apart.

"He beat you?" I said, amazed and angry at the same time.

Silence. Then the door spoke again. "Yes, that's when I left him. A week later I met you. I thought you were different," she said accusingly.

"I am," I stated. Hell, if anything, I was certainly different. I could think of a few more adjectives to describe myself but kept them to myself.

"I love you," I said after another period of silence. "When you realize I'm not Alex, I'll be in the garage." I turned away and started down the hallway. I'd be damned if I was going to be compared to Alex. I wondered what his last name was and where I might find him, but the brew was wearing off, and the safety was on. I entered the garage, feeling angry with myself and depressed with Joan for even comparing me to Alex. Maybe I would feel better if I went for a drive and looked up old Alex and got to know him better in a purely physical sense. Then I remembered all my cars were at Rick's. I wondered where Joan's little convertible was and decided not to ask her just now. I was standing there, in the dark, wishing I had something to kick, when Merlin turned on the ceiling lights.

"Hey, what's up, dude?" he invited. His slang was improving in direct proportion to the amount of TV he watched.

"Not me," I muttered.

"I know, I heard, what a bummer, man."

"What are you watching?" I thought I knew.

"A *Cheech and Chong* movie."

I knew it.

"Your marijuana is similar to Altairian tobacco; why is it illegal?" he asked.

"People here just don't know when to stop a good thing, you know, like alcoholics, who just don't know when to stop drinking."

"But that's not illegal," he said baffled.

"Nope, but it was once, it didn't work though, people still found a way to drink. Check prohibition, in your computer, it's all there, not to mention the politics that legalized it."

"Politics, that's a strange subject too."

"You got that right," I answered, smiling for no reason.

"Do you want to come on board?"

"Nah, I might be to tempted to leave then." And I might not come back.

"We could go find Alex?" He was such an instigator.

"No, I'm going back inside and try and work this out with Joan, go back to the movie." As I turned, the lights went out.

I awoke to the blinding light coming through the curtains, half open, and immediately noticed Joan was not in the bed with me. She always woke before me, nothing new, and I didn't figure she was still mad at me since we had talked it out last night and then made love again before going to sleep. Making love after making up is always great; it's almost worth getting into a fight just to make up, almost. I climbed out of bed and went into the bathroom and went through the routine, dressed in some very comfortable jeans and an old favorite T-shirt and went into the kitchen to find her. She was sitting there drinking a cup of coffee, and I waved her back down into the chair as I grabbed a cup and joined her.

"How did you sleep?" I asked, giving her a kiss first.

"Not as good as you, you chainsaw."

"Was I snoring?" I snored really loud. Blame it on hayfever and allergies.

"No, not really, I'm just kidding; I really did sleep good, especially after what you did to me with your tongue." She gave me the happy look.

I smiled at the thought. I had done a good job of that, come to think of it.

We sat for a while in silence, drinking and smiling. All was good. Too good.

The phone rang. The ring was evil.

"This is the devil, who in hell do you want?" I said into the receiver.

"Jim, this is Rick." His voice sounded distant.

"Yeah, what's up?" There goes my day off; I could feel it.

"I'm out in Doddridge County, at the Bailey well, at the little carryout about five miles north of West Union, just past the cut and the big red farmhouse on the curve, do you remember?"

This is the way you give directions in West Virginia.

"Yeah," I replied slowly. I knew what it meant when he told me exactly where he was; it meant, meet him there.

"Great, I need you to pick up an overshot from the office, we've got a string of tools hung in the hole, and bring it out to me, OK?"

I looked over at Joan with a "what can I do" look and shook my head. "Sure, how am I supposed to get there?" The office was downtown, on Market Street, a good fifteen miles from my house. I certainly wasn't going to walk.

"Shit, I forgot, all your trucks are parked there, and you're cars are at my house." He sounded rattled. Wonder what he did last night.

"Joan, do you have your car here?" I said, turning to her. I didn't remember seeing it.

She shook her head.

"Hell, I brought her home from the garage, Steve's, yesterday," said Rick, answering for her. "He's supposed to tune it up Monday, shit." Again he sounded rattled.

"I'll just have to come back into town and get the overshot myself, never mind, Jim." He sounded like he wasn't looking forward to a three-hour round-trip. I didn't blame him; I wasn't either.

"Hang on, Rick," I exclaimed before he could hang up, "I'll figure something out and be there shortly. I think I remember where the well location is, so I'll meet you there, is that all you need?" I wasn't making two trips, plus the back room of the office was a freakin' toolshed and lab for Rick and his drilling samples—little cloth bags of dirt from the well bores—that he examined with a microscope for evidence of petroleum deposits. Just walking in it could be hazardous to your clean clothes; raw petroleum products stain everything permanently.

"I think so," he sounded relieved. "If that doesn't do it, we'll have to shut down anyways."

"See you in a while," I returned, hanging up the phone. I looked over at Joan. I was about to fuck up another Sunday, and I half expected her to be pissed.

"Take me with you," she said happily, "at least we can be together."

"OK, yeah, that sounds good, let me get my boots from the basement and my gloves and we can leave, OK?"

"Yeah, but how, is Samantha coming to get you?"

"Damn, why didn't I think of that," I blurted out. I knew why. I smiled.

She reached for the phone and called Rick's number. His machine answered. She hung up.

"No way, she's at church," I said, pointing at the clock.

"Then how"—she stopped in midsentence; she knew—"Merlin?"

I nodded. Parkersburg would be deserted this time of day. I flashed to the basement and was back upstairs in a heartbeat. I was looking forward to getting out into the field again. I could almost smell the oil and gas, then I realized I was smelling it, off the outside of my boots. My nose came alive, sending a readout of the smell to my brain for analysis. I could almost tell you which well I had been at by the smells. I decided to put them on when we got there and signaled Joan to follow me as I headed for the garage.

Merlin was up for it, as long as we got back in time for him to watch the *Indianapolis 500*. I hadn't even known it was on today. He was chattering about the drivers as we exited the garage and climbed into the sky. Joan was sitting next to me, beaming like a kid, looking all around the ship, taking in everything. I tried not to imagine what Crouthhamel would say if he knew what I was doing.

"We won't mention this trip to anyone, Merlin," I suggested.

"No way, man," he replied in a voice identical to Cheech's.

"Especially Mr. C," I reminded him.

"For sure," he slanged, "dude, I dig it. By the way, I did receive a short message from him." So much for Cheech's voice.

"Oh yeah," I said suspiciously.

"Yeah, man, he's reached Jebis, in the Jurda system, and Wolf is going to be OK." More Cheech.

"Great," I exclaimed, forgetting to yell at him about not giving me my messages, "did he say anything else?"

"Only that he hoped you got a lot of rest."

"What does that mean?" said Joan, looking over at me for the first time.

"I don't know," I lied. She bought it and returned to watching the screen in front of us as the ground flew away behind us. The city came into view, the downtown area, with its tall buildings began to fill the screen until we rose over them. I turned the screen so the picture was under us and watched as Merlin settled between our office building and the one on the other side of the parking lot. I looked over my trucks, neatly spaced behind our office, and briefly thought about driving one out there. Maybe on the way back I could stop and pick one up, bring it out to the house, wash it maybe. They were all covered with dust from sitting so long. I shook my head. This Guardian business was more than I had bargained for, that was for sure. Joan waited while I went inside.

The overshot, a cylindrical device that operates like a Chinese fingercuff, was almost five feet long and weighed about three hundred pounds. I dragged it to the door where Merlin could get an exterior claw on it. He picked it up like it was paper and not heavy steel.

Of course, anyone watching would have seen it rise from my hands and disappear from sight into thin air. I returned to the back room and filled a milk crate with an assortment of collars and was about to leave when the phone rang. I listened to Rick as he left a message and picked up before he was done.

"Yes, I got all the collars," I scolded him for doubting my common sense, "and we'll be there in a few minutes."

"Merlin?" He was quick.

"Yup, although I should be driving one of my trucks from the looks of them, they haven't been run much lately."

"Yes, I've been turning them on and off since you left."

Now we were even, at least in the common sense department. We hung up after a few more exchanges of friendly scolding, and I boarded Merlin a moment later.

"You should have waited," Merlin informed me.

I looked at the screen and saw a police car sitting at the entrance to the parking lot. I watched the officer behind the wheel look over at his partner and shake his head.

"Let's go, Merlin, I want to catch the Indy too, if possible."

Suddenly the screen changed to a picture of the raceway, I assumed, at Indianapolis. Joan looked severely disappointed.

"That's all right, Merlin, let's watch the trees go by," I ordered, smiling over at Joan, "and take us up a little bit higher."

"We'll have to stay under the Allegheny flight path unless you want to take down a commuter," cautioned Merlin, "remember—"

"Yes, yes," I cut him off, "just do it."

Following the interstate, Route 50, we arrived at the cut off for Route 16 and, within seconds, had centered ourselves over the rig location where Rick was pacing in circles, watching the sky above without trying to be noticeable about what he was doing. It was comical.

"Is there a clearing where you can let us off?" I asked Merlin, panning the screen around, making myself dizzy.

"Nope." He seemed miffed that I didn't want to watch the Indy.

"Well then, let us off here," I said, smiling at Joan, who was busy adjusting her boots and giving me a great cleavage shot through the neck of her shirt, "but just before you open the hatch, why don't we make a tree fall down across the location, kinda draw their attention."

"Cool, dude," snapped Merlin.

I slammed on my boots and was in motion toward the hatch when it started to open, and I grabbed Joan's sleeve lightly and pulled her after me down the steps as they formed under my feet. We could still hear the tree crashing down into the undergrowth as we stepped onto the ground, and the hatch closed behind us. We walked up to Rick as he stood staring into the woods, probably expecting to see us walk out of it. Behind us, Merlin had sat the collars and overshot softly on the ground. Thank God it hadn't rained lately; these locations turn into quicksand when that happens. We'd be digging in the mud for it.

"Hey!" I said loudly.

Rick almost jumped out of his boots as he turned around and saw us standing a few feet from us. His look of shock made both of us laugh. "You prick," he swore, and then smiled, as he figured out what had happened with the tree falling. Then he realized Joan was with me and gave her one of those "I'm so jealous" looks.

She smiled sweetly, savoring the small triumph.

"Helluva way to greet your partner," I scolded him. He looked past me, turned, and signaled to someone on the rig to join us. A couple of mud-covered rig hands came striding down off the rig platform and headed toward us. I thought I knew one of them.

"What's up?" said the one I knew. His name was Gene; I had seen him a couple of other times when we hired his crew to do a hole.

"Grab that stuff," said Rick, pointing to the equipment behind us, "and take it to Tiny." Tiny was the one in charge of the rig. Every rig had a "Tiny" on it. He was always the biggest guy.

Gene and his buddy grabbed hold of the overshot and began dragging it toward the rig. He saw me watching and a puzzled look came over his face.

"How did you get this up here?" he asked between breaths. "And where's your truck?" He was smarter than the average hand.

"I left it at the bottom of the hill, Gene," I bluffed him. "I decided to carry it up the hill for the exercise; you know, gotta stay in shape."

Joan smiled beside me but bit her lip to keep from laughing. Rick was looking around for Merlin, unsuccessfully.

"Damn," muttered the other guy, obviously impressed with my strength.

Joan waited until they were out of range to laugh, poking me in my stomach playfully.

"So what's going on?" I asked Rick. "Why didn't you call me at three this morning?" My sarcasm was not lost on him.

"Oh, fuck you," he swore at me jokingly. "Those idiots shut the rig down last night with the drill string all the way in the hole."

"Not at the bottom?" That was crazy, and definitely a no-no.

He nodded. "And the hole collapsed during the night. Tiny claims the tools were hanging high up the hole and someone let them down during the night."

"Who would do that?" asked Joan for me.

"Tiny claims we're drilling on Indian land and there is supposedly some kind of curse on anyone who disturbs it."

"Really," said Joan, excited at the prospect of a good ghost story.

"Don't get too excited," I cautioned her. "We've heard that claim a hundred times, with no explanation." Nobody knew exactly why a person should be scared.

"So the cable finally broke and now we're fishing; that is, we will be, once we get the overshot into the hole." Rick sounded exasperated, and a little tired.

We walked over to the rig's wooden platform and climbed the few steps up to the doghouse and went inside, away from the noise and commotion. I couldn't stand people getting in my way, so I tried real hard not to get in theirs. Rick's samples from the hole were scattered around the floor of the semitrailer-sized room, and the ultraviolet light of the microscope made them look like little animals huddling in groups away from the light. It seemed like a lot of samples for the depth they were at now.

"Why so many samples?" I asked, looking around the room.

"Prickford wanted samples pulled every three feet," answered Rick; his real name was Bickford, but everyone called him the other name behind his back.

"No shit," I muttered. By the time they reached the right depth, this room would be full to the brim with little bags of dirt from way underground. Good God, Prickford, whoops, could be a real pain. I made a note to be careful with his name.

"He's the boss, it's his well," argued Rick. He was right. It was my lease; Rick was the geologist, and Prickford had hired him in order to buy the drill site from me.

"So is it looking good?" asked Joan, always trying to find the positive in something.

"Yeah," replied Rick excitedly, "it is looking good. The shallow formations had quite a bit of fluorescence under the scope," he added, gesturing toward the microscope. I let him walk Joan over to it and watched them as he showed her how the minerals in the dirt looked under ultraviolet light. Then I turned to the wall and signaled Merlin with a single hello into the sensor on my wrist.

"Yes, what do you need now?" Merlin sounded a bit put out.

"Gee, am I bothering you?" I retorted.

"No, Jim," he apologized, "I just got involved in that Indy race, and, well, I was hoping Sneva would win, except he just blew his pit stop. It could cost him the lead." He was incredible in his humanity.

"Why does that upset you so much? You got a bet on it or something?" A terrible thought crossed my mind, but I dismissed it.

"Oh, no, anyways, what do you need me to do, pull that stuff out of the hole?" He sounded so matter-of-factly about it. He was lying.

"Yeah, that's the general idea," I answered, trying not to sound too impressed. I wondered if he had placed a bet somewhere.

"OK, then have them pull that mast off the hole so I can cut everything loose with the Disorganizer." He sounded like he was chomping on something, and it was getting the better of him. Maybe I should have named him Nascar.

I explained to Rick what Merlin was going to do, and we walked out onto the rig platform and waved Tiny over to us.

"What are you going to tell him?" asked Rick cautiously, as Tiny strolled toward us. He was not a happy camper at this point.

"What he wants to hear, a lie." I smiled.

Joan had given up the microscope and joined us. I turned and winked at her, pulling her by the hand, into the conversation.

"What's up, boss," breathed Tiny, who was not known for his walking or exercising for that matter. He reminded me of Mackie, ugly and huge. "I have the overshot on cable, we can start fishing any time," he added, catching his breath. He had a hard time keeping himself from staring at Joan, probably the first woman he had seen of normal size and weight in quite a long time. Unless you count the porno he had stashed all over the doghouse and the truck he drove around.

"That's good," answered Rick, "but I think Jim wants to try something first."

"Oh," he said with an obvious surprised look on his face. He even pulled his eyes from Joan and fixed them on me.

"And what are you going to do?" he asked, a smirk crossing his otherwise stupid face. He didn't patronize me like he did Rick. Rick had a reputation that the old timers like Tiny respected. I didn't.

"Well, TINY," I said, stressing his name for effect, "I'm going to summon an ancient sorcerer to drive the spirits away from this area and make the string of tools rise up out of the hole." I thought Tiny was either going to swallow his tongue or shit himself. Rick turned away to hide his smile. Joan choked down a laugh.

"You think you're pretty funny, don't you?" he said, regaining his superior attitude. He was King Shit on the rig. He also thought I was crazy, which was the only thing anyone ever said about me, so I really couldn't say I had a reputation, except for being crazy, that is. He was eyeing me to judge my reaction, probably figuring I was bullshitting him, and glancing over at Rick as if to say, "How can you put up with this ignorant person?" Tiny felt anyone who didn't grow up around a rig was ignorant and shouldn't be near one.

"You had better move that mast, or it might just get caught up in the lightning," I warned him.

"Get the hell outa my sight; I don't have time for this shit," he scoffed, turning to Rick as if I no longer existed. He even stopped drooling over Joan. Apparently I had insulted his professionalism.

"Tiny," began Rick, delicately, "I think you had better move the mast." That snapped the big guy's head straight back. He hadn't expected Rick to go along with me. He still thought I was joking. By now, his rig crew had come over to our little circle. They all looked tired and dirty. Not a good crowd to joke with, but then I wasn't joking.

Tiny turned to them and quickly explained what they were supposed to do. They grumbled back at him. Moving the mast was a real pain. Finally Tiny turned back to Rick, Joan, and I. His eyes sparked with anger.

"OK, Mr. Funnyman," he warned me, "we're going to move the mast off the hole, but if you're fooling around, God help you when they get a hold of you." He waved over at the crew as they scrambled around the mast, disconnecting cables and lowering the high bar extension.

With a huff, Tiny turned and walked back to his crew. By now, they were disconnecting the cables that were connected to huge spikes that surrounded the hole to steady the mast.

"He's not a big fan of yours, is he?" asked Joan sarcastically.

"Not at all," confirmed Rick, turning to me.

"Have them back away from the hole," I ordered, ignoring the friendly sarcasm.

Rick motioned for them to move away as they finished up the lowering of the mast. They looked over at me like I was crazy, and also like they were going to kill me if this didn't work. I smiled and walked toward the hole and inspected the surface casing as I jumped down from the platform and stood next to the hole. I looked back at Rick and Joan, winked, and turned to the crew and bowed. Tiny took the opportunity to spit in my direction. Only Gene, the rig hand who knew me, gave me a positive look and a thumbs up sign.

With the rig shut down, the silence was almost overwhelming. When it's running, you can't hear yourself think, and when it's off, well, let's just say the silence is eerie. Damn eerie. I raised my arms into the air, gesturing to the sky, which was as blue and cloudless as I've ever seen it.

"Oh Great Sorcerer Merlin," I shouted emphatically, "help us to remove that which is below me, that which is lodged in this hole and must be removed by only one as great as you!" I turned to Rick and Joan and smiled. Nothing happened. I waited. Somewhere a clock was ticking; I could hear it in my head. A few minutes went by, still nothing.

"Oh Great Merlin!" I shouted.

The silence was overwhelming. I could hear the crew grumbling, and Tiny curse me under his breath. My name came up several times.

"Merlin, I command you to give me a sign!" I was shouting a bit angrily now. I couldn't believe he wasn't answering me, the prick.

Silence.

"You'll pay dearly," I whispered into my sensor, "especially if I get the shit beat outa me."

More silence.

Now the crew, even Gene, began to shout at me, describing what they were going to do to various parts of my body, if, in the next few seconds, the ground didn't come alive and spit that string of tools onto the rig platform. Even though it was a cool day, I felt myself perspiring. And now I was worried too.

Suddenly the Disorganizer erupted in the sky above me, and a thin beam shot past me into the hole. It appeared to come from a point about a hundred feet above me, and I jumped backward as I felt the power of the tiny beam as it sizzled in front of me. I looked over at the crew and saw nothing but true believers in the crowd. I smiled at them. I was sure some of them would be cleaning out their shorts after this.

"Sneva's in the lead again," quipped Merlin, as he turned off the beam, "and Crouthhamel wants you to give him a shout when you're done here."

The last part of what he said kept me from lambasting him. "What?" I exclaimed, "you didn't tell him what we're doing, did you?" I sure hoped not; it was a clear violation of the order. A rather big one.

"No, stand back, I'll explain later, right now I'm activating my gravity beam, and there's quite a load of mud coming up the hole."

I jumped back onto the platform and motioned everyone back.

Ever so slightly, the ground began to vibrate, in turn vibrating the platform under our feet. Everyone seemed to be watching me as the vibrations increased in intensity and the hole began making a rumbling noise. The noise increased, which made everyone, including yours truly, step back away from it. Nobody was looking at me now, although Joan had a death grip on my left arm that was making it go numb. Suddenly we were all treated to a visual explosion of mud as it gushed from the hole and cascaded like a giant fountain almost fifty feet high down onto the rig and the platform, splashing everywhere, covering some of the crew that froze in their tracks, and just missing us as we ducked into the doghouse.

"Holy shit!" barked Tiny, following us inside, obviously shocked at what just happened.

"Come on," I urged them, as I went back out the door, just in time to see the drill string float slowly out of the top of the surface casing and turn horizontally toward the platform. Merlin set the string down on the platform. I felt my sensor vibrating, something Merlin did when he knew I shouldn't be talking to him, and I ducked around the corner of the trailer-shaped doghouse and signaled him back.

"You had better cap that pipe off, and quickly," he cautioned.

"What?" I almost didn't feel it, and then I did feel it. The ground was moving again. "Oil?" I said out loud.

"And gas, they must have been almost into a salt sand formation," added Merlin. "Better hurry, Jim."

I turned and sprinted to Rick, who was already signaling Tiny, who was moving at speeds far beyond the known Tiny speed.

"What the hell did he do?" asked Rick over the rumbling sound now coming from the well.

"He said you were almost into a formation," I shrugged.

"Is the well going to erupt?" asked Joan from behind me.

"I . . ." I never got a chance to finish my sentence.

Tiny and his crew had been feverishly yanking a collar onto the casing and had almost set the blowout preventer when the oil, driven by an ungodly pressure, burst from the hole and straight up into the sky. It didn't seem like it was going to stop anytime soon, which presented a real problem since the force of the oil had ripped the blowout preventer off the top of the casing before the crew could finish tightening it down. Oil fell everywhere, raining down on us as we tried to dodge the blackness as it fell.

"Ohh, Jimmy, ohh!" yelled Joan, wiping the crude from her face and pulling her hair backward, wringing the oil from it as more fell upon us. I tasted it in my mouth as I screamed for help from Merlin.

"Are you sure you want me to help?" he asked.

"Hell, yes," I spit, wiping my eyes. I yanked off my coat and threw it over Joan, who was already looking like a drowned rat. She took it with a nasty look.

"OK, boss," said Merlin. Suddenly the blowout preventer lifted off the ground and righted itself over the hole, spraying oil sideways at us, coating us further, in places I didn't think it could possibly reach. Just as suddenly as it started, it stopped. I cleared my eyes and looked around me; everyone else was doing the same thing. The sides of the rig and every square inch of ground, except where we were standing, was black and gooey. Unrefined oil is loaded with paraffin too.

It looked like a Spitter's convention as everyone wiped and spit, coughed, and then spit some more. I looked at Joan, realized what a mistake that was, and turned to Rick. His look wasn't that much nicer, but I knew he would ultimately be happy with the whole situation once we secured the preventer and cleaned up ourselves and the rig. Oil was everywhere; it must have blown a hundred feet in the air. I looked up, and what I saw startled me. The oil must have struck the bottom of Merlin, and some of it was still hanging from him. Yet with him in deceive mode, it looked like the oil was floating all by itself above us, a thin cloud, waiting to fall earthward.

"Merlin," I whispered, "you're covered with oil." I looked around and noticed that almost everyone except Joan—she had run for the doghouse to hide—was watching the cloud of oil.

"I know," he hissed back through the sensor, "but I can't move until you secure the damn valve. I have the thing positioned correctly, so get them to twist it down over the casing, and I can shake myself loose from here long enough to clean off my exterior. You should consider doing the same by the way."

"Funny, real funny," I griped at him and turned to Rick. "We need to tighten the preventer down." He heard the seriousness in my voice and signaled to Tiny as we both leapt from the platform and sloshed toward the hole. The crew finally began to move again, and followed us, wrenches in hand. Moments later, the wellhead was secure, and we all moved back onto the platform and sat down on one of the benches along the wall. The cloud rose and disappeared from sight, a spectacle followed intently by everyone, except Joan and I. She was inside the doghouse, plotting my demise no doubt. Oh baby.

We all sat there in silence, removing articles of clothing, and looking at each other furtively, especially me. I think if I had yelled "boo" right about then, one or two of them would have fainted. They did respect me now, more than they did before, plus now they were scared shitless of me. Except Rick, who knew what had happened. He followed me into the doghouse, and we found Joan wiping her face and arms with clean sample bags lying next to the microscope. She scowled at me but threw me a bag and continued wiping. I turned to Rick and smiled.

"Got the tools out," I announced. Man, was I covered.

"Yeah," he agreed, "and then some." The oil didn't bother him either.

"Obviously a good well, hey?" I asked, skinning myself lightly with the coarse cloth bag. I couldn't wait to drill an offset to this one. I turned to Joan and laughed at her. She looked so pissed that it struck me right in the old funny bone. Looking back on the whole afternoon, I know it probably wasn't the smartest thing I've ever done. But she took it pretty good and only threw the box of sample bags at me before I reached her and grabbed her into my arms.

"What do you think is so funny?" she screamed at me. "I just had my hair permed Friday." She tried to squirm away from me, but I held on for dear life.

"No sweat," I assured her. "We'll grab a laser shower, and you'll be as clean as a newborn baby's butt." This seemed to calm her down some, but I knew she was disgusted with the whole thing. I let her go and stood back a little.

"Why didn't you warn me?" she moaned, trying to run her fingers through her hair, unsuccessfully I might add. Rick approached us. He was being cautious; he was too smart.

"Merlin must have somehow drilled farther down the well," he said, trying to help me out of my dilemma with Joan, "because we still had a couple hundred feet to go before we reached any formation that could do this."

"Vertical stress fracture," Merlin informed us. "I may have used the Disorganizer a bit heavily, but the real cause of the well-making fluid is a fracture directly under the location."

"See, honey," I reasoned, "it wasn't anybody's fault."

"Gee, I feel so much better knowing that," she sassed me.

Something told me it was time to leave and get her cleaned up. Call it male intuition, I like to call it my survival instinct.

"We're going to walk down the hill and catch a ride home." I said, turning to Rick.

"My job is done here," I joked.

He smiled and nodded. He knew. Looking at his watch, he said, "It's time we all went home. Tomorrow we can set some tanks and see what this well will produce naturally. I expect it will turn to gas but who knows." He certainly knew the way Mother Nature worked better than anyone else. I nodded agreement and started toward the door, hoping Joan would follow my lead. She slowly straightened her sweater, pushed her hair back again, and joined me.

Rick went out the platform door as Joan and I went out the rear door of the trailer and began descending the hillside toward the road. I could hear the crew yelling at each other and knew that Rick had told them all to go home for the day.

"I'm sorry, babe," I apologized, trying to brake the icy silence surrounding us. It wasn't cold out, but it felt like zero degrees in between us. She stopped, and I looked over at her.

She looked over at me and saw the sincerity in my face and smiled just a tiny bit, almost mischievously and closed the distance between us, grabbing my oily hand affectionately.

"I accept your apology," she answered, turning her lips toward me for an oily kiss.

I was stunned but not too surprised, after all, we had worked out quite a few things the other night, and I felt like our relationship had progressed to a higher level afterward.

"You're a good sport," I commented, coming to a halt on the hillside, bringing my lips up to hers. She was slightly above me on the slope, having stopped first and towered over me as she bent to kiss me. I closed my eyes as our faces almost met, don't ask me why; I'm not an eye-closer as a rule, and that's when she got even with me. Remember, Joan knows Akido or some other self-defense training and caught me by surprise too. Am I making excuses?

"OOPS," she said, sweeping her leg into mine, causing me to lose my balance and fall into the leaves. I tried to grab her as I went down, but she stepped back, smiling a most wicked smile. The ground underneath the leaves was nothing but slippery clay, so as I tried to stand up, I slipped again and fell into the leaves, which of course stuck to me or rather the oil all over me. The natural paraffin in the oil only made things worse. Then she booted me in my butt, and I slid off down the hill, screaming back at her as she stood there watching me and laughing. I must have rolled twenty yards before a well-placed tree rammed me in the side and knocked the wind out of me. I looked like a living pile of leaves as I lay there coughing and gasping for breath. My side felt like the tree had been a truck too.

I heard her rush by me, calling Merlin's name and laughing.

"Merlin," she chortled, "Merlin." More laughter.

I sat up on the slope and watched her disappear down the hill. I was sorry I had chosen the steep side of the hill now, but I had picked it so we could reach Merlin before the crew came down the road on their way home. I felt my side and brushed some of the leaves off my front as I climbed to my feet. Below me I could see her head bobbing above the slope, and I knew she was almost to the road. I trudged after her like an abominable creature, eager for revenge. Oh baby.

When I got to the road I found myself alone. I called her name, thinking she was hiding, then I called Merlin's name. Remembering my sensor, I signaled him with it, and squatted down by the bank and began to clean more of the leaves and clay from my clothes. In the distance, I could hear the sound of trucks coming closer and knew they were coming down off the hill in a hurry. A few minutes later, the crew, in two of the most beat-up trucks I had ever seen, swept by me. I hardly expected them to stop, and sure enough, they didn't. In fact, if I'm not mistaken, I do believe they even sped up when they saw me by the road. I watched them vanish around the turn and went back to calling Merlin. I had pretty much concluded that he was in cahoots with Joan, and the two of them were most likely directly overhead, watching and laughing.

"Come on, you guys," I begged, "I really want to get cleaned up."

Nothing, and I mean nothing. I had never paid much attention to Merlin when he was in deceive mode, mostly because I was inside him when he engaged it or busy trying to stay alive when I wasn't. I made a note to listen real hard next time.

I hoped next time came real soon, a crotch full of oil doesn't do a thing for me.

Rick's Bronco came down off the hillside, and he pulled up alongside me, smiling down at me from the driver's seat.

"What," he joked, "you weren't messy enough covered with oil?" He glanced down at the mess I call clothing and then glanced around the area, probably expecting to see Merlin. His attention returned to me, reluctantly.

"Joan," I said, pointing to myself, "she tripped me on the hill."

He laughed. "Boy, she was pissed at you . . . so where is she?"

"I don't know, probably having a grand time watching me stand here." I could feel the temperature dropping, and my humor along with it.

Rick thought it over and nodded at me. "Well, I'll see you later." He put the Bronco into drive and waited for me to nod. I started to nod and wave him off when the hair on the back of my neck kinda moved, like something was wrong with the whole situation. I almost felt like panicking, almost. Weird, huh?

"Maybe I should go with you," I suggested. I had a strange feeling that something was wrong, and I had no intention of walking all the way back to Parkersburg.

"Like that?" asked Rick incredulously. His truck was one year old and still looked new. He had already cleaned himself off and changed. Probably stowed his oily clothes in the back. He was very picky about letting people ride in his truck when he was out in the field. His look told me to fucking forget it.

"Look," I explained, "I can't explain the feeling I'm getting, let's just say I think something is really wrong, like Merlin left me behind or something." I was closer to the truth than I knew.

"You must be kidding." He wasn't.

"No, really, Rick."

"You'll ruin my seats, Jim."

"I'll take off my clothes, I don't care at this point."

"Well, I do, you're not riding in my truck like that."

"Come on, damn it!" I yelled as he started to pull away.

He stopped and looked back at me. Moments passed as he considered whether to leave me or not. I tried to look even more dejected than I was feeling. I think it's called the "puppy dog" look. It worked, hallelujah.

"All right," he agreed, "I'll meet you at the store, you can get cleaned up there." With that, he gassed his Bronco and began disappearing down the road.

The look on my face went from supreme happiness to pissed off at the thought of walking a mile or more down to the hard road and the store. *Shit*, I thought, *what if it's closed*. He might leave without me. He still believed Merlin was going to pick me up any minute. Maybe he thought I was trying to make Joan worry.

"Wait, Rick," I screamed, "what if it's closed!" It was too late; he was out of sight around the same turn that everyone else had disappeared around. I surveyed the location of the setting sun and decided it might be better to jog than walk. Shafts of light were already catching the edge of the opposite hilltop, and pretty soon, the hollow would be dark. It was still early in the evening; hell, it was only late afternoon, but I knew from experience that these hollows could be pitch-black in no time when the sun settled low enough in the sky. And it wouldn't be long now. Shit, shit, shit, I cussed, as I started jogging, or should I say, slopping, as in pigsty.

I was busy jogging along the ruts of the well road, thinking about a hot shower; that is, a hot shower with Joan, when I heard the trees rustling behind and above me. Rustling far to loudly for it to be an animal or even a person. I slowed to a walk and acted like I was out of breath, without turning around. I grabbed the side that had collided with the tree trunk and acted like it was hurting. I could play games too. I heard tree branches breaking on both sides of the road as something large descended behind me.

*How obvious*, I thought, *they must want me to hear them*. Joan's probably sitting in my command seat having the time of her life. I stopped and bent over, acting as if I was out of breath. Any minute now she would announce to the whole hollow that she was right behind me. I decided to fall to the ground when she spoke, act as if she had frightened me, then jump up when the hatch opened and rush her. I hoped she was already showered so I could rub myself all over her.

Then whole trees on both sides of the road began to fall over, cracking and splintering as some unearthly force pushed them down to the hillsides to make room for itself. Merlin wouldn't do that I said to myself, turning around in the road, preparing to give him hell. *Man*, I thought, *the State Mining boys would have our asses for tearing up the hollow like that*. We would never get another permit in this state, that was for sure, not to mention what it was going to cost me to fix it. I thought about how hard it had been to get my drilling bond, and my blood began to boil.

"Merlin, this is not funny; Joan, please, it's not funny." And still it continued. I stopped in the middle of the ruts and screamed, "STOP, GODDAMNIT!"

The more I looked at the trees falling behind me, the angrier I became, until I was sure my ears were smoking. Then, realizing that maybe they couldn't stop, I calmed myself down and considered the situation. I was a born problem solver; maybe I could help somehow, and suddenly it hit me, like an ice-cold shower on a hot summer day. The oily little hairs on my neck stood straight up, and somehow I knew I was fucked.

Because the trees were too far apart for it to be Merlin. Something or someone in a much larger ship was creeping closer and closer to me. And who ever it was, was definitely not a member of Greenpeace. By now, the sound of the trees being splintered and broken like little toothpicks had filled the hollow with a deafening percussion. I put my hands over my ears. Then as if I had commanded it to stop, it stopped.

Silence overcame the hollow as the last of the trees crackled and thudded into the hillside. I stood in the road, paralyzed at what I couldn't see, paralyzed because whatever it was, hovering there in deceive mode, was definitely not Merlin. My legs were screaming for me to run, yet my brain was overriding them because I knew I wasn't going to get away from whatever was there. The air crackled with static.

I saw the beam coming at me, and it came way too quickly for me to move out of its path; but just before it struck me, just before I lost consciousness, I yelled. I don't remember whose name I called, but I do remember my last word, as a huge Tayhest Battlecruiser appeared at the other end of the beam. I remember it, very well, because it echoed around me as I fell into a black void, and I heard it a thousand times, over and over again in my head. Beating into my brain like a hammer on a railroad spike. The word no one else heard, "HELP!" The last word.

# CHAPTER 12

## The Devil, an Owl, and the Pussycat

Waking up on a Tayhest ship is like waking up in the back of a garbage truck. The place was filthy. I don't mean dirty; I mean shit filthy. Apparently the Tayhest must shit just about anywhere they decide to, with little regard for where that might be, and then go on about their business as usual. Add rotting meat, broken pieces of metal, and whatever else they discard when it breaks, not to mention clothing that they no longer want, and if they don't want it, no one does, and I think you get the idea. And if that doesn't do it for you, picture this. These monoliths of ugliness drool worse than a St. Bernard, so everything they touch is covered with an assortment of body fluids, even some that don't come from their mouths. Their personal hygiene is reason enough to exterminate the whole freaking race, although I can think of even better reasons.

Like waking up upside down for one. It tends to disorient you, not to mention give you one helluva headache. Twirling, did I mention twirling? Well, I was twirling too, which was making me quite sick to my stomach. My arms were hanging down into the mess on the floor below me, scraping around in the crap as I twirled. I tried to raise them, but I couldn't find the energy; full of blood, they felt as heavy as my legs. When I finally brought them up off the deck, I could only hold them up for a while anyway, so I let them drop into the mess and tried to focus on the doorway as I circled and circled. I had lost track of time, but it was shortly after I blew lunch down, or should I say up the front of me, that I saw the door open, and an ugly pair of Tayhest legs advanced on me.

The arm connected to the legs grabbed me by my hair and lifted me until I could see the face connected to the rest of the ugly prick, which I'm sure was just as ugly too. I particularly disliked having my hair pulled, not just because it hurt like a mother, but because my family, the male relatives I knew, didn't seem to keep theirs very long after reaching middle age, and I didn't have far to go, I hoped.

"Well, what do we have here?" spat the Tayhest in my face. He didn't seem the least bit bothered by my hands grabbing his arm and relieving some of the pressure on the old scalp.

"If it isn't a puny Taran. How would you like to be dinner for me tonight?" He didn't see the relief I felt when I realized that without my uniform he didn't know who I was or that I understood the version of Hortic that he was speaking.

"Don't you make noise?" he said, lifting me even higher, until my face was even with his snout. He grabbed my throat with the other paw, and I thought I was going to die as he jerked his arm loose from my weakening grip and held me up to him to watch me turn purple. I knew I had to do something, or I was going to be leaving this world or wherever we were real soon.

"Please don't kill me," I gurgled.

He laughed at my sounds and tightened his grip with his other paw. While he was enjoying himself, and with every last ounce of strength in my arms, I took my Bic lighter out of my pocket and lit it. He spotted the flame and laughed even harder. "Oh, you're going to burn me with that?" he roared. He made no move to grab it from me, which I had hoped, the arrogant bastard. Instead he tightened his grip, which I thought was impossible, and laughed a slobbering laugh at me.

Now it was up to my lungs to keep me alive long enough for my lighter to heat up. You see, butane lighters, after they heat up long enough, don't explode; they melt the little valve on top of the butane supply and then flare up in a moment of glory. Kinda like lighter suicide, if you get my drift. I popped the hot metal collar off it and flicked it again.

I tried to imagine the little valve getting hot and melting off the top and brought the lighter toward the Tayhest, timing, if I was very lucky, the flare up to coincide with reaching his butt-ugly face.

He watched the whole thing, letting me bring it to his face, laughing at me with typical Tayhest arrogance. He threw his head back in an apparent fit of laughter. It was when he lowered his head back into place on his ugly shoulders that the lighter suddenly gave that little twitch it makes just before flare up, and I thrust it forward toward his eyes. The flame splashed directly into his eyes along with a dose of liquid butane that momentarily escaped ignition only to ignite most of the top half of his face. Tell me there is no God, go ahead, tell me.

I really can't describe his scream, but it washed over me like a wave from hell as he let go of me, and I swung away from him, filling my lungs with much-needed air. At the bottom of the arc, my hands plowed into the trash on the floor, and I feverishly hunted as I swung through it for something to use as a weapon. Just when I thought I would come up empty-handed, I felt something hard hit my left hand, some piece of metal or something. I knew it was hard, but I missed it as my swing carried me upward, but I did clear the crap away from it, so I actually spotted the end of it as I started back down like a pendulum. By now, the Tayhest had stopped screaming and, from the top of my view, was in the process of coming to slaughter me.

He stopped as I swung back toward him, certainly contemplating my demise, wiping his beady little eyes, and looking like a creature from hell's toilet bowl. I scraped through the trash and latched onto the piece of metallic trash that I had desperately tried for the first time and, without even looking, pulled it to my stomach as my swing brought me back to him. As he reached out to grab my head, I felt over the metal in my hand while trying to lower my head and make him bend down for it. One end of the metal felt very sharp, knifelike almost, while the other end felt like the handle of a gun. It also felt very much like my only chance.

In the next instant, a very quick instant, he grabbed my head from behind, and as he started to squeeze it like an orange, I brought the metal object straight up into his crotch. I had hoped to stick it in his eye, which I thought was the only vulnerable place to hurt one of these goons, but his reaction told me that there was apparently at least one other spot that was tender. The knife disappeared clear to the handle, and my hand was doused with a hot purplish black fluid, which spilled from the wound. He grunted a deep painful grunt and let go of my head like it was on fire. For a second, I hung there by the handle of the knife, and then it slid free, and away I swung, struggling to see where he was positioned in case, by some miracle, I got a second shot at him.

My gyrations caused me to spin, something I didn't want to do, and it panicked me into slashing hopelessly around, which made me spin even more wildly. As I spun, I kept catching quick looks, like watching an old nickelodeon machine, one picture at a time, until the quicker you watch them, the more it looks like a movie. By now, I was getting dizzy, so dizzy that I didn't see him drop to his knees until I almost spun into him.

He was holding his crotch area, huge amounts of fluid from the wound had already poured onto the floor, and it looked like he might fall over any second. I swung into him, slashing the weapon harmlessly against his shoulder area; and then my momentum carried me away from him, only this time I was swinging sideways, so I could see him trying to stand up.

*Shit*, I thought, *what did I do, wake him up?*

He reached his feet, and his face settled on mine; his eyes were glued to my eyes, and pain was there, seared to his bony forehead and pouring from his crotch. Yet there he stood, watching me swing back and forth in front of him, clearly calculating when I would be directly in his path. Each swing seemed like an eternity to me because I was helpless to do much but swing down through the trash and then back upward away from it. I wasn't swinging far enough to reach the walls, and I couldn't see how that would help me anyways.

"Well, come on, you big cocksucker," I said to him in Hortic, "let's see if you can catch the puny Taran." God, did I need a miracle. The reaction to my taunting was that of surprise, followed by uncontrollable, full-blown rage. You know, like a charging bull—nostrils flaring, feet pounding, and horn-tipped violence that only a stone wall three feet thick can stop. Only his pounding feet never really reached the point of pounding because he slipped in his own body fluids and fell facedown, grabbing at me as he fell. He must have some kind of luck because I swung right into his waiting arms, and he grabbed me around the waist as his feet went out from under him.

Now it was my turn to scream in pain, as I thrashed wildly at his chest and stomach areas, while his weight began to pull me apart. He wasn't trying to squeeze me to death; I think he was really just trying to pull himself up, and then he would squeeze me to death. My back felt like it was being broken in half; I could actually feel myself stretching. Little intense flashes of pain were going off all over my body as the Tayhest continued to pull himself upward. I had to do something before he reached my crotch and yanked on the wrong body part. Unfortunately the only part of him within reach was his torso, and my weapon was bouncing off his uniform like it had steel underneath it, and he was already at my hips. He must be gaining his feet because his weight seemed to be easing up. His breath was hot on my front.

No, I thought, he's getting that damn tail under him and using it to push himself upward; thank God, I was beginning to wonder how I would look as a seven footer. Another thought hit me, and I grimaced. What if he bit me. The last time I had seen a mouth like that was when I had been in a museum looking at the dinosaur exhibits. If he bit me now, I would have to change my name, and Joan and I would be girlfriends. Slowly his weight and grip eased up until I felt him lean back away from me, and I swung back away from him. I noticed his crotch was really pretty messy, so I figured it wouldn't hurt to try that spot again, especially since I didn't know what he was doing at the moment; and I had swung up, so I really couldn't see much more either. I swung back down toward him.

I lunged with both hands on the weapon and nailed him in the crotch for the last time. This time my lunge and his forward motion combined perfectly, and the weapon buried itself along with my hands deep inside him. He fell into me again, this time grabbing me around my legs with a grunt that told me everything.

He was history; I could hear it in his voice, feel it in his grip, and see it as I pulled my hands free from the area that used to be his crotch, and a huge bundle of guts and fluid poured out onto the deck. The smell was awful. I felt him slowly sliding down me, and I dropped the weapon and pushed myself against his legs. That's when I noticed the bundle of guts on the deck was still wiggling around in the fluids.

*Damn,* I thought, *this one was pregnant, real pregnant from the looks of that thing on the deck. No wonder it bled so much.*

As if answering my thoughts, it fell away from me to the side and landed on its back, its face only a matter of inches from mine, and spoke to me, gurgling fluid from its mouth.

"How did you know Taran?" it gurgled.

"I didn't," I answered back in Hortic, "but then you should know better than to fight with a Guardian." I suppose I shouldn't have said that, but my mouth always did have a mind of its own.

The word "Guardian" caused a look of anger to cross over the face of the Tayhest, and it, she, whatever, struggled to grab at me as I fought off its huge paws with arms that were running out of strength. Using its tail, it rolled over at me until it was almost on its stomach under me. I thought it was going to try to stand up again, and then it stopped moving; its arms flopped to the deck followed by its tail. It was dead, and so were my arms. I let them flop onto the creature and wondered what would happen when another one came into the room. Bet he wouldn't shake hands with me. I suppose that thought was what gave me the incentive to make my aching arms move once again, I don't know; all I know is that I didn't want to be upside down any longer.

Using his body as a platform, I pushed myself upward in one last attempt to free myself from my predicament.

As near as I could see, my feet had some kind of collar on them, and the collar was hooked over the end of one of two prongs that were attached to a ceiling bracket. I always felt my arms were big enough and strong enough to do whatever I needed to do, but somehow, doing a handstand wasn't part of the plan. In other words, it was a struggle to lift myself straight up and far enough up to unhook the collar from the prong. Even though it was downright cold in the ship, I immediately broke out in a sweat as my arms sank into the back of the creature further shortening the amount of clearance I so desperately needed to unhook. This brought on a series of grunts and curse words, until finally, with one final tantrum, the collar popped off the prong, and I tumbled down onto the deck. I laid there in catatonic relief, staring up at the prong triumphantly. That's when I noticed that there had originally been three prongs, and it suddenly occurred to me where my weapon had come from.

"Must have been one big heavy son of a bitch," I muttered to myself as I stood up for the first time in God knows how long. My whole body hurt from being stretched, my head felt very spacey, and my legs felt wobbly; but by God, I was on my feet and still breathing. Now to free myself from that damn collar. I found a magnetic lock on one side of the collar, and after a quick search of the dead Tayhest, I found the mechanism to release it. I love it when a plan comes together. Now for the door and whatever lay beyond.

This was my first time on a Tayhest Battlecruiser, but doors are doors no matter where you are, and these were no different. Locks only keep an honest person out, remember that. Or in this case, an honest person in; so consequently I had the door open in seconds, and I cautiously stepped into the corridor, which seemed deserted. Two steps down the corridor, I heard someone or something coming and ducked into the first doorway I could find and, using the same key I had lifted off the Tayhest, entered the room. It was dark, not pitch-black, but darker than the corridor, so it took a few moments for me to see where I was, and what was in there with me. Whatever it was, it was big. I approached it slowly since it appeared to be hanging upside too.

"You're a big sucker," I muttered, patting the side of the dead cow. Beside it hung another one, equally dead, hanging upside down, eyes bulging, tongue distended. Apparently this Tayhest ship was on a hunting trip of some kind when they picked me up too. But what the hell were they doing so far from home? Certainly they didn't come all the way to Earth for a sirloin dinner;

they weren't that discriminating a race. Hell, they ate most living things as far as I knew, probably roadkill too. I decided to exit the room and was about to turn and leave when I heard a sound coming from behind the cows. A groan, not a scary one, but definitely a human one. I decided to investigate, what the hell.

"What the hell are you doing here?" I said, standing in front of Gene, the rig hand I knew, who obviously hadn't made it home yet.

"Jim," he groaned, coming out of the gravity beam fog, "is that you?" He was hanging from the third prong! And he didn't look like the two heifers next to him.

"Yup, help me, Gene," I grunted, lifting him upward to free him from the prong. It took him a moment to figure out what I was doing, and then he helped me by straightening his legs and popping the collar free. I laid him down on the deck and knelt down by his ankles and freed him from the collar.

"What the hell is going on?" he asked, rubbing his ankles and inspecting the collar I removed. Gene was a good ole boy from the hills of West Virginia and just a bit freaked out by the whole thing. He sat there looking around like a foreigner.

"What do you remember last?" I countered, trying to figure out how to explain this to him. He was a good rig hand but definitely not a Rhodes scholar.

"I was gettin' in my pickup, yeah, I was just getting in my truck, when a bright light hit me," he stammered, looking up at me and then around the room again. "Hey, where the hell are we?"

"Well," I stalled, "you're probably not going to believe this."

"Try me," he drawled. He seemed braver than I thought he would be, thank God.

"OK, you've been chosen as dinner by an alien race from a galaxy far away, who just happened to be hunting on Earth for their next meal."

Silence. I could almost see the gears turning in his head.

"What the fuck," he said finally. "Are you shittin' me? 'Cause if you are, I don't 'preciate it one damn bit."

I pointed to the cows behind him. "Ask your roommates."

He jumped up off the floor when he saw them and turned to me, a look of horror on his face. He stood there confused, his mouth working silently as I turned and went back toward the door. I didn't have to tell him to follow; he caught up with me real quick. I turned and put my finger up to my lips for him to be quiet.

"Where are we going?" he said, forgetting the finger and letting his terror get the best of him.

"Look," I whispered, "we can't stay here in this food locker; sooner or later, one of these creatures is bound to come looking for"—I hesitated—"food." I didn't think it was a good time to tell him that I had iced one of them. "So be quiet and follow me, and stay close, OK?"

This time he nodded and, when the door slid open, followed me into the corridor, sticking to me like glue. Oh yeah, he was scared out of his wits when he saw the passageway and knew I wasn't joking about being on a spaceship. If I'd have farted, he would have gagged; he was so close to me. I really wouldn't have minded except I had no fucking idea what I was going to do, and I hated like hell to lead him from the frying pan into the fire. After he bumped into me a couple of times, I motioned for him to back off, or I was going to deck him. This seemed to help, and we slithered down the corridor past my cell, sliding along the curved sidewalls, hugging the bulkheads whenever we could, and jumping at every sound we heard. Not that I was spooked, mind you.

"Where are we goin'?" he whispered. "Is there a way outa here?"

I pulled up next to a bulkhead flange that ran the length of the wall and motioned him next to me. I peeked around the corner, inspecting the corridor ahead while trying to figure out a good answer for him. Unfortunately, there wasn't one.

"I don't know," I said finally, not wanting to lie to him. Hell, if the truth be known, I really didn't have an answer for that, or what the hell were we going to do when we got there either. I reached down to my ankle, it was time for help, and removed the extra sensor from inside my boot and slapped it on my wrist, motioning Gene not to ask.

"Merlin," I whispered, "can you hear me?"

I jumped when he answered me, making Gene jump also. What a pair.

"Yes," he exclaimed, "are you all right? We lost contact with you after they kidnapped you, we thought you were dead." Joan must be with him.

"Well, we're going to be, if we don't get off this ship."

"We?" he asked dumbfounded.

"I found one of the rig hands," I explained quickly, "hanging from a hook just like mine, only in another room. Tell me, does this ship have escape pods or something like that on it?" That was a prayer.

"No way, they're not allowed to do that," he chided me, "you know, fight to the death and all that good stuff. Are you in a safe place?"

"Not really," I said, looking around the corridor. "I don't think there is a safe place on this shit bucket."

"Well, see if you can find one, let me know when you do. And Joan says to be careful." His voice faded to silence. He loved playing spy games.

The coast looked clear, so we slithered down the wall to the next doorway, and after what seemed like an eternity, I slid the door open, and we jumped through it. Almost instantly it slid shut, capturing us in one of the awfullest smelling rooms I have ever been in, except maybe the locker room at the school I played football for, which I won't mention. Gene started to gag, either from the smell or the sight in front of us. Bigger than the rooms we had been in and warmer than they were, it was filled with rows of upside down animals in various stages of decay. Animals, I should add, that weren't from Earth and some of which probably weren't animals. In fact, the more I studied some of them, the more I became convinced that some of them had been caught from some kind of ocean. I left Gene and wandered down the first row, inspecting the alien creatures, especially the ones with appendages hanging down to the floor. Gene had gotten control of his stomach and caught up with me.

"What the hell are these things?" he gagged, swallowing hard.

"I don't know," I replied. "Creatures from another world somewhere, captured just like we were, only not recently, that's for sure." I held my nose as I walked past a real stinky one.

We walked past a whole bunch of jellylike masses that were hanging like snot from the hooks above them, past a few more sea creatures, and turned the corner, hiding ourselves from the doorway and anyone who might decide to enter. I was about to signal Merlin when I heard something and turned toward Gene.

"What did you say?" I asked.

"I didn't say anything; I thought you said something."

I looked in every direction, not wanting to believe my ears, and I heard it again, only this time, I was looking in Gene's direction, and his mouth didn't move. Someone, somewhere, had said help, not in English, mind you, but in some dialect I knew but couldn't name right at the moment.

I repeated the word to myself.

"Geee cha," came the reply. Help was what it meant.

Gene looked at me like I had blown a fuse but followed me as I started down the back row muttering "geee cha" every few steps. The answers were getting louder as we went, though not in our ears but in our heads, which made it all the more freaky. After several carcasses of ugly bloated creatures, we came to a whole slew of bluish green sea creatures with huge fins hanging to the floor, protruding eyes and flat faces, whiskery, almost catlike in appearance. They looked like something Dr. Seuss would invent. I reached out and touched one and felt the skinlike body. It was dried up and starting to split apart.

"Geee cha," came the sound, almost a scream now, as if I had touched it.

*Where are you?* I thought. Gene was freakin' out next to me, especially since he didn't know what the creature had said to us. He only heard the sound, and it made no sense to him. I decided to explain it, then it "spoke" again.

"Close" came the word into our heads, this time in English. It kinda freaked me, but I didn't let on to Gene, who had turned instantly white with fright. I decided not to explain anything to him just yet.

"Are you one of these things?" I said out loud, touching the next one.

"Yes, the last one."

I worked my way down the row, counting at least twelve of them until I got to the end of them. The last one was alive all right; it let its fin open and close as a signal to me.

"I am dying; even the creature next to me will no longer sustain me."

I looked between it and the blob of a creature next to it and saw how the creature had burrowed into the soft stomach of the creature next to it. I looked at the thing, and it reminded me of the huge mouse with horns that I had seen on the Mothership. It was split from top to bottom, like a Ginsu knife had gotten loose in it. I looked at the fins of the creature and back at the gaping hole in the mouse and slowly stepped out of reach of the creature. Its idea of help might not match mine. Gene was still on his feet until he looked at the carcass of the giant mouse and promptly fainted onto the floor. I started to drag him clear when the sea creature spoke to me.

"I will not hurt you" came the voice into my head. "I only opened the creature after it expired to absorb its body fluids, which until now have kept me alive; now I fear I am dying from lack of fluid as my other brothers have died."

*What can I do to help?* I thought. I looked up at the hook and saw that it had two leglike limbs that joined into one large fin at the end, which had been slung over a hook by the Tayhest, and they were slowly ripping apart. It must hurt like a mother.

I couldn't imagine what this room had been like when all these creatures had been hung up alive only to die a slow death. It must have been horrible.

"Yes," it communicated, "it was terrifying at first and then heartbreaking. Do you have any body fluids you can spare?"

"What?" I stammered. I had been imagining the sounds of the dying creatures, and it had caught me off guard.

"Do you"—it paused as if tired—"have any fluids?"

I thought about it and answered, "You mean like blood?"

"No"—another pause—"more like water; I cannot absorb blood very fast, as I learned from the creature next to me; it only kept me from drying up on the outside."

*Shit*, I thought, *what does it want me to do, piss on it?*

*What is that?*

*Urine, waste water*, I thought. I was no longer talking out loud.

*Please try*—another pause—*to piss on me.*

I stood there for a minute, thinking about what it had just asked me to do. I looked over at Gene who was still zonked out.

*OK*, I thought finally, *I'll do it on one condition.*

*What?* It sounded completely exhausted.

*That you watch those fins; I don't want to lose any body parts.*

*Yes, yes, now please, piss on me.*

I stepped toward it and unzipped Mr. Happy, who wasn't very cooperative, for which I couldn't blame him, and finally managed to coax a stream of piss out of him. I couldn't believe I was doing this.

*Too bad I haven't been drinking beer all day*, I thought, *then it would get a good drenching, hey wait, Gene had probably downed a few brews, all rig hands drink like fish, no pun intended.*

*Is that good?* It did look bluer now that I was done.

*Yes, I do feel better; the ammonia in your waste piss was very helpful, can you give me more?*

*Never happen*, I thought back at it. *I'm bone dry, but let me see if I can wake old Gene up; in the meantime, don't say anything, it will freak him out, okay?*

*Yes.*

I walked over to Gene and bent down, shaking him lightly on the shoulder until he started to move on his own. He sat up and looked around.

"Not a dream, huh?"

"Nope."

"Sorry I fainted, this is a bit of a shock for me. How do you handle this so well? You act as if this is not your first time here."

"Well, Gene," I began; boy, maybe he's not as dumb as I thought, "I watch a lot of horror movies, so nothing shocks me." Maybe he would buy that.

"Bullshit."

"Say, Gene," I said, changing the subject, "how about doing me a favor and piss on that blue creature over there." I pointed to the talker.

"What the devil," he retorted. "Why the hell do you want me to piss on that thing for?"

"Just do it, OK?" I said, persuasively pulling him to his feet. I was bigger than he was, so I guess I intimidated him a little bit too.

"Well, I guess I could do it," he complained. "Ain't nothin' funny goin' on here that I don't know about, is there?"

"Let's just say you're doing a friend a favor; I'll even turn my back." I turned around as he commented on faggots in general, and in no time, I heard the sound of piss splashing over the creature and dripping on the floor.

*That was very good* came the words into my head.

I turned to Gene and the creature. He was busy zipping up and jumped at the voice in his head. He looked at me suspiciously but didn't act like he was going to faint, then his look changed to "how about telling me what's going on here before I get pissed" look. Not that it would do him any good.

"OK," I answered his look. "What we have here is a telepathic creature who needs fluid to stay alive. I know it looks like a cross between a fish, a man, and a cat," I said, raising my hand for silence, "but it's also highly intelligent and might help us get out of here." That seemed to make him feel better, but I doubted it was going to be of any help to us.

*Yes,* said the creature to Gene, *I can read your mind. All of my kind can do that; that is how we communicate on our planet.*

*You look bluer now,* I thought.

*Yes,* it replied, *but I still need more fluid or I will still die shortly. Is there any fluid on this vessel?*

"Not that I know of," I said out loud.

"What about those giant jellyfish over there," remarked Gene, pointing back toward the first row.

"It's worth a try"—I nodded—"if you'll help me get it down off the hook and carry it over there." He had a lot of common sense.

*We're going to move you to some creatures in the next row that look like they came from some ocean somewhere; maybe their moisture will keep you alive until we get off this hellhole.*

*I will not hurt you, but do not touch my fins, as you call them, they are very . . . sharp.*

I put my arms around what I guess you would call the midsection of the creature and lifted to test the thing's weight. It was lighter than I thought.

*I have lost a lot of fluid, but do not squeeze too hard; I have no skeleton as you do.*

"Right," I voiced, "give me a hand, Gene; you lift it up, and I'll take the end with the fins." Gene jumped right into the task, shaking off his earlier fright, and gently lifted the creature upward. We laid it on the deck.

Almost immediately the thing began to shorten and compress, changing rapidly into almost a round ball; its fins unfolded at its sides momentarily, and then it stretched back out again, though not as long as it had been a la hook.

*Feel better?* I think Gene and I both thought it at the same time.

*Yes, oh yes, the stretching from that hook was torture to me.*

Carefully we moved it across the floor and around the rows to the jellylike creatures. When it was almost under them, we stopped and stood back.

*Should we hang you between them?* I thought.

*No, I can climb up myself. I think these creatures are loaded with fluid. You may have saved my life; I am in your debt.*

While it was communicating to us, it stretched upward toward the closest one, and I saw a set of arms with claws on the ends appear from under the fins, and it used them to grip the jelly thing, pulling itself up the side of the thing.

*Where had I seen claws like that?* I wondered.

"This is wonderful," it answered, "but I cannot answer your question."

"What did you ask it?" asked Gene.

"Oh, nothing important," I shrugged. "Merlin, did you hear any of this?" I decided that this room was as safe as we were going to get.

"Who are you talking to?" asked Gene. "Is it the same guy who talked with you earlier and told us to hide?"

"Yeah," I said, motioning him to be quiet.

*Can he help us?* thought the creature.

*I won't know until I talk to him*, I thought, *but if he can't, then we got big problems. So give me a minute, will you?*

*Yes, please, go ahead and talk with . . .*

"Come on, Merlin, talk to me," I muttered into my sensor, ignoring the thoughts of the creature, who seemed to have at least got his talking energy back.

"Yes," said Merlin's voice from my sensor, "stay put where ever you are. Crouthhamel is almost here, and he's got a plan."

*Somebody is approaching*, warned the creature.

I almost didn't pay any attention to the thought, then it hit me what the creature had just said to us.

"Gene," I exclaimed, "wedge yourself in between a couple of these dead creatures and keep your feet out of sight!" I pointed to two huge carcasses, and he jumped in between them as I ran down the row, searching for my own cover.

Just as I disappeared around the first row, I heard the door slide open. I ran past the rest of the blue sea creatures, knowing I needed a place to hide desperately and unable to find two creatures big enough to hide behind. Without a moment's hesitation, I made my mind up and climbed into the open underbelly of the creature that the sea creature had cut open and dragged my feet up off the floor without causing it to swing. I don't think I need to describe what it felt like or smelled like; just take my word for it, it was the most disgusting thing I think I have ever done. Well, almost anyways.

*Can you hear me?* I thought to the creature.
*Yes, very faintly.*
*Tell Gene to act dead.*
*I will.*

It got real quiet after that; apparently the creature could select which person he wanted to communicate with, and stuffed inside the belly of this giant mouse, I couldn't hear a damn thing either. Nevertheless, I found myself straining to hear if the Tayhest that entered the room was still here. It seemed like hours had gone by before I finally heard Merlin on my sensor. God, his voice sounded loud.

"Jim."
"Ssshh."
"What?"
"Quiet, someone's in the room with us." Then I heard Gene's voice from nearby. I stuck my head out of the cut, and Gene almost fainted again. He had been walking down the row, looking for me.

"Coast is clear," he advised me, watching me climb out of the carcass, shaking his head. This was one trip he wasn't going to forget for a long time.

"Whatever it was that came into the room, left right away," he explained, "and the creature told me that it went away from here. It also told me that you killed one of the things."

"Yeah, well, it was me or it, and frankly, I like me a whole lot more than a fucking Tayhest." We walked back to the blue creature; it had burrowed into the jelly blob next to it and was even brighter blue now.

*So you did kill the Tayhest*, it thought.

*Yes, damnit*, I thought back, *it was me or him, make that her.*

*We cannot kill another living thing; we are forbidden even to save our own lives.*

*Maybe that's why there's a dozen of you hanging from hooks on a Tayhest ship*, I shot back. *Besides, I'm a Guardian, so I'm allowed.*

*You are a Guardian, an Alpharian Guardian?*

*Yes, is there something wrong with that? I guess I am a bit grumpy. I always get that way when I'm covered with blood and guts, sorry.*

"Jim," interrupted Merlin, "Mr. C is here, along with some other Guardians."

"Where is here?" I said quickly.

"Just outside the Darassin system, now be quiet and let Mr. C explain what he wants to do." Merlin sounded a bit annoyed with me, which was not unusual.

"Go for it," I stated. *And I hope it's a good plan*, I thought. What the hell were we doing outside the Darassin star system?

"Jim, this is Crouthhamel, in just over two of your Taran minutes, the ship you are in will pass directly into the path of the interstellar transport beam from Altair."

*Here comes the good part*, I thought sarcastically to myself.

"They finally got it operational?" I said out loud.

"Yes, listen, will you?" he chided me. "We have disabled the warning buoys and the advanced warning signal that precedes the transport beam, and if our calculations are close enough, we should be able to materialize the cargo right in the ship and probably around it."

"You mean the shipment that is being sent from Altair to another star system?"

"Yes, when that happens, you will need to be near the outer wall of the room you are in. Merlin says he has your location. He will breech the ship and take you on board. We cannot risk a direct confrontation with the ship as it has the anti-Disorganizer material on it. Only Merlin can get through that, and I'd rather we sneak you out than try a direct attack, which might kill all of you."

"OK," I answered, "what are they shipping with the transport beam?"

"You don't want to know," answered Merlin matter-of-factly.

"Yes, I do." That had to be the really bad part; I knew it.

"No, you don't, just get to the wall away from the door," joined in Crouthhamel, "and hurry, you don't have time to argue, now go!"

*Are you coming*, I thought, motioning Gene toward the wall.

Silence. For some reason, the blue thing wasn't talking now.

I shoved Gene toward the wall and turned back to the creature.

*Why aren't you coming?* I thought. *Is it because I'm a Guardian?*

*Yes, we are forbidden to talk to Guardians. I will stay and die with the rest of my kind.*

*Oh, no you're not*, I thought, grabbing it between its legs and dragging it away from the jelly blob and across the floor to the wall. It flopped and clawed at the floor, but true to its word, it didn't try to hurt me.

"We're at the wall, Merlin," I announced, not releasing my hold on the blue thing, which had stopped struggling. It felt heavier.

"Thirty seconds, Jim; on my command, take a deep breath and hold it," he advised.

"Not until you tell me what's being transported." I bluffed.

"Water, happy now," answered Merlin as Gene looked at me like I was wrong to give our saviors a hard time. He didn't know Merlin like I did, and I smelled a rat.

"What kind of water, not that shit water from inside the Nephid, tell me that's not it." Oh, shit. I looked at Gene like "I told you so!"

"Take a deep breath, here it comes," laughed Merlin, giving me my answer.

"You fucker!" I yelled, and then I stopped. Directly across from us, the door opened, and a whole squad of Tayhest burst into the room. They didn't look happy either. Out of the corner of my eye, I saw Gene start to freak out at the sight of them, and I didn't know whether he was going to faint or run, so I grabbed him with my free arm and pulled him to my side. He started whitening and then fainted, pulling me to the floor with him. I felt one of the creatures fins brush against my leg and saw the blood gush from my leg before the pain hit my brain. Then we were suddenly underwater, a nutrient solution they had called it on Pyritium, though I had another name for it.

I don't know what happened to the Tayhest, but less than a second after being submerged, the wall dissolved behind us, and Merlin's claw came out of nowhere, searching for my hands. I wasn't going to let go of either Gene or the blue creature, so I swung my legs around and bumped the claw. Instantly the claw closed around my right ankle and, just as quickly, pulled the whole bunch of us through the opening. The next thing I knew, we were being dragged into Merlin through a wall of water, and then we were on the floor of my ship, gulping for air and wiping "nutrient" from our eyes. My leg was bleeding badly, and my other leg felt broken. I let go of Gene, and he sat up sputtering, but when I let go of the blue thing, it just laid there.

"Commencing firing," said Merlin.

Suddenly I felt Merlin shake, and I knew he had just destroyed the Tayhest ship with the medal in his nose.

"Target eliminated," he again spoke. "All that's left is water, Crouthhamel."

*So that's who he's talking to*, I reasoned. *No wonder he sounds so professional.*

I felt a hand on my gashed leg and cleared my eyes enough to see Joan kneeling at my side. She was wiping my wound clean and trying to stop the bleeding. Gene had stood up and was looking around the room.

"Hi, baby," I said casually, "fancy meeting you here."

"Honey, you're cut real bad. I can see the—"

"Don't tell me," I stopped her. "Merlin, tell Crouthhamel I need the Bonemender real quick." I looked up at her. "I think my other leg is broken too."

"Ooh, baby," she comforted me, giving me a hug and a kiss. I loved it when I was hurting. And she didn't care if I was covered in "nutrient" either.

Gene had gone up to the command chairs and was taking it all in but not touching a thing. I lay back down next to the blue creature and looked over at it. It was still quite blue, so I knew it wasn't dead.

*Still not talking*, I thought.

*You should have let me die.* The voice was loud and bitter, no, not bitter, but rather accusatory, like I had a plan for it.

Joan jumped at the voice, not knowing where it was coming from and not wanting to accept the obvious source.

"Telepathic," I explained, pointing. "Hates Guardians too."

*I don't hate you.*

"Docking with Mr. C, Jim," broke in Merlin.

"Thanks for saving us, Merlin," I replied. Never hurt to compliment someone.

"Good to have you back, pal."

Through the pain, I smiled. Yes, it was good to be back, very good.

The hatchway slid open, and Crouthhamel strode in, cool as a cucumber, saw the blue creature, and did a doubletake. Behind him, a furry dog growled and rushed around him. It was Wolf, looking just as he had before being burned. He got almost to me, tail wagging, and stopped. He looked at me affectionately and sniffed the air as if to say, "I'll wait 'til you're cleaned up before I lick your face."

Crouthhamel turned and spoke to someone behind him and stepped aside to let Alzador see the blue creature. He looked at the creature and then at me, then he clicked his mouth and shook his head. Gene had come back to us when the hatch had opened, and now he stood gaping at Crouthhamel and Alzador.

"Did you bring the Bonemender?" I snapped. "I'm bleeding to death and . . ."

Crouthhamel silenced me by pulling the device from his belt and handing it to me. Quickly I turned it on and applied it to the gash. Almost immediately, the pain in that leg began to subside as the wound began to close. My other leg was killing me but not losing blood like a Delta faucet. I went to work on it finally, finding the ankle broken and not paying attention to who entered the ship from Crouthhamel's ship. But I heard her.

"Jimmy," cried Tamee, rushing around Crouthhamel and Alzador, looking very excited to see me and looking quite pregnant, before stopping at Wolf's side. She sniffed the odor of the nutrient and came no closer to me. She blew me a kiss.

"Hi, Tamee," I said, catching the look on Joan's face out of the corner of my eye, "what are you doing here?" *Besides screwing up my life on Earth*, I thought.

"We all came running when we heard you had been snatched by the Tayhest. There must be a dozen ships out there, ooh, what is that?" she added, pointing to the blue thing.

"A Teeber," answered Alzador. Which meant nothing to me but made Tamee step quickly back toward him and Crouthhamel, which made me wonder what the hell I'd gotten myself into this time. *And now for some more shit*, I thought.

"Are you Joan?" asked Tamee, looking over at Joan and then Gene who was taking it all in, not wanting to believe what he was seeing.

"Yes, I am," she said, smiling back at Tamee, and walked over to join the group, leaving me sitting on the floor. "Jim didn't tell me there were female Guardians too."

"Well, not many," answered Tamee. "I knew that was you. Jim has told me so much about you; I've been dying to meet you." Then they hugged each other.

I suddenly understood how a bigamist feels when he's caught, and I laughed right out loud at my predicament, which made everyone stop talking and look down at me.

"Care to share the joke with us?" asked Joan coyly. They were huddling now.

"Later," I said, finishing up mending the ankle Merlin broke with the claw when he snatched us. I stood up and tried it.

I left Joan and Tamee talking and walked over to Alzador and Mr. C, pocketing the Bonemender rather than giving it back, and found they were whispering about the Teeber.

"Thanks for saving my ass," I said to both of them. Wolf and Gene had followed me over to them, leaving the two women alone, a move that seemed dangerous, if you know what I mean.

"No problem," said Crouthhamel, "but I think, after you get cleaned up, that we should talk."

"About the Teeber?"

"That and other things," he said. "Why don't you and your friend get cleaned up, and then we can figure out a good plan of action."

"Sure," I said suspiciously. Wonder what I've done now.

Gene had wandered back to Joan and Tamee. Wolf was still sniffing at me, so I bent down and rubbed his back, making his tail start wagging.

"Are you glad to see me?" I asked him. I knew he was, but I wasn't ready for him to answer me.

"Yup," he said quietly, so only I could hear him, "but you smell too bad to lick."

I stood there bent over, my mouth almost hitting the floor with surprise. I couldn't believe I just heard my dog talking to me. Maybe I hit my head somewhere, and I'm actually unconscious.

*No, you're not unconscious*, thought the Teeber.

Both Crouthhamel and Alzador jumped at the voice; they must have thought the Teeber was dead.

*You don't look so blue*, I thought. *Are you in need of more fluid?*

*No, let me die.*

*No. I cannot do that, regardless of what you think of Guardians; we do not kill at random or without just cause.* Forgetting about Wolf, I stood up and called to Merlin.

"Yes, boss of bosses," he answered pleasantly sarcastic.

"Can you make a tub for the Teeber and fill it with the nutrient solution?"

*Why are you doing this?* asked the Teeber.

I chose not to answer.

"Yes, as long as you and Gene get cleaned up, so I can get this room cleaned up, and we can all sit down and talk, ha," smirked Merlin.

Gene was talking to Joan and Tamee as I walked over to them and motioned him to follow me, something he was getting good at, and the two of us headed for the shower. All in all, I'd have to say he was handling all this pretty good. I couldn't wait to be alone with Joan. I hoped that Tamee had not spilled the beans about our little lovemaking episode. Then it hit me, and I stopped dead in my tracks. Tamee was pregnant, holy shit! It couldn't be, no, could it be that she's carrying my child? And I left them alone to talk. What, was I crazy? That's for sure, fucking crazy as a loon. And not much smarter either.

"Something wrong, Jim?" asked Gene, who had stopped walking when I did, not knowing if he should go farther or not.

"Nothing you need to worry about, so let's get cleaned up, shall we?"

Now I knew why Merlin had laughed. My head was spinning, imagining, and trying to comprehend everything that was happening around and to me. I needed a shower, a drink, and a smoke. Big time.

I gave Gene an ordinary uniform, his clothes were ruined, and we rejoined the rest of the party, looking and feeling refreshed and, above all, safe. Well, Gene felt safe; I felt worried, especially when I walked into the room and found the two women still talking and having a wonderful time together. Wolf came up to me and licked my face and said hello, something I still found very disconcerting. And both Tamee and Joan commented on how nice and clean I looked and then gave me a big hug together, not separately, but together. I got Gene and I a drink. Merlin had already seen to the ladies, and then I went over to the tub that Merlin had formed next to the side wall and inspected the Teeber.

*How are you feeling now?*

*I am completely recovered.*

*Good*, I thought, and I turned to walk away.

*Jim*, the Teeber thought to me, *I am grateful for being rescued, and I do believe you are a good and decent being. I also must tell you, you have a destiny far greater than you can imagine; I see it now, you will do great things.*

*But?* I asked. *There had to be a 'but.' There was always a 'but' in my life.*

*Perhaps we can discuss some things later, when you have sorted out your other problems.*

*Sure, wait a minute, what other problems?*

"Jimmy," said Joan, a bit sardonically, standing quietly behind me, "why don't you join us. Crouthhamel and Alzador will be back in a minute, and then you'll probably have to go talk to them, and I won't see you for who knows how long."

I turned to her and swirled the drink in my hand. "You sure you want me to join you?" I put on my best sympathy look, the beagle look. Our eyes met.

"Why not, you intergalactic stud, you," she laughed.

*Uh-oh, I was in trouble now,* I thought.

*No, you're not,* thought the Teeber. *I sense a feeling of wonderment from your female and also a little regret that the child-carrying female, the Nack, is not herself, but no jealousy, very interesting.*

*Thanks,* I thought.

"Jim," said Tamee, "are you going to join us?"

"Oh, yeah, sorry, I must have been spacing off," I lied. I noticed that Gene had grabbed a seat next to Joan, leaving me a seat between them. Thanks a boatload, buddy. I sat down, a bit disconcerted.

"Tamee was telling me," began Joan matter-of-factly, "that this is her last outing until after the baby is born."

"Oh," I replied, "Gene have you been introduced to Tamee?"

He nodded but said nothing. What a brilliant conversationalist.

"What the hell was that Tayhest doing in the Taran system?" I asked Tamee, trying to ignore the huge bulge where her tiny waist used to be.

"I'm not sure," she answered. "Crouthhamel has been very quiet about the whole thing, so I suspect there's more to it than we think."

Joan pinched me, and I jumped. "What did you do that for?"

"Don't you want to know when the baby is due?" she smirked.

"Yes," I said, turning to Tamee, giving her a warm smile while my hand reached under Joan's butt and pinched her back. She smacked at it but said nothing.

"The babies are due in one cycle; I can't wait to see what they look like. Joan wants you to bring her to see me, will you?"

I was trying to figure out the Nackan cycle length when her words finally registered in the old cerebellum.

"Babies?" I said stunned. Oh my god, what have I done now?

"Why, yes, Jim," confirmed Tamee, "we Nacks always have multiple births, sometimes as many as nine or ten."

"Nine or ten?" I said, dazed. Joan laughed, and I turned to her; my face said it all, and she laughed harder. It was nice to know she was enjoying this, ha!

"But according to my sister, I'm not expecting more than four; here, want to feel your children kicking?" answered Tamee, grabbing my hand and placing it on her exposed swollen stomach. Gene had just put it all together and choked on his drink to let us all know that he knew who the father was. He looked at me strangely.

I placed my hand on her stomach, and sure enough, I could feet the little rug rats moving around inside her. Did I say "rug rats"? Holy shit and Shineola.

*She will give birth to three very large Nacks*, thought the Teeber.

*Will she be all right?* I thought back.

*Yes, but don't get real close to her for a few days afterward.*

"Ha,ha,ha," I laughed. "I can feel them moving," I added, covering up what the Teeber had just relayed to me. It had a dry sense of humor.

*I wasn't trying to be funny*, it thought to me. *Nacks can be very emotional for a brief period after giving birth.*

Oh, I thought, *you mean like violently emotional? Jesus Christ.*

*Something like that, but I'm being sanguine.*

"So can I go see Tamee?" asked Joan. "Tamee says it will be about two weeks more."

"No, I mean sure," I replied, making them both smile, "as long as I'm not off somewhere doing God-knows-what." I pulled my hand from Tamee's stomach, and she zipped up the front of her uniform, barely getting it over the kids. I groaned watching her struggle. Somehow her fleshy stomach wasn't doing it for me today.

"Nine or ten?" said Gene out loud. He looked at me like I was, you know.

Joan laughed again and went to fill her glass, patting me on the back as she did so.

"Three," I answered, "only three."

"How do you know that?" asked Tamee. "From feeling my stomach?"

Joan had stopped in her tracks, listening to our exchange.

"Let's just say a little bird told me," I fibbed.

"Did your little bird tell you that what you two have done has never been done before," asked Joan, continuing across the room, "and that Tamee's whole planet has been following her pregnancy since her copulation with the mighty Guardian Jim, holder of the Medal of Uhlon Bathor and the Claw of Catau?"

*God, she loved to tease me*, I thought, looking over at her filling another round for all of us, smiling like the cat that ate the canary. Then I noticed the Teeber was literally going crazy in his tub.

*What is wrong?* I thought, not knowing whether I could direct my thoughts with any accuracy.

*The Claw*, it screamed in my head, *you have the Claw?*

"What's wrong, Jim?" said Joan, as I held my hands up to my head.

The Teeber was screaming at me in his own language, so loud and so quickly that I couldn't follow what it was so upset about, and its voice was actually hurting me. It felt like my head was going to burst.

*Stop, you're hurting me*, I thought back. *Please, I know nothing about you or the damn Claw, so settle down, and we can talk about it.* Suddenly the pain went away, and as I pulled my hands from my head, I found everyone staring at me, looking at me like I was crazy.

"I'm OK," I said slowly, "but it would seem that my possession of the Claw has really upset the Teeber." I shook my head, and it suddenly dawned on me where I had seen another Claw like the one I had on my wall; I had seen it on the Teeber. Boy, I couldn't wait to find out what that was all about. I was about to find out when Crouthhamel and Alzador came striding back into the ship through the airlock, looking and acting very tense.

"I hate to break up the party, but we have to leave immediately," growled Crouthhamel, motioning to Tamee to move it. "Jim, go on home. I'll get back to you later; there is no time to talk now, but stay in touch with Merlin at all times."

"Gotcha, boss," I said, standing up and saluting him. Gene stood up and walked over to him and stuck out his hand.

"Thanks for rescuing us," he spoke, looking at the three of them, Tamee, Alzador, and Crouthhamel. He was getting used to the tall red man, but when Alzador's arm came out from under his wing, and his clawlike hand extended toward him, he hesitated before grabbing it firmly. Alzador smiled, a rare occurrence, and Tamee gave him a quick kiss on the cheek, which made Gene blush profusely. *I think he likes her*, I thought. I looked at Joan, and she winked slyly at me, to let me know she had picked up on it also.

"No problem," said Crouthhamel. "I'm just glad it worked out OK."

"Jim," said Tamee, as the other two disappeared into the airlock, "it was good to see you again. I missed you, please come see me." She said it all bluntly and honestly, and I walked over to her and gave her a hug and a kiss. She entered the airlock and turned to Joan, who had come over to us, and gave her a hug too.

"We'll be there," she said to Tamee, as the hatch closed in front of the smiling Nack. Motherhood agreed with her, that was for sure.

Joan put her arm around me, and we turned back around toward Gene, who by now was acting like a seasoned space traveler, busily mixing himself another drink at the synthesizer.

"Well, Merlin," I said sighing, "what do you say we head home?"

"Sounds like a good idea." He probably couldn't wait to get back to TV land.

"How about you, Gene, ready to go home?"

He nodded.

"Me too," said Joan, "I've had all the excitement I can handle for one day."

"Me too," I said, looking over at the Teeber. I knew there was a story soon to be told, and I wondered if I really wanted to hear it. I got no reaction to my thoughts, so I turned my attention to Gene and Joan.

I took Joan to the left command chair and left her in Merlin's hands and walked back to Gene, who was helping me straighten up the table and chewing down the last of the appetizers that Merlin had made while we were showering and changing.

"Man, Jim, these little meatballs are tastier than deer meat," he complimented me. "What the heck are they made from?"

"Garf," I said, pressing a button on the wall, which made the table disappear into the floor and the chairs dissolve also. Gene took it all in and finally asked me.

"What's Garf?"

"You don't want to know," answered Merlin for me.

"Is that your computer?"

"Oh, he's much more than that," I commented, "and he's right, you don't want to know."

Gene laughed for the first time, a real hee-haw of a laugh. "You don't know either, do you?"

"No," I laughed, "and I don't want to either."

I had Merlin form a more comfortable chair for him, one that faced the forward screen, and I had him strap himself into it, just as a precaution. I started to head for my seat, and I thought of something and turned back to Gene. Wolf had already settled himself beside my chair.

"Of course, you realize that everything you saw and heard here today can never be spoken of again to anyone," I warned him dead seriously.

He looked up at me and smiled, then he laughed again.

"What?"

"Well, I could probably convince my wife that I had been kidnapped by aliens; she might believe me about that," he explained and then stopped, shaking his head.

"What, what," I egged him on. I was good at that.

"Nobody, and I mean, nobody would believe me if I told them I had been rescued by the devil, an owl, and a pussycat." He laughed, I laughed, hell, I think even Wolf and Merlin laughed. Joan was giggling as I strapped in next to her.

"Did he say what I think he said?" she asked, still laughing.

"Yup," I answered, "the devil, an owl, and a pussycat!"

# CHAPTER 13

## Drunk and Ugly

Once you pass through the crap surrounding our solar system, the Oort Cloud, I think they call it, the first thing that hits you is how bright the sun really is, and how far out into space the "flames" from the sun actually reach, something you can't see from Earth, for whatever reason. This proved to be very exciting for Joan and Gene, as well as Wolf who quietly commented to me on how hot it looked. Without letting Gene hear us, I managed to carry on a small, or should I say limited conversation with Wolf; it took me a while to discover finally that although he could now speak, thanks to the wonderful things they did to him on Jebis, he was still a dog with a dog's brain. It did, however, now give him the ability to say yes and no to me, which is at times a real blessing and other times not a real blessing, to say the least.

"This is a real hoot," commented Gene as we circled Saturn for a second and final time and headed for Mars, so they could see the cuts in the planet surface.

"Fascinating, just fascinating," replied Joan, reaching over to squeeze my hand affectionately. She seemed quite happy that I was soon to be a daddy, something I couldn't seem to get used to, all things considered. Maybe space made you happy, who knew.

"Pretty balls," quipped Wolf. He was fascinated too.

"Wolf, be quiet," I said quickly, but not quickly enough.

"Jim," said Gene carefully, "I could have sworn your dog just said something like "pretty balls"; tell me I'm not hearing things."

"Yes," answered Wolf, turning his head toward Gene.

Gene was silent for a minute and then laughed.

"I get it," he said finally. "What a great trick. I had no idea you were a ventriloquist. But how do you get him to turn his head?"

I could see Joan was about to bust open with laughter, and I had to hold myself back from laughing too. Somehow I had to teach Wolf when he could talk and when he couldn't; otherwise, it might become a real problem.

"Timing, Gene, it's all timing."

"Timing," mimicked Wolf, rolling the word around in his mouth and saying it again, "timing."

Joan, if not for her straps, would have been on the floor by now; she was laughing so hard. I looked over at her to be quiet, but she was lost in the laugh, and it was contagious too.

To Wolf, this was a sure sign that I was happy to see him again, so he stood up and walked around to the front of my chair and put his front paws on my lap. I looked down at him and smiled, remembering some of the things we had done together.

"Wolf and Jim!" he said, smiling back at me as best a dog can smile, tail wagging, waiting to have me pet him.

"You're a good dog," I said, pulling him upward so I could reach the spot on his back that he loved to have scratched more than any other spot. I dug my fingers into his fur and began the ritual.

Mars went by us, and Earth appeared ahead, followed by a chorus of oohs and aahs.

Gene's truck was still at the location even though we had been gone Monday and most of Tuesday. The rig had vanished, but from the looks of it, Rick must have had them moved to an offset location, and in its place, a three-tank battery had been installed. Rick's truck was parked next to Gene's, and he appeared from behind one of the tanks as we settled a few feet above the location. He motioned to me and pointed to where he had just come from, and we all scrambled down the hatchway steps so Merlin could close up and remain invisible. He wasted no time in reaching us.

"Bickford's checking out the meter site we set yesterday," he said hurriedly, "and I don't think he wants to see you right now; it's a damn good well"—he gestured—"and he's a little pissed that you're offsetting it so quickly, and where the hell have you been for three days?"

"Why's he mad at me?" I exclaimed. He was so cantankerous.

"Because I permitted the offset in your name," replied Rick, smiling.

"Oh, I get it." I laughed; the prick had put it in my name. "You prick!" He knew I meant it good-naturedly; we always swore at each other.

"So where the fuck have you been?" That's all he wanted to know.

I was about to explain how I had been abducted after he left my ass on the road when old beak nose Bickford came out from behind the tanks. He saw us and stopped momentarily and then charged over to us, like we were trespassers and he was the Sheriff. I looked at Joan and Rick and shrugged my shoulders. Gene had wandered to his truck and was looking at it like he'd like to switch it for Merlin. I looked at Bickford; his face always looked like someone had just stuck a corncob up his ass.

"Edwards," he began, without so much as a hello, "when I bought this lease, we agreed that I would have first option on the rest of it."

"That's right," I agreed.

"Then what the fuck are you doing, offsetting my well?" he sputtered, obviously annoyed, which was normal for him.

"This is the Collin's lease, correct?" I asked, smiling up at him. He was tall but nothing like Crouthhamel.

His eyes bulged as he leaned down at me. "You mean that offset is on another lease?"

I nodded, still smiling. "If I may," I remarked, "quote you on what you said when I offered you the entire package of leases in this hollow, 'I'm only buying this lease because I may need another location if I can't drill another well on the Simmon's lease and, and'"—raising my voice—"'this area is no damn good anyways.'" He knew he had said it. Now he was really glaring at me.

"Well, you should have offered it to me; haven't I bought enough goddamn stuff from you?" he argued back at me.

"No, not really," I said, "although you made several promises and certainly put me through the ringer while you were at it."

He smiled, which startled all of us. Apparently he was one of those people that liked to be argued with and probably liked to be tied up while having sex too. I smiled at the thought.

"There are plenty of excellent offset locations," offered Rick, the sly devil.

"How so," demanded Bickford, stalling around while he thought of a way to get his bony hands on the rest of the leases.

"Well," said Rick, pulling a small version of a land map out of his back pocket and unfolding it, "your lease is right in the middle."

I thought Bickford had swallowed his tongue for a minute.

Joan poked me in the side, and I nodded. I was pretty tired too.

"Why don't we discuss this tomorrow," I said, smiling, looking up at the western ridge and the disappearing sun. "I'm sure we can work out something."

Bickford had grabbed the map from Rick and was studying the rest of the acreage. It made me just a bit angry since I had gone over it with him several times in his office. Now he was paying attention or, should I say, paying for not paying attention.

"When are you leaving," I said to Rick.

"Well, we just finally set the rig up this afternoon, so I guess we could call it quits, it's your quarter."

I pulled him aside, away from everyone. "How many quarters do I have left?" I asked. It was our drilling fund, not just mine, but I started it in my name.

"You don't want to know, let's just say, enough to drill in the offset but probably not enough to do much else."

"Ouch," I replied. I needed to spend a little time on the ground that was certainly obvious.

"Well, let's shut down for today, I think you and I need to go over all this, and I need a good night's sleep if I'm going to lock horns with Prickford tomorrow."

Rick nodded and set off toward the new location, leaving us with Bickford. I walked up to Bickford and smiled. He smiled, almost.

"Let's get together tomorrow, Mr. Bickford," I offered.

"My office, say, ten o'clock," he replied, going for the power position.

"Nah," I replied casually, "let's meet at noon at my office."

He nodded agreement, knew I had him, and smiled, as he turned and walked to Rick's truck.

The ride back into town was a very quiet one, primarily because old man Bickford was with us, sitting up front with Rick, who desperately wanted to pump me for info on where I had been and why Gene, of all people, was with me. To make matters worse, the old coot was pumping Rick for all the free advice he could get out of him about geology. I thought I was the only one allowed to do that. Joan was unusually quiet, not cool quiet, like she was mad, more like she was waiting to be alone with me and had something to say of great importance, and because she couldn't say it now, and because it was occupying her thoughts, she said nothing at all. I knew she wasn't mad at me, her smiles and actions confirmed that, but I knew something was bothering her. It wasn't Tamee, I knew that, although it should have been, and that sorta bothered me. But worst of all, since the old coot was with us, I couldn't risk boarding Merlin, so we had decided to go with Rick. Consequently, the trip took us back through the hollow, what a fuckin' mess, and two hours more before we dropped Dickfuck off at his office. Then we headed for Rick's place, averaging twenty questions per mile. My car was sitting in the grass alongside his driveway when we pulled in, and I noticed the grass was cut underneath it.

I deposited Joan in the passenger's side and climbed into the driver's side after promising to call Rick later. My keys were in the ignition, and the engine, a smooth 400, fired up on the first crank. To me, this was going to be so enjoyable, driving my car for the first time in so long, I couldn't remember. I backed down the driveway, feeling like a kid with a new toy and swung out into the street. I shifted into drive and turned my head toward Joan.

"Wanna get some dogs on the way home?" I asked, feeling hungry for real food.

"No," she said softly, "I'm not really hungry," then she added, "but we can stop, and you can get something to eat."

"What's a matter," I joked, "eat too many Garf balls?" While I was waiting for her to answer me, my hand felt for my wallet, and I realized I had left it in the pants that I had been wearing earlier. I wondered if it was still in the back pocket or somewhere outside the Darassin system, floating around in the nutrient water. I started to ask Joan if she had any money when she answered me.

"They shifted my territory on me," she blurted out, sounding as if she was going to cry.

"What does that mean?" I asked quietly. I knew; I just wanted her to tell me. It felt icy cold in the car, a cold that runs up your spine and makes your hands shake too.

"I have to move to Los Angeles," she said it sadly; the implications went unstated, but we both knew them. She was leaving, as in, forever.

"You have to move?" I asked. "Why don't you quit and stay with me."

She sat there silently for a couple of minutes and finally spoke. "Jim, you know this job is my career, and besides, you may leave at any moment and not be back for six months. I can't sit around waiting for you to come back, wondering if you are even coming back and, most of all, not knowing if you are dead or alive."

I nodded; that made sense. Then why did I get the feeling she wanted to go?

"When are you going?" I knew that answer too. Pronto, baby.

"Tomorrow," she said slowly. "I have to be there by Thursday." We sat in silence the rest of the way home. I had nothing to say; hell, what was left to say. She wasn't just leaving West Virginia; she was leaving me for good too. I almost decided to propose to her, but something made me keep from asking her; something told me to be quiet as far as that was concerned. But part of me also had to know if she still loved me or not.

We entered the house, going our separate ways, mine to the bathroom, hers to the phone where I heard her booking her flight. I fled to the shower and let it run for quite a while, trying like hell to figure out how our relationship had gone to hell so fast. While I was sitting on the bed, putting on clean jeans, she entered the room and sheepishly began to pull her stuff out of the drawers, laying them on the bed next to me. I had a lump in my throat the size of a baseball.

"Did they give you a bigger territory?" I asked, trying to keep the conversation light and trying not to probe too conspicuously.

"No," she answered finally, "it's a promotion." She kept on sorting and folding. "I am being made vice president and national director of the retail division."

"No shit," I gasped, "that's fantastic; when did you find out?"

"I knew some time ago that I was in the running for the position, then when you didn't show up with Rick, I had Merlin take me home so I could check the messages on my machine and then your house too. There were no messages from you, but there was one from my home office, telling me to call them immediately. Merlin made the connections while we were looking for you; that's when they told me that I had been chosen. I had wanted to spend a couple days with you, Jim, but now there is no time left."

She didn't say it to make me feel guilty, but it did. All the space travelin' is what did this to your relationship, you idiot. What did you expect her to do, wait?

"I'm sorry, Joan," I said finally, after scolding myself.

Merlin knew; no wonder he was so quiet. I glanced at my sensor and thought about thanking him, but I knew it wasn't his fault. Plus, he really hadn't had time to warn me anyways; besides, what could he say, "Oh, by the way, your girlfriend is about to dump you"? She seemed happy to talk about the promotion, so I let her talk away.

"I won't be out on the road anymore. I'll have my own office," she rambled pleasantly, "with my own staff and everything."

I grabbed her as she walked by me and pulled her to me. "I'm very proud of you," I said, nuzzling her neck. She didn't pull away from me, but she didn't seem quite in the mood for a roll in the sack. "When you get settled in, I'll come see you." There, I had said it; now I would find out if I was welcome.

"Sure," she said unconvincingly, standing up and continuing her routine. I hadn't realized how many clothes she had at my house, but the pile on the bed was still growing.

"Will you get my suitcases from the storage room downstairs?" she asked, searching my face to see if I was convinced.

I nodded and smiled back at her. She didn't have to say anything else, and I didn't want us to end up parting on bad terms, so I kept my big mouth shut for once and headed after the luggage, knowing deep down inside that it was over between us.

"Jim," said Wolf, who had been so quiet on the way home in the car, "Wolf hungry." He had sensed something and left us alone, preferring to settle on the carpet by the front door.

I reached down and rubbed him on the head. "OK, buddy, let me get Joan's luggage first, and then I'll feed you."

"Jim sad?" asked Wolf, following me downstairs and into the back room.

"Yes, smart guy," I said, still a little surprised at his new faculty, "Joan's leaving." I pulled out her two suitcases, wondering how she was going to fit all her clothes into them and decided to give her one of mine too.

"Jim go too?" he asked bluntly. Maybe he was smarter too.

"No," I said, reaching the landing and turning up the stairs to the upper floor of the house, "I don't think I'll ever be going." I looked up, and there stood Joan. She must have heard me banging the cases around or had changed her mind and decided to help. She looked down at me, and I thought she was going to cry.

"You know I love you," she blurted out, grabbing a suitcase from me and heading back toward the bedroom. "Why did you say that?"

"And you know I love you," I said carefully, following her back into the bedroom. I set the cases down and stood there. All of a sudden, the words I wanted to say just wouldn't come out. "I don't think you have to ask me that," I replied.

That's when she began crying. Wolf disappeared like a shadow, a smart shadow. I walked to her and took her in my arms; we hugged each other, stood together wordlessly, and cried. There was nothing to say; it was the last time we would really hug each other, and we knew it. We didn't cry because we were going to be apart; we cried because no matter how far our relationship had gone, it wasn't going to go any further and would never be the same again. The dull ache in my chest only confirmed what my mind told me. No matter how much we loved each other, our careers came first. Joan's because she needed an identity and self worth, mine because this is where I hunted for oil and gas. End of story, game over.

I took her to the airport in the morning and watched her fly off, waving like an idiot long after the plane was gone from sight. We had managed to talk things out after the hug, drank a few beers together, and even made love for the last time, though it wasn't my best, that's for sure; yet we both loved to have sex, so even though we hadn't planned on making love, we did just that, like two animals who are locked up together. Wolf nudged me as I stood there on the tarmac, leaning against the fence, wondering if part of me just flew off too.

"Plane gone," said Wolf. Several people who had gathered in the fenced-off waiting area outside the lounge of the tiny airport stopped talking and stared at him.

*She had respected my job and never asked me to quit,* I thought. She never asked me to give up my oil company and move out to LA. I wondered if I would ever find anyone as loving and giving as she was to me.

"Jim," nudged Wolf again, "plane gone, we go now?"

And she hadn't even asked me to quit being a Guardian, and we both knew that had a lot to do with our relationship ending; I nodded to myself.

"Hey, mister," said a little boy, staring at my dog, pulling himself free from his mother who was watching an incoming plane land, "does your dog talk?"

"Huh?" I said, rejoining the real world. "What?"

"I heard your dog say something."

Suddenly I became aware of other people around me and realized it was time to leave. I had no idea how to answer that question; my brain was somewhere else.

"Dogs can't talk, silly boy," answered Wolf and nudged me toward the exit.

"No, Johnny," said his mother, pulling him back toward her, "he's a ventriloquist; he's making it seem like the dog is doing the talking. He's silly."

Wolf looked up at her and cocked his head to the side as if thinking.

"Come on, Wolf," I ordered him, "let's go home."

Wolf followed me toward the lounge but couldn't resist turning as we reached the door for one final comment.

"Good-bye, Johnny!" he yelled back at the little boy.

"Thanks a lot," I said, as we crossed through the lobby toward the doors to the parking lot. "I thought you weren't going to talk in front of strangers anymore."

"Only boy," he snapped as we hit the sidewalk and headed for the car.

"Only boy," I mimicked him as I opened the car door. "Only boy may have parents who could cause trouble for Wolf and Jim."

"Sorry, Jim," he apologized as I placed the seatbelt around him and slammed the door a little harder than he deserved.

By the time we came to the Mini-Giant convenience store, he had me feeling so guilty for scolding him that I stopped and bought us both beef jerkies. God, does he love beef jerkies probably almost as much as me. Boy, was I down on myself.

My next stop was the office, my office, though I hadn't been there in so long; it felt like the same feeling you get when you return to your old high school or something. Rick was in his office; we shared a common reception area, and I planted myself in one of his chairs after giving Betty, our girl Friday, a big hug. Wolf lay down next to me; I let him come in providing he promised not to say one single word to Bickford when he showed up at noon. Last night had been to heavy to talk business, so we had decided to meet earlier than noon at the office and go over what we wanted from the asshole, Bickford. To make a long story short, we hashed out a deal that would replenish the old checkbook and keep us busy for the next twenty-four months or more. Now all we had to do was get Bickford to go along with it, which didn't look like a tough problem, considering how much money he had already made off the oil and gas from the first well. When I finally got up and went into my office, to find my desk buried under mail and messages, Wolf stayed behind to get a good scratching from Rick, who couldn't believe how good Wolf looked since being burned so badly by the Nallie. I had instructed Wolf that he could talk to Rick only when the two of them were alone or with me, so I was quite prepared for Rick's yell of surprise when in the course of talking to Wolf, Wolf answered back. I counted to three, and my phone's intercom light came on and buzzed me.

"Yes," I said into the receiver, like nothing was going on out of the normal.

"Is this some kind of trick?" gasped Rick into the other receiver.

"Why don't you ask wolf?" I laughed. I hung up and went back to my desk, knowing full well that I had to have it cleared off by noon. I didn't hear another word from Rick's office, and since he had taken care of a lot of my business for me, it wasn't long before I could see the top of my desk, and finally it was all cleared off. The last chore was an examination of the company checkbooks, both mine and ours, which is what I was busy doing when Betty buzzed me and announced Bickford's arrival. No sooner had I hung up the phone than in walked Rick and Wolf. I wanted to share in the fun Rick was having with Wolf, but my mind was a jumble of Joan and finances, so the two of them sat down and waited for me to look at them.

"OK, I'm ready for him," I sighed, tossing the checkbooks into my desk and picking up the phone. Rick nodded, and I buzzed Betty to bring him back to us. I looked down at Wolf, and he looked up at me from beside the desk.

"Remember, no talking while he's here," I cautioned him. Bickford must have heard me from the hallway and entered the room like a charging bull.

"What do you mean, no talking?" he asked, clasping my hand almost too cordially as he entered the room. Betty had tried to keep up with him but only managed to close the door behind him after giving him a dirty look behind his back for my benefit. I smiled at her as she left and pulled the door shut behind her.

"Has he got you lip locked," he said to Rick, crossing the room to shake his hand and join him on the couch I called my second home. Bickford always tried to separate partnerships when he did business with them, hoping to get a better deal as a result. From what he heard, I'm sure he thought I was talking to Rick.

"No, Austin," replied Rick, motioning toward Wolf, "he was talking to his dog." He smiled at me, always ready to help, the troublemaker.

Bickford already thought I was nuts, so he laughed and settled back into the couch.

"So, your dog talks, eh?" he remarked, eyeing me critically.

"Yeah, three languages," I sassed back, "but only after you rub his balls, wanna try?" Rick and Wolf both looked like they had choked on something, but I ignored them and went to my map case for the maps of the leases that Bickford was about to buy. Bickford ignored my question and followed my gaze to the maps I unrolled in front of him on the coffee table as I settled into the easy chair across from him.

I had set my office up to resemble a hotel room but with no bed although the couch did open up, so when I did business, I could get out from behind my desk and join whomever I was dealing with in a more comfortable setting. As I unrolled the last map, a list of the properties unrolled with it and fell on the carpet. I handed it to him and, in the process of sitting back down, stepped on Wolf's tail. Graceful.

"Ouch!" yelped Wolf, jumping up, more startled than hurt.

"Sorry, Wolf," I said, leaning over the arm of the chair to rub his head. He looked at me like he wanted to tell me how clumsy I really was but decided not to and settled back down to the carpet. I turned back to Rick and Dickford, hoping they had been too busy to hear Wolf.

"You're a little off in the head, aren't you? asked Bickford, assuming I had made the "ouch" word somehow come out of Wolf's mouth. I should have known; no matter what Wolf said, Dickford would never believe he could talk, only that I was responsible in some way. I smiled and pointed to the map.

"Let's cut this deal, Austin," I replied. "I got a rig running, and you've got investors to talk to, I'm sure." I was damned sure he hadn't told them about not optioning the remaining acreage, and his look told me I was right. That meant he already had the money in escrow to drill the acreage surrounding the well we had already drilled for him; he just didn't own the leases. I did. Oh baby.

An hour later, option papers in hand, he stormed out of my office, which is exactly the way I wanted it. After he left, Rick congratulated me with a hand slap and handed me a Bud from the minifridge, and we toasted each other. This was going to be a good day after all. I bent down and played with Wolf's ears.

"Man, you stuck it to Prickford," commented Rick, as we sat and sucked down the cold Buds, passing his check for $700,000.00 back and forth between us.

"I wouldn't say that." I smiled. "Seriously, he optioned almost seven thousand acres, and I only hit him for a thirty-second." That meant a thirty-second override in all the wells he drilled on the land, a fair percentage. The way I stuck it to him was by making him buy all the land at one time. I pointed that out to Rick.

"He could have bought the leases one at a time when I first offered them to him." I observed. "But he didn't want them then, say, let's check with Merlin and see if he can scan the whole field for reserves."

"I already have," came Merlin's voice out of my wrist sensor, "and it looks like most of the area is blanketed quite heavily in fossil fuels, so you should do well. Rick, if you would like to see the sensor results, just have JR bring you out to the house sometime, I'm chained in the garage, but I'll be glad to show them to you."

"OK, cool," answered Rick, nodding his head at what Merlin had said.

"Wait a minute," I spoke up, "who said you were chained? And how did I get the name JR?" I tried to sound hurt.

Rick laughed.

Wolf started saying JR and walked out of the office, probably to go outside to relieve himself or chase a pussy, sorry, whatever.

"Actually," began Merlin, happy to be included in the discussion and suffering from a mild case of diarrhea mouth, "it should be Guardian JR; you're not doing so bad bagging Tayhest either. In less than a year, you've managed to take the lead and set a new record. A record that took over forty years to compile."

I smiled at Rick and shrugged. What could I say, it was them or me.

"How many? What did you kill?" asked Rick curiously.

"Tayhest warriors," cut in Merlin. "Unofficially, the count stands at thirteen, four at the Zalo base, one on the mother ship, then the ones you whacked in the Pheren galaxy."

"OK, OK," I interrupted him this time, "who cares how many?"

"You should," argued Merlin. "Each confirmed kill has a bounty that gets added to your Guardian balance, oh wait, I forgot, you got credit for the shipload that kidnapped you too."

"So what's the bounty?" I said. Rick nodded too. I wondered why nobody had told me about this before, but then, things were always so hectic when I was involved; nevertheless, I would have to talk with old Mr. C about this. I wondered if they had a catalog for the nearest Zalo base. Someone say toys?

Rick handed me another beer as Betty came to the doorway on her way to lunch. I handed her the check just as Merlin spoke up.

"A thousand triple tres," he announced, "and get this, you are getting a bounty for all the Betas that are iced in this parsec too, although you should share a portion of that with the other Guardians."

"Put it in the bank," I said to Betty.

She left with the deposit, giving me one of her famous looks that I'm sure she only reserves for crazy people who talk to their wrists.

"It's in the bank, Jim," returned Merlin. "How did you think you paid for all that Chaga brew you bought on the Mothership?"

No wonder everybody wanted to drink with me; I was buying, and nobody told me. I laughed out loud, and then Rick laughed as it dawned on him why I was laughing.

"Buy a few drinks?" grinned Rick.

"About half the ship," said Merlin, laughing, at my expense, I should add.

Wolf came back into the room, looking like he had accomplished the "whatever." He flopped down next to Rick and fell asleep almost instantly.

"Wolf," I teased, "was she good looking?"

"Foxy," he answered sleepily.

We all cracked up.

"So," inquired Rick, pulling another round from my minifridge, "you get rewarded for killing the enemy?"

"Apparently"—I nodded—"although it's news to me."

"Oh, come now, Jim," scolded Merlin, "don't you remember? Crouthhamel talking to you about it, after you had that argument with him, and the two of you got toasted on Altairian cigars?"

"No, and that's probably why," I agreed. "Those fuckers are strong."

"Smoke?" said Rick, picking up on the word "cigar." We had some bad habits, and twisting up a joint every now and then was one of them.

"Yeah, but you won't be walking afterward," I informed him. "In fact, the last time and the only time almost killed me. Nevertheless, I did manage to bring back a small supply of them." And later tonight, I planned on getting into it.

"So do I have a positive balance?" I asked.

"Oh, you better believe it," replied Merlin. "It will carry you well into the next century, even if you never bag another Tayhest, which is highly unlikely since you are worth so much to them . . . alive or dead." He just had to add that.

"What's a tre worth?" asked Rick.

I had been wondering that myself. "Yeah, what'd he say," I joked.

"Tres are worth quite a bit in your currency," answered Merlin, "and the exact amount is hard to calculate . . . let's just say about a thousand bucks."

"So a triple tre is worth three times that?" I was impressed and rich from the sounds of it.

"No, that's a factor of three," answered Merlin.

I looked at Rick, and he whistled. I was worth fucking millions, holy shit.

"That check that Betty just took to the bank is peanuts compared to what you've made as a Guardian," he concluded, shaking his head in disbelief.

"Yeah," I answered, "but tres are hard to spend here."

"You haven't done so bad spending your tres," replied Merlin. "The equipment you had them install in me cost a small bundle, not to mention your energy bill on the Mothership."

"OK, OK," I said, stopping him, "don't tell me, I'm enjoying my wealth right now." And then I added, "But give what you think is proper to the other Guardians, OK?"

"I think that's an excellent idea," he said. "I'll do it right now."

We sat there and bullshitted the rest of the afternoon, something we hadn't done in a long time. Not once did Rick ask me about Joan, so I figured Samantha had known and told him too. It didn't matter; there was nothing I could do. Just enjoy what memories I had and get on with it. Around about five o'clock, Betty had said good-bye for the day, so it must have been five; we pulled ourselves up from the couch and found it had gotten quite drunk in the room. I was mangled, and Rick didn't look much better off. I wished Merlin were here to take me home instead of my Trans Am. I needed an autopilot bad, sorry MADD. Not once did I think about pulling the sofa out, duh.

I really don't remember the ride home; at five o'clock the traffic must have been bumper-to-bumper downtown and not much better out on Route 2, but nevertheless, I managed to make it home without killing Wolf or myself and made a note not to do that again. Damn. I remember stumbling to the couch, a feat I don't always accomplish. I must have dozed off at that point because it was a little after seven o'clock when Wolf bit my hand to wake me up and feed his ass. He usually did that after licks and nudges, so I must have been really zonked.

"Ouch," I said, rubbing my hand, which had only little red marks, no punctures, which was lucky considering the mood he gets in when he's hungry, "what did you do that for?" I sat up and felt my head pounding softly, a sign of things to come.

"Wolf hungry," he muttered, looking at me like I was stupid. Maybe he always did that, I don't recall, but now he definitely looked that way.

"OK, OK," I said, rising to my feet. I noticed the TV was on and wondered which one of us had turned it on, then the picture caught my eye as I walked by it. I stopped and let the words sink in as I viewed the screen. Wolf realized something was up and stopped too.

"And a tremendous midair collision was avoided by the two wide-body jets with less than fifty feet to spare." The picture changed to that of a newsman standing in front of what looked like LA International, a newsman I recognized but couldn't place just yet.

"Yes, Chip," the newsman was saying, "today was a very lucky day for myself and several hundred other passengers aboard the two jets. The FAA has confirmed that there was no human error involved but rather a freak computer accident that put the two planes in the wrong place on the controller's screen."

I wondered if Joan's plane was one of the near misses, what a ride that was.

"And had it not been for two really fine pilots, I don't think I would be standing here reporting to my old friends back in Columbus. This is Stacy Bolton, for WKLA, signing off."

It hit me like a ton of bricks.

"All right, thanks, Stacy," joked the one who must be "the Chip." "Maybe someone was trying to tell you to stay in Ohio and not move to LA."

*Son of a bitch*, I thought, *that's the guy that Joan had been seeing in Columbus.* Suddenly the two newsmen sitting there at Newscenter Ten, bantering back and forth, impeccably dressed, witty beyond their collective intelligence, really pissed me off. I stepped up to the TV and brought my leg back to kick it, and Wolf grabbed the material of my trousers, jerking my leg out from under me. I fell, cursing the TV, flat on my face. It knocked the wind out of my lungs and the anger from my brain. I lay there gasping for life as Wolf sat down next to me.

"Joan gone, Jim." He licked my hand where the bite marks barely showed now.

I didn't answer. He was right, damnit, he was right. I suddenly felt very unhappy and very sad.

"Jim," whispered Wolf as he licked my face, "stop crying; JRs don't cry."

"Yeah, OK," I said finally, after I regained my breath. "Come on, I think I hear a steak calling our names." I rose slowly to my feet and noticed that Wolf had positioned himself between the TV and me. I shook my head at his obvious strategy and again secretly wondered if they had done something to his brain too.

He was always a smart dog, but now, he was sounding like Freud, no, Merlin maybe. Yeah, Merlin, he would know how to find out about Joan.

"How about checking those flights, Merlin."

"Just finishing, yup, she was on the flight with pretty boy," he said quietly. I stood there for a second. "Come on, Wolf, I could eat a horse."

Wolf looked up at me. "OK, Wolf try horse too."

We ate out on the breezeway; the kitchen was still too full of Joan and all her little womanly touches. I made a note to hire a housekeeper and quickly forgot what I was thinking as Wolf and I battled to see who could finish their steak first and claim the last piece. He won, even though I made him give me a handicap because I was using silverware, and he wasn't. I even cheated on the ten-second head start too. I knew he couldn't count, or maybe he could?

"Mine!" he said triumphantly, eyeing the last piece on the platter and smacking his lips.

"Oh, go ahead," I said like a loser. I didn't have the heart to tell him I was full; it would spoil the taste of that last piece if I did that. I watched him grab hold of it and drag it off the platter, splattering juice on the floor around his plate.

"You're a pig," I commented. "Why didn't you wait for me to put it on your plate?"

"Dog, not pig," he answered me, chewing and smiling, if that's what you want to call it.

The phone rang in the kitchen, and I knew who it was, or rather, part of me hoped it was her. I decided to let the machine get it; I didn't know if I could even talk to her. Maybe it would hurt her a little to leave a message, knowing I was home and listening. I stared resolutely out the windows into the backyard, watching the fireflies and moths buzzing against the screens. Suddenly the phone stopped ringing, and I spun around in my Adirondack to see if I should get up and check it out. I sat there half expecting to hear my own message, and nothing happened. Now I had to get up, something told me, and I knew I didn't want to hurt her just because I was hurting. I rose slowly from the chair, feeling the Chaga brew that I had consumed with dinner, losing my balance just slightly. *At least I wasn't going to have a damn hangover*, I thought. I thought I heard Wolf talking as I tripped up the steps into the kitchen.

"Here he is," remarked Wolf into the receiver. Quickly he scampered away from me as I swatted at him for answering the phone. I thought I heard him laugh in the living room.

"Hello?" I said. The hand piece had slobber on it.

"Hi," said Joan cautiously, "I just wanted to let you know I made it OK."

Now I remembered; I had made her promise to call me.

"Great, that's good." I couldn't think of a damn thing to say. "Nice."

"Wolf said you saw my plane on the news; he said you got upset?"

"He did, did he?" That prick.

"It really wasn't that close, at least I didn't think so; it made the news, huh?" She was fishing for a reaction, I could tell.

"Oh yeah, at least the Columbus channel," I tried to sound indifferent.

"Oh?"

"Yeah, Joan"—I shook my head at her—"didn't pretty boy Bolton tell you about his live broadcast from the LA airport?" Now she knew I knew, but I wondered if she knew he was there. If she did, then the whole thing was a setup all along.

A puzzling silence came out of the receiver.

"I saw him for the first time at the airport in Columbus, Jim, it wasn't something we'd planned, at least I didn't, I swear it."

"I believe you," I said softly, "so where are you staying?" Time for good-byes, I could feel it coming. My heart was ripping in half.

"I'm at the Hilton on Century Boulevard, all by myself, OK?"

I felt foolish now. "Joan, you don't have to explain anything; I have no right to ask you. I'm truly sorry, really." I was too.

"Listen, I have to go now," she began the ending, "but I'll call you as soon as I get a place, OK?" Now she sounded sad.

"OK, yeah, sure," I stammered, trying to think of something to keep her on the phone a little longer, anything.

"Good-bye, Jimmy, take care of yourself and that crazy dog," she continued the ending; suddenly she brightened up. "And don't forget, we're supposed to go see Tamee, after the kids are born, you stud you."

"You still want to come?" I thought she was bluffing earlier.

"Yes, as long as I can get the time off, you know how that goes."

"Yeah, OK, I'll look forward to hearing from you; call me when you find a place. You going to look this weekend?"

"Yeah, Patty, an LA employee, met me at the airport. She's real nice; she offered to help me."

"Great, OK, I'll see ya, call me anytime, I . . . miss you." There, I said it.

"OK, me too."

"OK, take care."

"You too."

"I will, you too." This time I laughed.

"OK, I love you, good-bye." With that, the line went dead. I felt so much better I almost jumped up and yelled. It was going to be hard letting go of her, maybe little by little; a call every now and then would help. I hoped so. I felt like a big baby.

But I felt so good that I decided to have another brew. I wondered if Rick was still coming out Saturday with Samantha, to celebrate the deal we closed. Damn, I forgot to tell Joan; maybe I should hop out there and surprise her. Nah, bad idea. I cleaned up the mess Wolf made and the kitchen too and found my way into the living room. I threw myself into my recliner. Time to surf.

Saturday evening found me back in the recliner, same position, different day. And I was shaved and showered too, ready to party, or whatever. I missed my party pal though and wondered what she was doing. Then I heard the front door close.

"I'm up here!" I yelled. "Get up here, you big mouth." It must be Wolf; I didn't remember seeing any headlights pull into my driveway. I was about to get up when the head of a dog came around the half wall overlooking the entrance. It was a big black dog, larger than Wolf, eyeing me cautiously until Wolf came around it, and the two of them headed into the kitchen.

"Company?" I asked. His pussy hunting was becoming legendary.

"Just a friend, mind if I open the Gravy Train?" responded Wolf without stopping, the other dog sticking to him like glue.

"Boy or girl?" I asked, although I knew the answer.

Wolf stopped and crooked his head back toward me. "What you think?"

I laughed and went back to the TV. I heard the cupboard door open, followed by the sound of a bag ripping open and little bits of dried food falling onto the floor. About that time, a set of lights pulled into the driveway. Moments later, Rick and Samantha were at the door. Since Cockhound was busy, I decided to answer the door like a civilized person rather than yell like I normally do. Rick entered like it was old home week, but Samantha entered cautiously, looking around and giving me the evil eye.

"No monsters or space people tonight?" she asked, still only two steps from the door, waiting for the right answer.

"No, Sam," I said, laughing, and then added, "not to my knowledge, but it's early."

She smacked me in the arm and followed Rick up the stairs, and I followed her tight jeans at a safe distance. She seemed a bit tense and still mad about the last time, no doubt. Oh well, she wasn't my girlfriend . . . but those jeans, wow!

About the time we all reached the living room, and I settled Sam on the couch and let Rick catch the remote for the stereo, a large growling commotion started up in the kitchen. I was on my way there and stopped dead in my tracks. I turned back to Rick and caught the look on Sam's face out of the corner of my eye. I shrugged my shoulders and headed for the kitchen, smiling to myself. Sam doesn't have the balls Joan has, that's for sure. Even in the dining room I could feel pieces of dog food crunching under my feet. What the hell had happened?

"Wolf," I yelled, "I'm going to take you back to Jurda and have your body replaced for a vacuum cleaner, you Shithead!" Sure enough, the Train was all over the kitchen, including both dogs who were stuck together by a Wolf boner. The big black one tried to get out of the kitchen and into the breezeway, but Wolf wasn't done, so the two of them tumbled down the three steps, still attached, and settled at the bottom with Wolf on top.

"I hope you're using a doggy condom," I said, closing the door to the breezeway, all the while crunching food with my boots. I poured three Chagas and headed for the living room. I didn't hear any more growling, but one of them was yelping pretty good. Maybe Wolf finally bit off more than he could chew.

"Here you go," I commented, handing Sam her brew and walking over to Rick, who was playing with my cassette deck.

"Wait til you hear this," he said, depressing the play button. "It's the latest AC/DC album." Almost instantly, a heavy-rock sound began to pound from the speakers. I made a note to spend more time with my music; that song sounded really excellent. That's when I decided to twist one.

At Merlin's urging and advice, I had let him synthesize a mixture of Mother Earth's finest and Altairian death weed, the stuff I almost OD'd on; I always keep a little under the couch in an upside down Frisbee, along with some papers and a clip, and it was only a minute or two before a substantial joint emerged and became engulfed in flames.

"Wow," remarked Rick, as he exhaled his first hit, "this stuff is out of this world!" Then he laughed, which surprised even him.

I kept my mouth shut until Sam had managed to take a tiny little "girl" hit, and then I put my "Hoover" to it. As I exhaled, I could taste the Altairian stuff just slightly; all in all, the taste was quite good. "Actually," I began explaining, "this is a mixture of this world and a world called Altair, a place I am looking forward to visiting again someday." The two sisters appeared briefly in my mind, which made me smile and then laugh. Which made Rick laugh, which made Sam laugh, until all of us were laughing like hyenas. I stopped myself just to see if I could stop.

"Man, Jim, this is killer shit," chortled Rick as he passed the ever-shortening joint to Sam, who uncharacteristically went for another hit, although she was having trouble smoking and laughing and couldn't decide which came next.

I nodded to him as I heard the front door open and close. I motioned to Rick to watch the top of the steps, and sure enough, who came dragging up them but old Wolf, looking like he had been dragged down more than the breezeway steps. He wasn't limping, just walking kinda funny, and of course, the effect on all of us was complete and total hysteria. Then, to top it off, he looked at us, with an expression I just can't describe, and proceeded to flop down on the living-room rug like he was dead. He just laid there looking at me; God it was funny. I thought I was going to suffocate from laughing and not stopping to breathe. Bad drug, bad, bad, bad.

"Hey Wolf," I giggled, "was she too much for you?" Everyone quieted down to hear what he was going to say; Rick and I because we knew he could talk, Sam because she must have thought he would bark or growl at me. Knowing Rick and the way he kept secrets, I just knew he hadn't told Sam about Wolf, so this might be real interesting. I looked down at Wolf and laughed.

"Too much for you," he mumbled back at me. It was hard to tell if he meant me, or he was just repeating what I said; either way, it broke us all up with laughter.

"Holy cow," said Sam, laughing, "this stuff is so good I swear I just heard your dog talking." She looked over at me and cracked up again.

"No way," I answered her. "You can't talk, can you, Wolf?"

His eyes were almost slits as he started to doze off, but he managed to look up at me and say, "Talk yes, walk, no."

"My god, he did talk!" exclaimed Sam, as Rick and I rolled on the floor laughing.

"I go to sleep now," explained Wolf, as his eyes closed slowly. He missed the look Sam gave me, but I didn't.

I explained what happened while Rick laughed and wiped the tears from his eyes. Sam gave him the same look, and it sobered him slightly.

"Really, Sam, it was nothing for the doctors on Jebis to create a better set of vocal chords for the Wolfman here." I leaned across the floor and rubbed his stomach.

"Wolf de man, wolf de man," uttered Wolf, from somewhere near dreamland.

And so he began to snooze, with AC/DC blaring and us laughing.

We were busy yakking about what had happened to Wolf, when the front door opened and closed ever so quietly. Wolf looked up and me and started to get up, but by the time we both wobbled to our feet, whose head should appear but Cluver the Darassin and his buddy Remonl, who was sporting a jug of Chaga under his long skinny arm. I caught the look Sam was giving Rick, but since Cluver looked like a human and not the devil, she seemed only mildly unnerved.

"Hey, how are you doing?" I exclaimed, forgetting not to handshake, which Cluver overlooked and grabbed my hand anyway, followed by a guardian salute to Rick and Sam. He gave everyone a Darassin smile, the huge face almost a cartoon.

"Good," he answered, spending more time saluting Sam than was really necessary. "Real good since my credits shot space high; that's why we stopped by, to thank you for your . . . fairness. You didn't have to do that."

"Think nothing of it," I replied, wondering just how much Merlin had shared with the rest of the Guardians in the galaxy. "After all, you saved my life once or twice already."

Remonl had been quiet until this point, but his eyes hadn't left the area surrounding Sam, and I half expected Rick to say something. I reached up and turned off the ceiling fan—Darassins are tall—and turned toward Remonl.

"Here," I said, diverting his gaze, "let me take that brew for you and get you a mug."

"Remonl," admonished Cluver, sensing the awkwardness of his staring, "you act as if you've never seen a Taran woman before; sit down and remember you're a Darassin." He pointed toward the loveseat, and Remonl complied. Rick broke the ice by handing him the remains of the joint, stuck in a smoking stone. He accepted it and hoovered the rest of it like he was smoking air. He sat there, puffed up like he was part blowfish, and smiled up at Cluver and I.

"Whoa," I laughed, "looks like it's time to twist another dozen."

"I'm Cluver," said he, stretching past me to offer his hand to Rick. A nice bit of diplomacy. Something I needed to learn.

"I'm sorry," I said to the whole group. "This is Cluver and Remonl, Guardians from the Darassin system, Milky Way galaxy."

"Pleased to meet you," said Rick, obviously enjoying the hell out of meeting people from another world. Sam was so stoned she even seemed to be enjoying herself too.

"I'll be right back." I left them to the task of small talking and crunched my way into the kitchen for more mugs, laying the jug on the counter, remembering that it didn't need to go into the fridge. I was busy filling mugs when Merlin piped up.

"I did as you instructed, but before you ask, what I shared with the rest of the Guardians was nothing compared to what you still have in your account."

"I know you look out for me, thanks, Merlin, what are you doing?"

"Watching the 60s." Merlin watched TV by the decade, all of it.

"Say, if I open the kitchen door, can you send one of your cleaning pods in here to collect this spilled dog food?" I sloshed a bit of Chaga as I turned to set down the mugs and open the door.

"Just the dog food?" inquired Merlin sarcastically, having heard the brew splatter on the floor.

"No, smartass," I answered, opening the door to the porch. I jumped back as the two Nacks standing there startled the shit out of me, which, of course, made them jump too. It was Cray the Guardian and a female Nack, a cute one I might add.

They finally entered the kitchen, looking a bit apprehensive.

"Cray," I exclaimed, "how are you doing? And what are you doing here? Is Tamee all right?" I watched his face for any sign of trouble.

"Yes, yes, Jim," answered Cray quickly, "she's fine although I wouldn't go near her right now. Nack females get a bit touchy just before they give birth. I came to thank you for your generosity; no one has ever done that . . . for me, that is."

I nodded. "No problemo," I said and then asked, "I thought that was after they gave birth?"

"It's even worse afterward," replied the female Nack. "I am Ffame, and you are the Jim?" She looked at me intensely and smiled.

"Yes," I answered, looking into her eyes, which seemed to glow. *Wow, I thought, this one's hotter than fire. Go, Cray.* I stepped back and noticed the little cleaning pod waiting patiently behind them to begin its job. I wondered why Merlin hadn't warned me about all these Guardians showing up tonight. I led them into the living room after filling a mug for them and grabbing the rest. All I needed was a skirt!

"Everybody," I announced, "look who's here, Cray and Ffame, from the Nack system." Cluver and Remonl rose and offered their seats to the two Nacks, more precisely Ffame, while Rick and Sam sat gawking at the furry heads and appendages visibly sticking out of their jumpsuits. They made a sharp couple. I believe from the goofy looks of everyone in the living room that I must have missed at least one, maybe two joints. Wolf had disappeared too, but that was normal for him, especially in his postcoital condition. I decided it was time to head for the downstairs Rec room, and I do mean wreck room, and handed out the refills.

"Everyone," I yelled over the music and talking, "follow me!" I turned and started down the steps just as the front doorbell chimed. "Now who could it be this time?" I said to myself.

"Alzador and Crouthhamel," answered Merlin, "you should see the ships that are hovering around here."

"I hope nobody else can," I said, confused as ever.

"Nope, only I, answer the door, the Jim." He laughed.

"Hello," I said, without surprise, to the astonishment of both Alzador and Mr. C. "Come in, come in," I said; behind me, the rest of the party was waiting patiently at various places on the steps, some not so steadily. All quieted upon seeing Mr. C.

"Hello, Jim," said Alzador, much happier than the last time we spoke. He stepped into the house and let Crouthhamel step past him. Mr. C saluted me and then gave me a hug, which caught me off guard, and wasn't lost on the rest of the group either.

"Hello, Jim," he said softly, "we all came to thank you for your generosity and help you celebrate fatherhood." He smiled a bit strangely. The crowd murmured.

"So you're behind this surprise party; that explains why Merlin, my trusted buddy, didn't say anything to me ahead of time." Then the fatherhood part registered.

"Don't be too hard on him; it's for a good cause. Just a few mespics ago, Tamee gave birth quite unexpectedly to three healthy Nacks, or should I say Nackarans."

Rick had led the rest of the party past us and down into the Rec room and must have been showing them how to play billiards as I could hear the balls colliding with each other. I motioned Alzador to go on down and saluted him again. His wings brushed by me, his claw slugging me playfully on the shoulder, another gesture not unique to Earth apparently.

"Daddy Jim," he whispered drolly. He vanished after the group.

"If you want to," I said to Crouthhamel, "go on down and join them. I'm just going to get a handful of mugs and the jug of brew, and I'll be right back."

"Let me help you," he offered.

"Sure." We both knew he wanted to talk alone, and I wondered what he had to say.

We entered the kitchen without a crunch; the floor looked so clean I'm sure you could have eaten off it. It hadn't been that clean since I put it down.

"What's up, boss," I asked, leaning against the counter.

He leaned against the other and sighed. "The Council wants you to share your knowledge of the anomies as they exist in the universe naturally; they know that Merlin has the Pheren maps stored in his memory, and they want them." He sounded as if he was reciting his laundry list. Or a job he didn't like to do.

"They're pissed because I showed up and watched them suck those Tayhest ships into that artificial anomy and then left without permission, right?" I wished he hadn't brought this up right now; I was really too blitzed. I really hated to mix business with a good high. Plus, I was a father, oh baby. I had to call Joan.

"That and the Teeber, although I agree with what you did; they are scared of the power of the Teeber as well you should be also . . ."

"Yeah, yeah," I replied, "tell me something, since you started this conversation"—my hairs on my neck were starting to prickle—"where did that Tayhest ship come from, the one I caught the joyride on, that fucker was a long way from home, and they weren't here looking for me either. I was just another piece of meat." Damnit, I didn't like the feeling I was getting, and I felt like I was sobering up. I poured us a mug while Crouthhamel decided how he was going to answer me.

"It doesn't matter."

"Yes, it does. But let me tell you, because I'm pretty sure I've figured out where it came from, and I just want you to nod when I get it right, OK?"

"I'm listening."

And drinking, I noticed, as he refilled his mug. "OK," I began, "the ship that snatched me was one of the seven I trailed when I came back into Guardian territory, some kind of supply ship for the other six, right?"

"Possibly, keep going." It was almost like he wanted but couldn't tell me.

"The artificial anomy they set up didn't work right, and instead of sending the Tayhest into the unknown, it sent them deep into Alpharian territory, so you've been running around trying to find the other six before they cause any more trouble, how am I doing?"

"It sounds possible."

"Which means it didn't send them where you thought it would, which means you thought you could send them to a specific location, and that means the whole experiment was a total loss. Oh, yeah, and—"

"Not just as a defense," cut in Merlin, "but as a form of point to point drive, which is what the artificial anomy was supposed to do in the first place."

I watched the look on Mr. C's face and knew it was true. "Let me guess, I was the first experiment, and the Tayhest were the second. Merlin, did you tell them about the maps?" Those bastards used me, what an organization, just like Earth.

"No, it was the Black Nallie up my ass that tipped them off; they must have figured out that I went through an anomy to get back here as quick as we did." Merlin had finished the puzzle. The Council had decided to experiment with a new drive system that could create anomies in the universe, and it had backfired on them. I knew the answer now; that's why they tried it on the seven Tayhest ships. They must have figured they would wind up in the same place I did, right outside the Aktagara galaxy. It was like a light went on in my head; I was so happy that I figured out what had happened to Merlin and I that I forgot to get angry with Mr. C. I refilled both of us this time.

"Most probable," he answered, "and it could also be possible that now that the experiment has been abandoned, the Council would like to recover some of their investment, like the investment they made in you and your ship."

"Oh, don't make me feel guilty. I've done pretty good for them so far."

"Yes, and for yourself, which is why they want the maps that Merlin has stored away." He sounded like he almost believed what they told him to say.

Suddenly another thought occurred to me, but I kept it to myself; I didn't want to spoil anyone's party just yet, even though I had a feeling mine was just about over.

"One question, no, two"—I was almost too drunk and stoned, almost—"who was in charge of the project, Councilman Phayton of Jurda?"

"Mmm, could be," quipped Crouthhamel; he was beginning to feel the Chaga.

Just then, Rick came into the room. "Everyone's out of brew, Jim," he stated. I noticed Sam wasn't with him. I wondered if she was still with us.

"No problem, we were just going to come down with this jug; come on, Mr. C, let's go liven up the party. Here, Rick, grab this jug while I let this little cleaning pod back into the garage," I said, opening the door to the porch ever so slowly, concentrating really hard on the Teeber and the message I wanted him to pass along to Merlin. Crouthhamel stayed close to me, or so it seemed to me, Mr. Paranoid, so I grabbed him around the shoulders and swung him toward the downstairs, and off we marched. He turned to me as we descended the stairs.

"What was your other question?" he asked, trying to be cheerful.

"Why, who else did you invite tonight?" I lied. My other question had more to do with what happens to Merlin and I, if we refused to give them the maps, and did that have anything to do with why my house was filled with Guardians, all of whom were my friends, people I wouldn't hurt, no matter what. Which would be a problem if push came to shove, if you catch my drift.

"I think Inrew is on his way."

"No shit, I can't wait to see him." He was a Zellen I knew and drank with on occasion, any occasion.

Ten minutes later, while I was in the middle of an awesome 8-ball game, he showed up with a wild Zellen woman on his arm, obviously pleased with himself and happy to call me . . .

"Daddy Jim," yelled Inrew, saluting me with passion, "how the hell fuck are you?" He had picked that up from me. I try hard to help others learn good English.

"Awesome," I lied, missing my pool shot as my eyes wondered over his date, who returned the look with considerable interest, "here, let me get you a brew, hey, everyone, look who's here."

Everyone who was doing something, like Cray and Ffame who were playing with my pinball machine and Alzador who was bowling his wings off on my old miniature alley, stopped to salute and wave to Inrew. I quickly filled a couple of mugs and returned to my game, though my heart wasn't in it. Maybe I was too straight.

With all the Guardians saluting each other, you would have thought there was a swarm of bees loose in the room. I glanced around the room and saw everyone enjoying themselves, what with the brew and the smoke and wondered why I felt so edgy. Yet I knew why; I couldn't let the Council have information that I shouldn't have had to start with, information that could expose the Pheren to anyone who wanted to gain power by using the anomies, the conduits, to enter Pheren territory unannounced, through anomies I remembered that were almost at my backdoor and Tarr's backdoor too. I wondered how high and mighty the Council would be if they knew how close the Pheren really were, or could be if they chose. Yup, just a quick step through a time corridor, and I could have lunch with Tarr.

"So, Daddy Jim," exclaimed Rick, bringing me back to Earth, "I hear you are the proud father of three!" He was enjoying this part.

"Yup, I was thinking with my small head that night," I joked, accepting the offered joint. It hit so smooth that I ended up taking much more than I had anticipated and suddenly found myself hunched over the edge of the pool table, coughing up a lung so to speak. I felt the room spin and vaguely remember handing the instrument of my undoing back to Rick as I sank into the waiting wings of Alzador, who had secretly stunned me. He snatched me up like kindling sticks and whisked me out of the room and down the short hallway into a back bedroom that was more a storeroom than anything else. I had all kinds of shit stacked up in it. Mr. C was waiting, and in his hand was a real good likeness of a Vega collar. While Alzador pinned me down, he slipped it on my head. My whole body went numb while my brain felt like a berserk Commodore 64 computer, no, make that a Gateway 2000.

"Jim," began Crouthhamel, a little sympathy colored his words, "this is not the way we wanted to do this, and I'm not entirely in favor of it either, but the Council runs the show and pays the bills." He sounded decidedly human and even smiled down at me as I lay helplessly on the bed.

"Why, aren't you Mr. Do Boy," I smarted back, apparently able to move my lips at will, even without my brain engaged.

"Ready, sir," he remarked into a wrist sensor, ignoring my comment.

Something told me to shut up, but I didn't. "So when the Council orders you to invade the Pheren, through anomies you didn't even know exist, do me a favor and go first, and take big bird here with you." I was about to add something else about how much I hoped they got their asses kicked when in walked the head asshole himself, Phayton of Jurda. He came at me swiftly and touched the collar on the side, and my lips went numb like I was at the dentist office. A cold breeze filled the room, and I suddenly hoped that Mr. C would stay in here with me. My eyes connected with Alzador's eyes, and I knew he felt bad about the whole thing, but then he left the room like a good little boy. *Good-bye, asswipe,* I thought.

"Hello, Guardian Jim," Phayton said smoothly, ignoring Mr. C, who looked over his shoulder at me, standing over both of us silently. "I had hoped you would cooperate with us, especially since we have been so kind and generous to you. Yet you won't, will you, yes, I can see that in your eyes, can't I? You think I don't know what you think of me? I'm really not the evil creature you think I am. I'm just doing what needs to be done, what must be done, and what will be done."

*Not if I have anything to do about it, asshole,* I thought. The words came out of the Vega collar, and I heard myself talking. OOPS. And OOPS came out too.

He leaned over me and slipped the sensor off my wrist as Mr. C removed the other one from inside my boot. Phayton missed the look on my face, but Crouthhamel didn't; he started to warn Phayton as Phayton began telling me that I wouldn't be needing these to signal my ship, nor anyone else, when suddenly from outside and above us came the sound of a huge object hitting the ground.

The Teeber had managed to pickup my telepathy and had warned Merlin of my concerns for our safety. I managed a smile despite the collar, and I thought I saw an itsy-bitsy smile wander across Mr. C's face. In my mind, I saw the garage door being opened quickly, as Rick had once explained, and Merlin slipping soundlessly into the sky and beyond, heading for a location only I could find with a little help from a friend.

Phayton rose from my side and motioned to Mr. C to join him in a private conversation as Alzador strode into the room. He must have confirmed what I already knew—that removing those sensors from my touch was a signal to Merlin to fly the coop. I filled my mind with pictures of Joan and waited.

Phayton came over to me and knelt down beside the bed. He did not look like a happy camper. "I'll make this brief, when I reactivate the audio, you will tell me exactly where the nearest anomaly is, and with Crouthhamel's guidance, you will begin to map all the other locations from your memory, and then you will command your ship to return here immediately and transmit its entire memory to my ship's computers. If you do not do exactly as I have instructed, I will hold you in contempt, and you will be tried as a traitor of the Alpharian Council." With that, he reached to the side of the collar, and I sat up mechanically. My buzz was nowhere to be found, and it pissed me off, though I was powerless to do anything.

"I understand," I heard myself saying, "but cannot comply with your wishes, Councilman Phayton of Jurda." I kept the pictures rolling.

He looked like I had slapped him. Crouthhamel looked somewhat shocked and relieved.

"And why can you not follow my orders?" asked Phayton, his voice rising with his temper.

"I do not know the exact locations of the anomies." I knew I was going to say that; hell, I never tried to memorize any of them. I knew my memory better than anyone, or should I say, oh hell, I forget.

"Then bring your ship back here!" he yelled in my face. He looked very upset now, angrier than I think I have ever seen him. He was getting as red in the face as Crouthhamel, who was fidgeting like he had to go to the bathroom or laugh.

"I understand," I heard myself say again, "but cannot comply with your wishes, Councilman."

"WHY NOT!" he screamed, totally exasperated by now. I can do that to people.

"I do not know the exact location of Merlin, nor can I reach him with any sensor or communication device." I heard myself again and loved every minute of it. I could almost sense Crouthhamel was too.

He looked over at Crouthhamel and then back at me; his shoulders sagged, and his demeanor suddenly reminded me of a whipped puppy. He grabbed the collar off my head and sat down on the bed next to me, apparently not worried about my immediate reaction. It caught me off guard. I no longer felt like smacking him; if it was a sympathy routine, it worked. I threw an arm over his shoulder, and he turned and sighed.

"You need a beer," I suggested. So did I, and another doobie.

"I need your help," he returned. "The Alliance is facing certain doom; the Point to Point experiment was a complete loss, and now we have no way of countering a most certain Tayhest attack, let alone, a full-scale invasion."

"Wait a minute, what's all this about? I thought the Alliance and the Tayhest were pretty evenly matched, give or take a weapon or two. Don't the Tayhest send small raiding parties into our territory all the time?" His depression was uncomfortable and so was the bed.

"That is true, although you have certainly heightened these attacks since you became a Guardian." He raised his hand to silence me. "I know it's not all your fault; you were provoked on a number of occasions. It is not the attacks that cause us concern."

"Then what?" I asked, feeling dry and badly in need of a brew. He seemed to be pondering his own answer, and I saw Crouthhamel slip quietly from the room.

"Do you remember the trouble you had with the Betas, when you first became a Guardian?"

I nodded.

"And how it seemed like they appeared all over the Alliance's territory, an age-old threat left behind by the"—he hesitated—"the Bojj and reactivated by the Tayhest!" He studied my face as I nodded again. Crouthhamel appeared with mugs in hand, slipping into the room and shutting the door behind him.

He looked thinner than normal; I made a note to ask him how he did it. At the sound of Phayton's voice, low and fearful, I snapped my head around and scanned his face as he said it to me again, allowing me to swallow first.

"The Bojj have returned." He looked at me, and I could see the fear in his eyes and face. There was more going on here than a little power struggle between Council members; I could see that now.

"Yeah, so . . ." I baited him. *Tell me more*, I thought. Suddenly I felt a little guilty for holding out the information on the anomies. Just a fucking little.

"And they are joining forces with the Tayhest," added Mr. C.

"Already have, we have confirmation on that," corrected Phayton, "but that is not the worst part"—he drank long and slowly from his mug and then looked at both of us—"they must have discovered or developed their own Point to Point and used it to send Betas all over the Alliance. Some of those Betas were prewar Cyborgs, but a few . . ." He stopped drinking and indicated his mug was empty.

Mr. C signaled to Alzador, and I saw his wing and claw appear at the doorway and grab the mugs before Crouthhamel closed the door again. Mine had been empty too. Phayton handed me back my sensors, and we exchanged smiles.

*Maybe he was OK after all*, I thought, *just lousy at interrogations.*

Alzador returned, and after another long drink, Phayton began again, "Some of the Betas we found were not adaptable; they were Immediates, inferior copies of the older ones, but there was so many of them failing to adapt, all over the place, that it quickly caught our attention. For that to happen, as quickly as it happened, and as unsuccessfully as they fit in, wherever they showed up—"

"They had to be shipped overnight," I finished it without any help. He looked at me and nodded. The fucking Tayhest were flooding the Alliance with bad boys by sending them through the anomies.

"Yes," he agreed, "either the Bojj figured out how to send them as we were trying to do, or they discovered the natural anomies that you came through on your way back from the Aktagara galaxy; either way, the Bojj are sending Betas, in Tayhest ships, over considerable distances, in the blink of a Horc's eye." He stopped and drank the last of his mug. He looked totally whipped.

"So you figure it won't be long before swarms of Tayhest start showing up the same way?" I really didn't need to ask that; my imagination was busy picturing Tayhest Battlecruisers swarming like bugs all over Earth and the rest of my galaxy. No wonder old Phayton was so bent outta shape. There would be no defense. Shit. I drank right along with him. Suddenly I felt really guilty. Well, almost really guilty, after all, he had used me as a guinea pig.

"You were expendable then"—he nodded, as if reading my mind—"but we knew, if anyone could come back, it would probably be the crazy Taran. Unfortunately, you didn't show up where we expected you to show up, and nor did the Tayhest ships go where we wanted to send them either; they just went farther into our territory, while you ended up on the other side of the universe as we know it."

Mr. C collected the mugs and opened the door, briefly searching for Alzador. Then I saw a wing and hand grab the mugs. Something triggered an alarm in the back of my mind, but I was getting pretty fried on the Chaga brew, and I brushed it aside. HAND! I realized I had seen a hand, not a claw on Alzador's arm or whatever. Nah, I must be getting really stewed, that's all. I'll check it out when he comes back.

"Merlin was expendable too?" I asked skeptically. Me, I could understand.

"We had to destroy the second Cyclone for its own good; it wouldn't stabilize, not to mention all the other problems, no . . . Crown Alpha will be the only ship of its kind for a long time to come"—then he laughed—"just like you will be the only Taran for a long time to come." I failed to find the humor, but I let it pass good-naturedly.

The door opened, and Alzador entered this time, handing the brews around to all of us. I tried to get a look at the appendage under the wing, but he was very careful not to show it.

*Maybe I was imagining it*, I thought. I noticed that as he stepped back from the rest of us, trying to be inconspicuous, that he certainly appeared bigger than life; man, I reasoned, I must be close to blotto or something. I caught him staring back at me, and I felt kind of funny.

"Why don't you join us, Alzador," I said, hoping he wouldn't be offended by my stares. "We're drinking to the Alliance, while it's still here."

Almost on cue, the door opened, and in walked Alzador again. We all exchanged glances until the first one looked down at me and said, "You're drunk."

I knew the voice; I couldn't believe I had heard it, but nevertheless, I answered him, "And you're ugly."

Before I reached him, before anyone could move a muscle, thank God, he changed shape. I grabbed his leg-size arm, and he pulled me to his side, musing my hair like I was child. He was still a little bent over even though my basement was built extra tall, and even now his body still grew larger. I turned to the group, to introduce them to my old friend, Tarr the Pheren. Phayton looked like he was going to faint, puke, or do both.

The real Alzador was ready to fight, but Crouthhamel, hell, he looked fascinated, having never seen a real Maglarr, and especially not in person. They don't look like daddies in battle either, according to Merlin; they look damn scary.

"Everyone," I announced, "this is Tarr. He is a Pheren." I said it slowly so no one would make the mistake of calling him a Maglarr. Probably saved a life or two.

Tarr nodded and looked down at me as I slouched under the load of Chaga in me.

"And this," he said, holding me up a little to the group, laughing as he hefted me, "is drunk and ugly."

# The End

Note to Jim's Readers

*The Projects* doesn't end here, but unfortunately Mr. Guardian of the Year has other things to do right now and has delegated this job to me while he's off playing games. Seriously, Jim wanted me to let you all know that as soon as he gets back, he will continue "writing." Dictating to me, that's the real story; it's always Merlin do this and Merlin do that. Excuse me, what was I saying? Oh yeah, right now Jim is headed for—no, you're not ready for that just yet. OK, let's just say that until Lover Boy gets back . . . you know, I ought to write a few chapters—no, I'd never hear the end of it. What did he say to tell you? "Hang in there, I'll be back!" How gauche. My advice is—wait, be quiet, Wolf, ever since you started talking I—OOPS! So the dog talks, big deal. Let's see him fly, ha! OK, here's my advice: Don't go away, it only gets better. And now I'm going to take Wolf for a spin of the solar system. See you later.

Merlin

Printed in the United States
123936LV00006B/136/A